MOBILE SUIT GUNDAM WING

BLIND TARGET

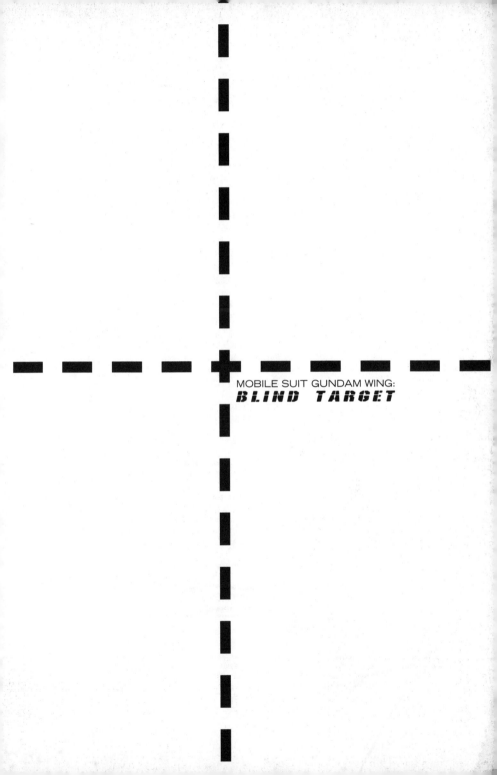

MOBILE SUIT GUNDAM WING:
BLIND TARGET

Mobile Suit Gundam Wing: Blind Target
This volume contains the Mobile Suit Gundam Wing:
Blind Target installments from comic issues #1 through #4 in their entirety.

Based on the anime TV series
Mobile Suit Gundam Wing

Mobile Suit Gundam created by Yoshiyuki Tomino/Hajime Yatate
Originally Broadcast in Japan as a radio drama

Adapted for comics by:
Writer/Akemi Omode
Art/Sakura Asagi

English Adaptation/Jen Van Meter
Translation/Lillian Olsen
Touch-up & Lettering/Bill Schuch
Graphic Design/Carolina Ugalde
Gundam Consultant/Mark Simmons
Editor/Ian Robertson

Managing Editor/Annette Roman
Director of Sales and Marketing/Dallas Middaugh
Editor-in-Chief/Hyoe Narita
Publisher/Seiji Horibuchi

©SOTSU AGENCY • SUNRISE
©HAJIME YATATE • YOSHIYUKI TOMINO • AKEMI OMODE • SAKURA ASAGI

First published in Japan Gakken Co., Ltd,. Serialized in ANIME V and LOOKER

New and adapted artwork and text
©2001 Viz Communications, Inc.

Printed in Canada.

Published by Viz Communications Inc.
P.O. Box 77010
San Francisco, CA 94107

10 9 8 7 6 5 4 3 2 1
First printing, November 2001

Call us toll free at (800) 394-3042 and ask for out FREE Viz Shop-By-Mail catalog!
Or fax: (415) 348-8936
Or logon: www.viz.com

VIZ GRAPHIC NOVEL

MOBILE SUIT GUNDAM WING:
BLIND TARGET

MOBILE SUIT GUNDAM CREATED BY
YOSHIYUKI TOMINO/HAJIME YATATE

ADAPTED FOR COMICS BY
WRITER/AKEMI OMODE
ART/SAKURA ASAGI

CONTENTS

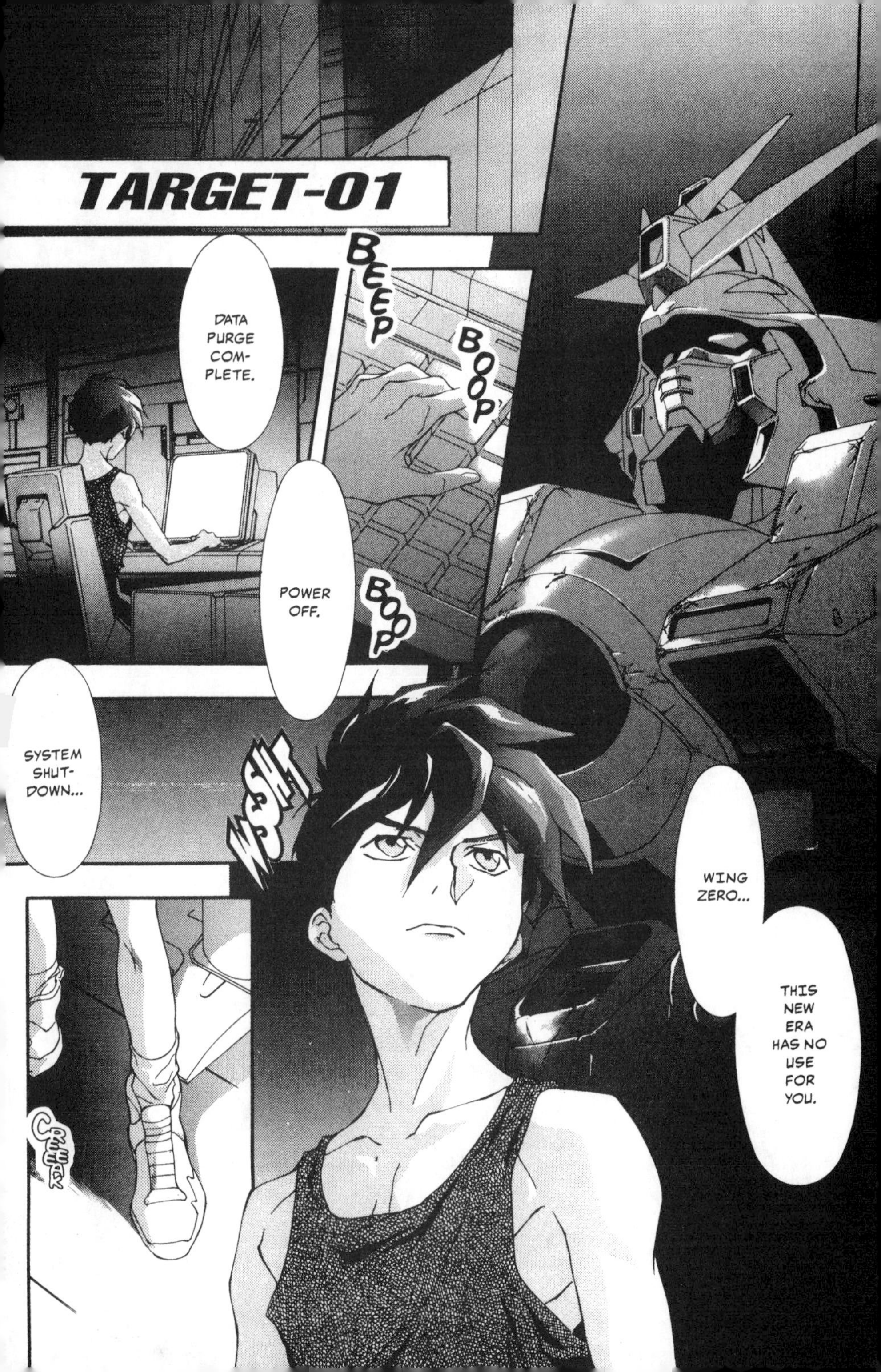
TARGET-01
DATA PURGE COM-PLETE.
BEEP
BOOP
POWER OFF.
BOOP
SYSTEM SHUT-DOWN...
CREAK
WOOSH
WING ZERO...
THIS NEW ERA HAS NO USE FOR YOU.

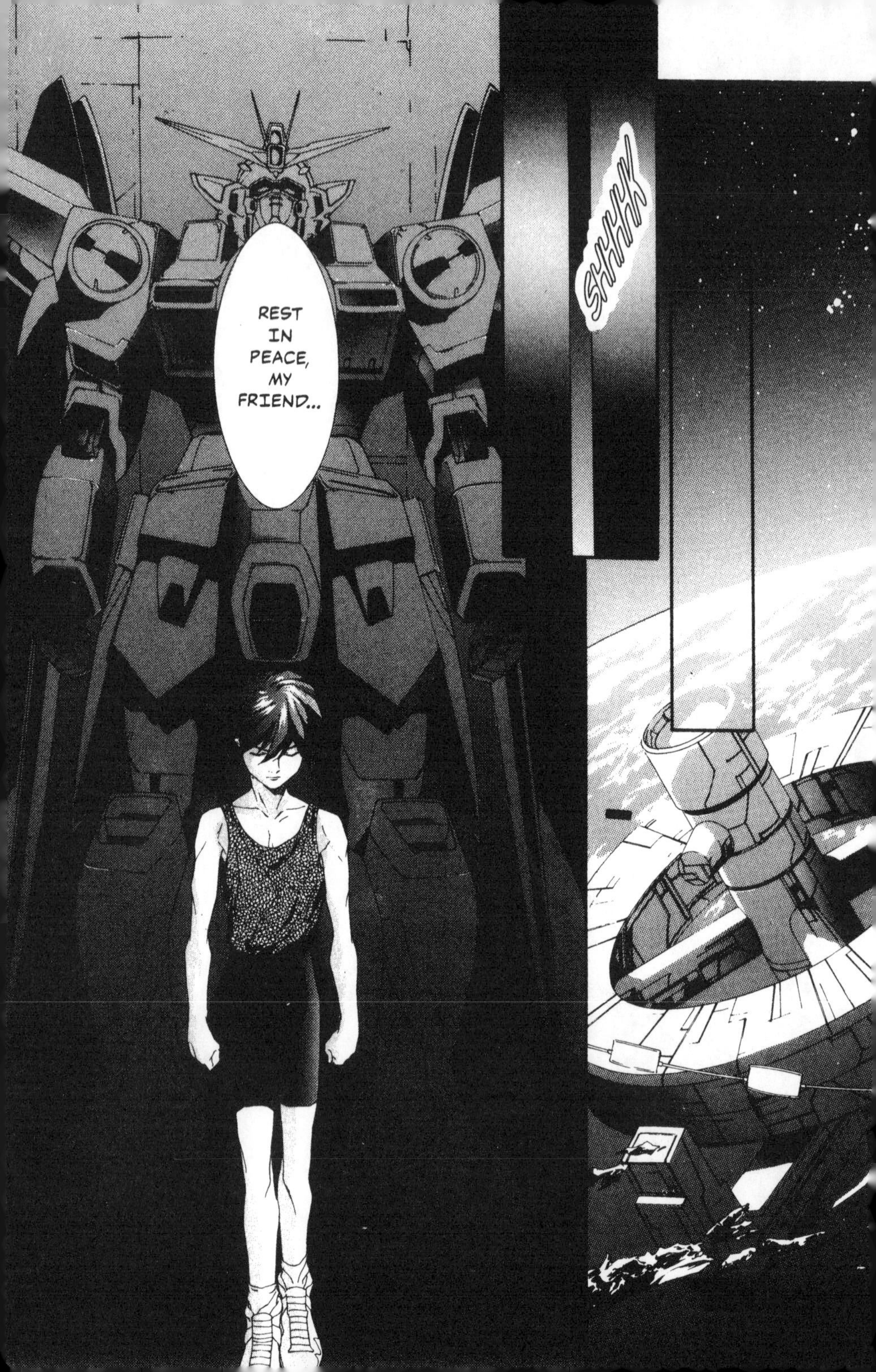
REST IN PEACE, MY FRIEND...
SHHHK

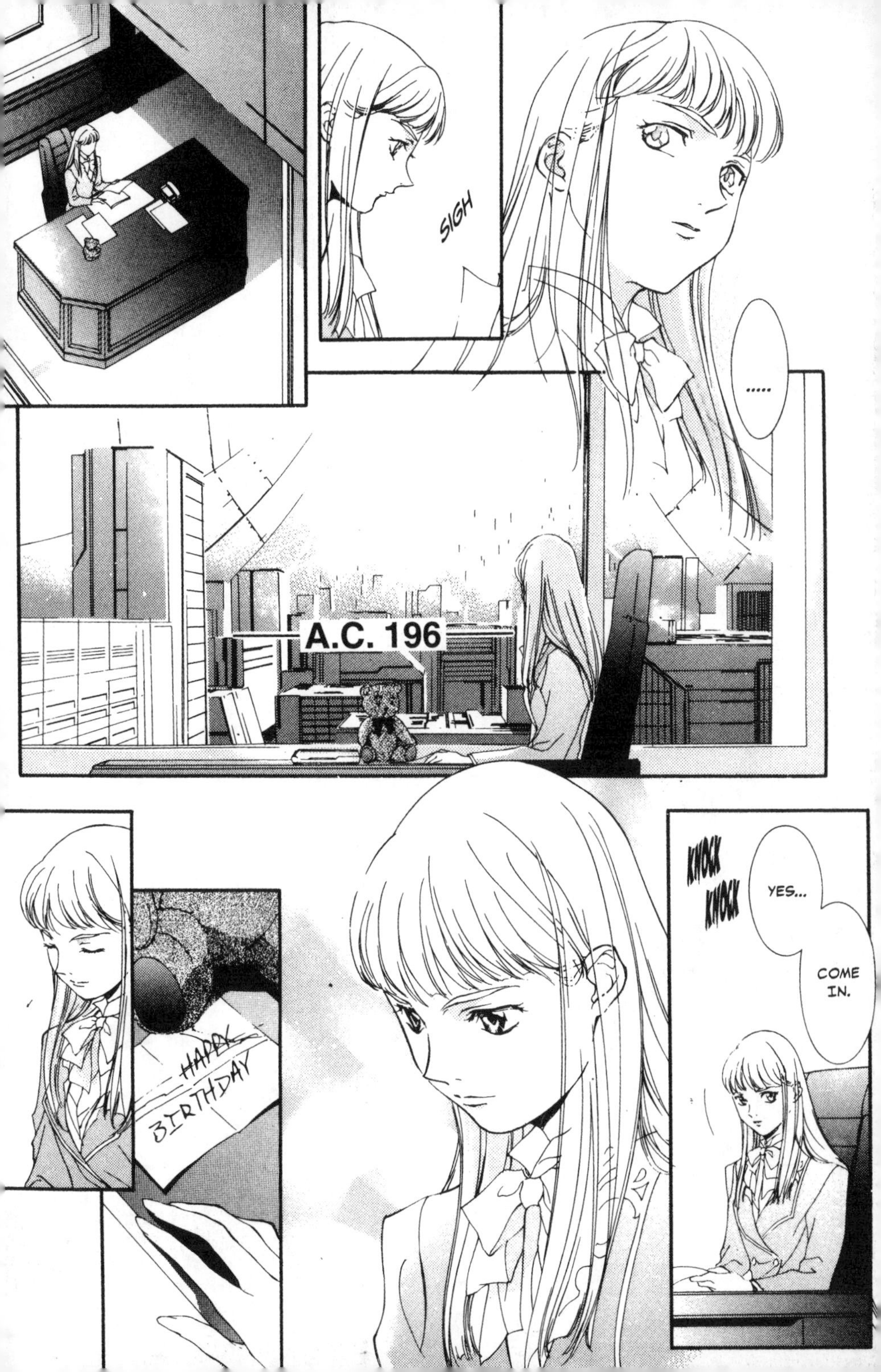
SIGH
......
A.C. 196
HAPPY
BIRTHDAY
KNOCK
KNOCK
YES...
COME IN.

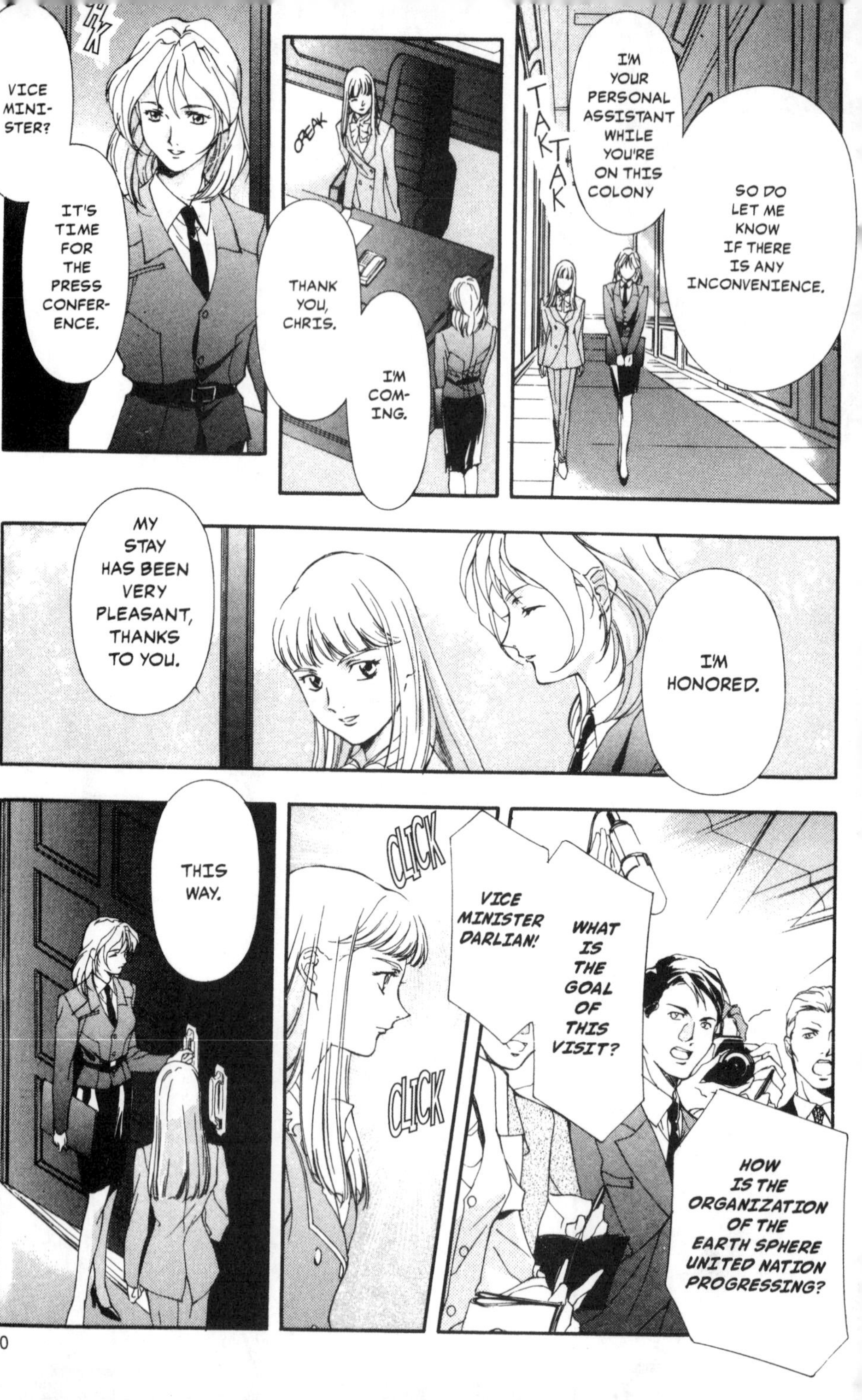
VICE MINISTER?
IT'S TIME FOR THE PRESS CONFERENCE.
CREAK
THANK YOU, CHRIS.
I'M COMING.
TAK TAK TAK
I'M YOUR PERSONAL ASSISTANT WHILE YOU'RE ON THIS COLONY
SO DO LET ME KNOW IF THERE IS ANY INCONVENIENCE.
MY STAY HAS BEEN VERY PLEASANT, THANKS TO YOU.
I'M HONORED.
THIS WAY.
CLICK
CLICK
VICE MINISTER DARLIAN!
WHAT IS THE GOAL OF THIS VISIT?
HOW IS THE ORGANIZATION OF THE EARTH SPHERE UNITED NATION PROGRESSING?

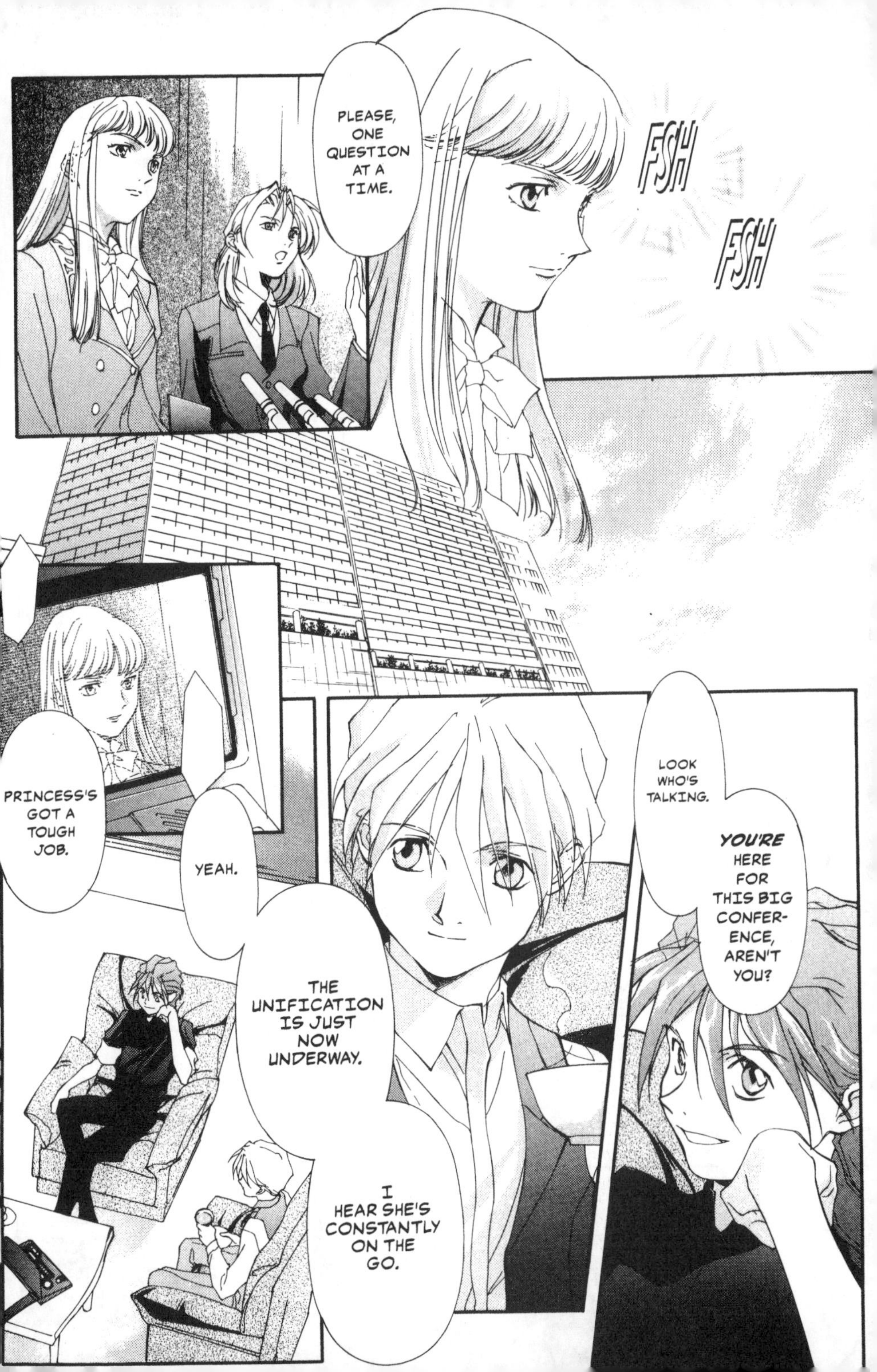
PLEASE, ONE QUESTION AT A TIME.
FSH
FSH
PRINCESS'S GOT A TOUGH JOB.
YEAH.
THE UNIFICATION IS JUST NOW UNDERWAY.
I HEAR SHE'S CONSTANTLY ON THE GO.
LOOK WHO'S TALKING.
YOU'RE HERE FOR THIS BIG CONFER-ENCE, AREN'T YOU?

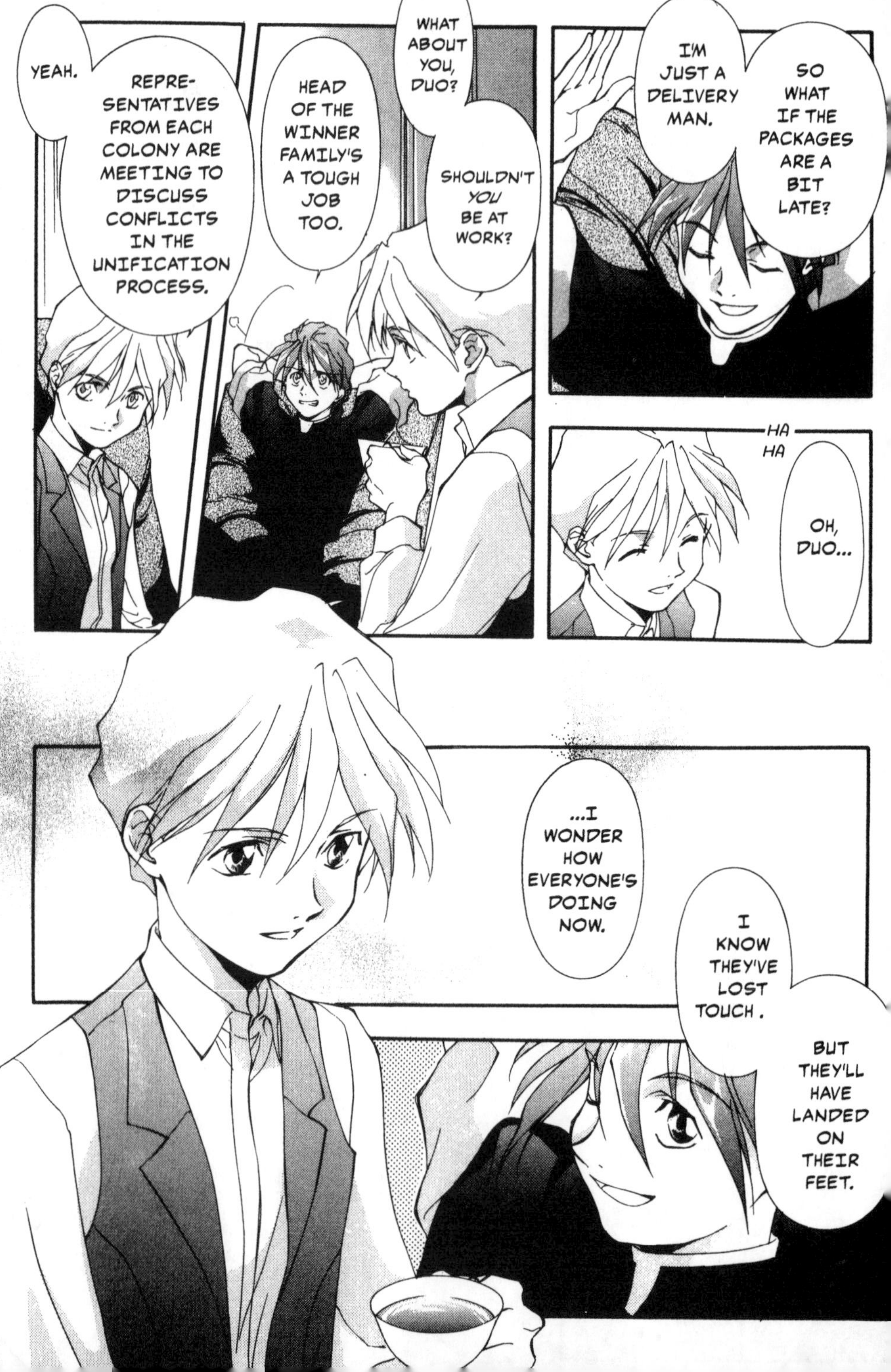
YEAH.
REPRESENTATIVES FROM EACH COLONY ARE MEETING TO DISCUSS CONFLICTS IN THE UNIFICATION PROCESS.
HEAD OF THE WINNER FAMILY'S A TOUGH JOB TOO.
WHAT ABOUT YOU, DUO?
SHOULDN'T *YOU* BE AT WORK?
I'M JUST A DELIVERY MAN.
SO WHAT IF THE PACKAGES ARE A BIT LATE?
HA HA
OH, DUO...
...I WONDER HOW EVERYONE'S DOING NOW.
I KNOW THEY'VE LOST TOUCH.
BUT THEY'LL HAVE LANDED ON THEIR FEET.

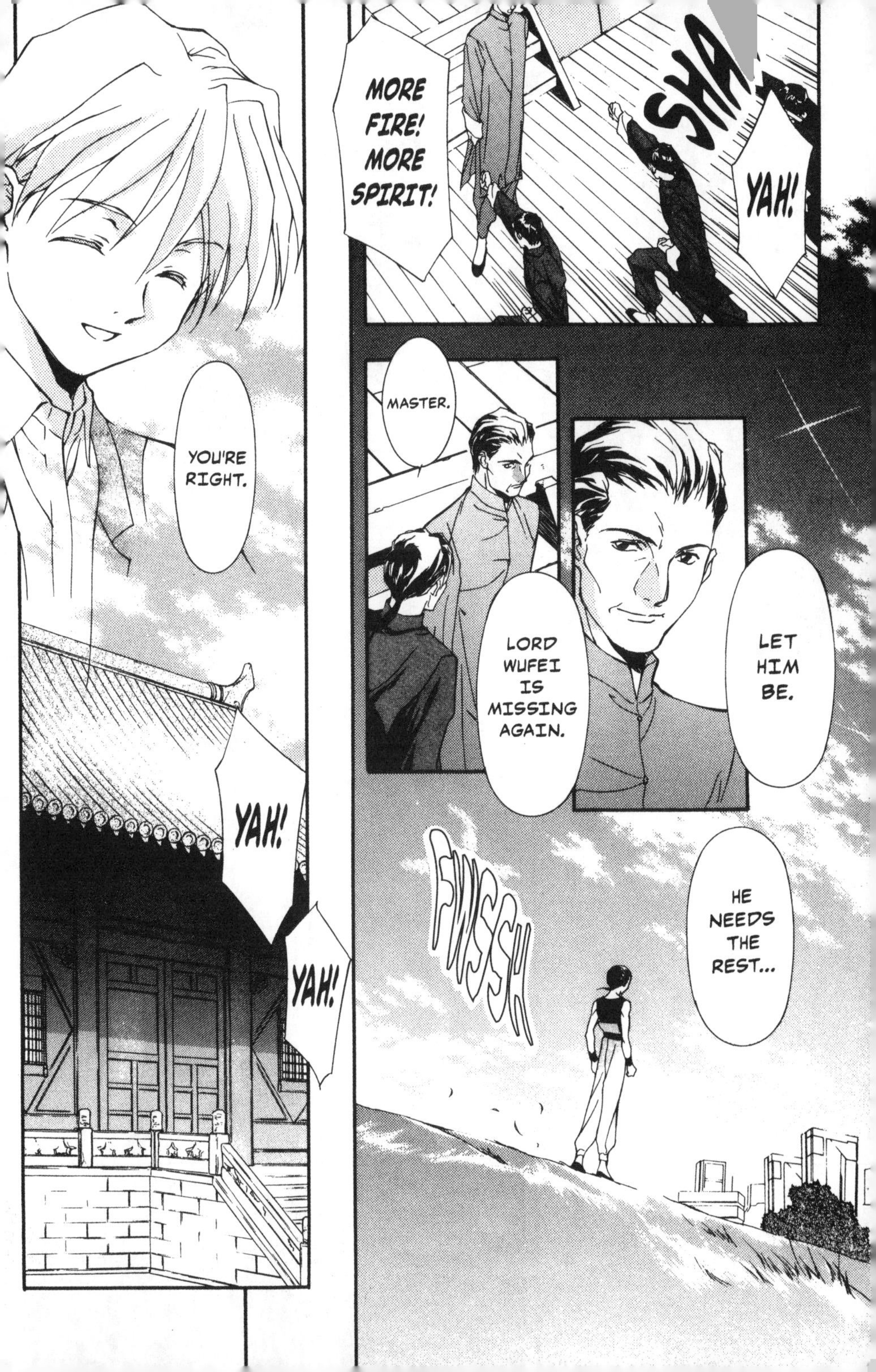
YOU'RE RIGHT.
YAH!
YAH!
MORE FIRE! MORE SPIRIT!
SHA
YAH!
MASTER.
LORD WUFEI IS MISSING AGAIN.
LET HIM BE.
FWSSH
HE NEEDS THE REST...

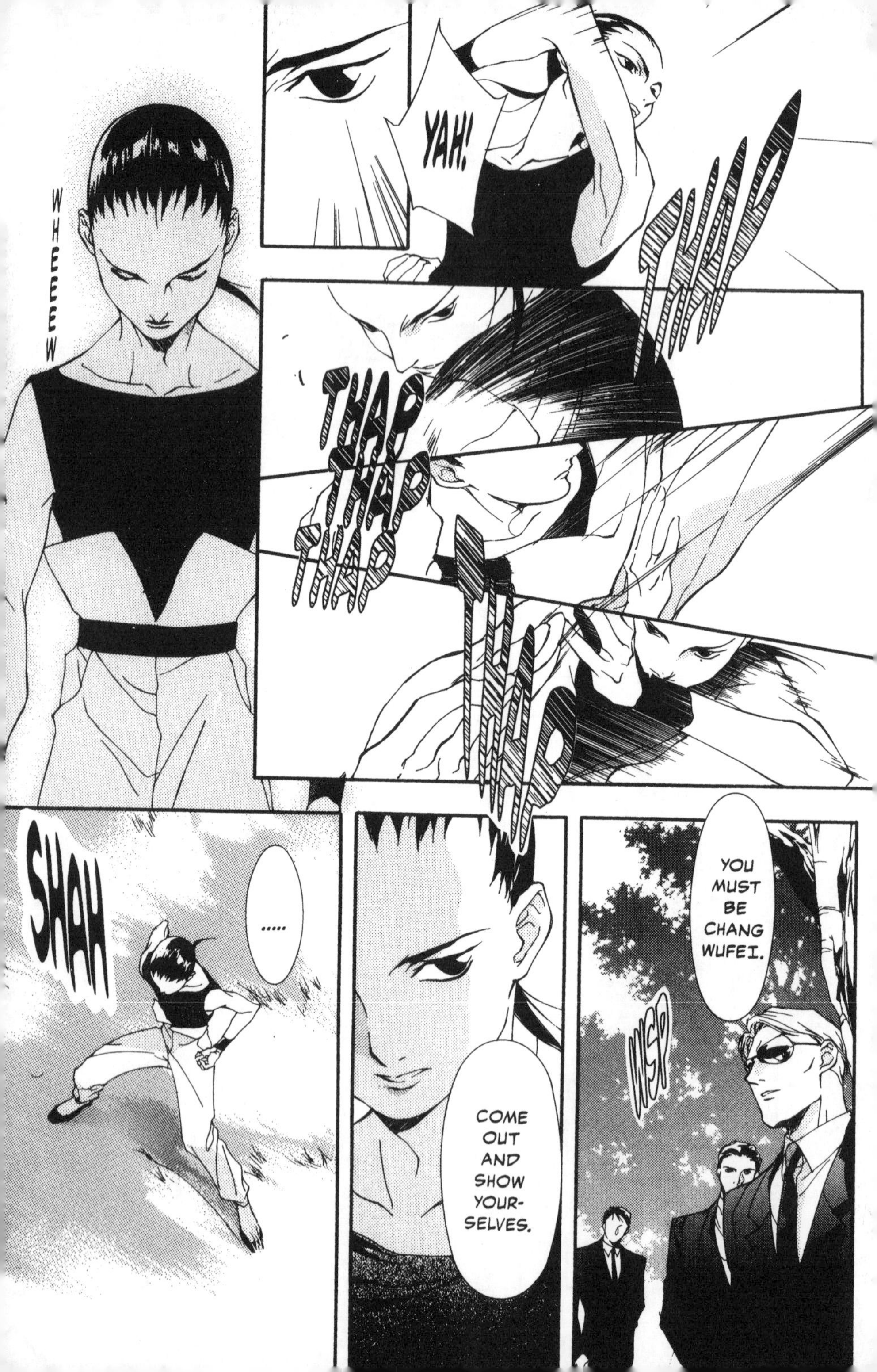
WHEEEW
YAH!
THAP
THAP
THAP
THAP
THAP
SHAH
.....
COME OUT AND SHOW YOUR-SELVES.
YOU MUST BE CHANG WUFEI.
WSP

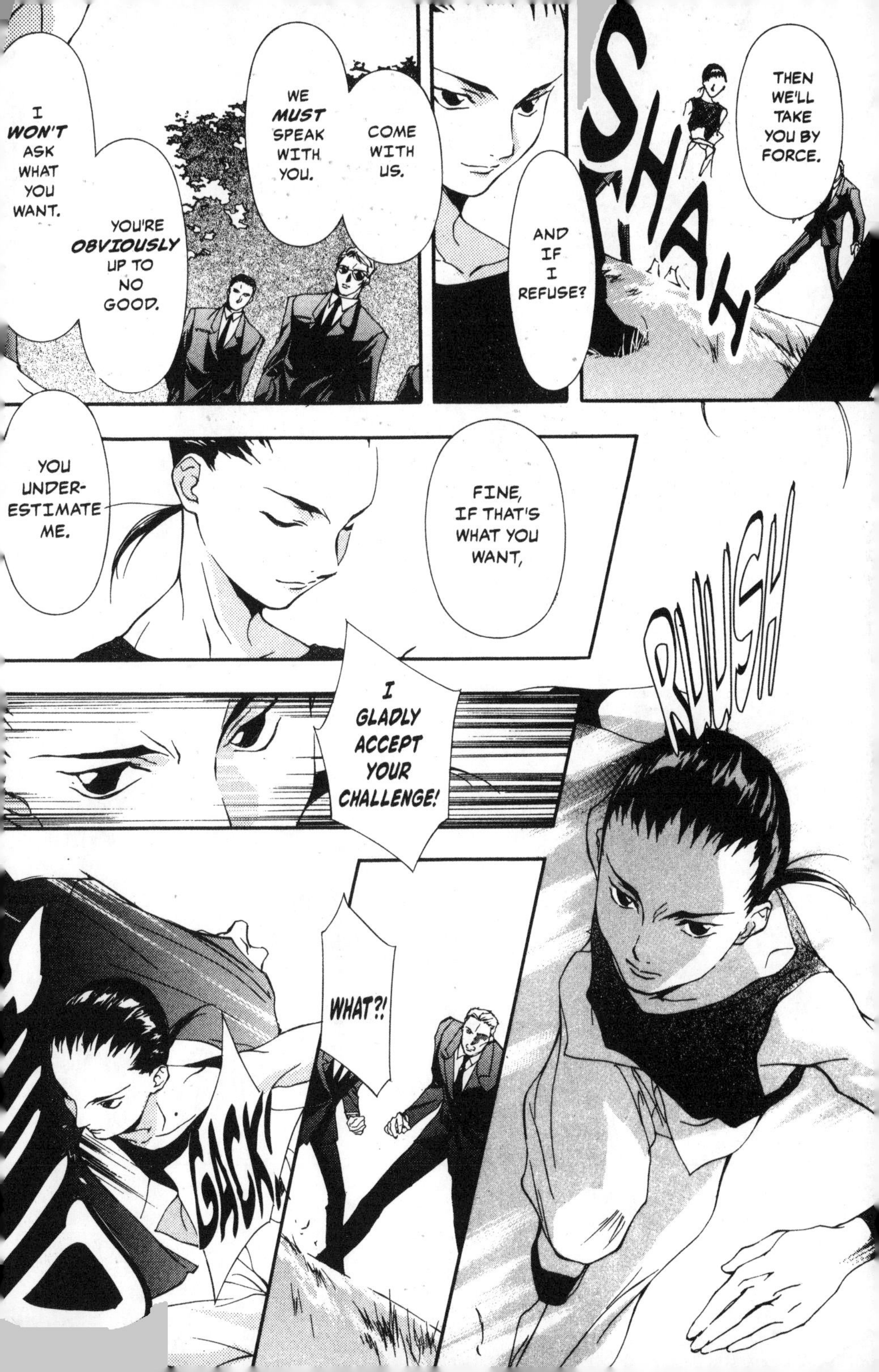
I WON'T ASK WHAT YOU WANT.
YOU'RE OBVIOUSLY UP TO NO GOOD.
WE MUST SPEAK WITH YOU.
COME WITH US.
AND IF I REFUSE?
SHAH
THEN WE'LL TAKE YOU BY FORCE.
YOU UNDER-ESTIMATE ME.
FINE, IF THAT'S WHAT YOU WANT,
RUUSH
I GLADLY ACCEPT YOUR CHALLENGE!
GACK!
WHAT?!

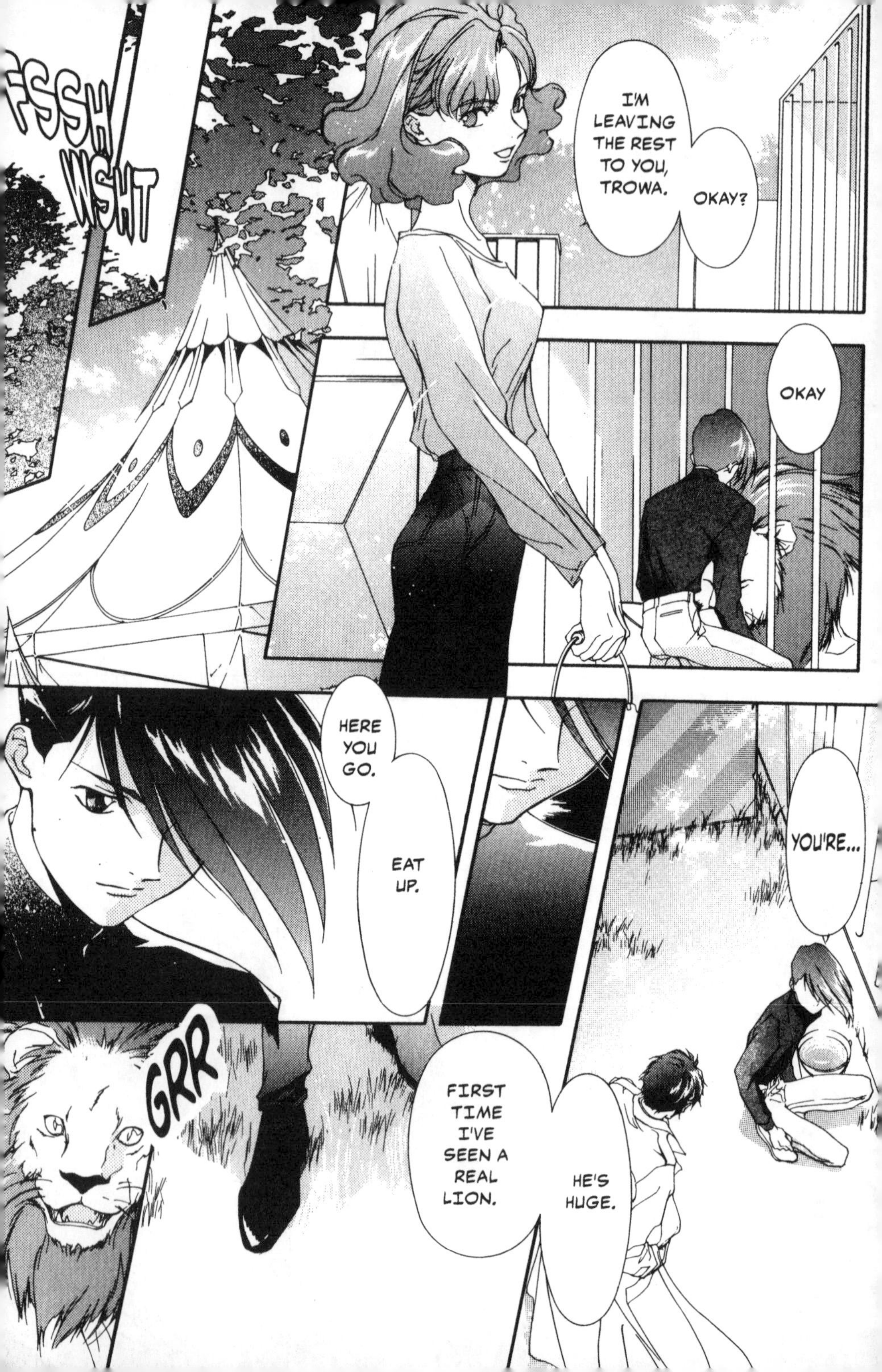
FSSH
WSHT
I'M LEAVING THE REST TO YOU, TROWA.
OKAY?
OKAY
HERE YOU GO.
EAT UP.
YOU'RE...
GRR
FIRST TIME I'VE SEEN A REAL LION.
HE'S HUGE.

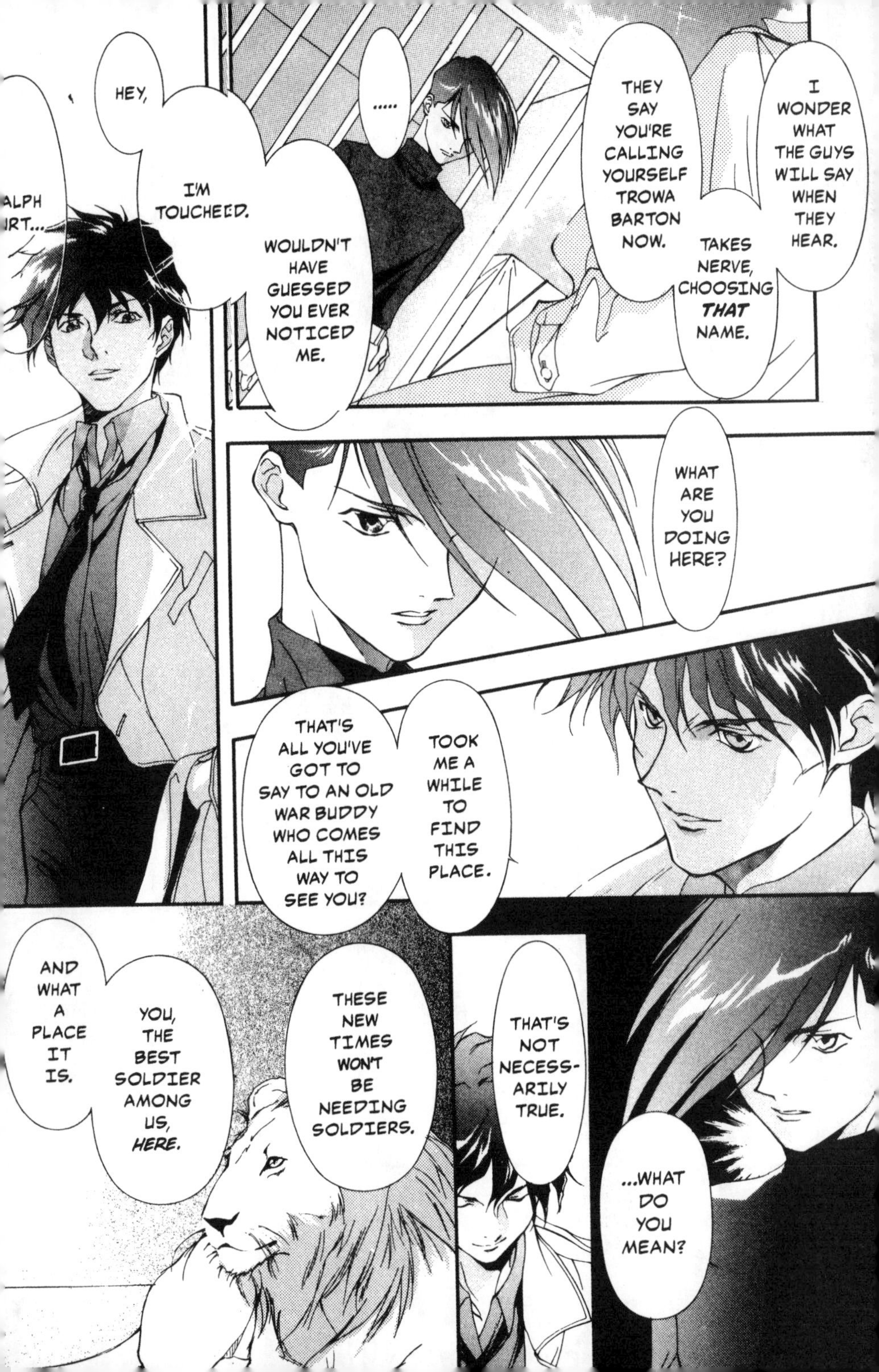
ALPH
RT...
HEY,
I'M TOUCHEED.
WOULDN'T HAVE GUESSED YOU EVER NOTICED ME.
.....
THEY SAY YOU'RE CALLING YOURSELF TROWA BARTON NOW.
I WONDER WHAT THE GUYS WILL SAY WHEN THEY HEAR.
TAKES NERVE, CHOOSING *THAT* NAME.
WHAT ARE YOU DOING HERE?
THAT'S ALL YOU'VE GOT TO SAY TO AN OLD WAR BUDDY WHO COMES ALL THIS WAY TO SEE YOU?
TOOK ME A WHILE TO FIND THIS PLACE.
AND WHAT A PLACE IT IS.
YOU, THE BEST SOLDIER AMONG US, *HERE*.
THESE NEW TIMES WON'T BE NEEDING SOLDIERS.
THAT'S NOT NECESS-ARILY TRUE.
...WHAT DO YOU MEAN?

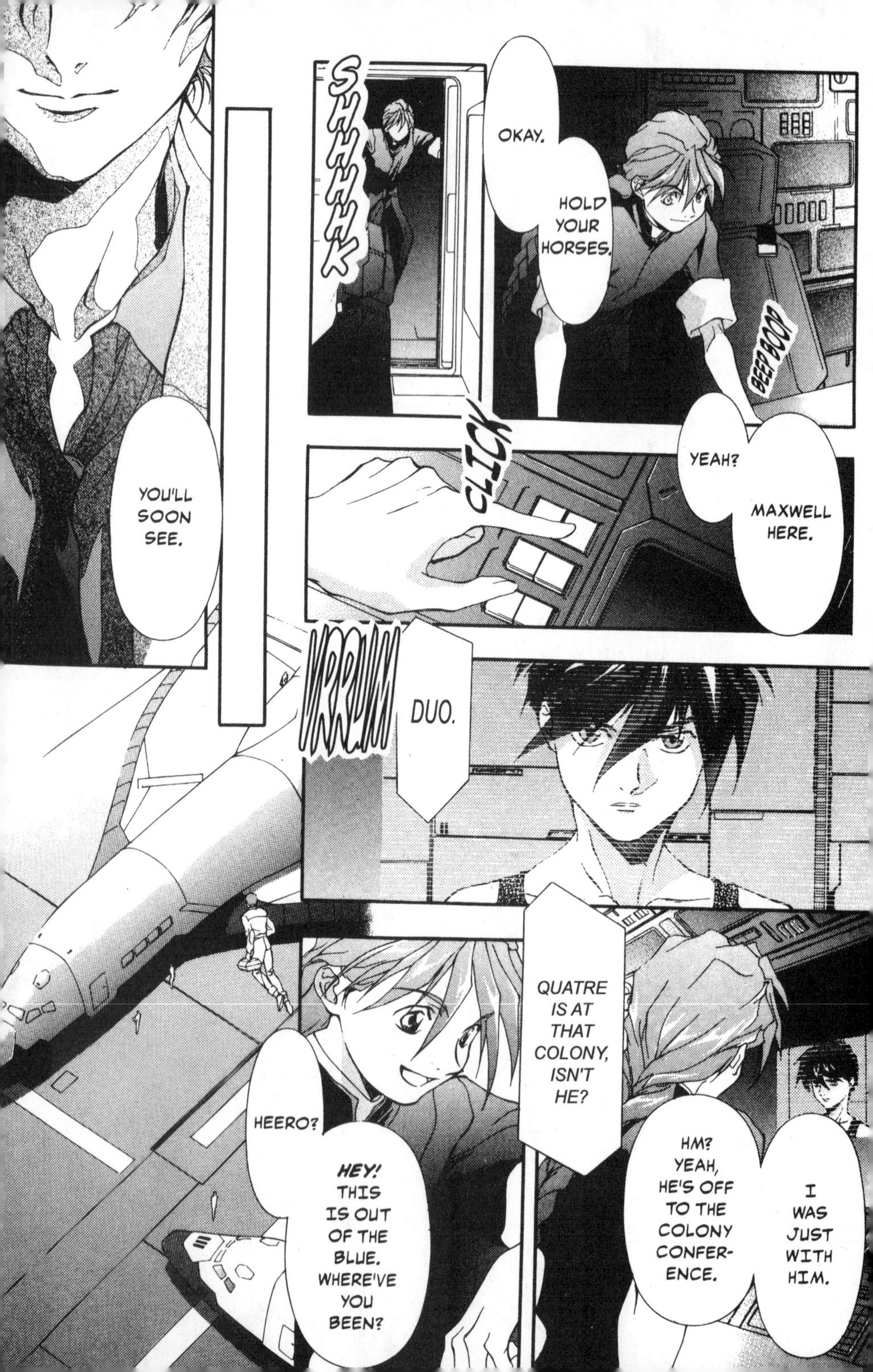
YOU'LL SOON SEE.
SHHHHK
OKAY.
HOLD YOUR HORSES.
BEEP BOOP
CLICK
YEAH?
MAXWELL HERE.
DUO.
QUATRE IS AT THAT COLONY, ISN'T HE?
HEERO?
HEY! THIS IS OUT OF THE BLUE. WHERE'VE YOU BEEN?
HM? YEAH, HE'S OFF TO THE COLONY CONFERENCE.
I WAS JUST WITH HIM.

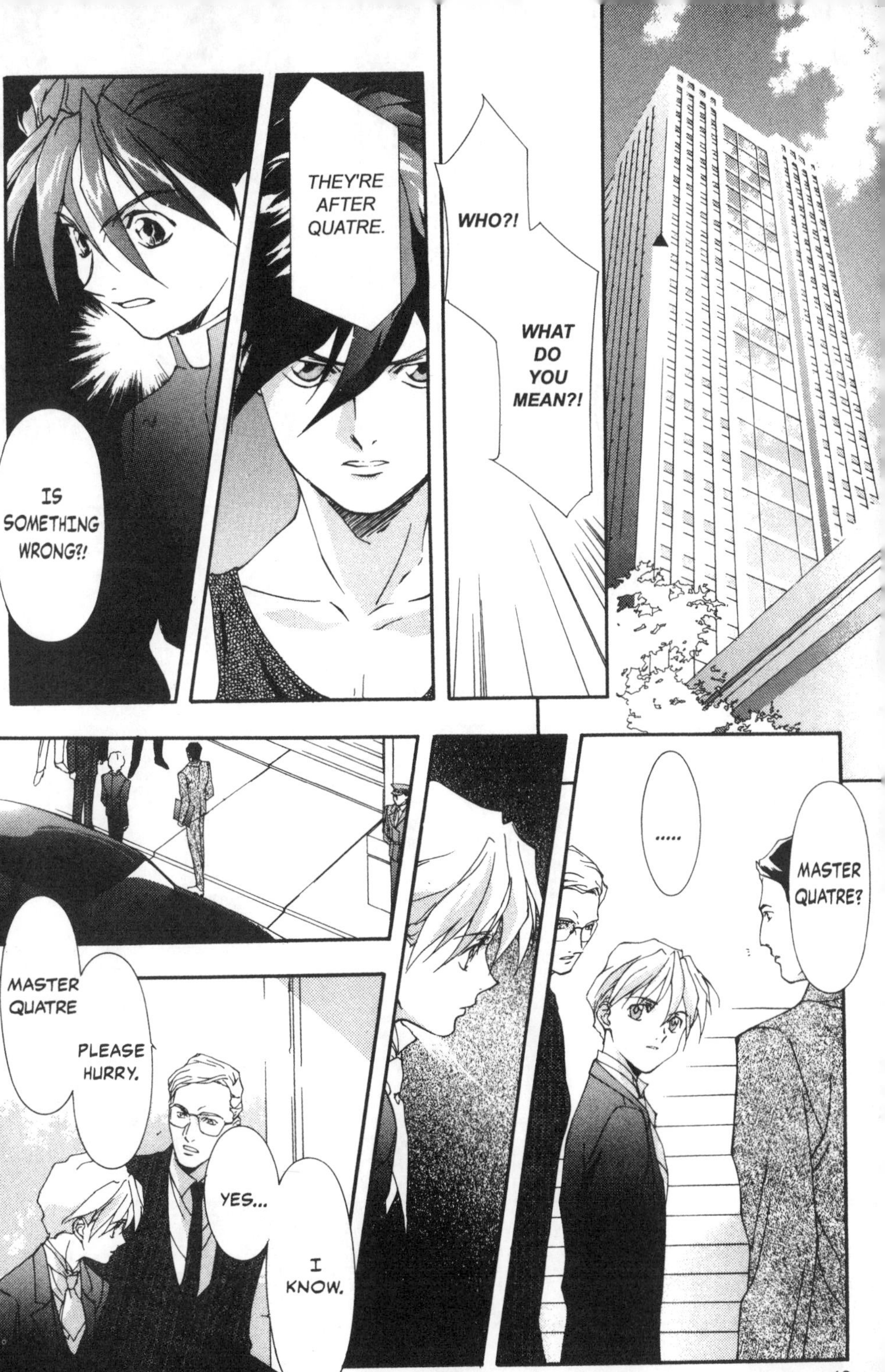
IS SOMETHING WRONG?!
THEY'RE AFTER QUATRE.
WHO?!
WHAT DO YOU MEAN?!
MASTER QUATRE
PLEASE HURRY.
YES...
I KNOW.
.....
MASTER QUATRE?

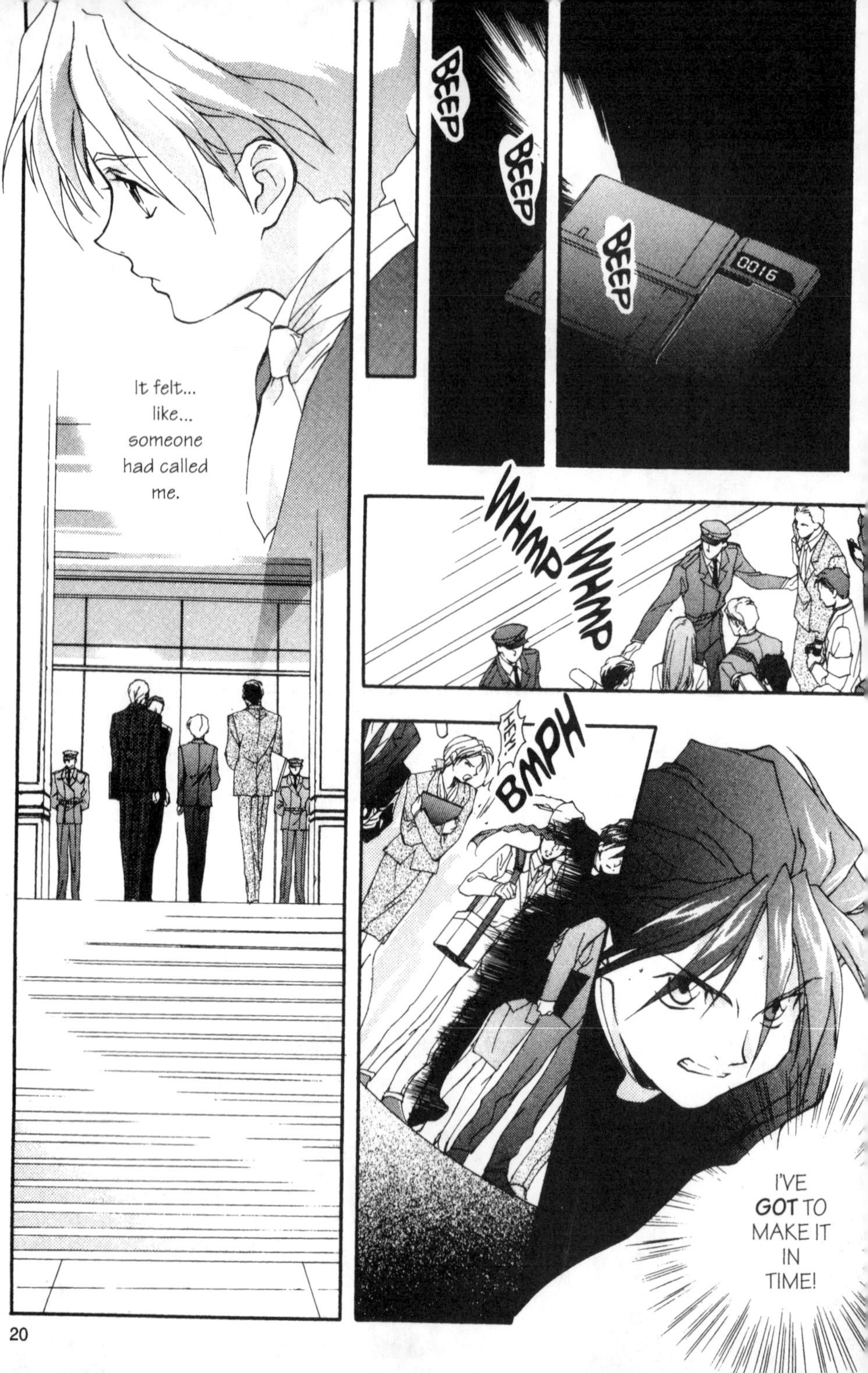
It felt... like... someone had called me.
BEEP
BEEP
BEEP
0016
WHAMP WHAMP
HEY!
BMPH
I'VE GOT TO MAKE IT IN TIME!

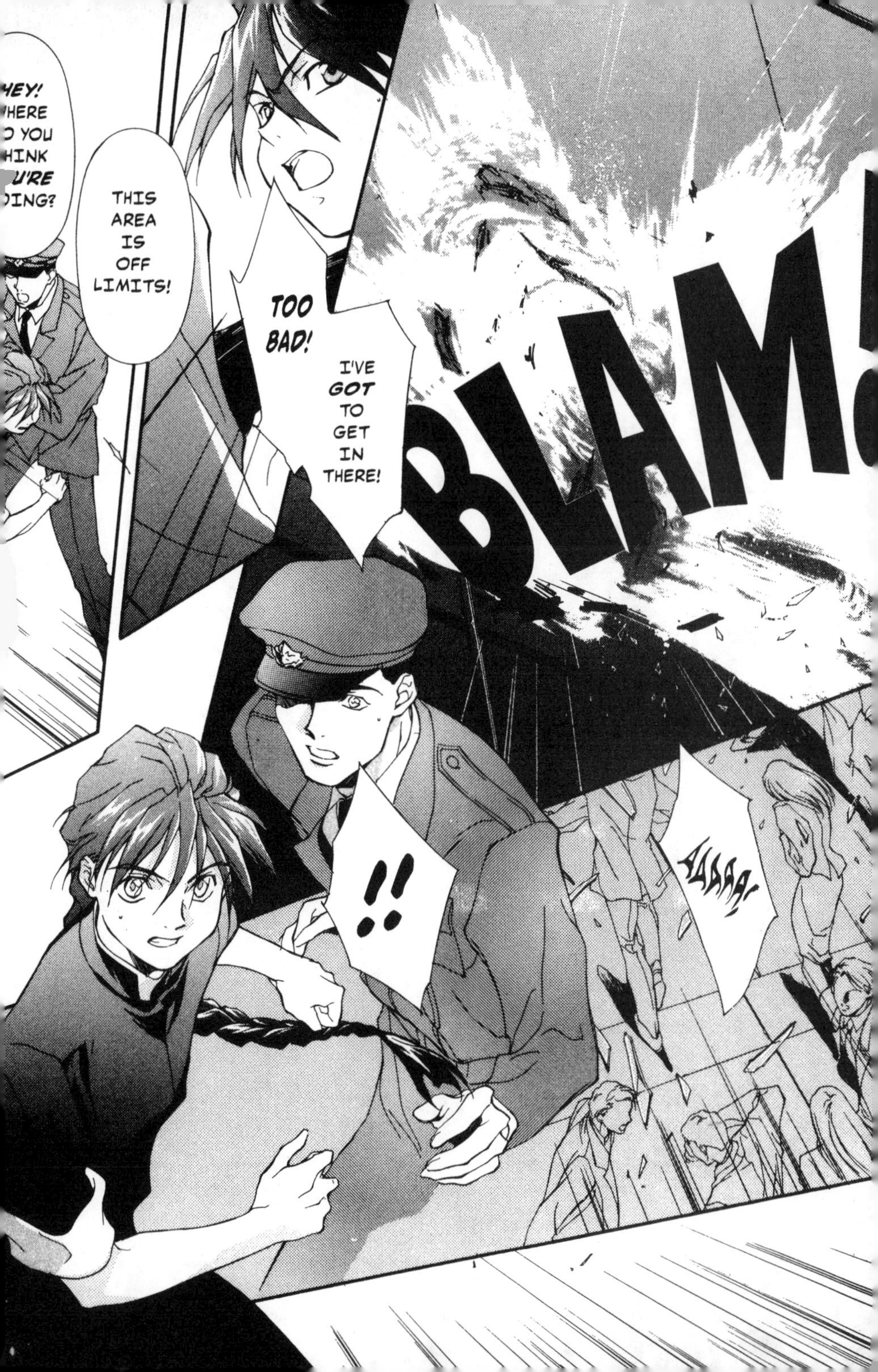
HEY! HERE O YOU HINK U'RE OING?
THIS AREA IS OFF LIMITS!
TOO BAD!
I'VE GOT TO GET IN THERE!
BLAM!
!!
AAAAA!

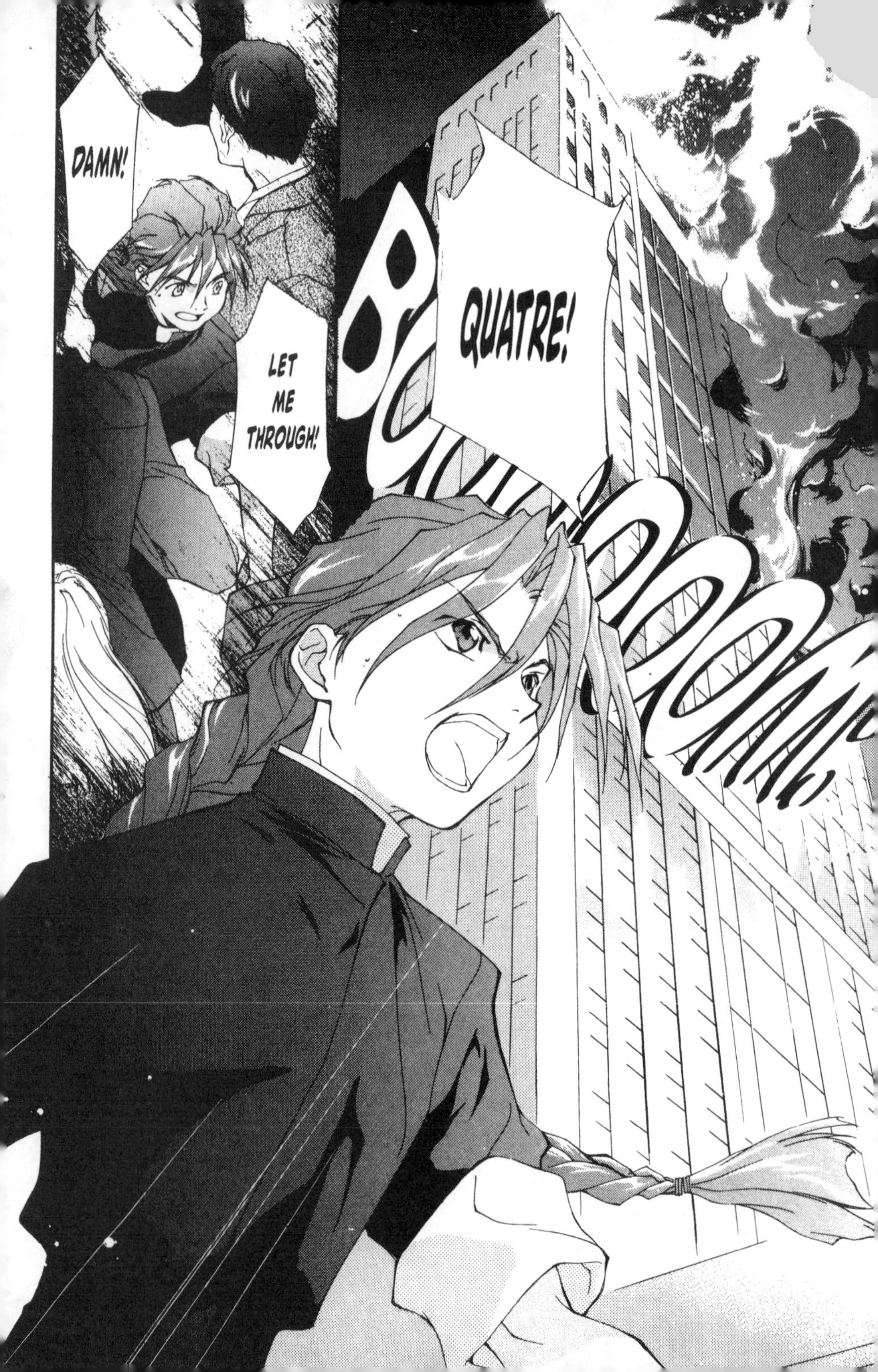
DAMN!
LET ME THROUGH!
QUATRE!

HERE'S A BRIEF HISTORY OF SOME OF THE GUNDAM CHARACTERS. WE'VE REMIXED THIS BOOK WITH THE VIDEOS AND OTHER PUBLICATIONS FOR A DYNAMIC VIEW OF GUNDAM WING EVENTS!

MOBILE SUIT GUNDAM WING REMIX I..........

LADY RELENA DARLIAN: TEENAGE WORLD LEADER

1

Lady Relena assumed office as the Vice Minister of Foreign Affairs when she was 16. It was an honorary title at first, but after the war she quickly gained a reputation as a skilled leader, diplomat and advocate of pacifism. Relena brought speedy resolution to many post-war colonial conflicts, and in the "Endless Waltz" she headed to Colony X-18999, which sought such a settlement. While her skills as a mediator are valuable, Relena herself is even more precious as a symbol of the peace she has wrought, so much that when she disappears in this book, it creates conflict between the colonies and Earth. When she declares her intentions to run for president, she becomes such an obvious target that Heero will have to act as her bodyguard. Leader of a country at age 15, Queen of the World Nation, Vice Minister of Foreign Affairs of the Earth Sphere Unified Nation and presidential candidate at age 16; impressive beginnings. Relena has earned her power and takes her responsibilities seriously; though still in school, she's put her studies on hold to work tirelessly for universal peace.
The teddy bear she keeps in her office, though, reminds us how young she really is.

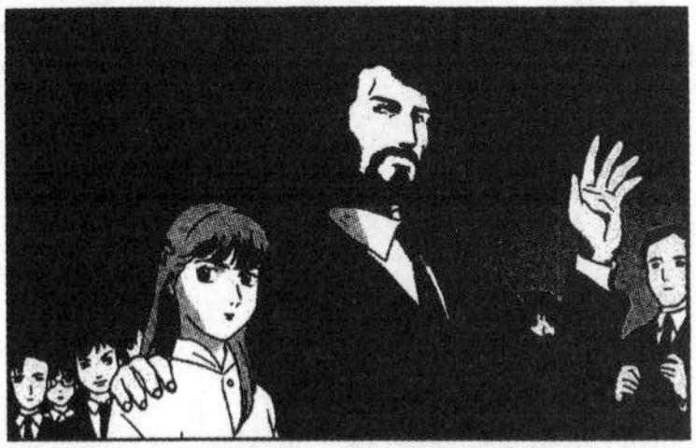
Relena Darlian assumed the office of her late father.She became Vice Minister of Foreign Affairs the day before her 16th birthday, and at 16 1/2 is running for president.

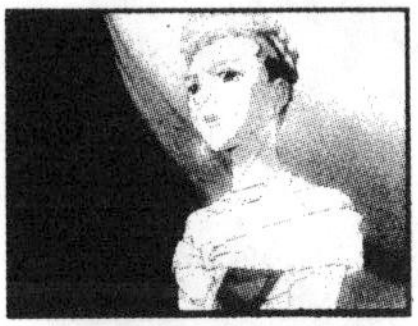
From princess of a country to queen of the world nation in 2 weeks. such a noble presence in one so young!

"TROWA BARTON": WHAT'S IN A NAME?

2

While a mechanic at the Heavyarms's secret factory, he saw Doktor S's assistant kill the real Trowa Barton. He took the name for himself and headed to Earth piloting the Gundam, Heavyarms. But the real Trowa's family could be a problem. The father, Dekim Barton, is the secret commander seen in the "Endless Waltz". The older sister was once involved with Oz leader Treize, who thought of the murdered man as his brother-in-law. What's more Treize doesn't know he's the father of Trowa's niece. Our Trowa may be surprised that the little girl whose picture the real Trowa showed him with pride has grown to be his enemy, cunning mastermind Mariemaia.

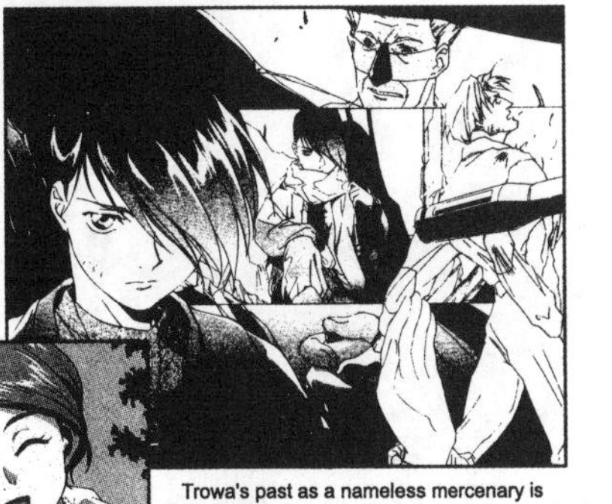
Below, Mariemaia as a child. the niece of the *real* Trowa.

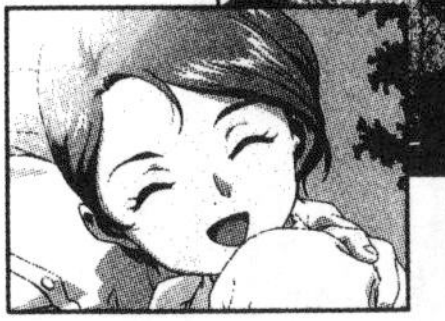
Trowa's past as a nameless mercenary is mysterious, but now he uses the distinguished Barton family name. It's a choice that could reshape history.

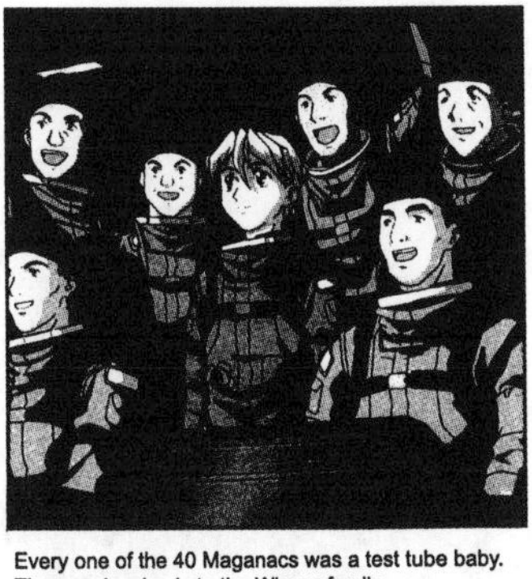
Every one of the 40 Maganacs was a test tube baby. They are loyal only to the Winner family.

THE MAGANAC CORPS: BODYGUARDS OF THE WINNER FAMILY

3

Wherever Quatre goes, there they are. In the "Endless Waltz" we get a glimpse of their bravery when they accompany Quatre on a dangerous mission to retrieve an abandoned satellite. In the current story, however, it looks like Quatre only brought a personal assistant; perhaps it's undiplomatic to bring 40 bodyguards to a peace conference? In any case, this new incident will make it far more difficult for the head of the Winner family to get much time alone. The devoted maganacs are likely to vehemently oppose master Quatre's independence in the future.

The pictures were taken from the TV series and "Endless Waltz."

MOBILE SUIT GUNDAM WING
BLIND TARGET

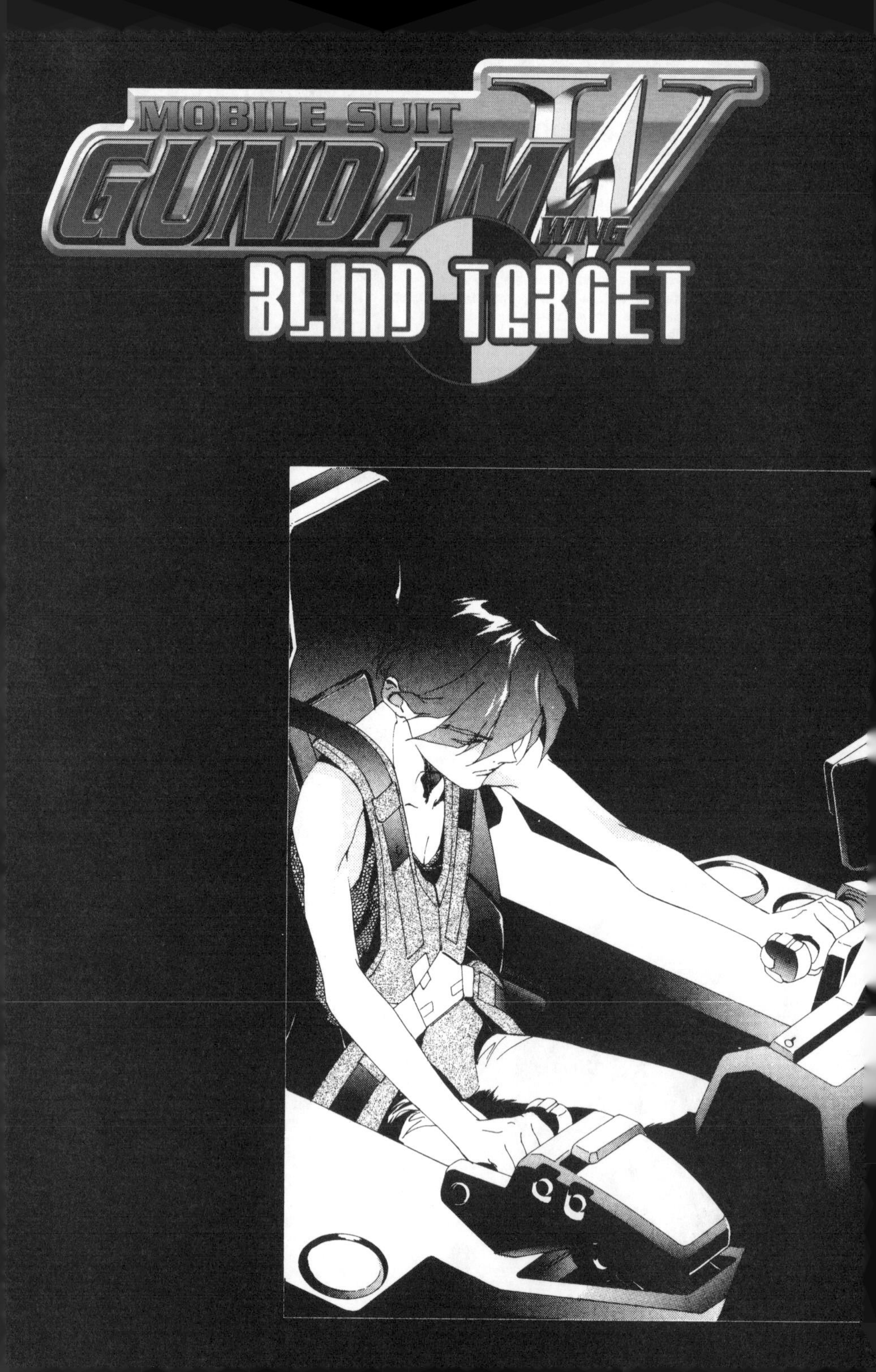

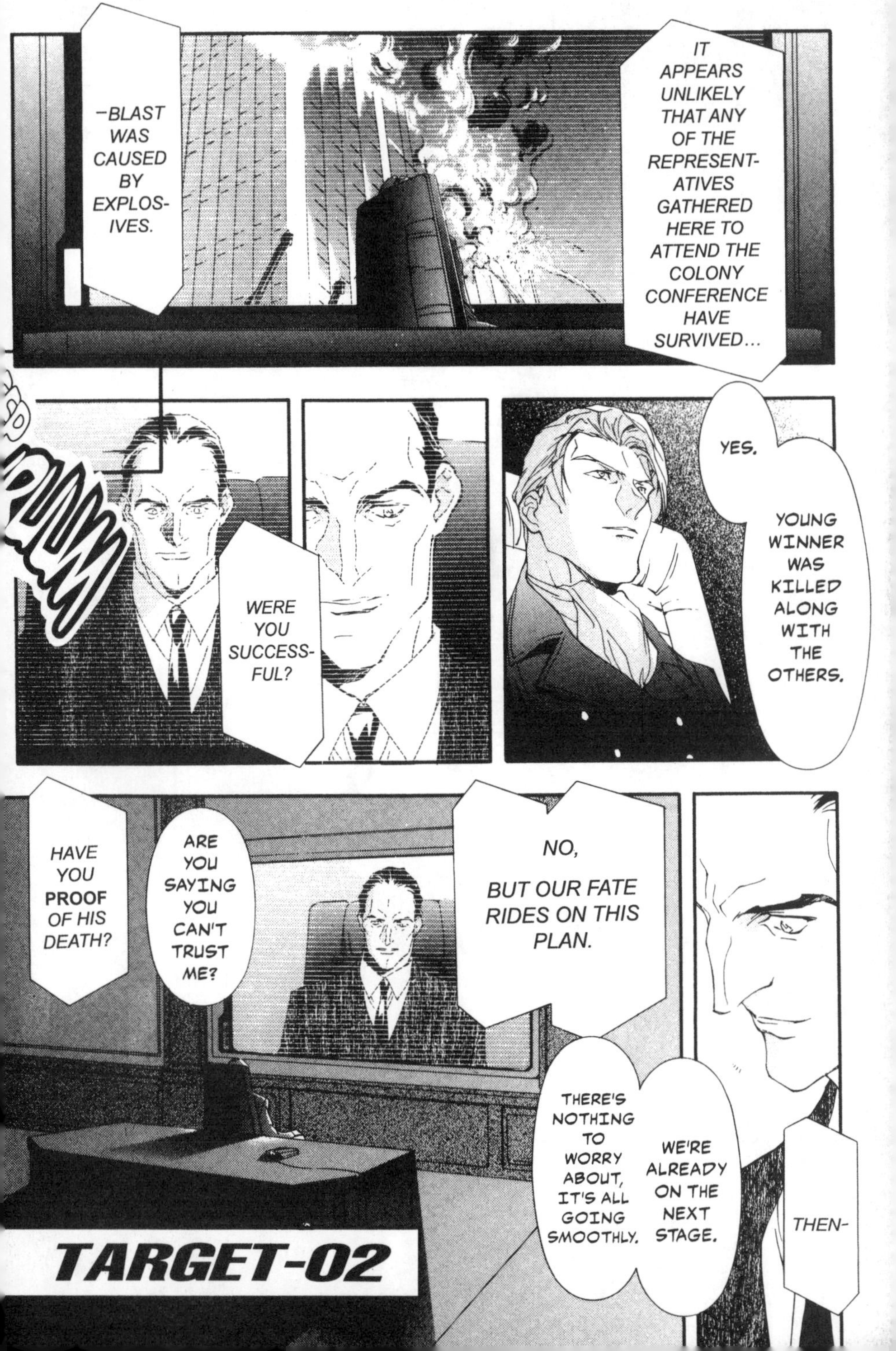
—BLAST WAS CAUSED BY EXPLOSIVES.
IT APPEARS UNLIKELY THAT ANY OF THE REPRESENTATIVES GATHERED HERE TO ATTEND THE COLONY CONFERENCE HAVE SURVIVED…
WERE YOU SUCCESSFUL?
YES.
YOUNG WINNER WAS KILLED ALONG WITH THE OTHERS.
HAVE YOU PROOF OF HIS DEATH?
ARE YOU SAYING YOU CAN'T TRUST ME?
NO,
BUT OUR FATE RIDES ON THIS PLAN.
THERE'S NOTHING TO WORRY ABOUT, IT'S ALL GOING SMOOTHLY.
WE'RE ALREADY ON THE NEXT STAGE.
THEN-
TARGET-02

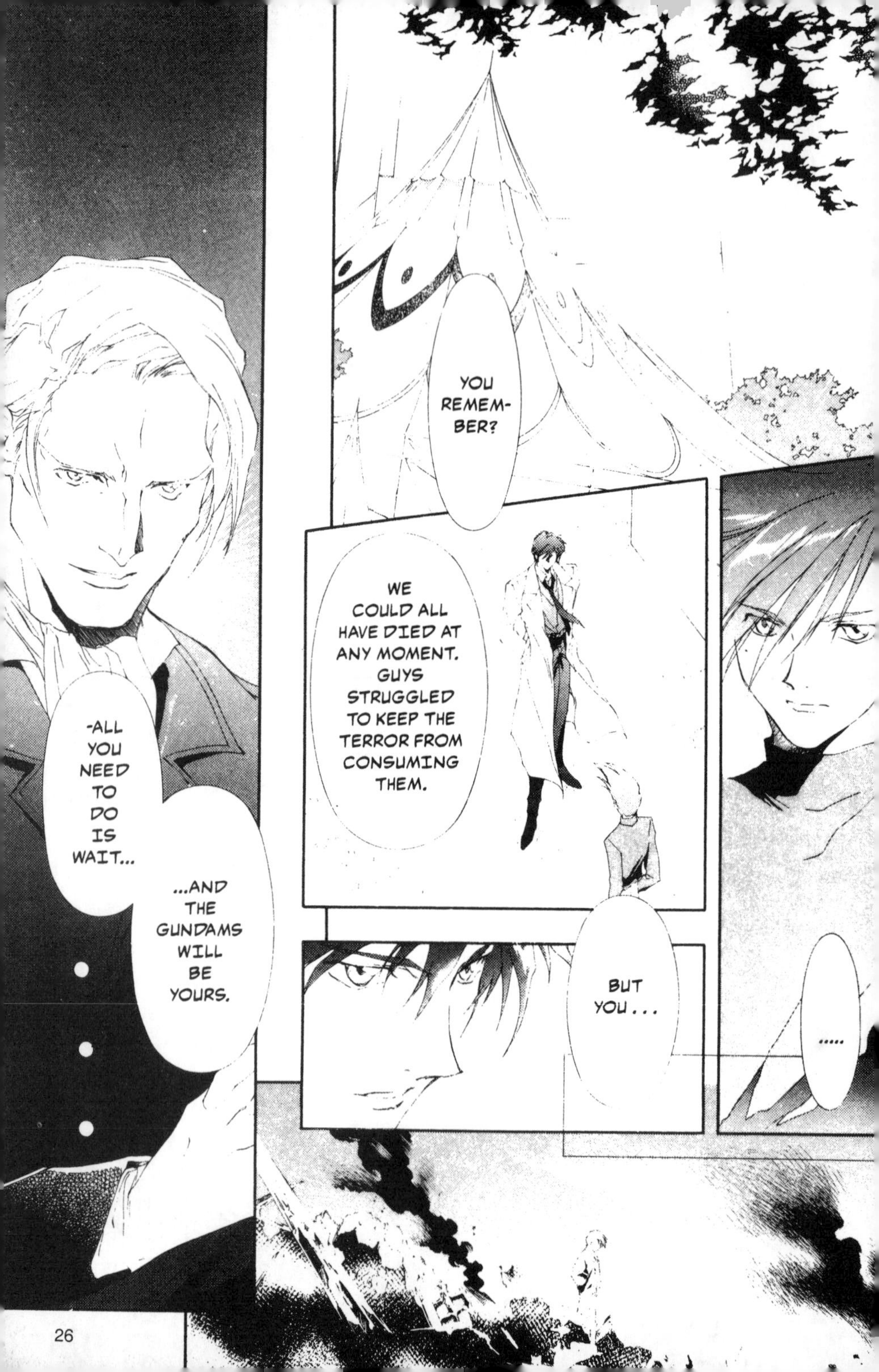
-ALL YOU NEED TO DO IS WAIT...
...AND THE GUNDAMS WILL BE YOURS.
YOU REMEMBER?
WE COULD ALL HAVE DIED AT ANY MOMENT. GUYS STRUGGLED TO KEEP THE TERROR FROM CONSUMING THEM.
BUT YOU . . .
.....

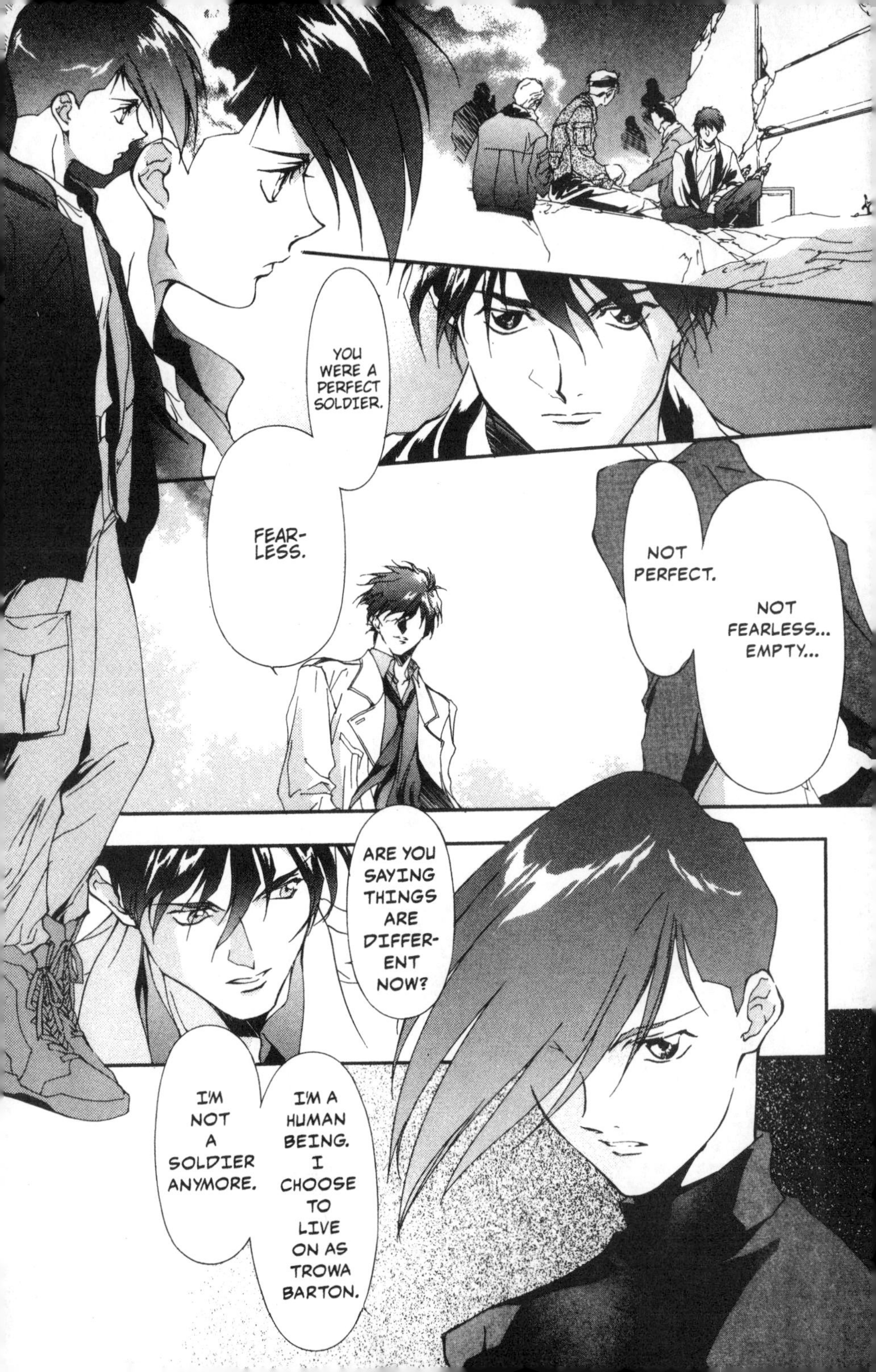
YOU WERE A PERFECT SOLDIER.
FEAR-LESS.
NOT PERFECT.
NOT FEARLESS... EMPTY...
ARE YOU SAYING THINGS ARE DIFFER-ENT NOW?
I'M NOT A SOLDIER ANYMORE.
I'M A HUMAN BEING. I CHOOSE TO LIVE ON AS TROWA BARTON.

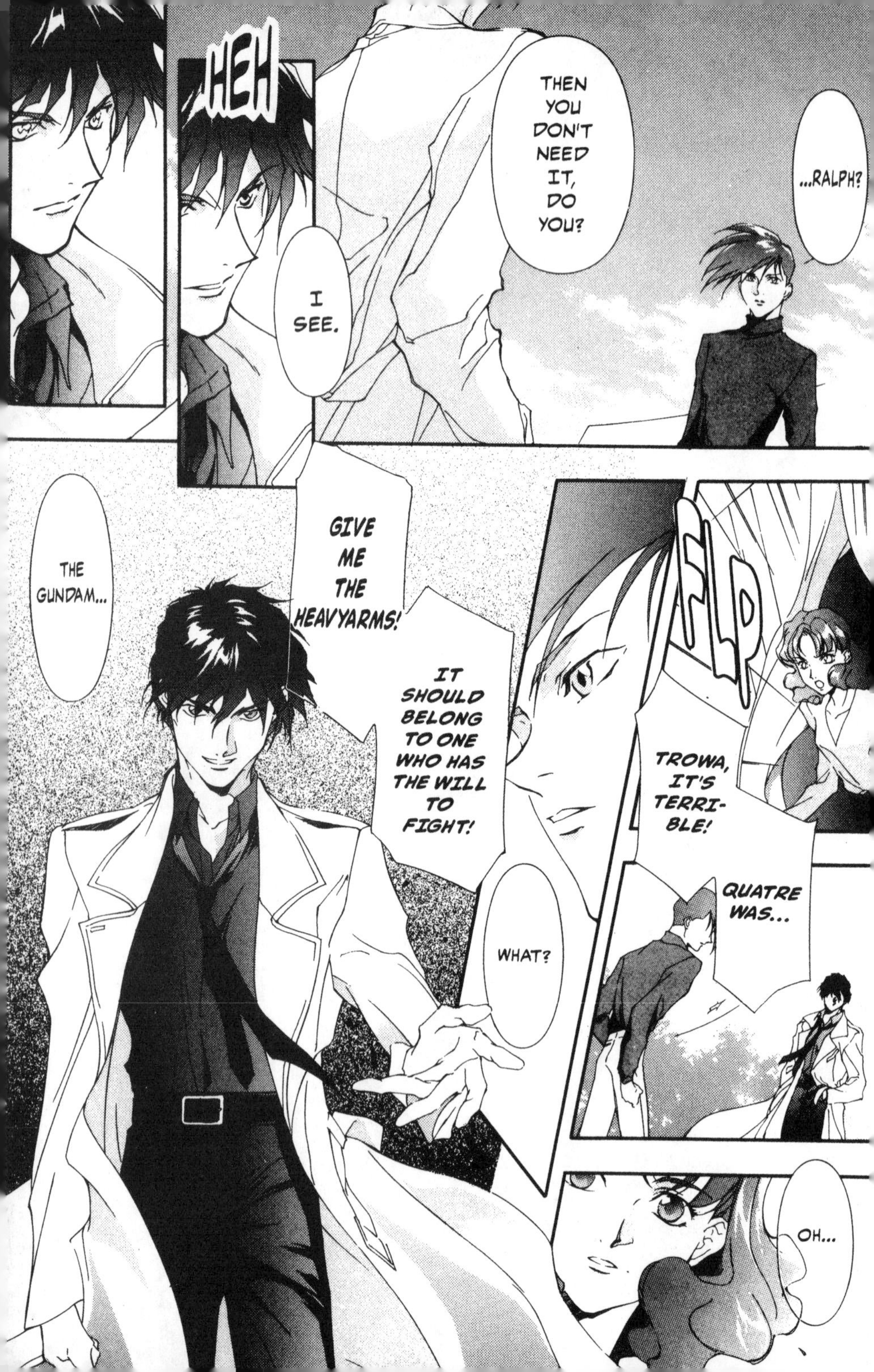
HEH
I SEE.
THEN YOU DON'T NEED IT, DO YOU?
...RALPH?
THE GUNDAM...
GIVE ME THE HEAVYARMS!
IT SHOULD BELONG TO ONE WHO HAS THE WILL TO FIGHT!
FLP
WHAT?
TROWA, IT'S TERRI-BLE!
QUATRE WAS...
OH...

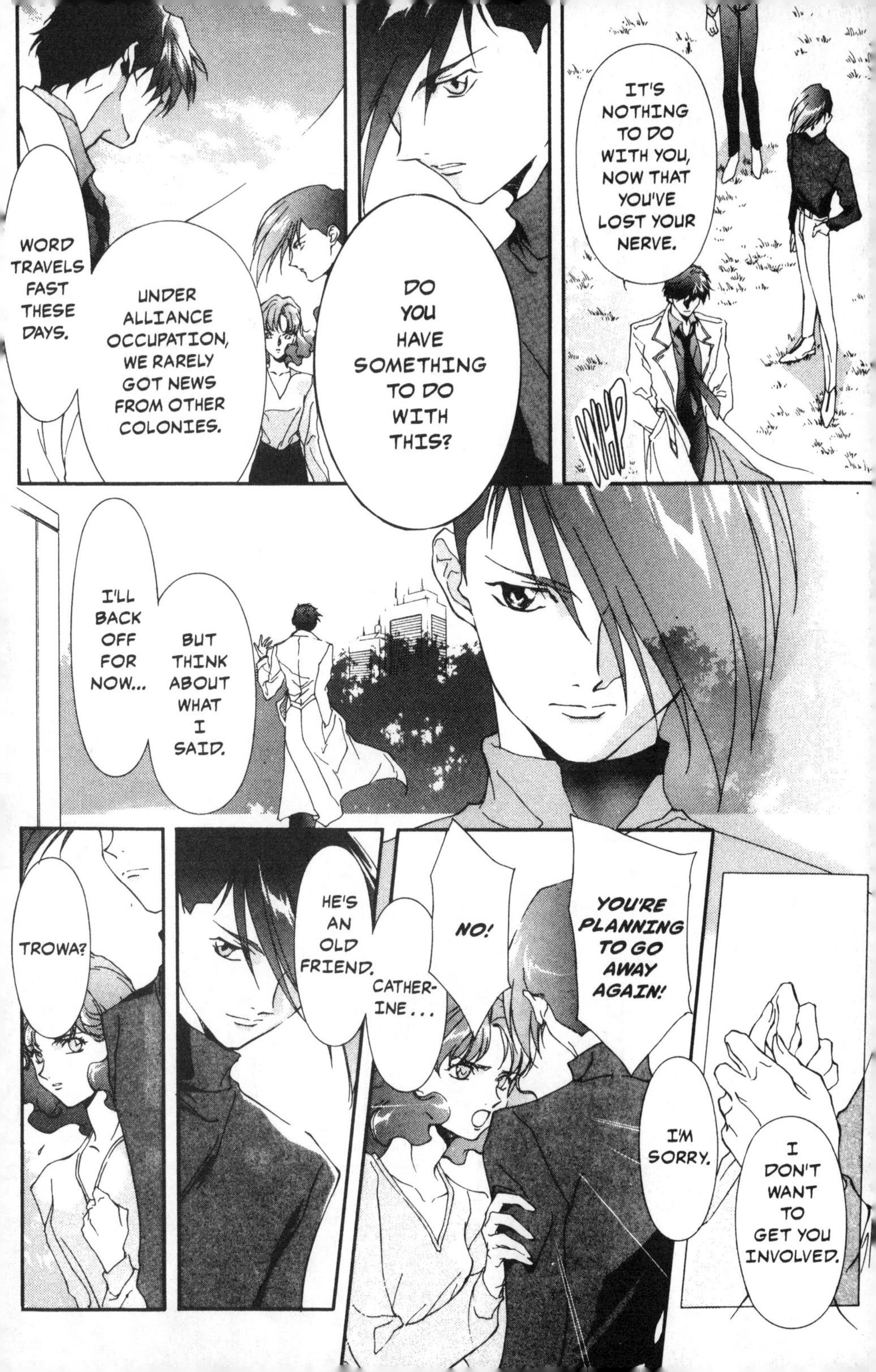
WORD TRAVELS FAST THESE DAYS.
UNDER ALLIANCE OCCUPATION, WE RARELY GOT NEWS FROM OTHER COLONIES.
DO YOU HAVE SOMETHING TO DO WITH THIS?
IT'S NOTHING TO DO WITH YOU, NOW THAT YOU'VE LOST YOUR NERVE.
WHIP
I'LL BACK OFF FOR NOW...
BUT THINK ABOUT WHAT I SAID.
TROWA?
HE'S AN OLD FRIEND.
CATHER-INE . . .
NO!
YOU'RE PLANNING TO GO AWAY AGAIN!
I'M SORRY.
I DON'T WANT TO GET YOU INVOLVED.

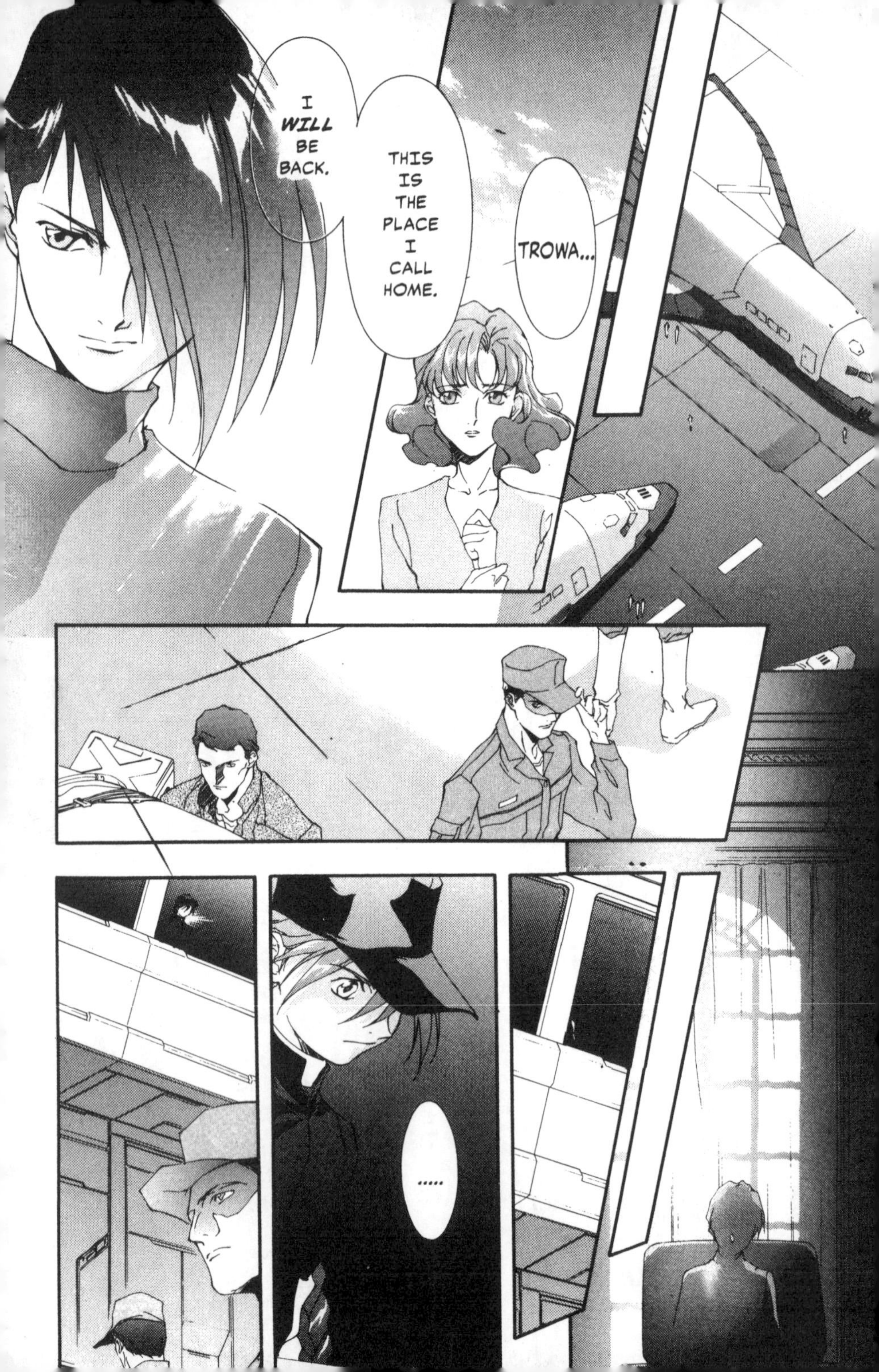
I WILL BE BACK.
THIS IS THE PLACE I CALL HOME.
TROWA...
......

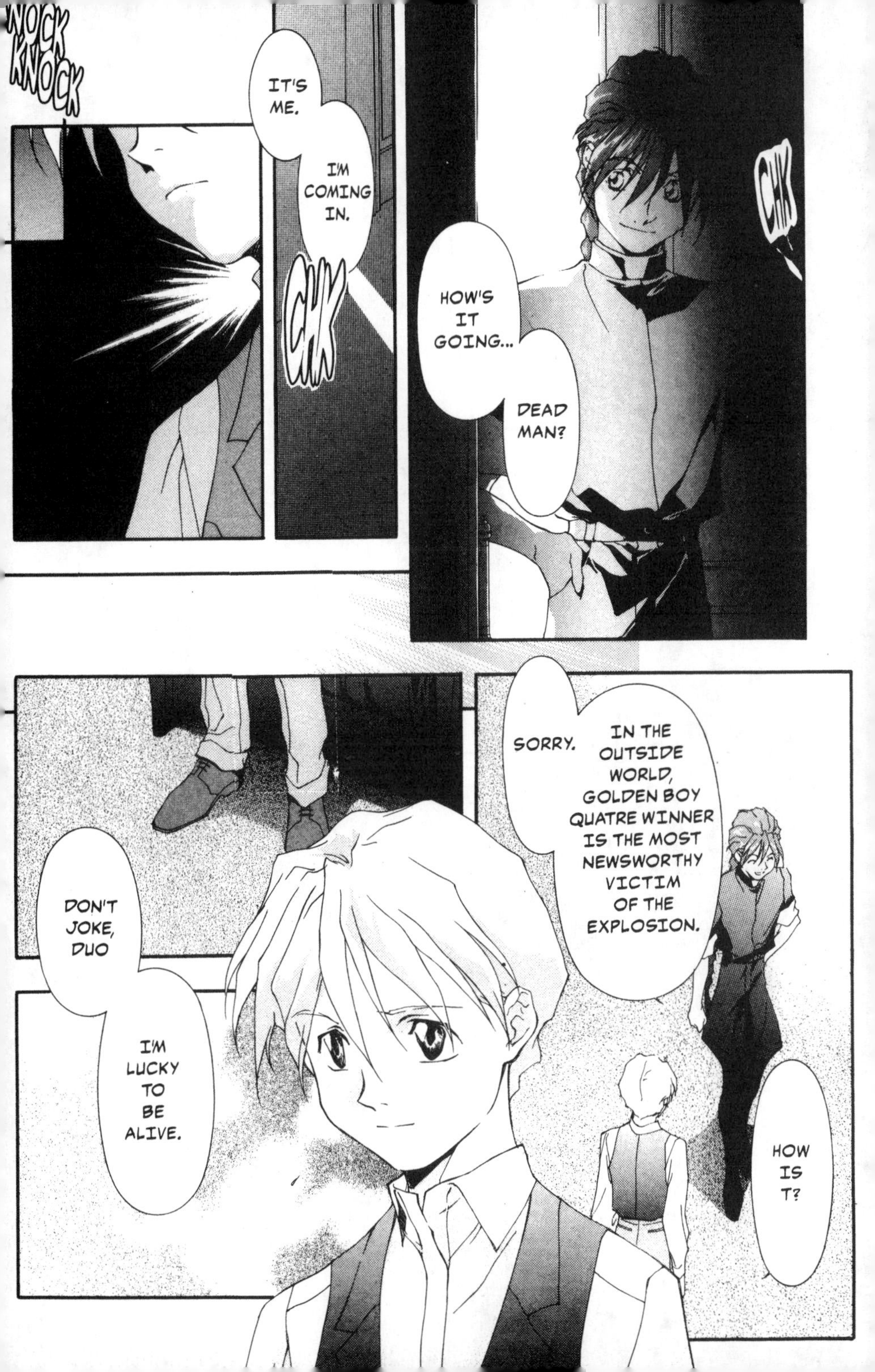
NOCK KNOCK
IT'S ME.
I'M COMING IN.
CHK
CHK
HOW'S IT GOING...
DEAD MAN?
SORRY.
IN THE OUTSIDE WORLD, GOLDEN BOY QUATRE WINNER IS THE MOST NEWSWORTHY VICTIM OF THE EXPLOSION.
DON'T JOKE, DUO
I'M LUCKY TO BE ALIVE.
HOW IS T?

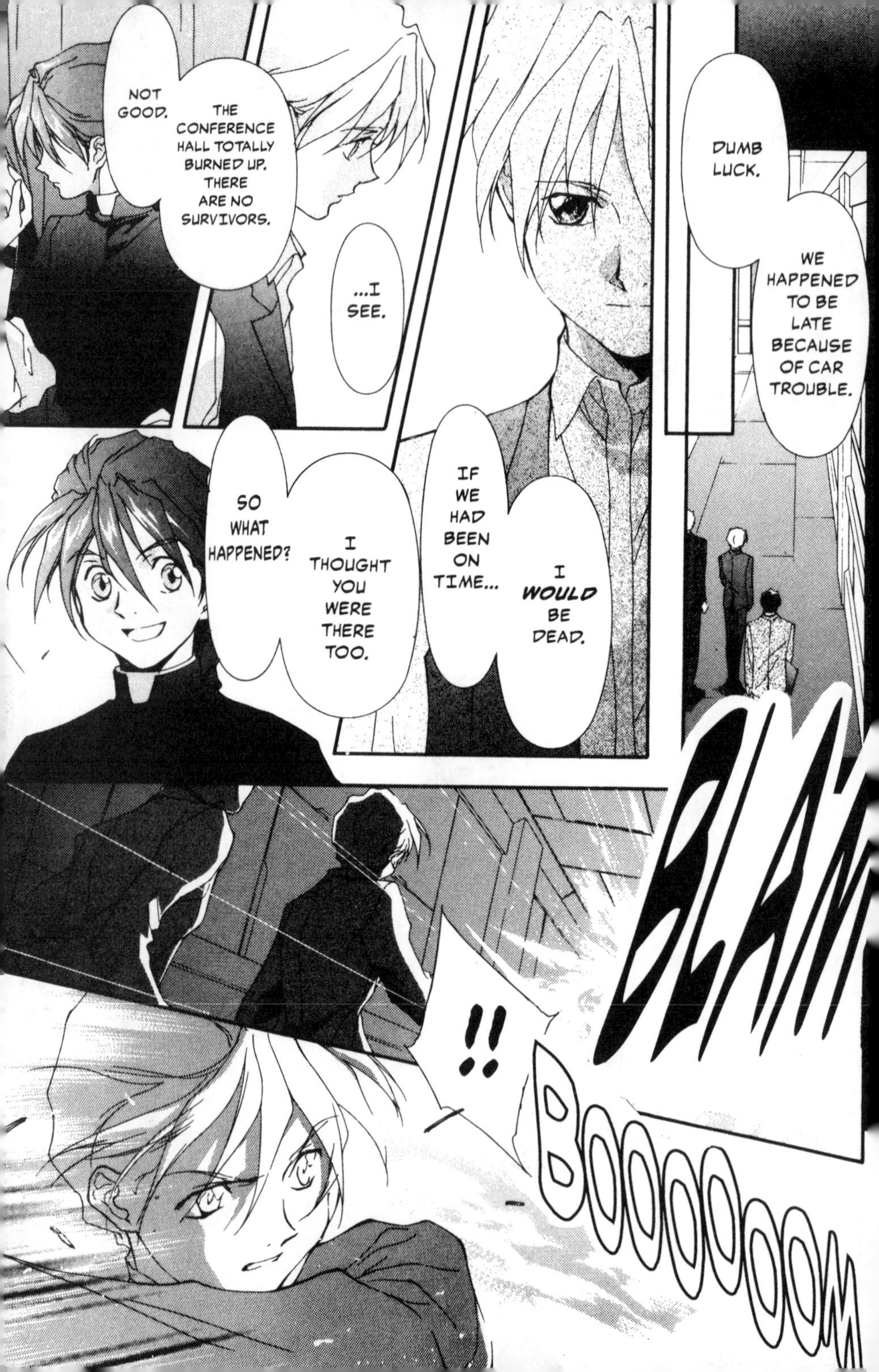
NOT GOOD.
THE CONFERENCE HALL TOTALLY BURNED UP. THERE ARE NO SURVIVORS.
...I SEE.
SO WHAT HAPPENED?
I THOUGHT YOU WERE THERE TOO.
DUMB LUCK.
WE HAPPENED TO BE LATE BECAUSE OF CAR TROUBLE.
IF WE HAD BEEN ON TIME...
I *WOULD* BE DEAD.
BLAM
!!
BOOOOOOM

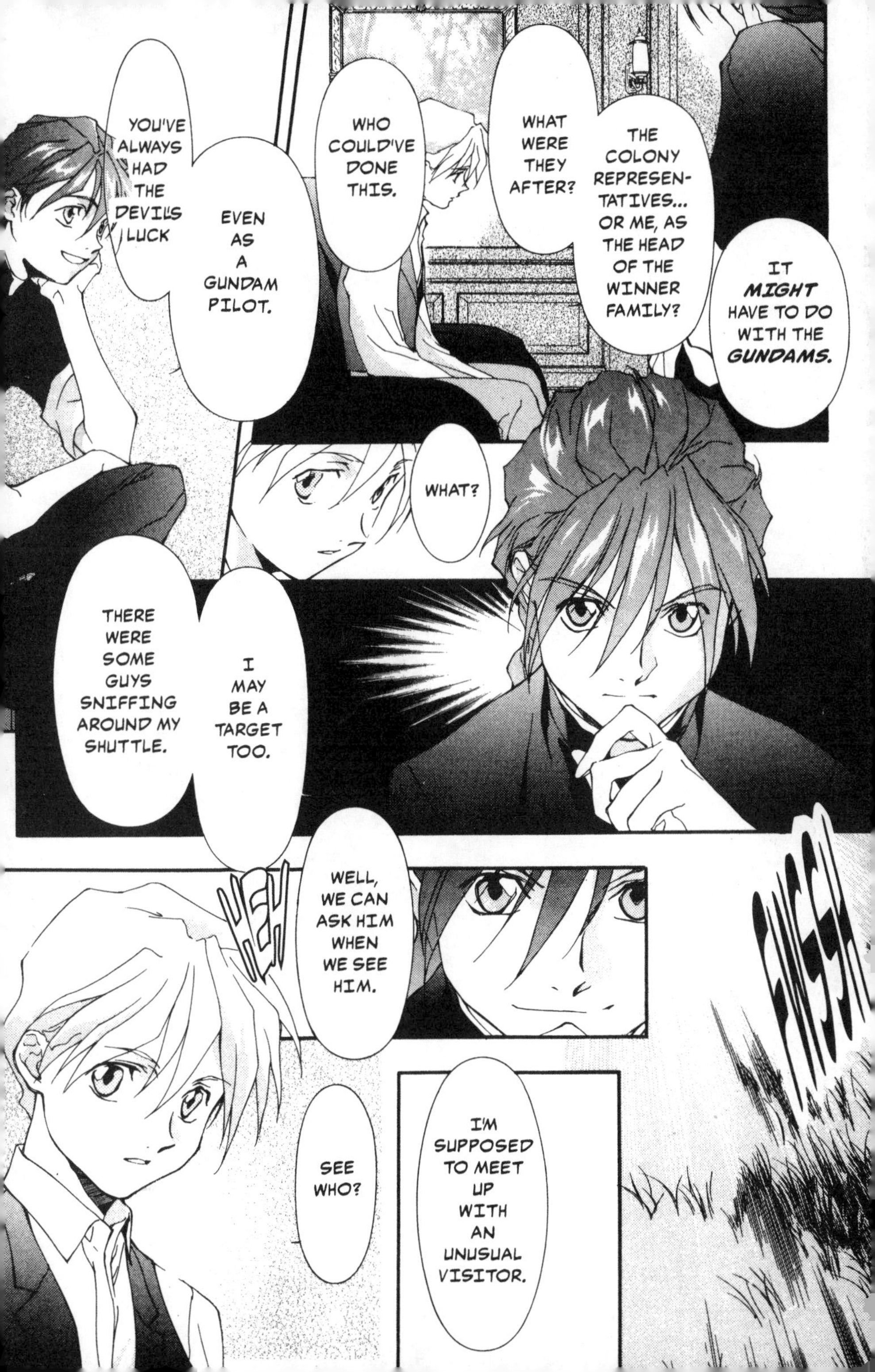
YOU'VE ALWAYS HAD THE DEVIL'S LUCK
EVEN AS A GUNDAM PILOT.
WHO COULD'VE DONE THIS.
WHAT WERE THEY AFTER?
THE COLONY REPRESENTATIVES... OR ME, AS THE HEAD OF THE WINNER FAMILY?
IT *MIGHT* HAVE TO DO WITH THE *GUNDAMS.*
WHAT?
THERE WERE SOME GUYS SNIFFING AROUND MY SHUTTLE.
I MAY BE A TARGET TOO.
WELL, WE CAN ASK HIM WHEN WE SEE HIM.
SEE WHO?
I'M SUPPOSED TO MEET UP WITH AN UNUSUAL VISITOR.

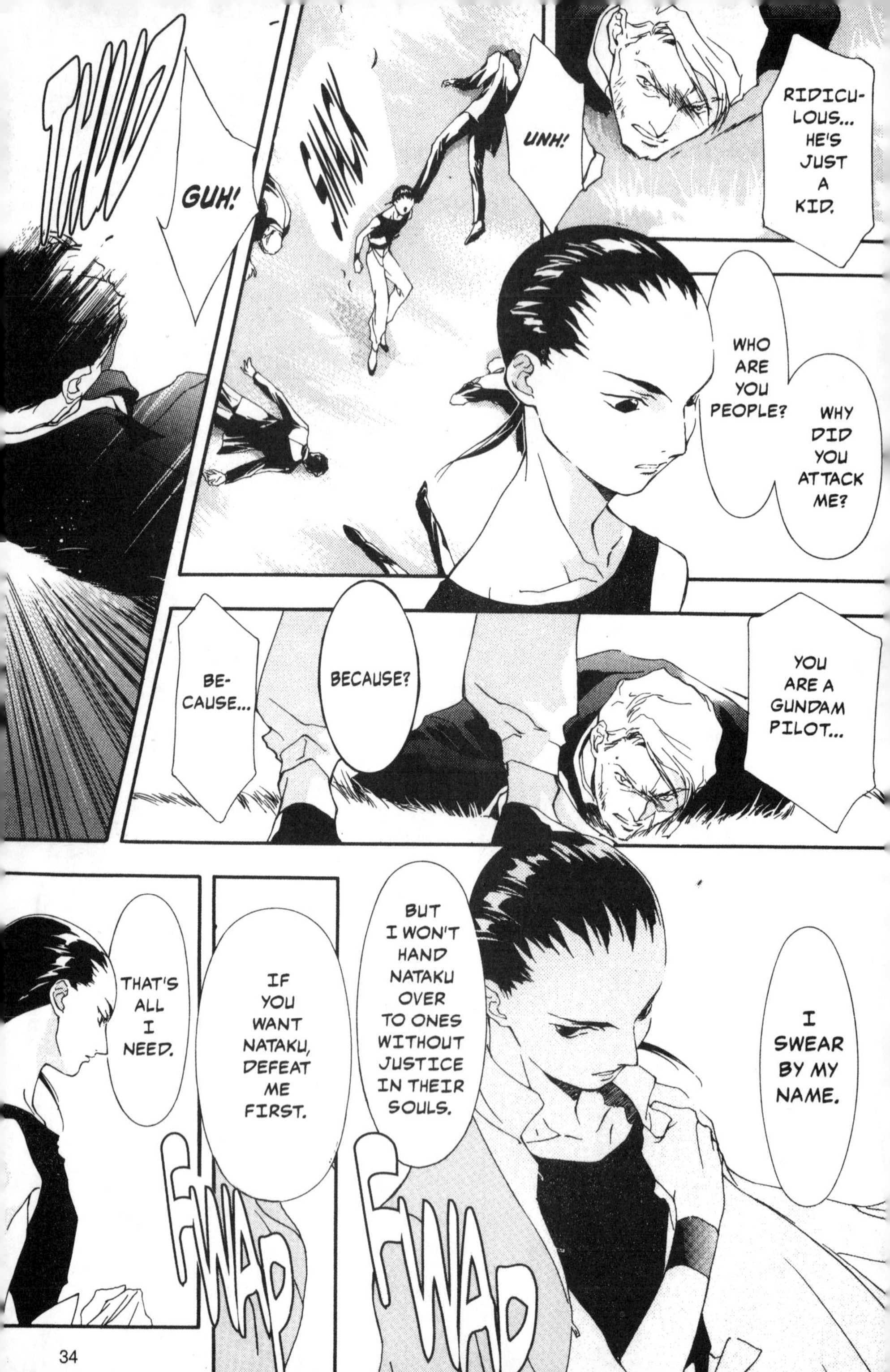

RIDICULOUS... HE'S JUST A KID.
UNH!
SMACK
WHO ARE YOU PEOPLE?
WHY DID YOU ATTACK ME?
GUH!
THUD
YOU ARE A GUNDAM PILOT...
BECAUSE?
BE-CAUSE...
I SWEAR BY MY NAME.
BUT I WON'T HAND NATAKU OVER TO ONES WITHOUT JUSTICE IN THEIR SOULS.
IF YOU WANT NATAKU, DEFEAT ME FIRST.
THAT'S ALL I NEED.
FWAP
FWAP

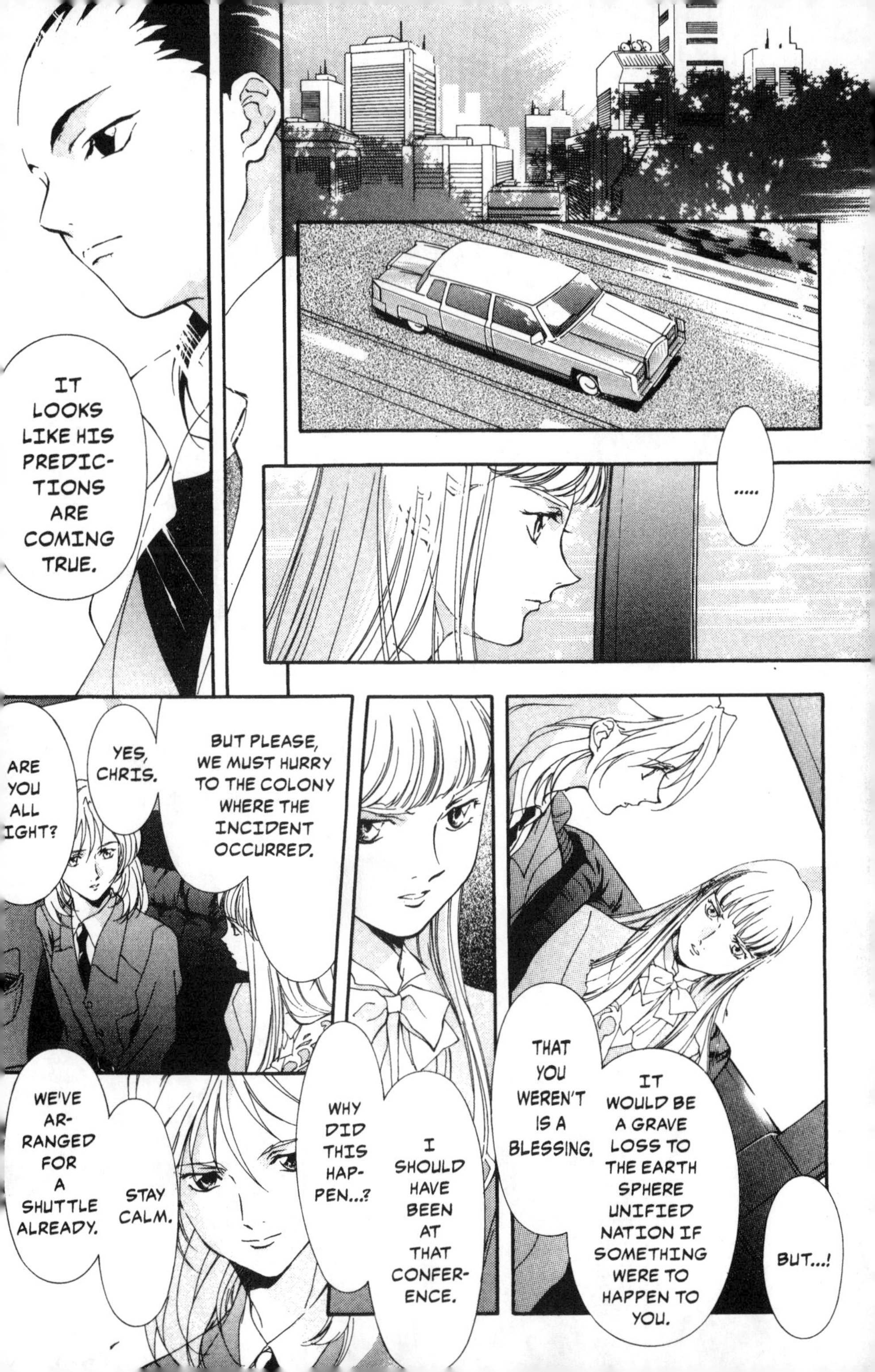
IT LOOKS LIKE HIS PREDICTIONS ARE COMING TRUE.
.....
ARE YOU ALL IGHT?
YES, CHRIS.
BUT PLEASE, WE MUST HURRY TO THE COLONY WHERE THE INCIDENT OCCURRED.
WE'VE ARRANGED FOR A SHUTTLE ALREADY.
STAY CALM.
WHY DID THIS HAPPEN...?
I SHOULD HAVE BEEN AT THAT CONFERENCE.
THAT YOU WEREN'T IS A BLESSING.
IT WOULD BE A GRAVE LOSS TO THE EARTH SPHERE UNIFIED NATION IF SOMETHING WERE TO HAPPEN TO YOU.
BUT...!

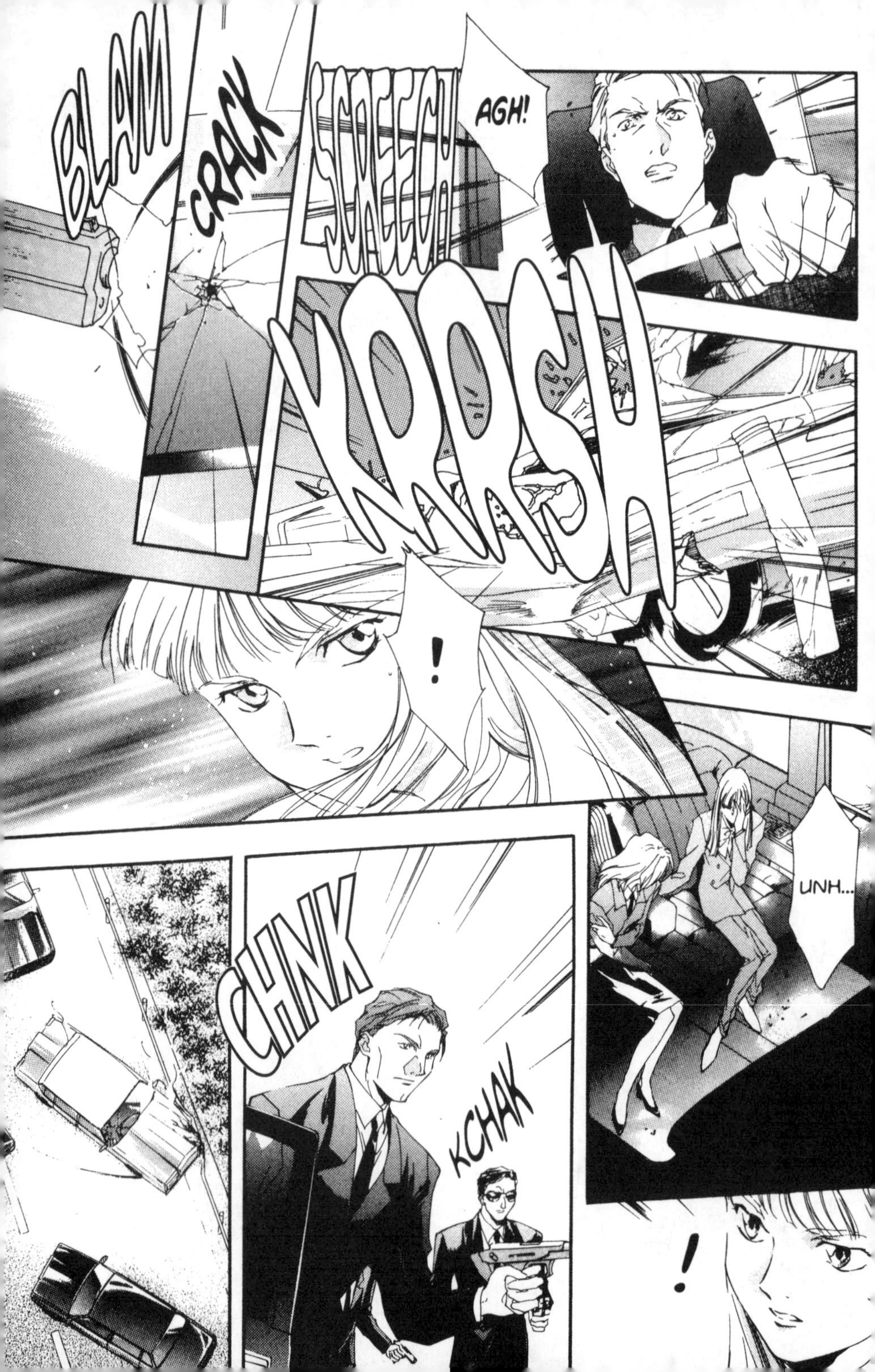
AGH!
SCREECH
CRACK
BLAM
KRRSH
!
UNH...
CHNK
KCHAK
!

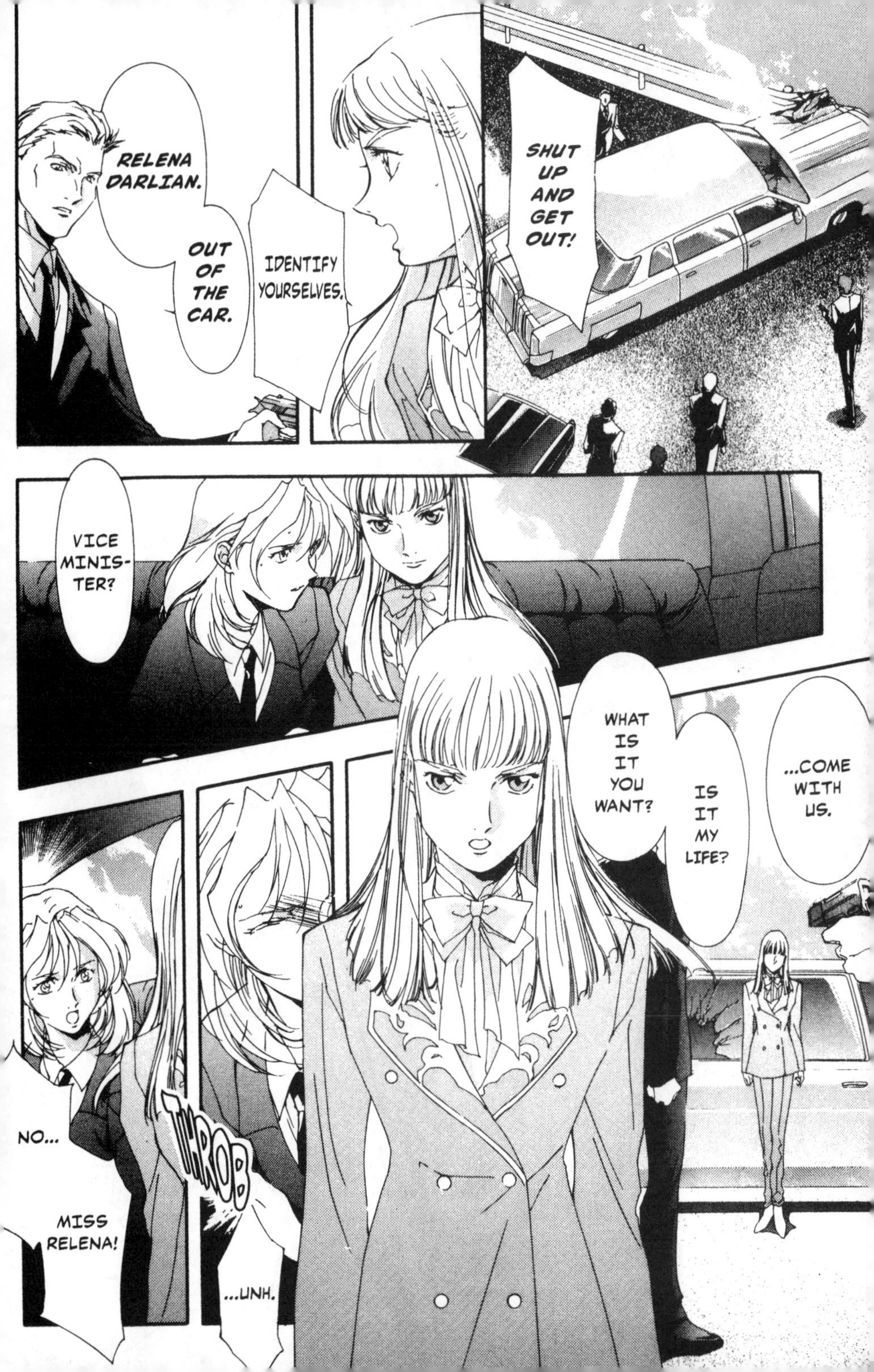
RELENA DARLIAN.
OUT OF THE CAR.
IDENTIFY YOURSELVES.
SHUT UP AND GET OUT!
VICE MINISTER?
NO...
MISS RELENA!
THROB
...UNH.
WHAT IS IT YOU WANT?
IS IT MY LIFE?
...COME WITH US.

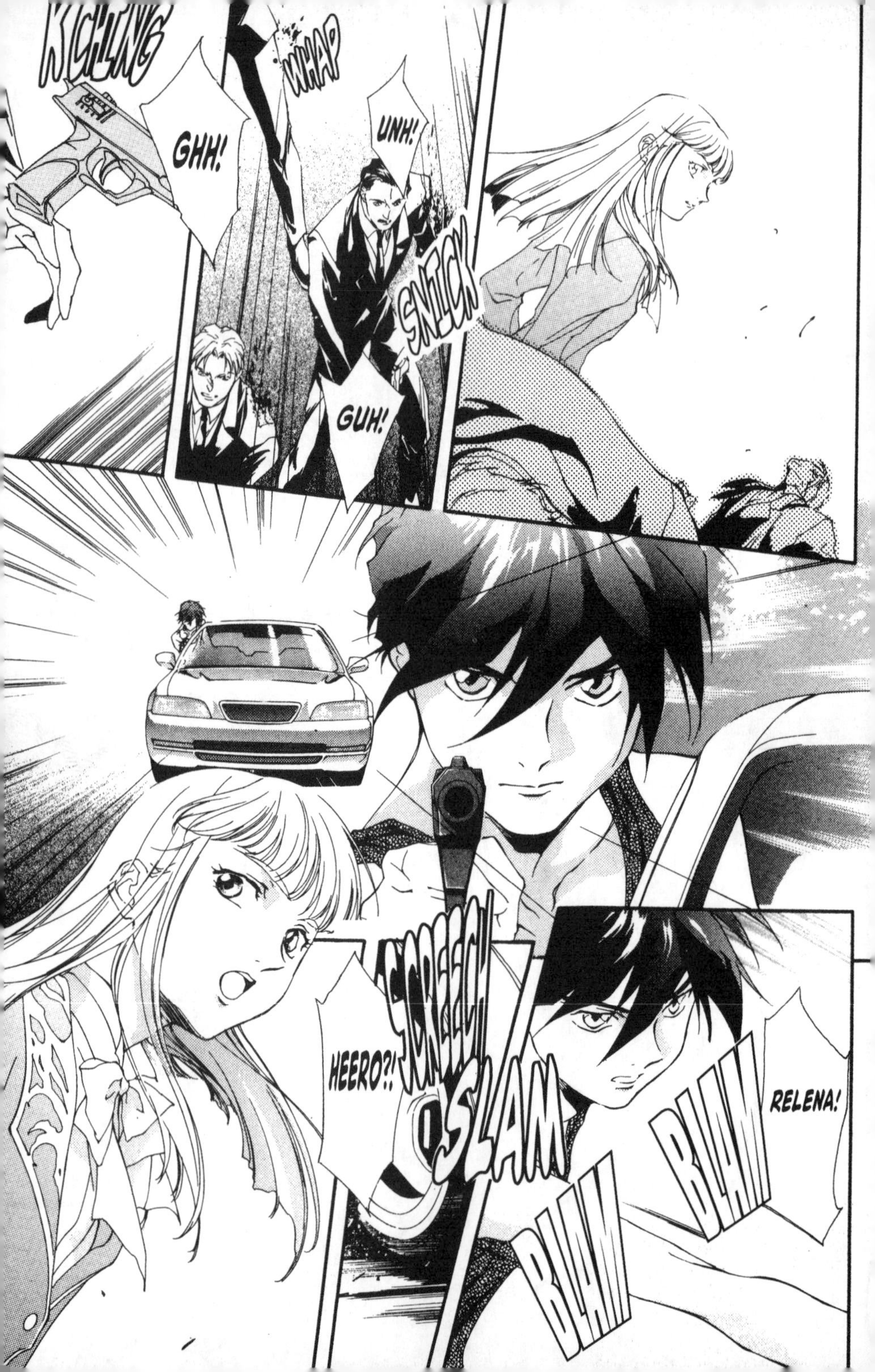

K'CHING
GHH!
WHAP
UNH!
SNATCH
GUH!
HEERO?!
SCREECH
SLAM
BLAM
BLAM
RELENA!

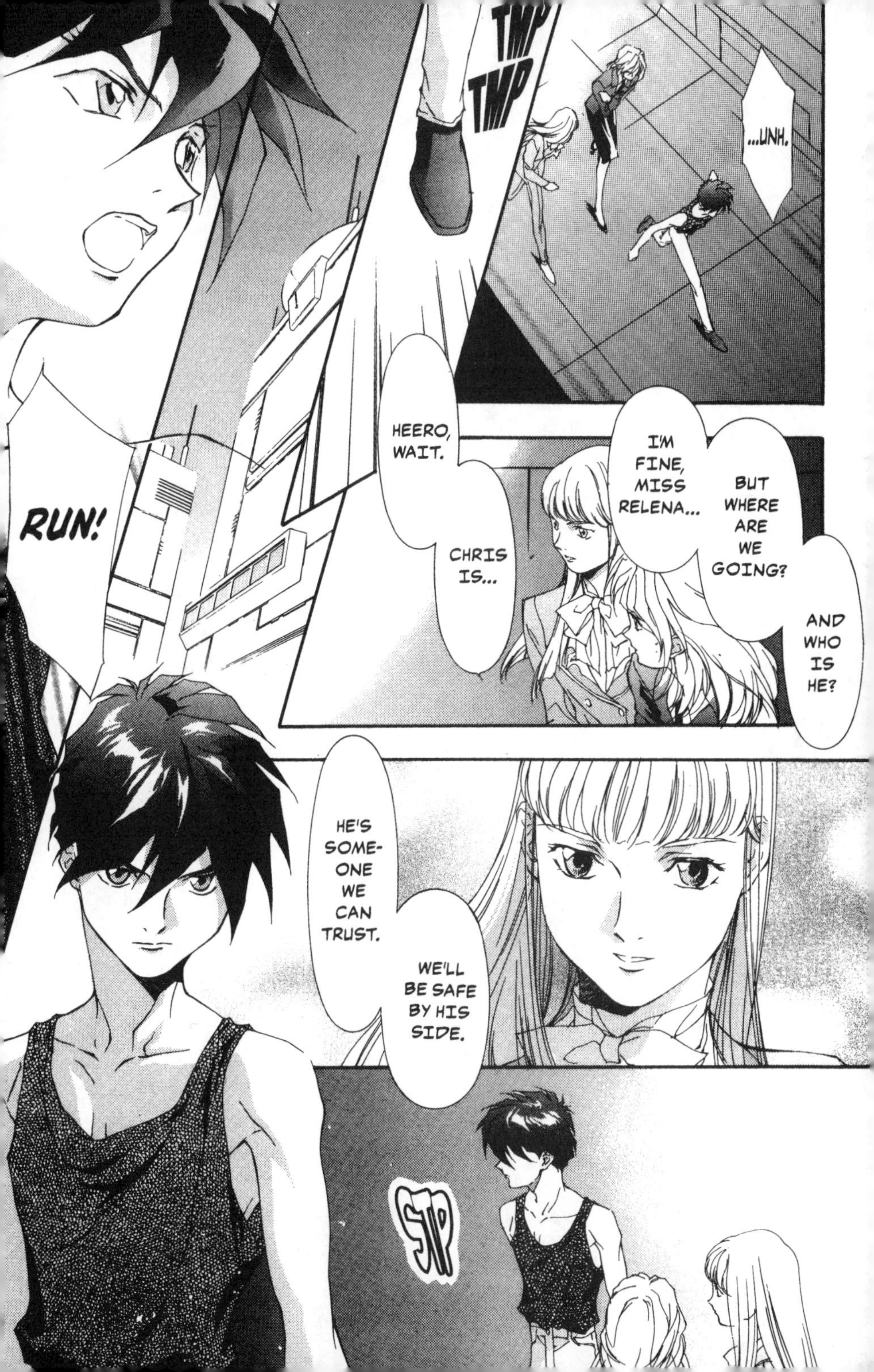
RUN!
TMP TMP
...UNH.
HEERO, WAIT.
CHRIS IS...
I'M FINE, MISS RELENA...
BUT WHERE ARE WE GOING?
AND WHO IS HE?
HE'S SOME-ONE WE CAN TRUST.
WE'LL BE SAFE BY HIS SIDE.
STP

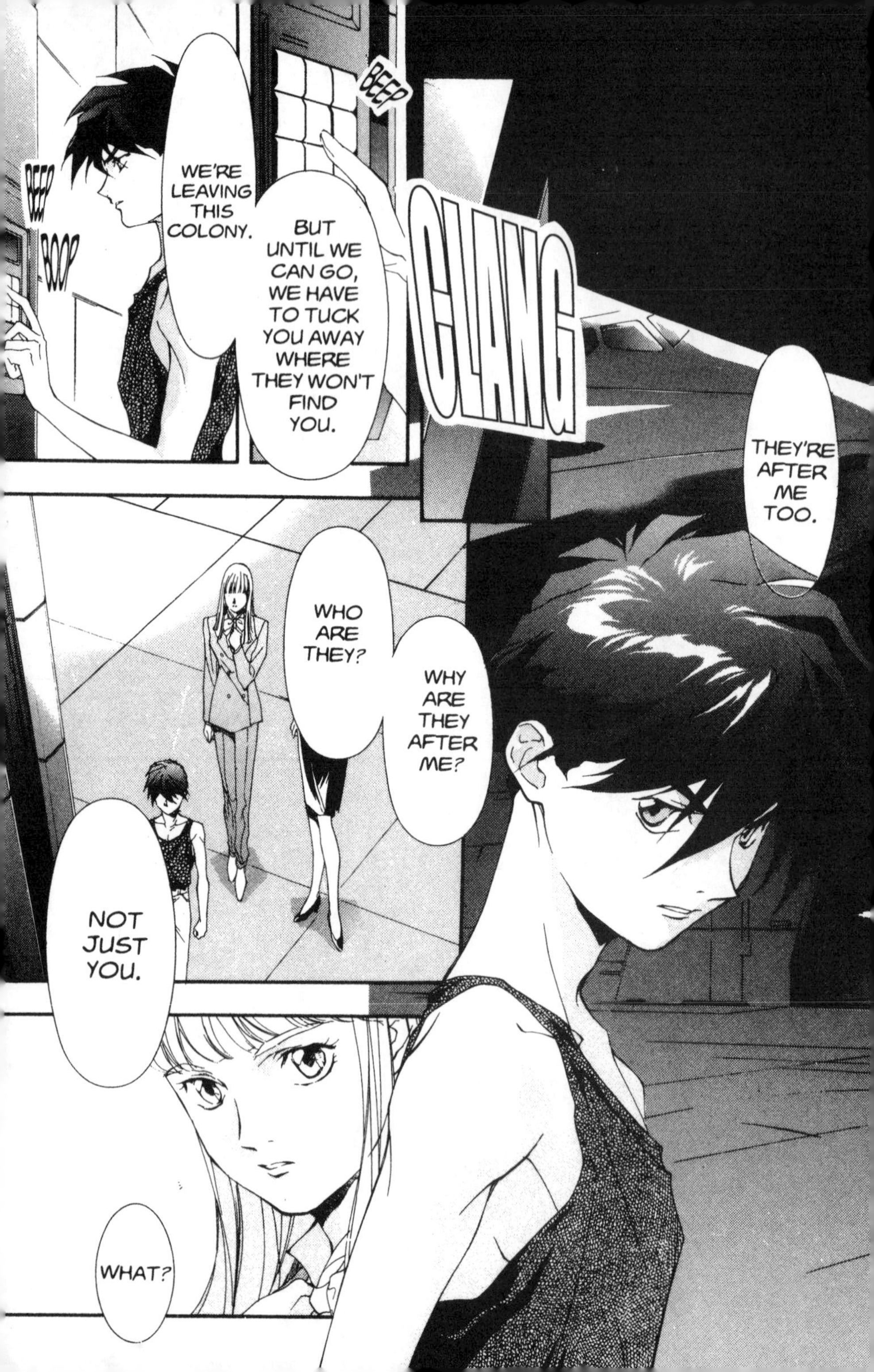
BEEP
BEEP
BOOP
WE'RE LEAVING THIS COLONY.
BUT UNTIL WE CAN GO, WE HAVE TO TUCK YOU AWAY WHERE THEY WON'T FIND YOU.
CLANG
WHO ARE THEY?
WHY ARE THEY AFTER ME?
NOT JUST YOU.
WHAT?
THEY'RE AFTER ME TOO.

SUBHEADER: A HEROIC DESTINY HAS ITS PRICE, AS OUR HEROES CAN PLAINLY SEE. BUT WHAT'S BROUGHT ON THIS LATEST ASSAULT?

MOBILE SUIT GUNDAM WING REMIX I I........

1

DUO XWELL: T YOUR ERVICE!

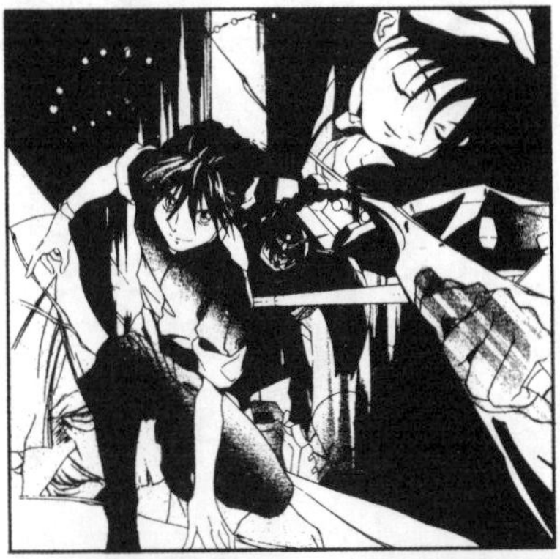

LIFE CAN BE LONELY AS A NAMELESS WAR ORPHAN, BUT DUO HAS SURVIVED BY HIS WITS, TAKING THE NAME OF SOMEONE HE MET ALONG THE WAY - LIKE TROWA.

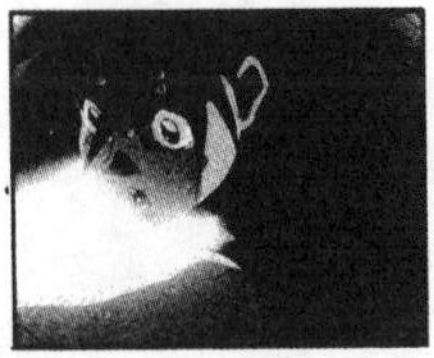

EVEN THOUGH HE KNOWS IT'S ▲ DANGEROUS, DUO NEVER HESITATES TO PUSH HIMSELF INTO THE ACTION . . .AND THE TROUBLE. ARE THESE THE ACTIONS OF A WORRYWART?

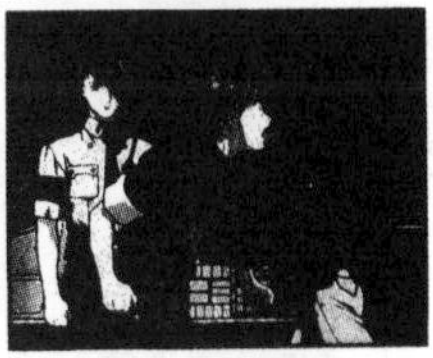

THIS FAMOUS PUNCH LEFT ▲ HEERO AND DUO "EVEN," BUT DUO DIDN'T HAVE MUCH OF A CHANCE.

Once a war orphan wandering through the colonies as a junkman, kind, optimistic. Duo has always gone to where the trouble is, and usually gets himself hurt in the bargain. As a mobile suit pilot and communications engineer, he's the tops, but as a fighter he's more about street smarts than strength or prowess--no match for warriors like Heero or Wufei. Ranked fourth on the team in fighting skills but first in good-natured generosity, Duo may feel even his friends are suckering him sometimes. In the "Endless Waltz", for instance, Heero got a fight started that he was sure to win, knocking Duo out and getting him thrown in jail; from Duo's side, it sure looked like the short end of the stick, but most of the time he doesn't see it that way. He is all to happy to do most of the hard work when storming Colony X-18999 with Heero, and in this story, we'll see him smile through every kind of crisis as he plays messenger, nursemaid and errand boy for the others. So, is he really a worrywart and a sucker, or is he using his wits: how does a lonely orphan best keep his new–and only—family together and safe?

2

TROWA: WHAT IS IT ABOUT HIS GUY?

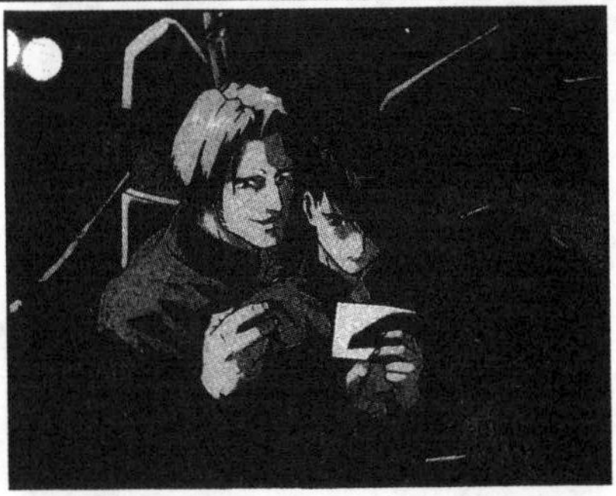

◀ THE REAL TROWA WAS IN HIS 20's WHEN HE BE-FRIENDED OUR MYSTER-IOUS MECH-ANIC.

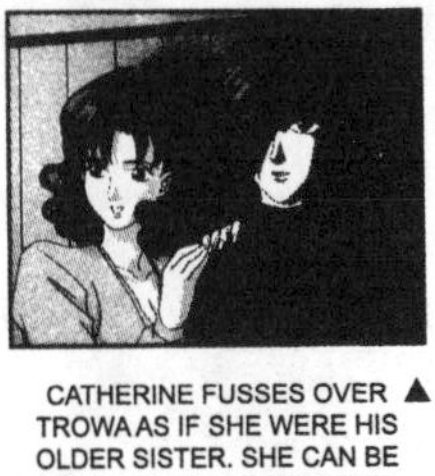

CATHERINE FUSSES OVER ▲ TROWA AS IF SHE WERE HIS OLDER SISTER. SHE CAN BE PRETTY OVERPROTECTIVE.

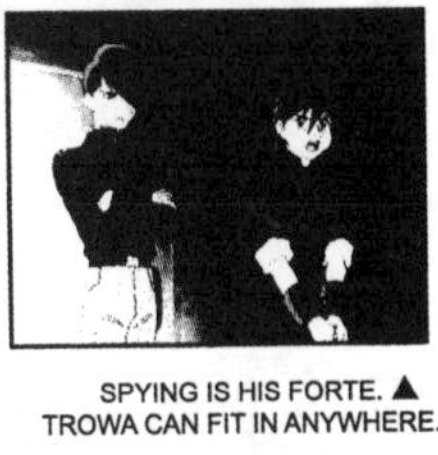

SPYING IS HIS FORTE. ▲ TROWA CAN FIT IN ANYWHERE.

He endures anything for the sake of the battle, speaks seldom and rarely betrays his emotions--it's easy to see him as little more than another surly teenager.
And yet, Trowa is surprisingly popular with his elders; the real Trowa was devoted to the nameless boy(our Trowa), telling him all about his family, proudly showing him pictures of his sister and niece, and at the circus, Catherine treats him like a favored younger brother. In the "Endless Waltz", Dekim Barton lets the boy into the army, even knowing him to be an imposter Perhaps his laconic nature instills a sense of security in others. And here's another thing: the Barton Foundation was behind Operation Meteor, yet the Gundam pilots never questioned Trowa Barton about his name. Why not? Well, Trowa tells only Quatre his last name (in the beginning of the TV series) and of all the members of the team, only Quatre doesn't know the name of the foundation behind Meteor. So what gives? The other three worked with Trowa all this time and never knew his last name. Should he have told, or should they have asked?

The pictures were taken from the TV series and "Endless Waltz."

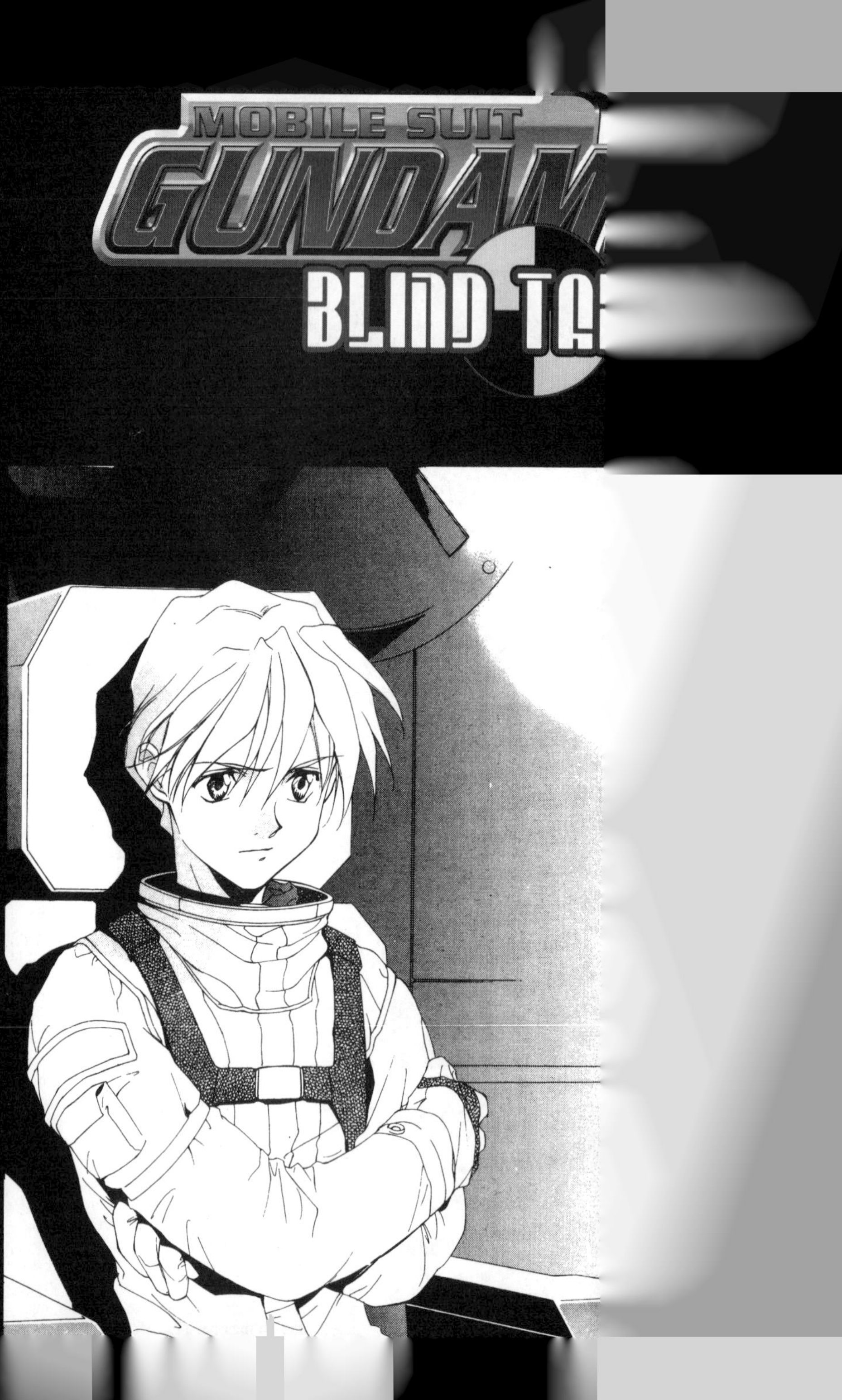
MOBILE SUIT

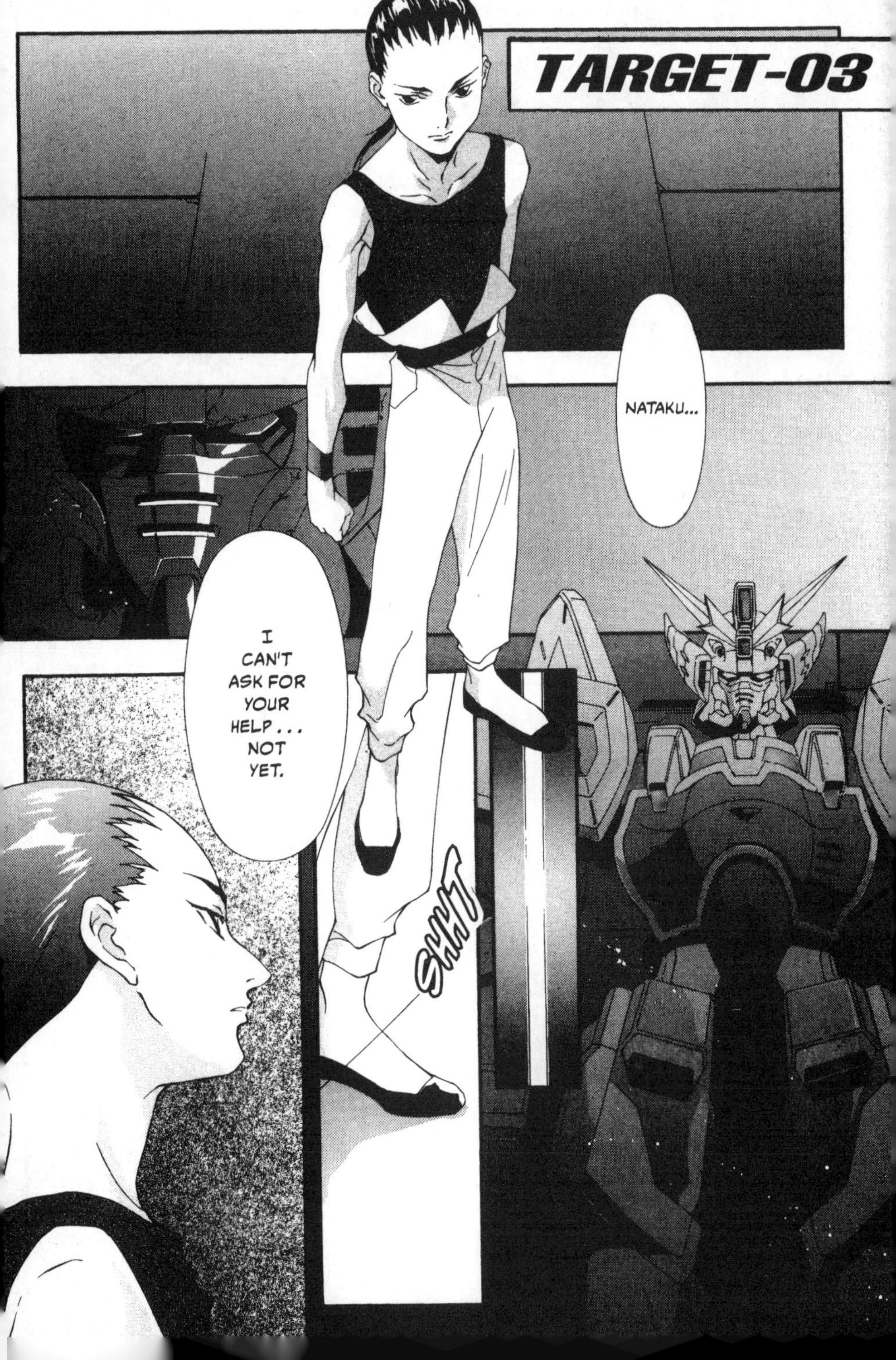
TARGET-03
NATAKU...
I CAN'T ASK FOR YOUR HELP... NOT YET.
SHHT

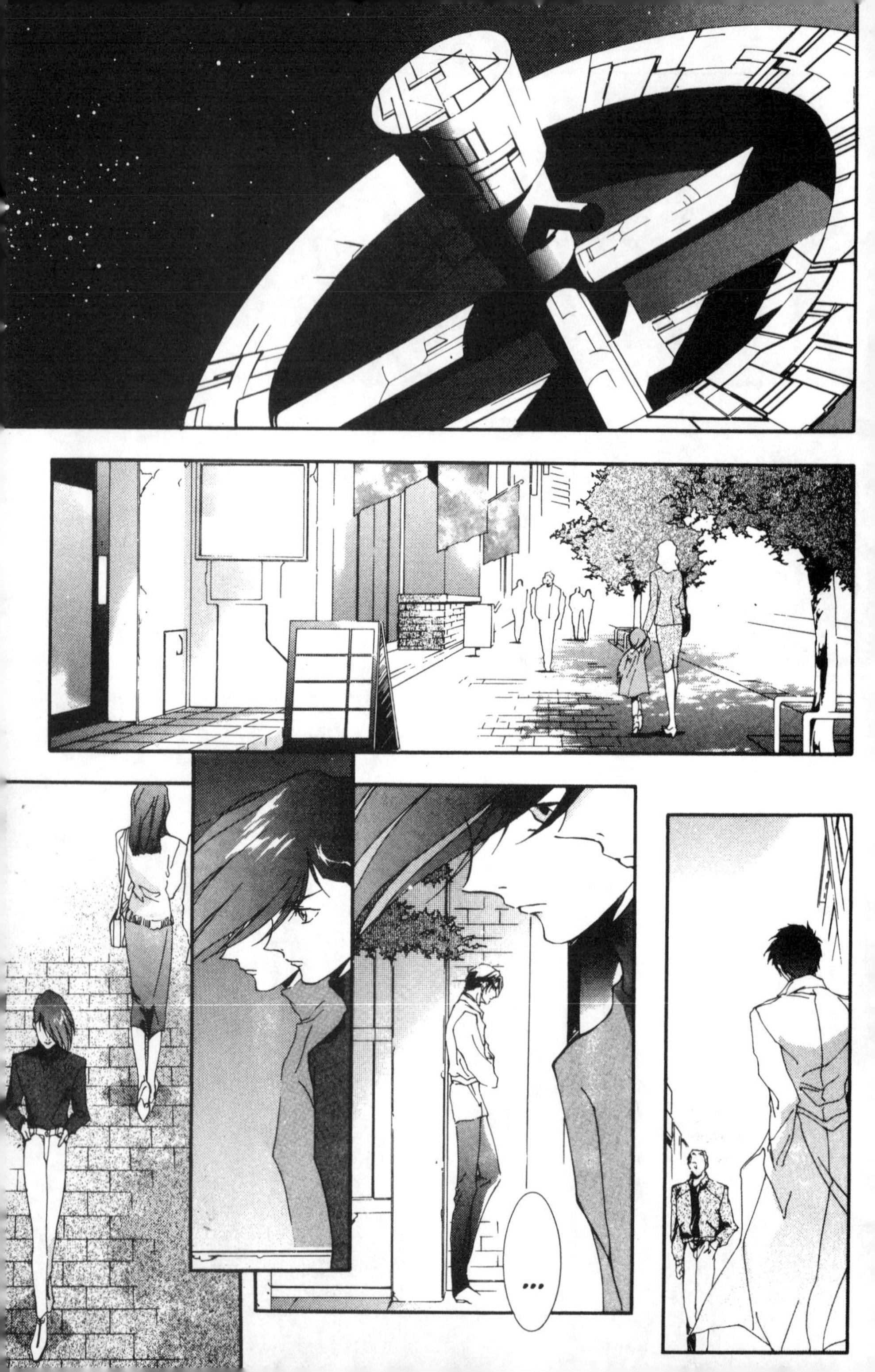
...

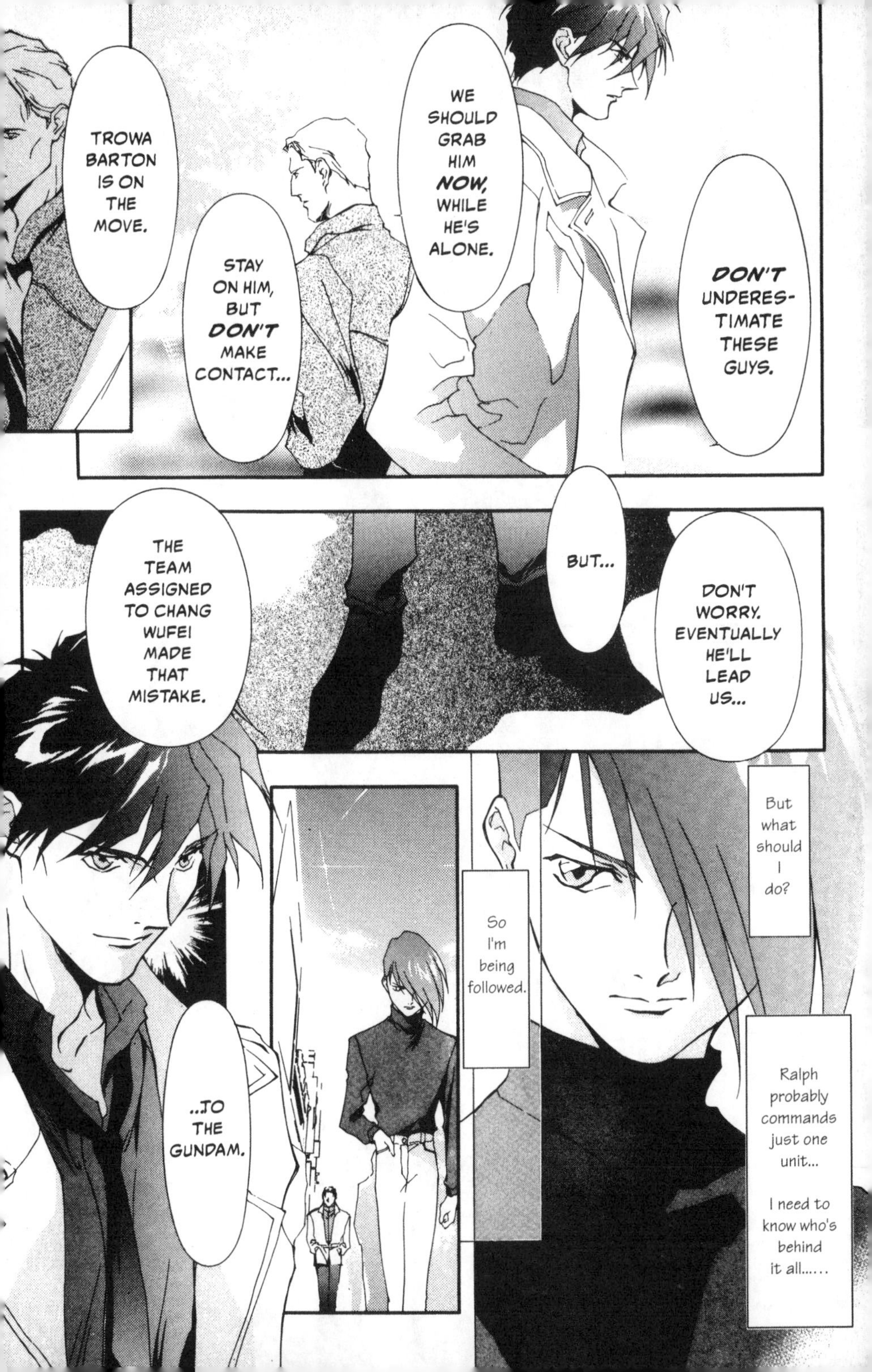
TROWA BARTON IS ON THE MOVE.
STAY ON HIM, BUT ***DON'T*** MAKE CONTACT...
WE SHOULD GRAB HIM ***NOW,*** WHILE HE'S ALONE.
DON'T UNDERES-TIMATE THESE GUYS.
THE TEAM ASSIGNED TO CHANG WUFEI MADE THAT MISTAKE.
BUT...
DON'T WORRY. EVENTUALLY HE'LL LEAD US...
..TO THE GUNDAM.
So I'm being followed.
But what should I do?
Ralph probably commands just one unit...
I need to know who's behind it all......

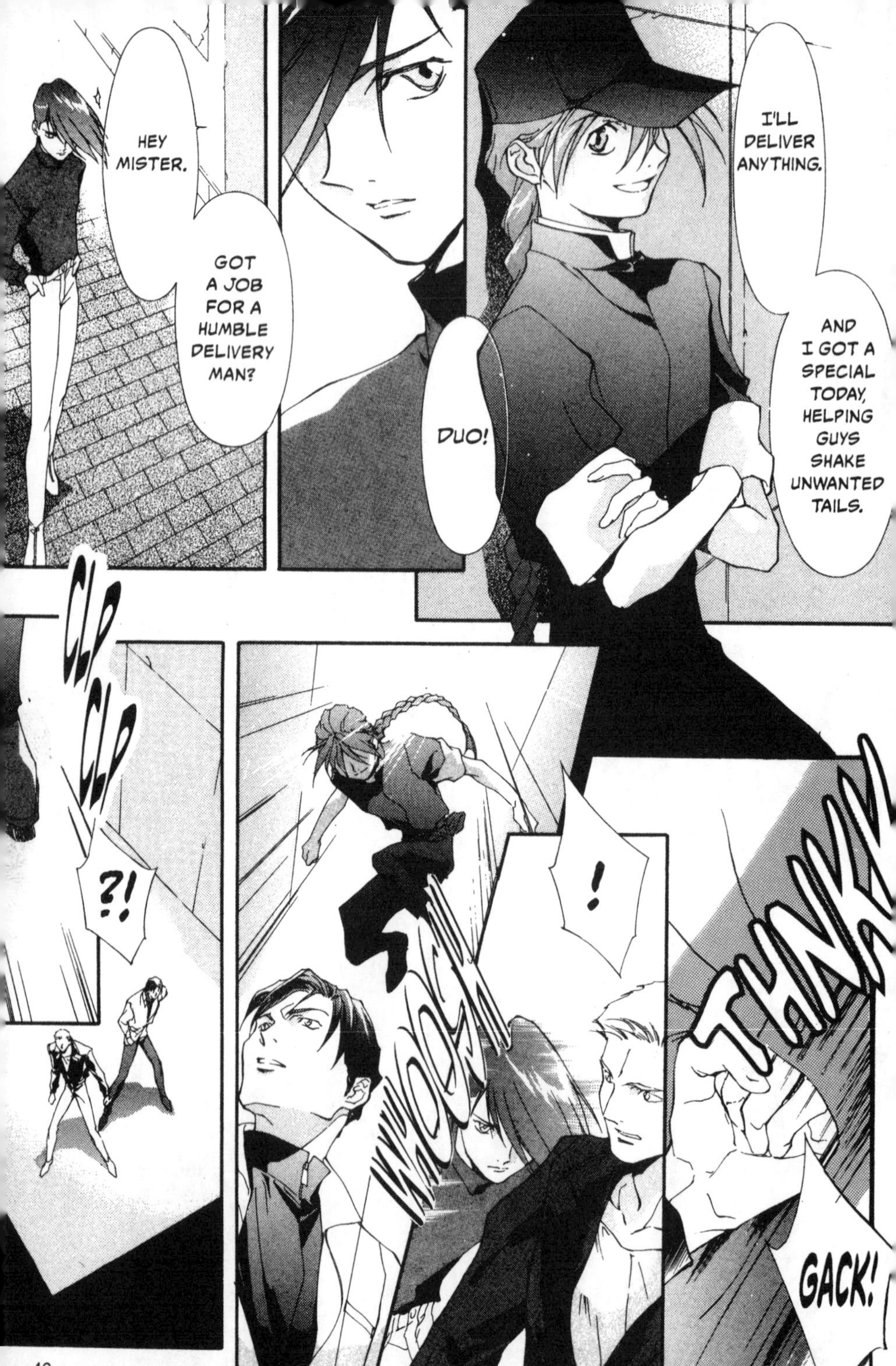
HEY MISTER.
GOT A JOB FOR A HUMBLE DELIVERY MAN?
DUO!
I'LL DELIVER ANYTHING.
AND I GOT A SPECIAL TODAY, HELPING GUYS SHAKE UNWANTED TAILS.
CLP CLP
?!
WHOOSH
!
THWAK
GACK!

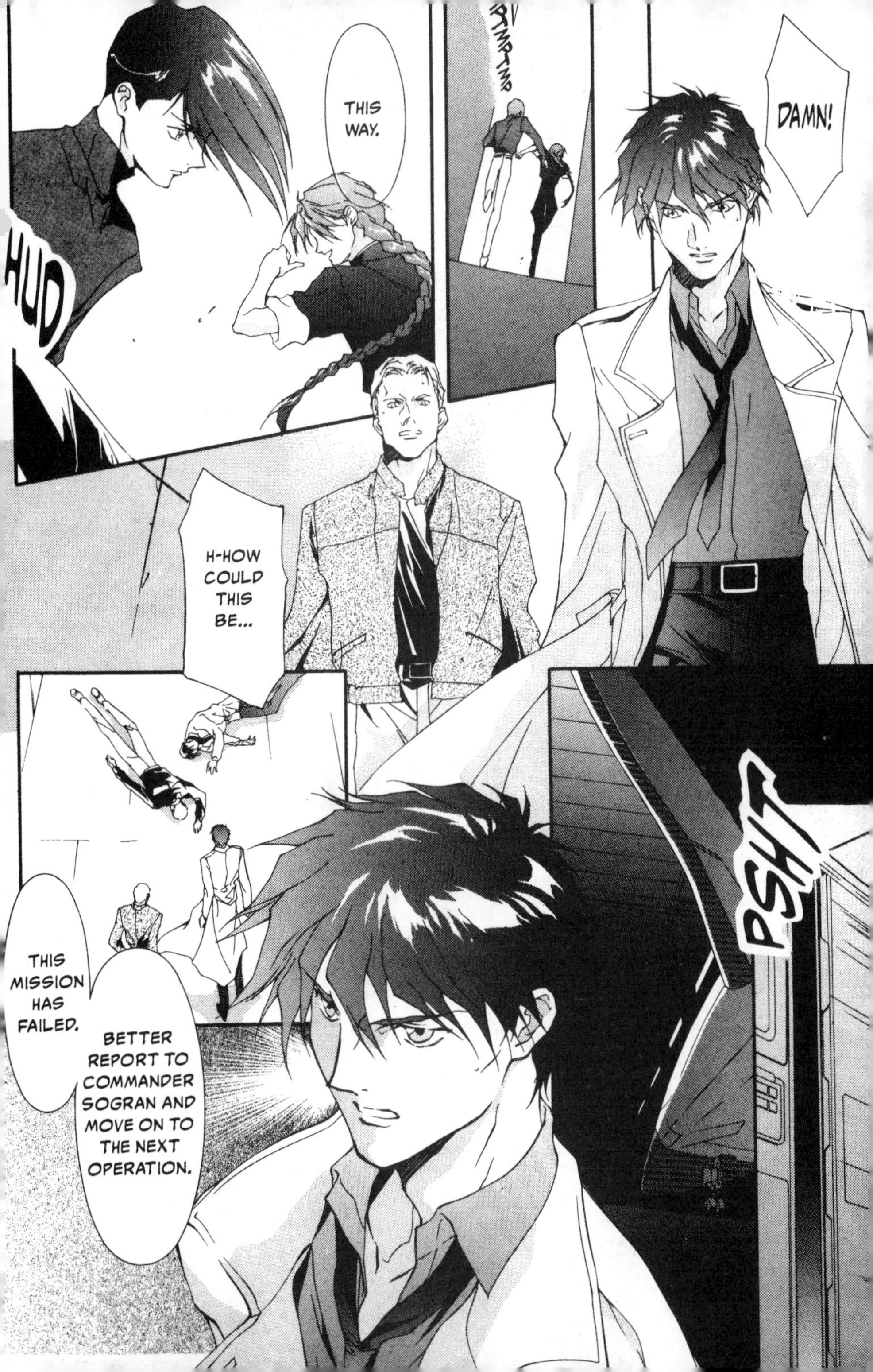
HUD
THIS WAY.
TMPTMP
DAMN!
H-HOW COULD THIS BE...
THIS MISSION HAS FAILED.
BETTER REPORT TO COMMANDER SOGRAN AND MOVE ON TO THE NEXT OPERATION.
PSHT

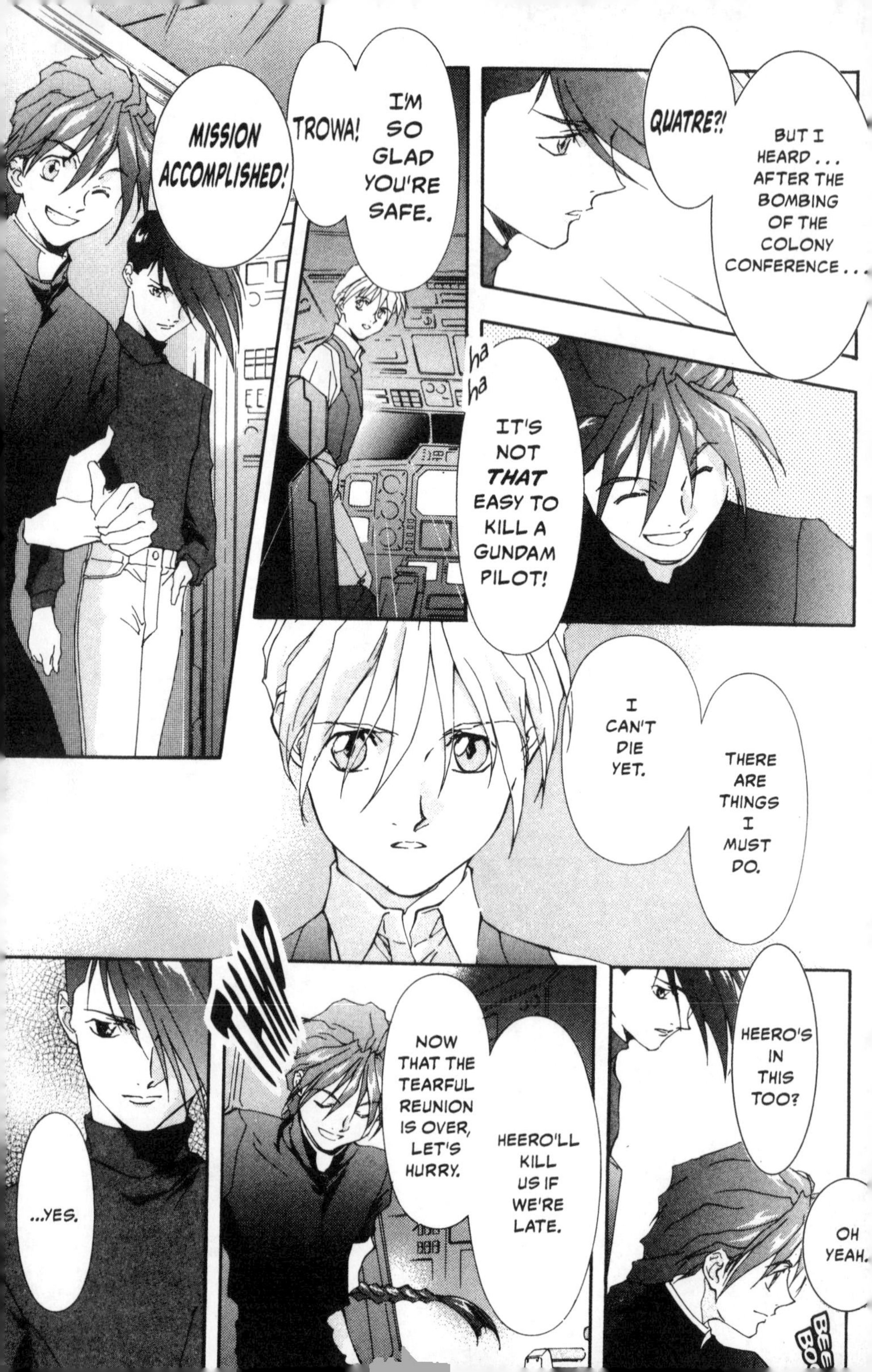

MISSION ACCOMPLISHED!
TROWA!
I'M SO GLAD YOU'RE SAFE.
QUATRE?!
BUT I HEARD... AFTER THE BOMBING OF THE COLONY CONFERENCE...
ha ha
IT'S NOT *THAT* EASY TO KILL A GUNDAM PILOT!
I CAN'T DIE YET.
THERE ARE THINGS I MUST DO.
...YES.
NOW THAT THE TEARFUL REUNION IS OVER, LET'S HURRY.
HEERO'LL KILL US IF WE'RE LATE.
HEERO'S IN THIS TOO?
OH YEAH.

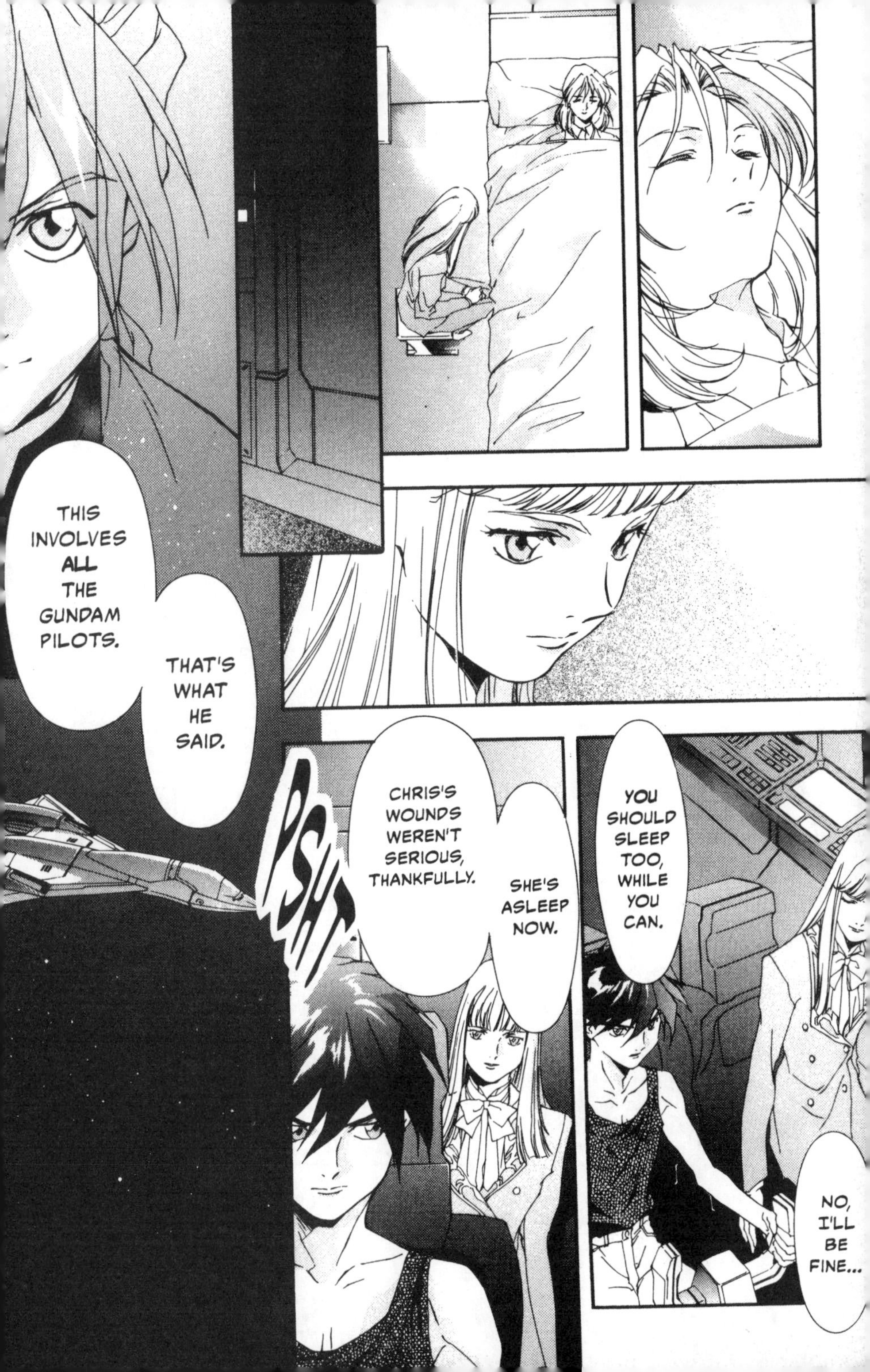
THIS INVOLVES ALL THE GUNDAM PILOTS.
THAT'S WHAT HE SAID.
PSHT
CHRIS'S WOUNDS WEREN'T SERIOUS, THANKFULLY.
SHE'S ASLEEP NOW.
YOU SHOULD SLEEP TOO, WHILE YOU CAN.
NO, I'LL BE FINE...

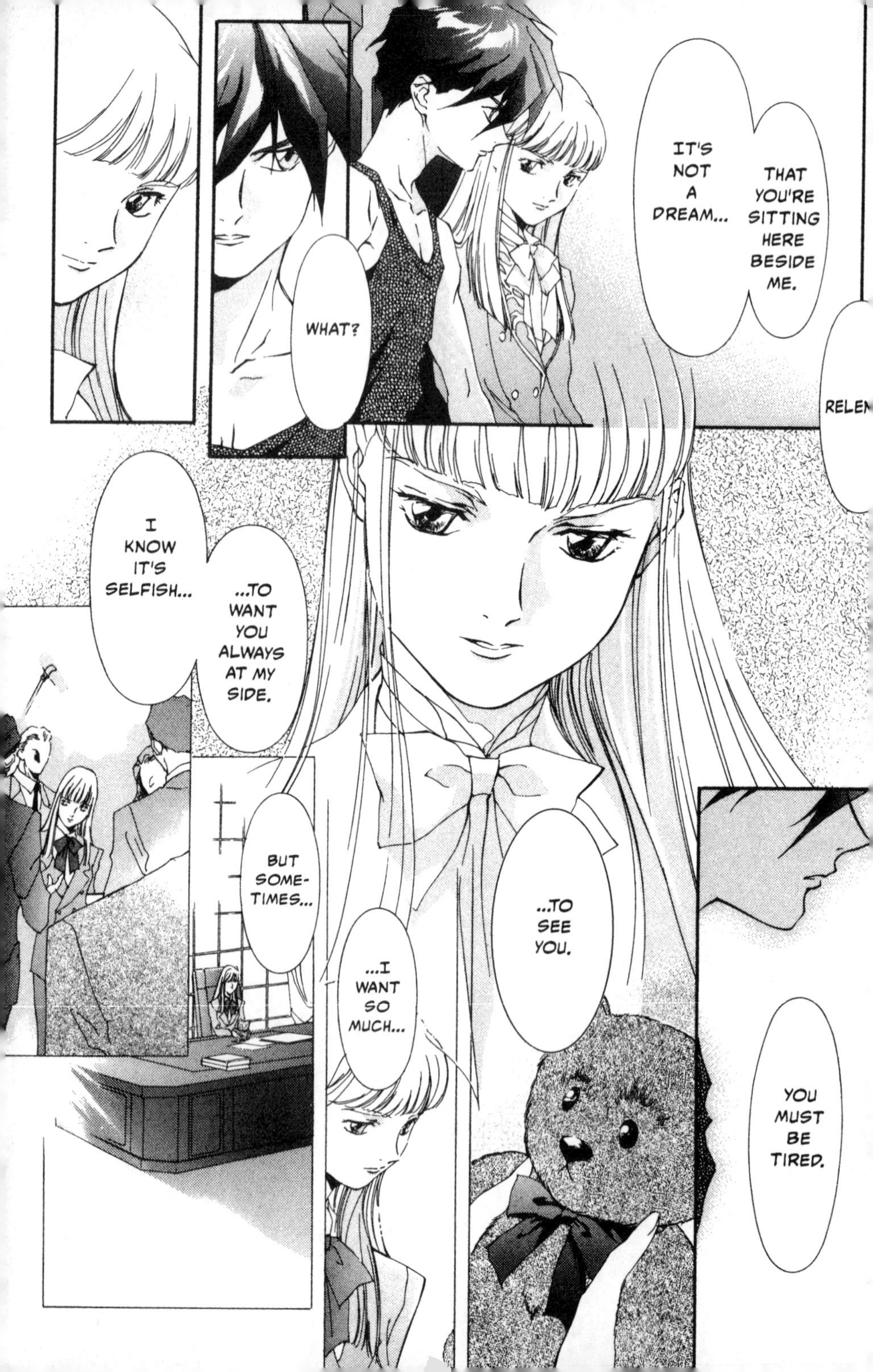
WHAT?
IT'S NOT A DREAM...
THAT YOU'RE SITTING HERE BESIDE ME.
RELEN
I KNOW IT'S SELFISH...
...TO WANT YOU ALWAYS AT MY SIDE.
BUT SOME-TIMES...
...I WANT SO MUCH...
...TO SEE YOU.
YOU MUST BE TIRED.

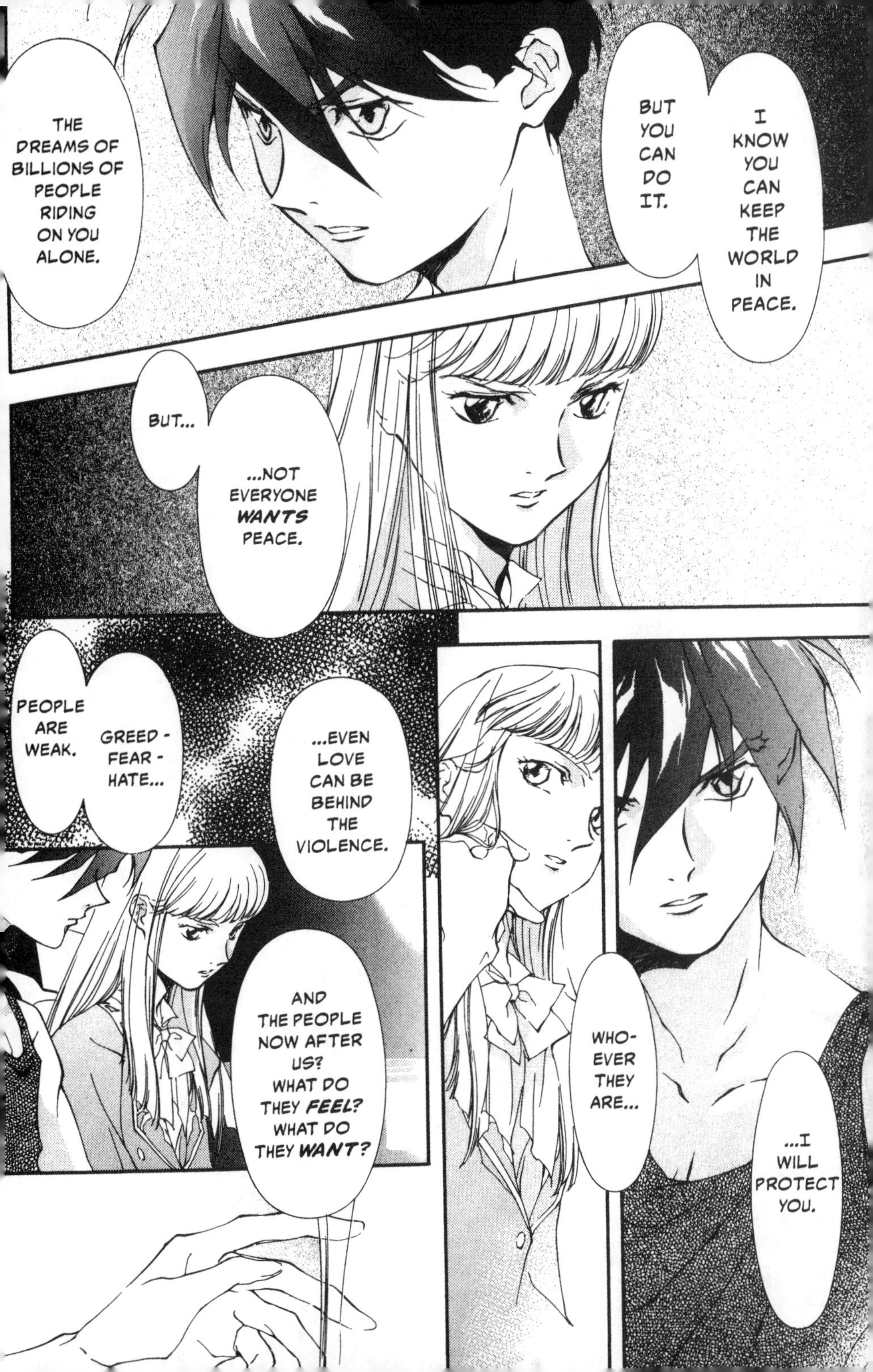
THE DREAMS OF BILLIONS OF PEOPLE RIDING ON YOU ALONE.
BUT YOU CAN DO IT.
I KNOW YOU CAN KEEP THE WORLD IN PEACE.
BUT...
...NOT EVERYONE *WANTS* PEACE.
PEOPLE ARE WEAK.
GREED - FEAR - HATE...
...EVEN LOVE CAN BE BEHIND THE VIOLENCE.
AND THE PEOPLE NOW AFTER US? WHAT DO THEY *FEEL?* WHAT DO THEY *WANT?*
WHO-EVER THEY ARE...
...I WILL PROTECT YOU.

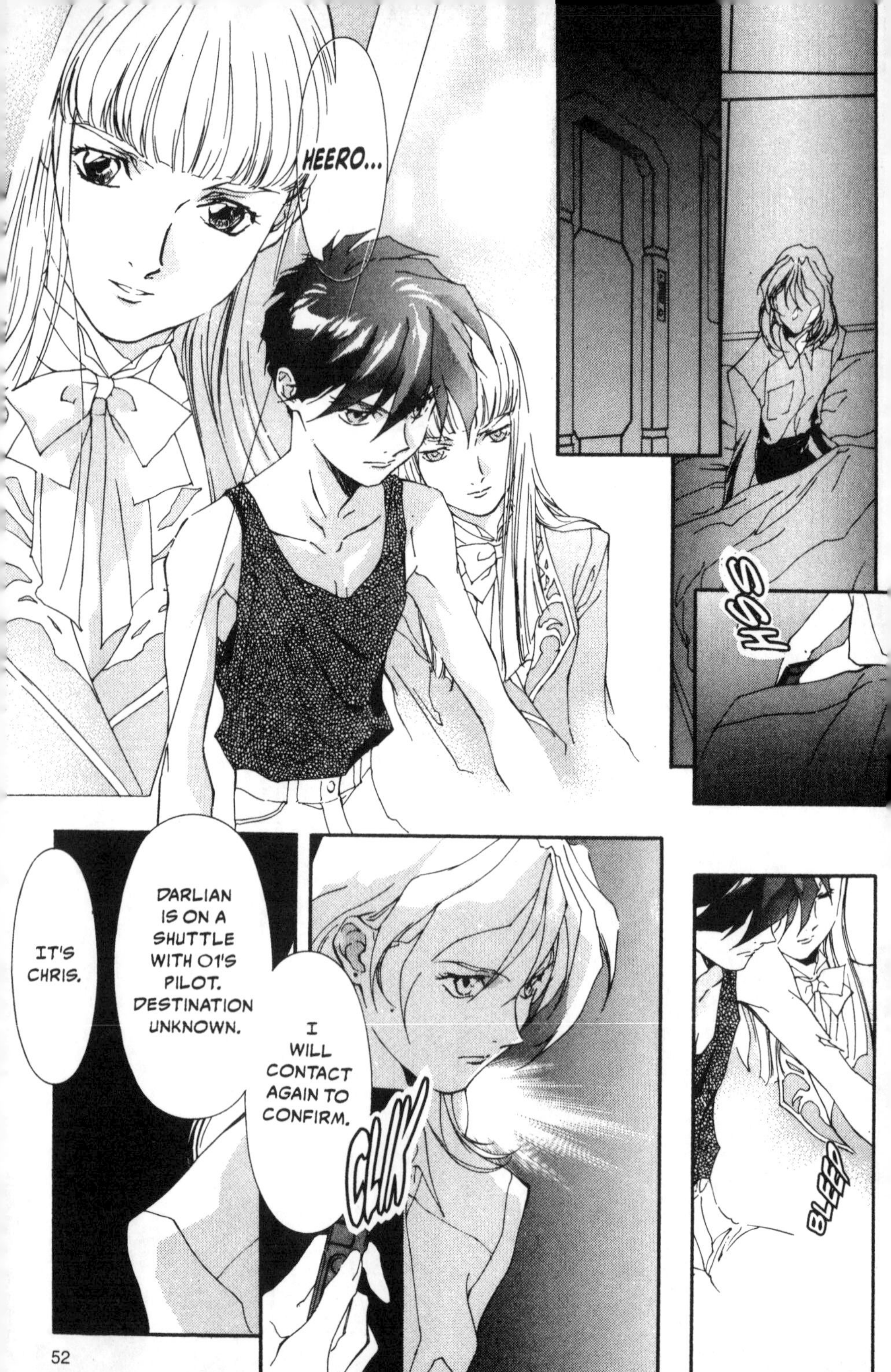
HEERO...
SSGH
IT'S CHRIS.
DARLIAN IS ON A SHUTTLE WITH 01'S PILOT. DESTINATION UNKNOWN.
I WILL CONTACT AGAIN TO CONFIRM.
CLIK
BLEEP

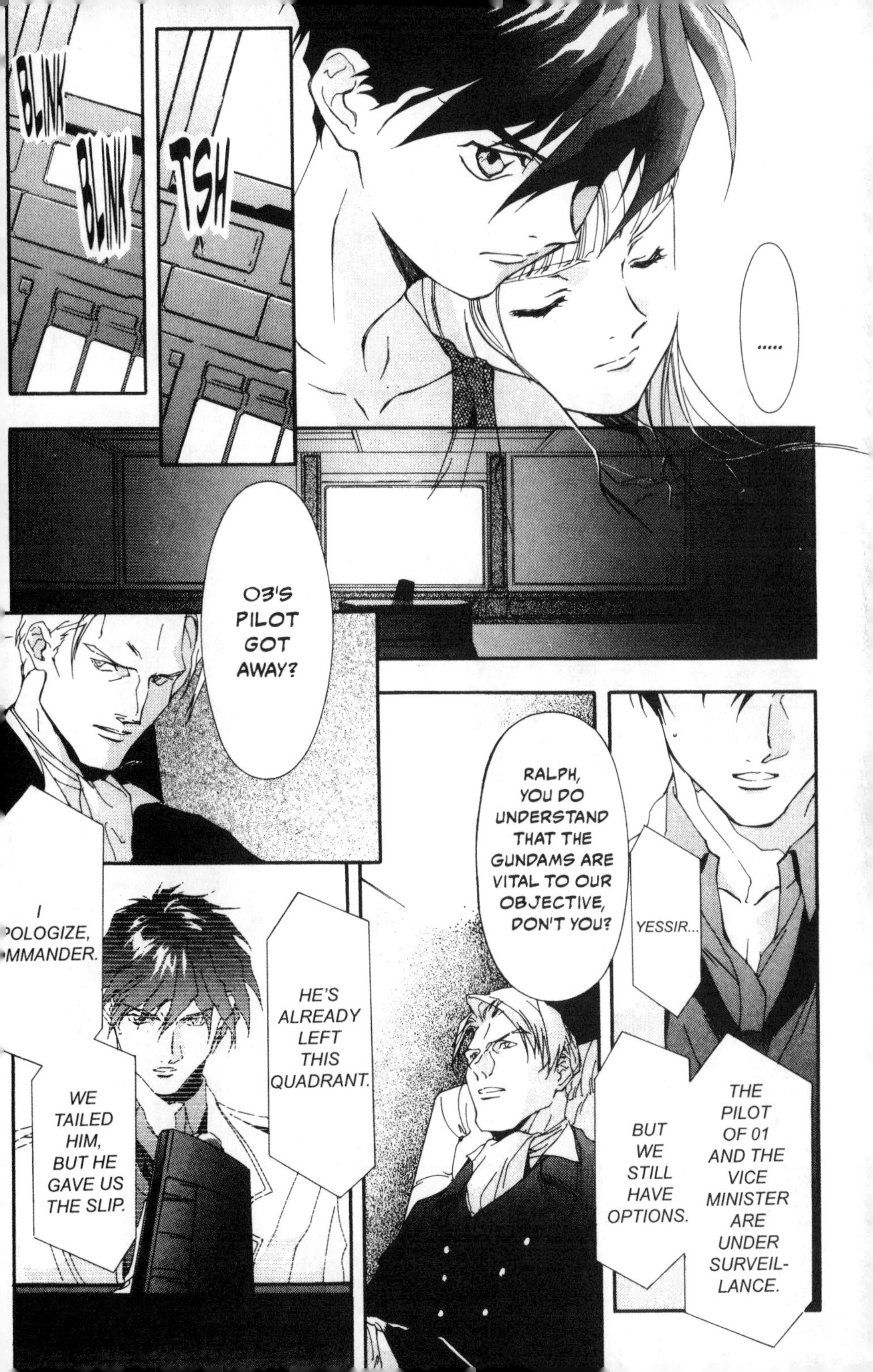

BLINK
BLINK
TSH
.....
O3'S PILOT GOT AWAY?
RALPH, YOU DO UNDERSTAND THAT THE GUNDAMS ARE VITAL TO OUR OBJECTIVE, DON'T YOU?
YESSIR...
I POLOGIZE, MMANDER.
HE'S ALREADY LEFT THIS QUADRANT.
WE TAILED HIM, BUT HE GAVE US THE SLIP.
BUT WE STILL HAVE OPTIONS.
THE PILOT OF 01 AND THE VICE MINISTER ARE UNDER SURVEIL-LANCE.

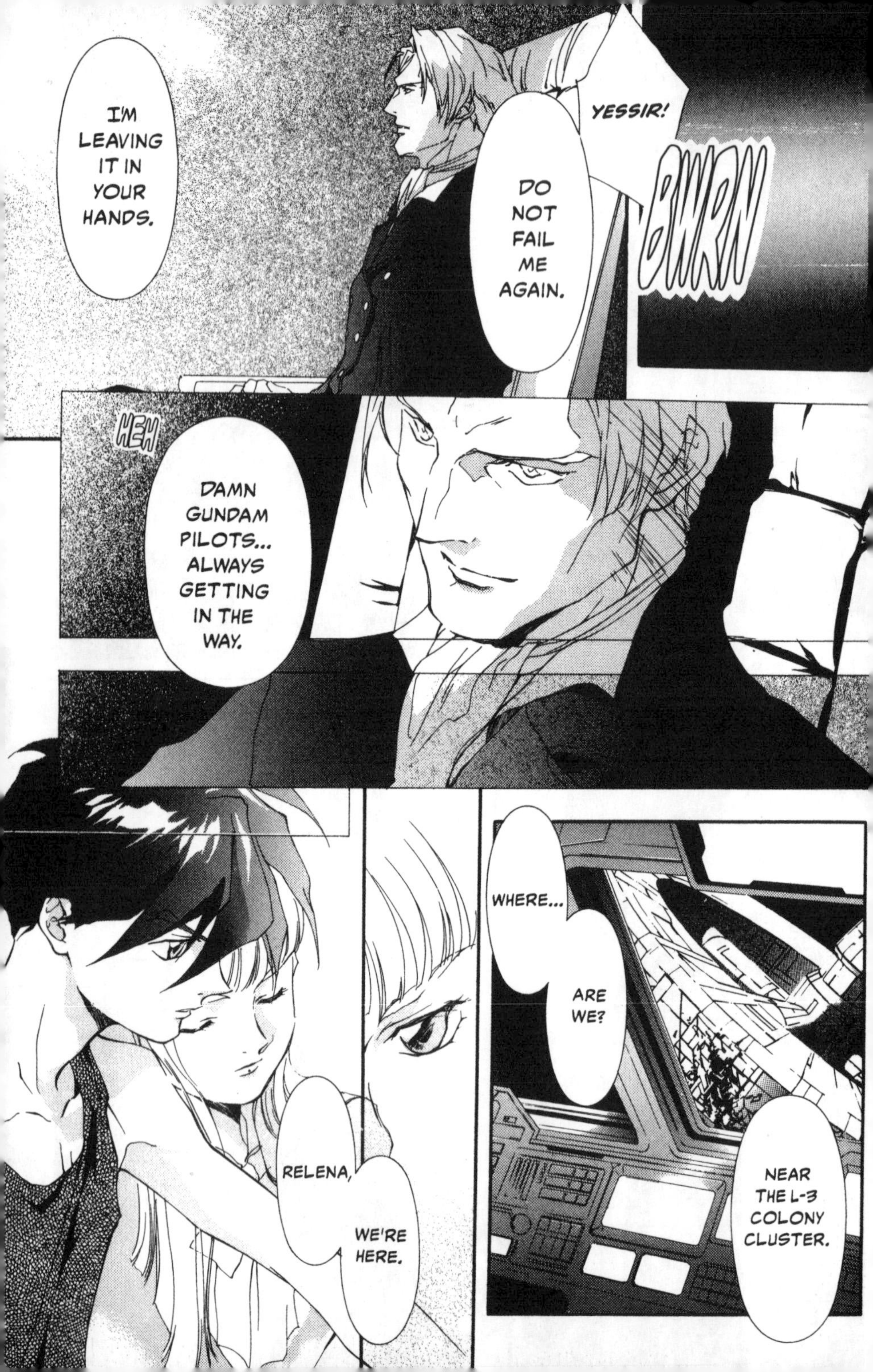
I'M LEAVING IT IN YOUR HANDS.
DO NOT FAIL ME AGAIN.
YESSIR!
BWRN
HEH
DAMN GUNDAM PILOTS... ALWAYS GETTING IN THE WAY.
RELENA,
WE'RE HERE.
WHERE...
ARE WE?
NEAR THE L-3 COLONY CLUSTER.

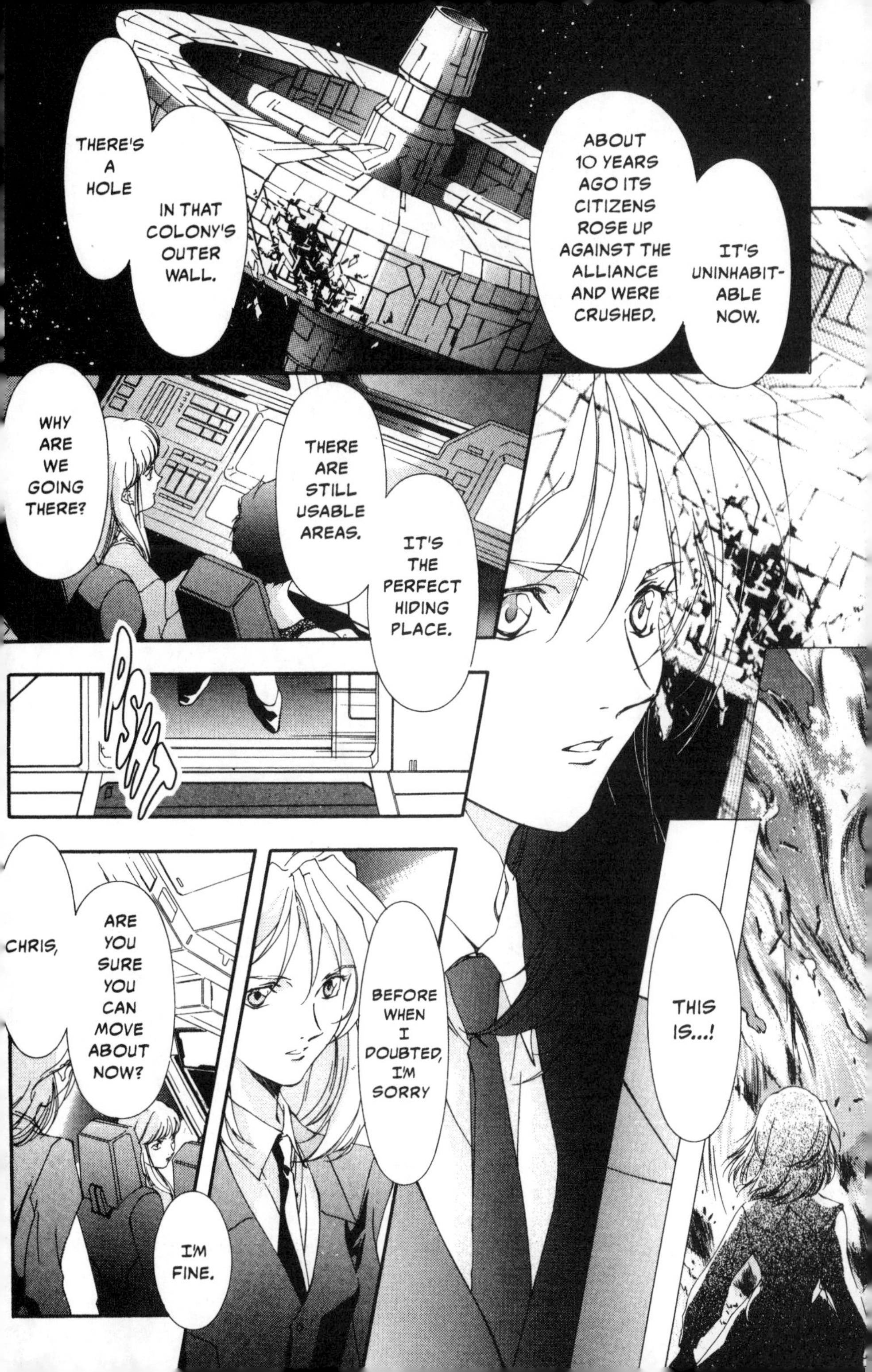
THERE'S A HOLE
IN THAT COLONY'S OUTER WALL.
ABOUT 10 YEARS AGO ITS CITIZENS ROSE UP AGAINST THE ALLIANCE AND WERE CRUSHED.
IT'S UNINHABIT-ABLE NOW.
WHY ARE WE GOING THERE?
THERE ARE STILL USABLE AREAS.
IT'S THE PERFECT HIDING PLACE.
PSHT
CHRIS,
ARE YOU SURE YOU CAN MOVE ABOUT NOW?
BEFORE WHEN I DOUBTED, I'M SORRY
I'M FINE.
THIS IS...!

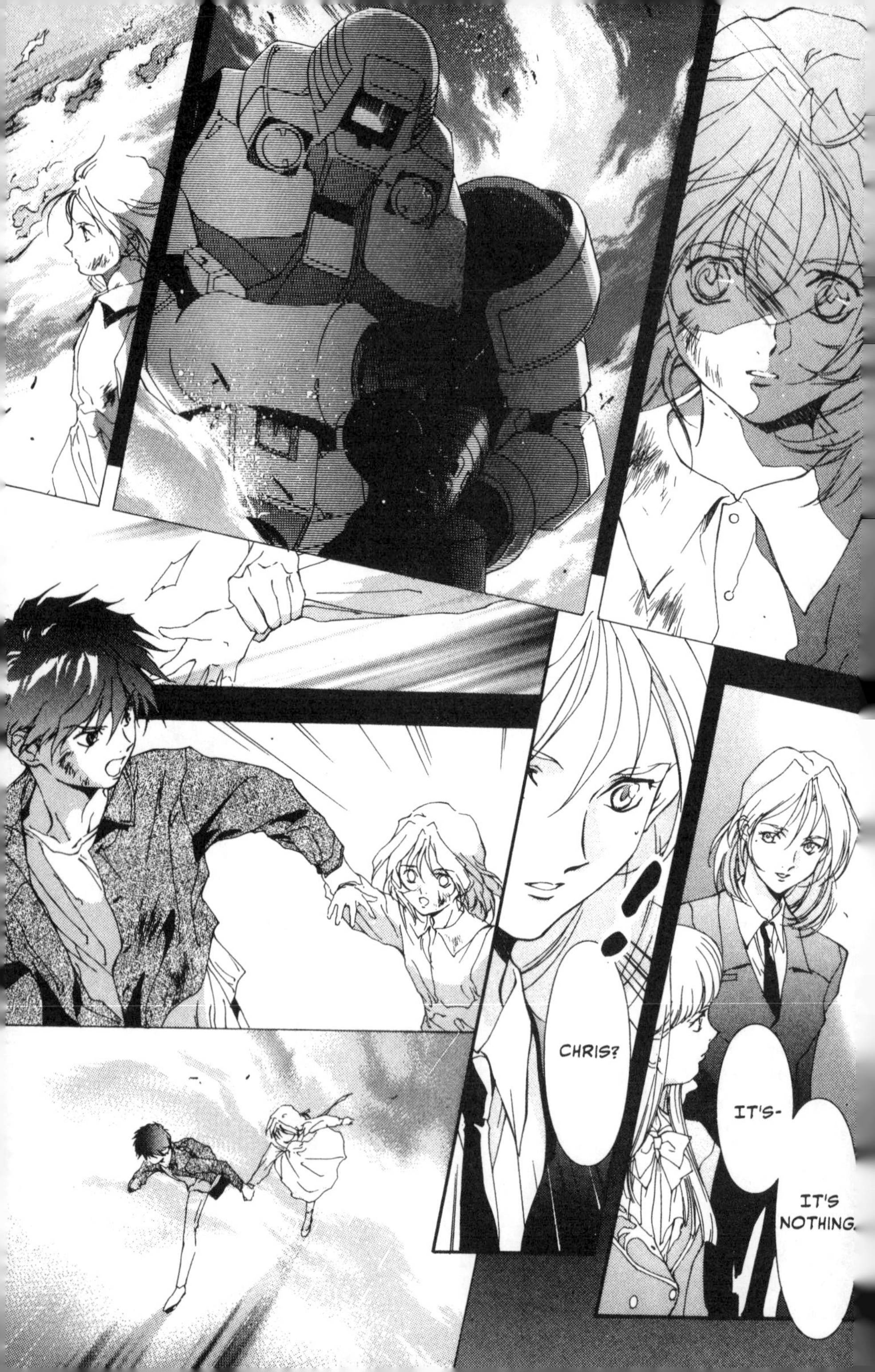
CHRIS?
IT'S-
IT'S NOTHING.

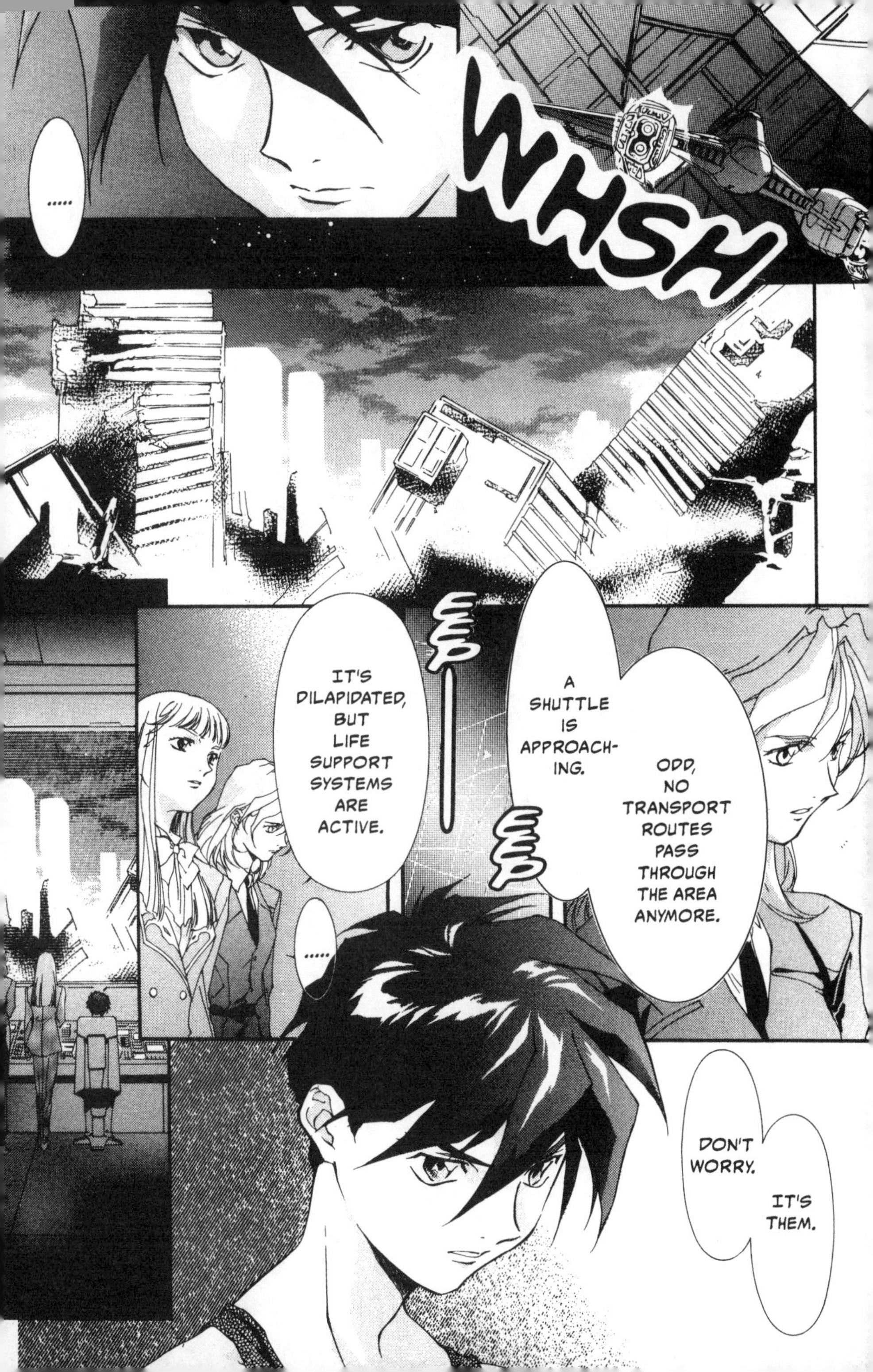
......
WHSH
IT'S DILAPIDATED, BUT LIFE SUPPORT SYSTEMS ARE ACTIVE.
EEP
EEP
A SHUTTLE IS APPROACH-ING.
ODD, NO TRANSPORT ROUTES PASS THROUGH THE AREA ANYMORE.
......
DON'T WORRY.
IT'S THEM.

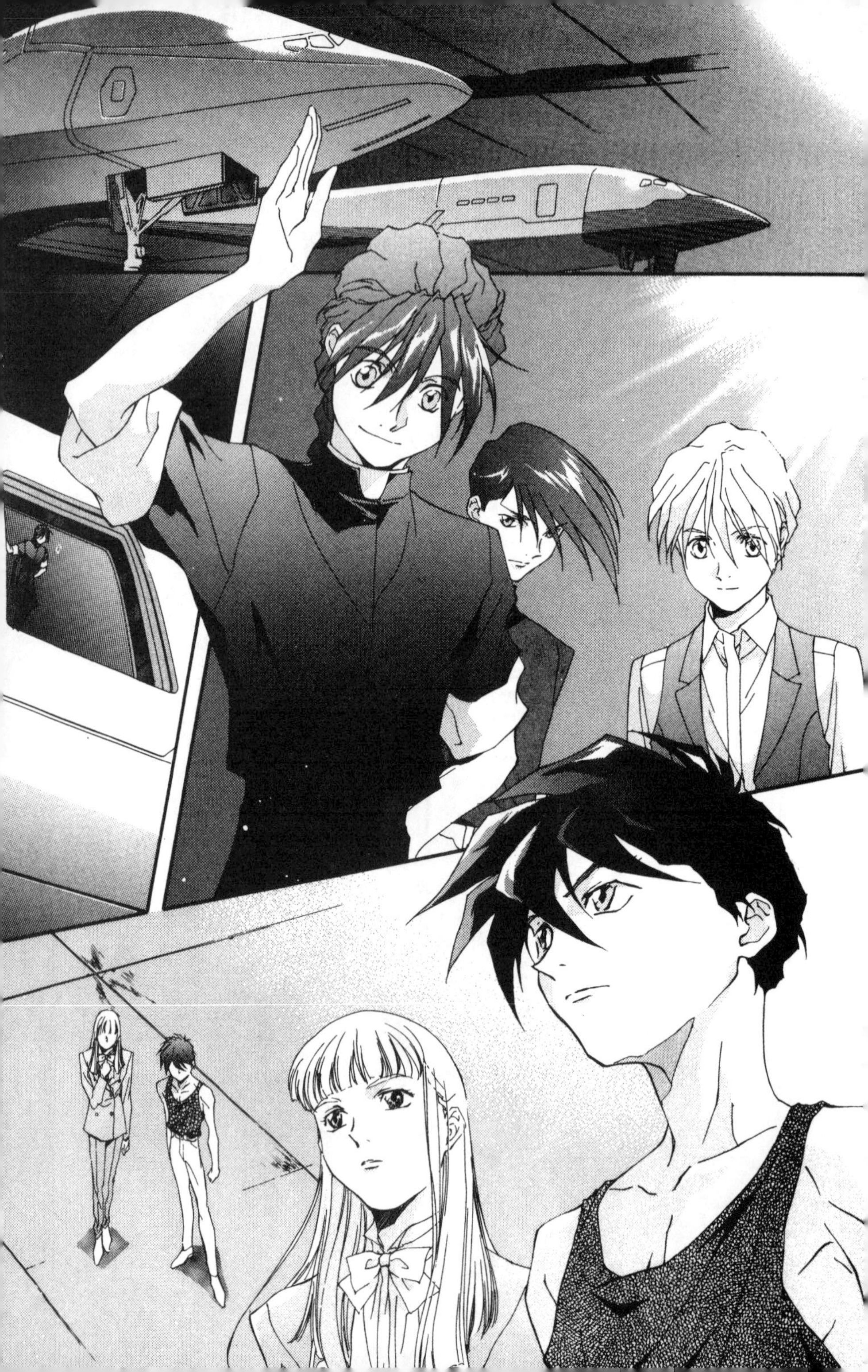

THIS TIME THE SPOTLIGHT IS ON HEERO, HIS SUBTLE RELATIONSHIP WITH RELENA, AND QUATRE'S CONFLICTING DESIRES.

MOBILE SUIT GUNDAM WING REMIX III........

HE BACKS UP HIS WORD WITH HIS LIFE: A PROMISE TO HIS SOUL

1

Once, he threatened that he would kill her, but now Heero is truly Relena's guardian angel, appearing whenever she's in danger.
It would seem that when he found he could not follow through on his plan to assassinate Queen Relena, he made a promise, if only in his mind, to protect her always. Now he risks his life to keep that promise. Some think there's more to Heero's feelings than just protectiveness; on Relena's birthday, he disguised himself in order to bring her a teddy bear, and he's taken crazy risks on her behalf, even for a bodyguard. Heero's matured over the years, but don't expect him to confess his deeper feelings for Relena any time soon.

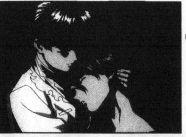

She turns to him for protection, he to her for comfort. They no longer seem to need vwords.

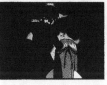

Heero intended to kill Relena, who could have blown his cover, but . . .

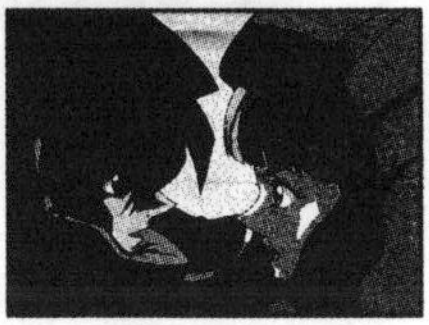

The perfect soldier, he believes Relena to be far mightier than himself.

HEERO YUY: KING OF THE ROAD

2

In the TV series, he used Duo's name in the colonies because his own name would stand out too much. And since the war? Looks like the all-too-recognizable Heero Yuy uses whatever alias serves his immediate needs, and moves whenever it suits him. We know he has recently been transferring between schools, probably under another alias, but since colony schools allow skipping grades, we can't be certain when he'll graduate, or from which school he'll do so. He lives from day to day, with no plans for what he's going to be doing tomorrow, or where. The only thing that's certain is that, when Relena is in trouble, he goes back to being her "Heero."

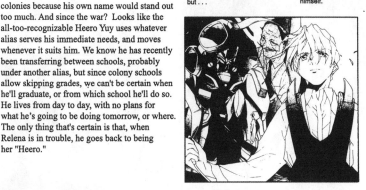

Quatre's father opposed militarization; their relationship was strained by Quatre's willingness to fight for right.

QUATRE RABERBA WINNER: WITH GREAT POWER COMES GREAT RESPONSIBILITY.

3

This young champion faces a constant inner struggle to meet with honor his many obligations. He has the political power to influence the fate of the colonies. A source of military power as tremendous as the Gundam he pilots demands that he use it carefully. As the head of a family as distinguished as the Winners, he's in no position to think only of himself; his every move could involve others. And yet, if he cannot stand up for himself, how can he stand up for anyone else? The path he has chosen is fraught with personal conflict; will he do what he believes he must, or what others - even his family - say he should? The pressure and loneliness of great responsibility is at the center of Quatre's saga here and in the "Endless Waltz".

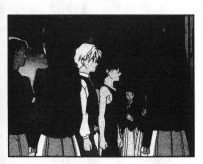

Heero gets treated as an attendant when with Quatre. He's not cut out for a royal lifestyle.

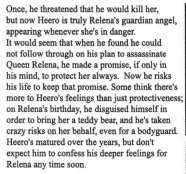

The pictures were taken from the TV series and the video series "Endless Waltz."

MOBILE SUIT GUNDAM WING

BLIND TARGET

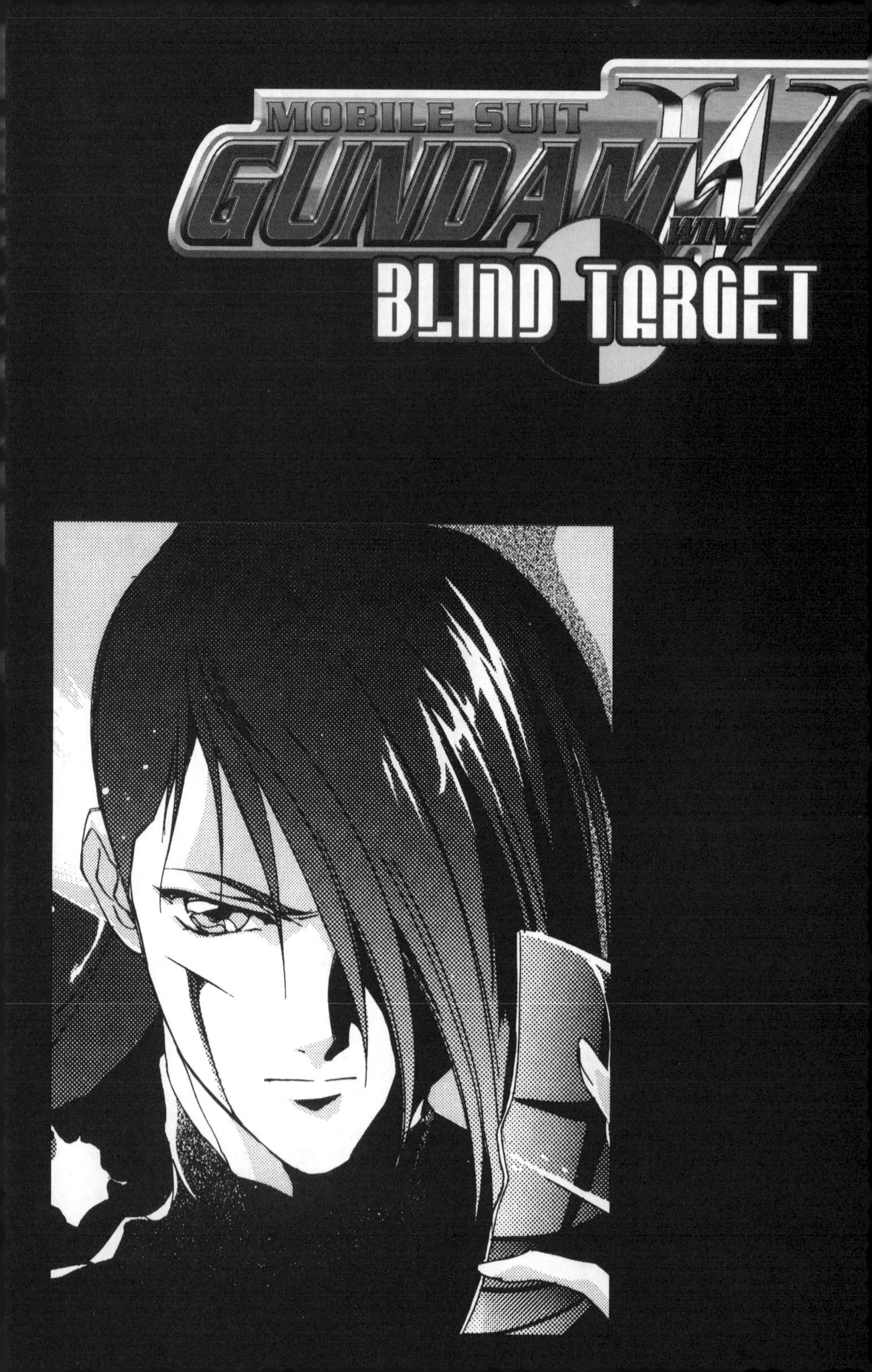

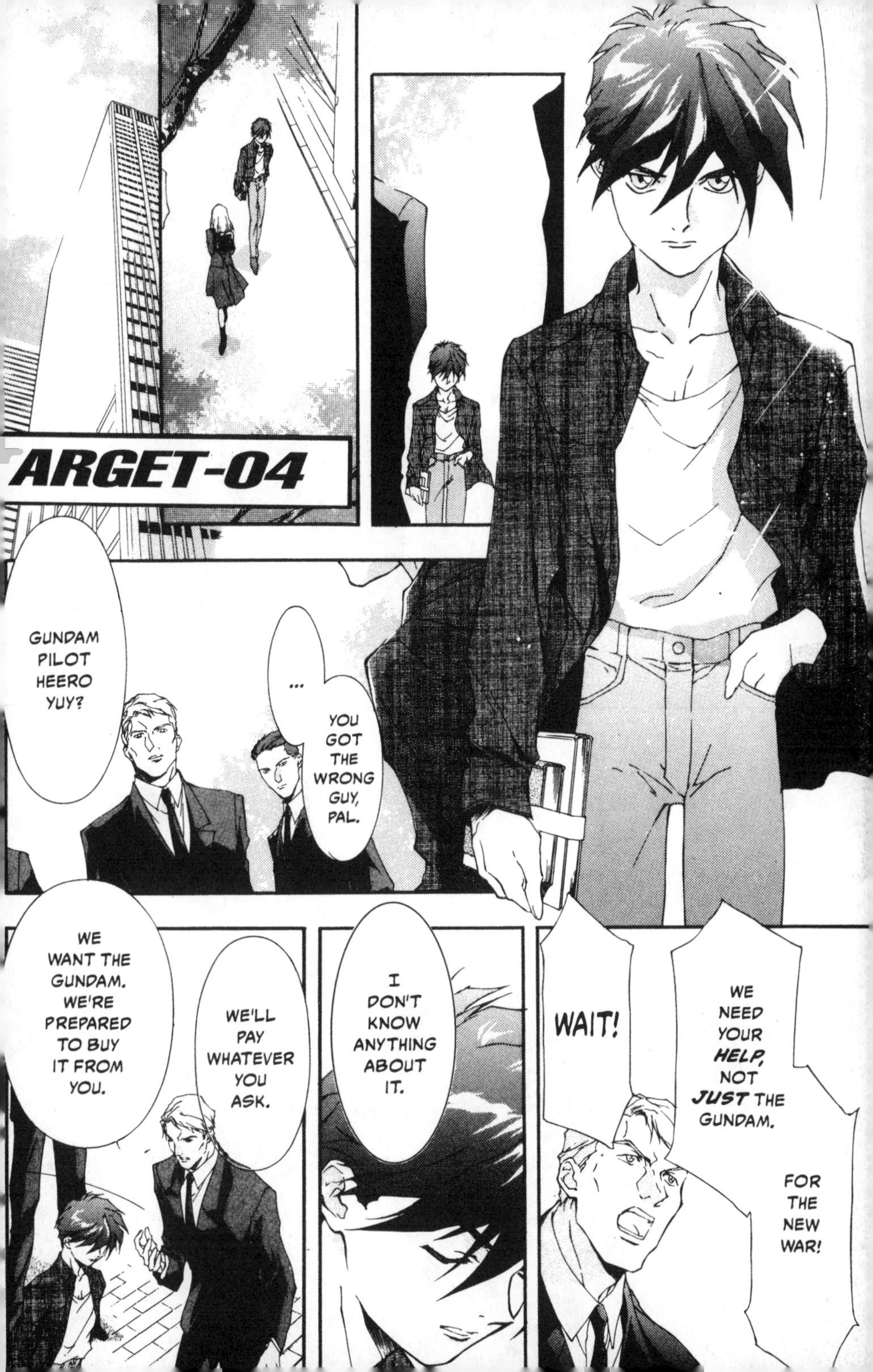
ARGET-04
GUNDAM PILOT HEERO YUY?
...
YOU GOT THE WRONG GUY, PAL.
WE WANT THE GUNDAM. WE'RE PREPARED TO BUY IT FROM YOU.
WE'LL PAY WHATEVER YOU ASK.
I DON'T KNOW ANYTHING ABOUT IT.
WAIT!
WE NEED YOUR HELP, NOT JUST THE GUNDAM.
FOR THE NEW WAR!

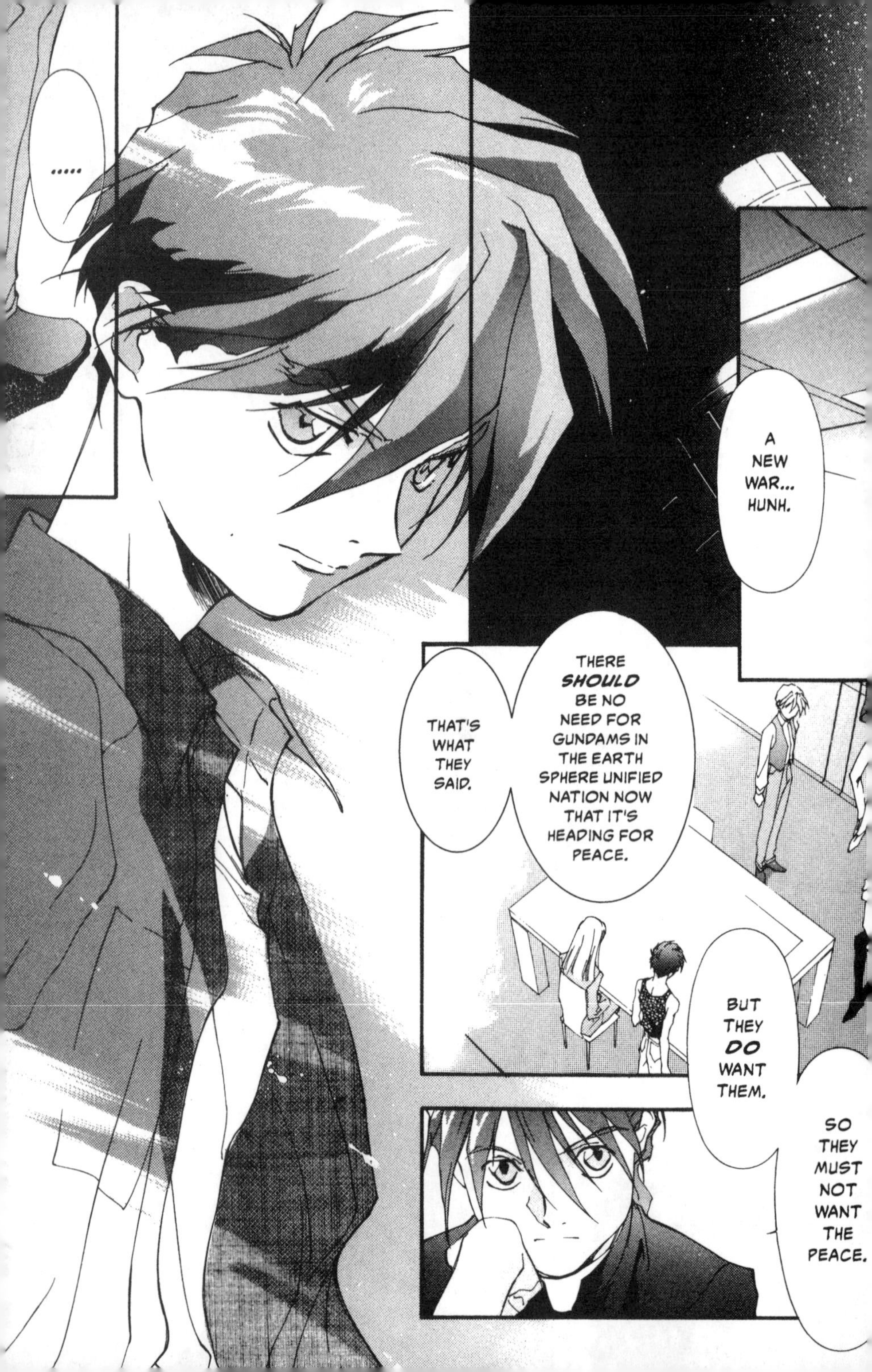
.....
A NEW WAR... HUNH.
THAT'S WHAT THEY SAID.
THERE **SHOULD** BE NO NEED FOR GUNDAMS IN THE EARTH SPHERE UNIFIED NATION NOW THAT IT'S HEADING FOR PEACE.
BUT THEY **DO** WANT THEM.
SO THEY MUST NOT WANT THE PEACE.

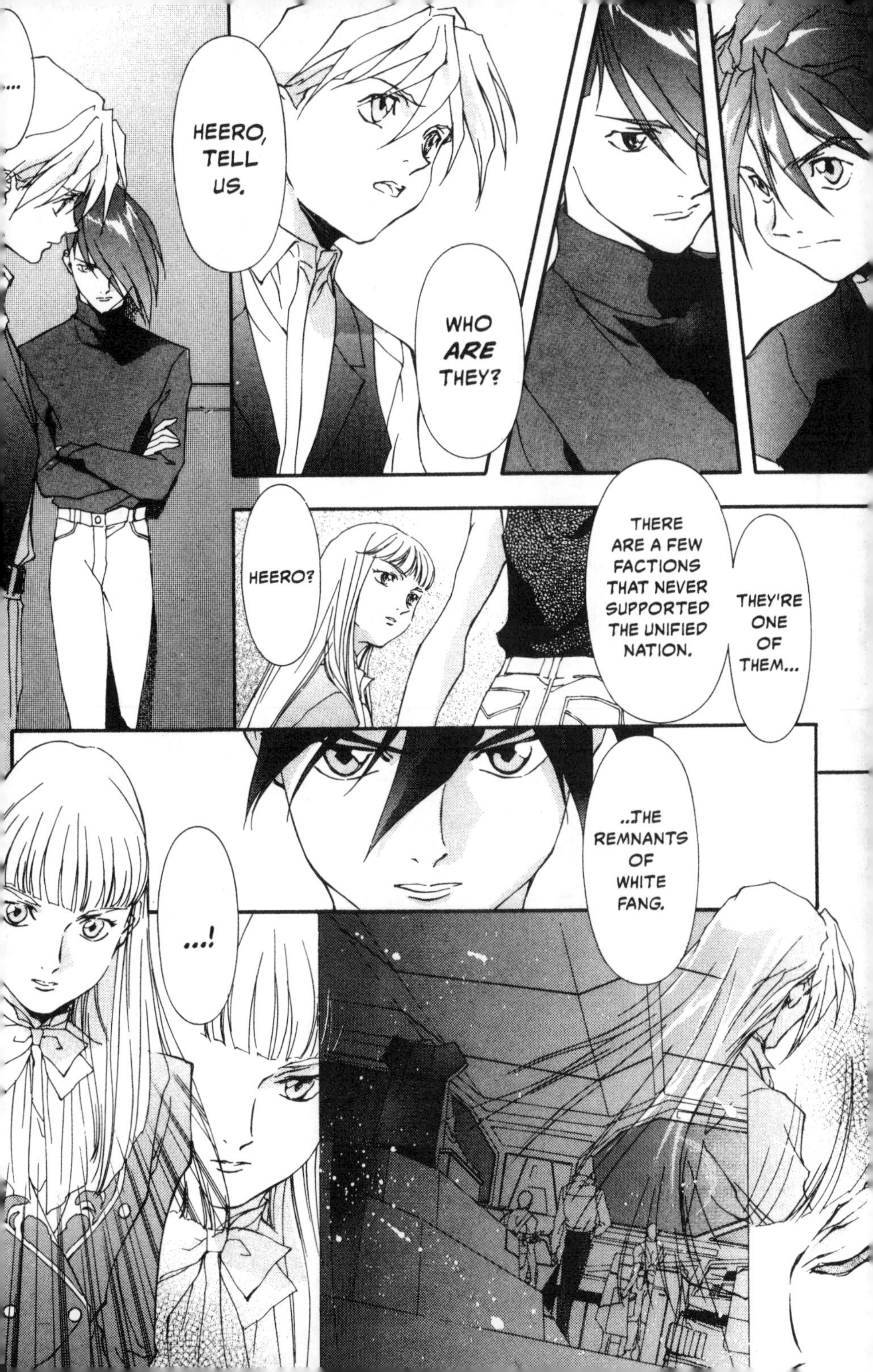
....
HEERO, TELL US.
WHO *ARE* THEY?
HEERO?
THERE ARE A FEW FACTIONS THAT NEVER SUPPORTED THE UNIFIED NATION.
THEY'RE ONE OF THEM...
...THE REMNANTS OF WHITE FANG.
...!

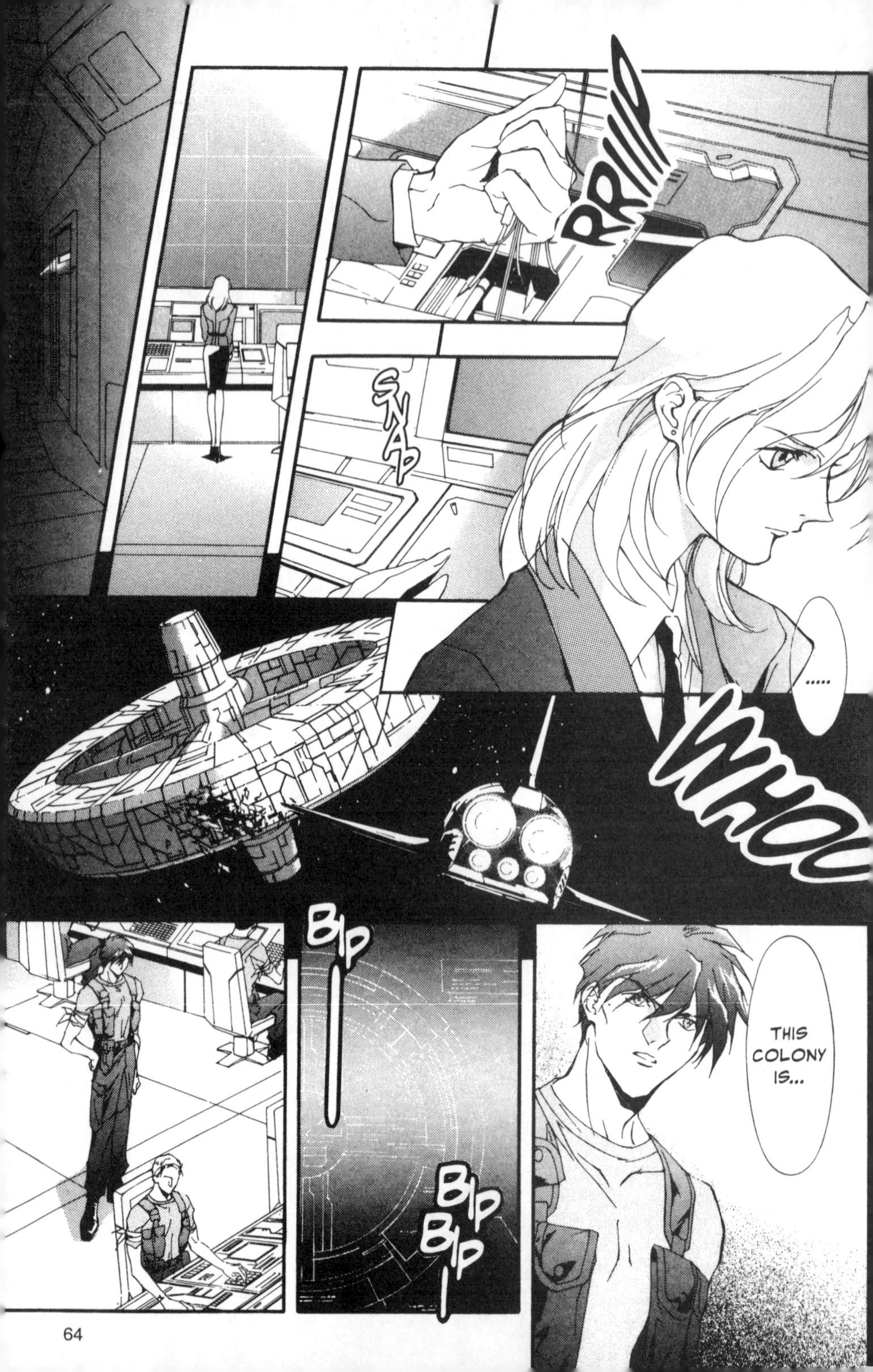
RRIIIP
SNAP
.....
WHOOO
BIP
BIP BIP
THIS COLONY IS...

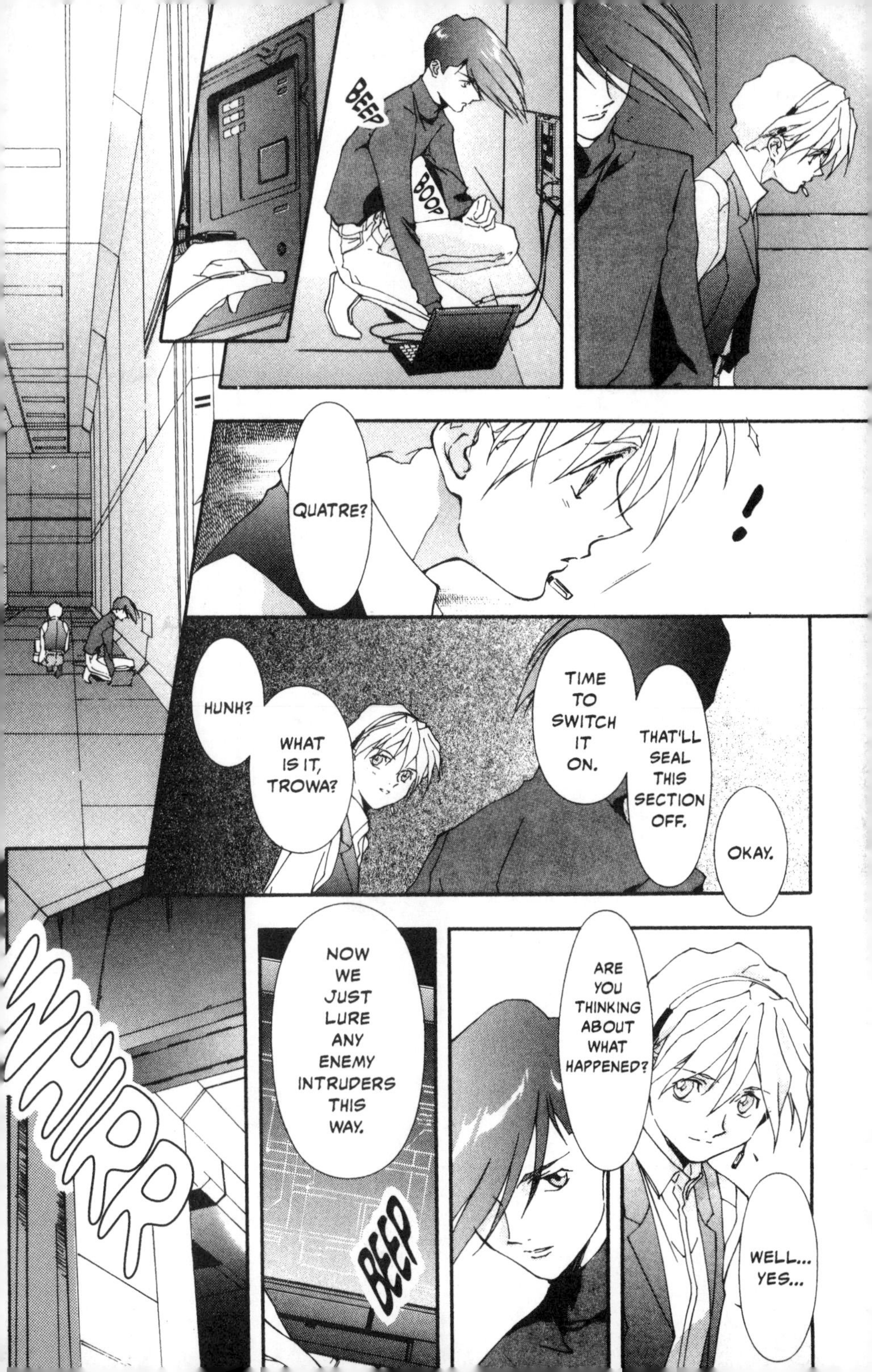
BEEP
BOOP
QUATRE?
!
HUNH?
WHAT IS IT, TROWA?
TIME TO SWITCH IT ON.
THAT'LL SEAL THIS SECTION OFF.
OKAY.
WHIRR
NOW WE JUST LURE ANY ENEMY INTRUDERS THIS WAY.
BEEP
ARE YOU THINKING ABOUT WHAT HAPPENED?
WELL... YES...

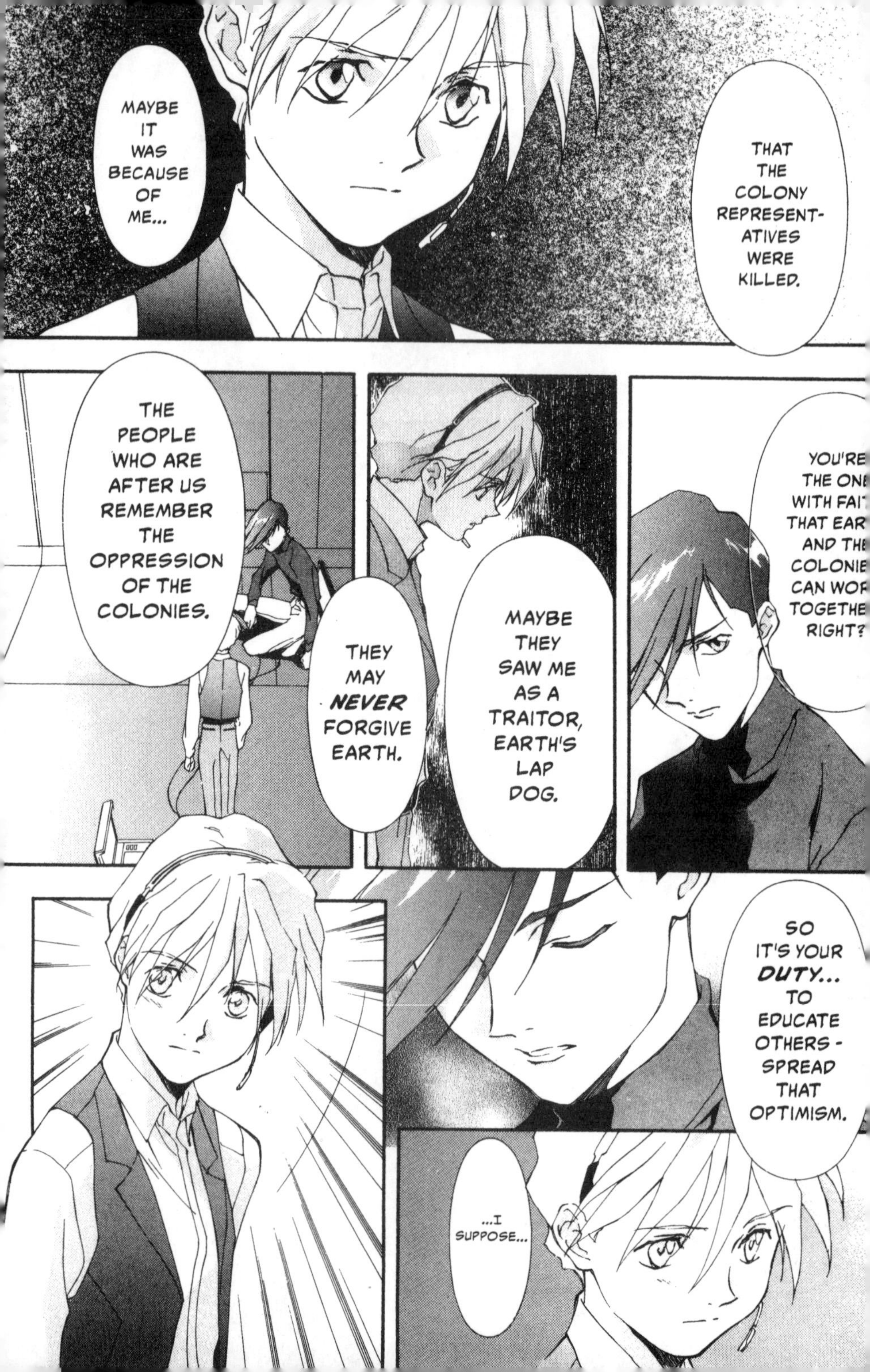
MAYBE IT WAS BECAUSE OF ME...
THAT THE COLONY REPRESENTATIVES WERE KILLED.
THE PEOPLE WHO ARE AFTER US REMEMBER THE OPPRESSION OF THE COLONIES.
THEY MAY NEVER FORGIVE EARTH.
MAYBE THEY SAW ME AS A TRAITOR, EARTH'S LAP DOG.
YOU'RE THE ONE WITH FAIT THAT EAR AND THE COLONIE CAN WOR TOGETHE RIGHT?
SO IT'S YOUR DUTY... TO EDUCATE OTHERS - SPREAD THAT OPTIMISM.
...I SUPPOSE...

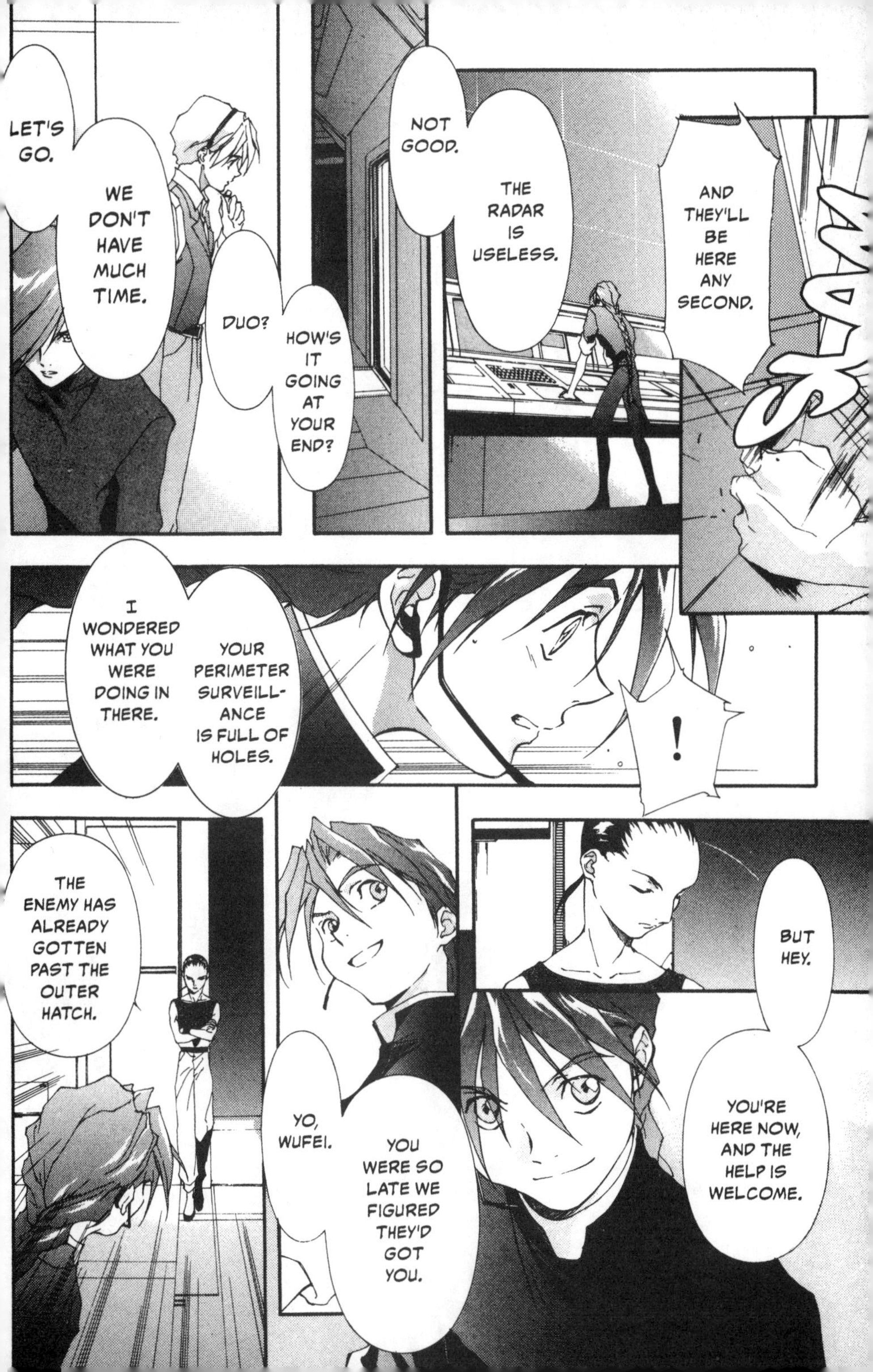
LET'S GO.
WE DON'T HAVE MUCH TIME.
DUO?
HOW'S IT GOING AT YOUR END?
NOT GOOD.
THE RADAR IS USELESS.
AND THEY'LL BE HERE ANY SECOND.
I WONDERED WHAT YOU WERE DOING IN THERE.
YOUR PERIMETER SURVEILL-ANCE IS FULL OF HOLES.
!
THE ENEMY HAS ALREADY GOTTEN PAST THE OUTER HATCH.
YO, WUFEI.
YOU WERE SO LATE WE FIGURED THEY'D GOT YOU.
BUT HEY.
YOU'RE HERE NOW, AND THE HELP IS WELCOME.

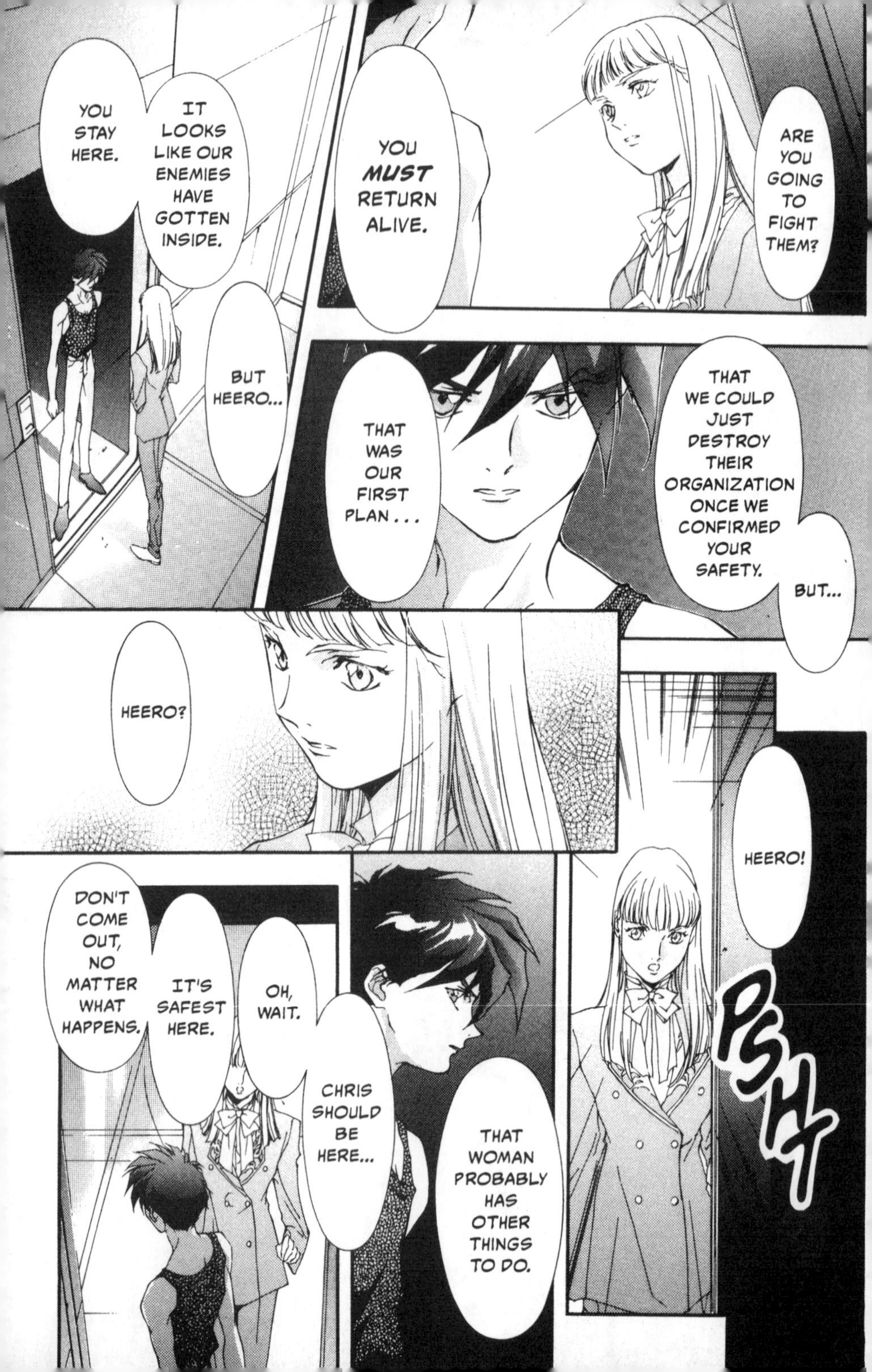
YOU STAY HERE.
IT LOOKS LIKE OUR ENEMIES HAVE GOTTEN INSIDE.
BUT HEERO...
YOU **MUST** RETURN ALIVE.
ARE YOU GOING TO FIGHT THEM?
THAT WAS OUR FIRST PLAN . . .
THAT WE COULD JUST DESTROY THEIR ORGANIZATION ONCE WE CONFIRMED YOUR SAFETY.
BUT...
HEERO?
DON'T COME OUT, NO MATTER WHAT HAPPENS.
IT'S SAFEST HERE.
OH, WAIT.
CHRIS SHOULD BE HERE...
THAT WOMAN PROBABLY HAS OTHER THINGS TO DO.
HEERO!
PSHH

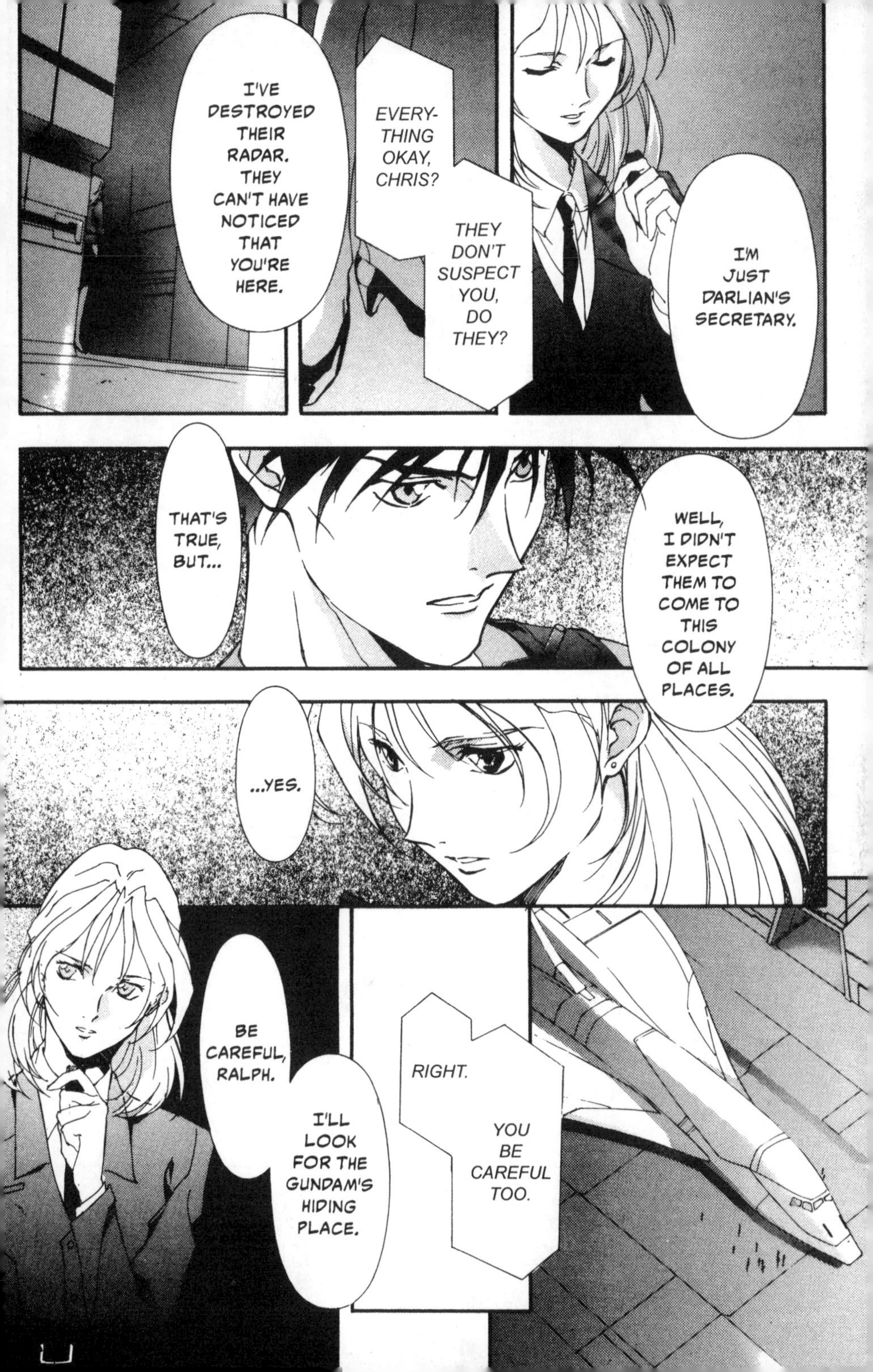
I'VE DESTROYED THEIR RADAR. THEY CAN'T HAVE NOTICED THAT YOU'RE HERE.
EVERY-THING OKAY, CHRIS?
THEY DON'T SUSPECT YOU, DO THEY?
I'M JUST DARLIAN'S SECRETARY.
THAT'S TRUE, BUT...
WELL, I DIDN'T EXPECT THEM TO COME TO THIS COLONY OF ALL PLACES.
...YES.
BE CAREFUL, RALPH.
I'LL LOOK FOR THE GUNDAM'S HIDING PLACE.
RIGHT.
YOU BE CAREFUL TOO.

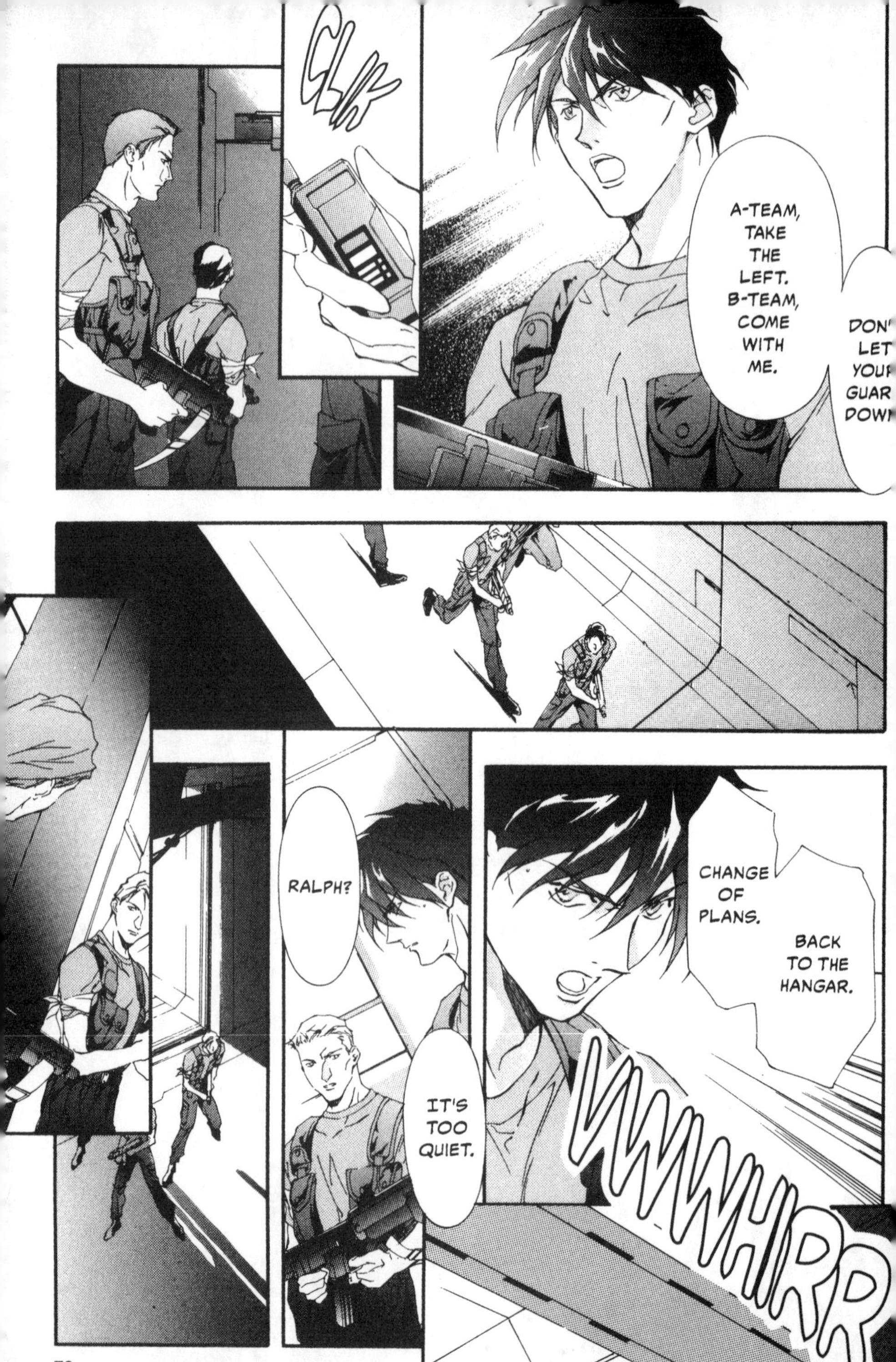

CLK
A-TEAM, TAKE THE LEFT. B-TEAM, COME WITH ME.
DON' LET YOUR GUAR DOWN
RALPH?
IT'S TOO QUIET.
CHANGE OF PLANS.
BACK TO THE HANGAR.
VVVWHIRR

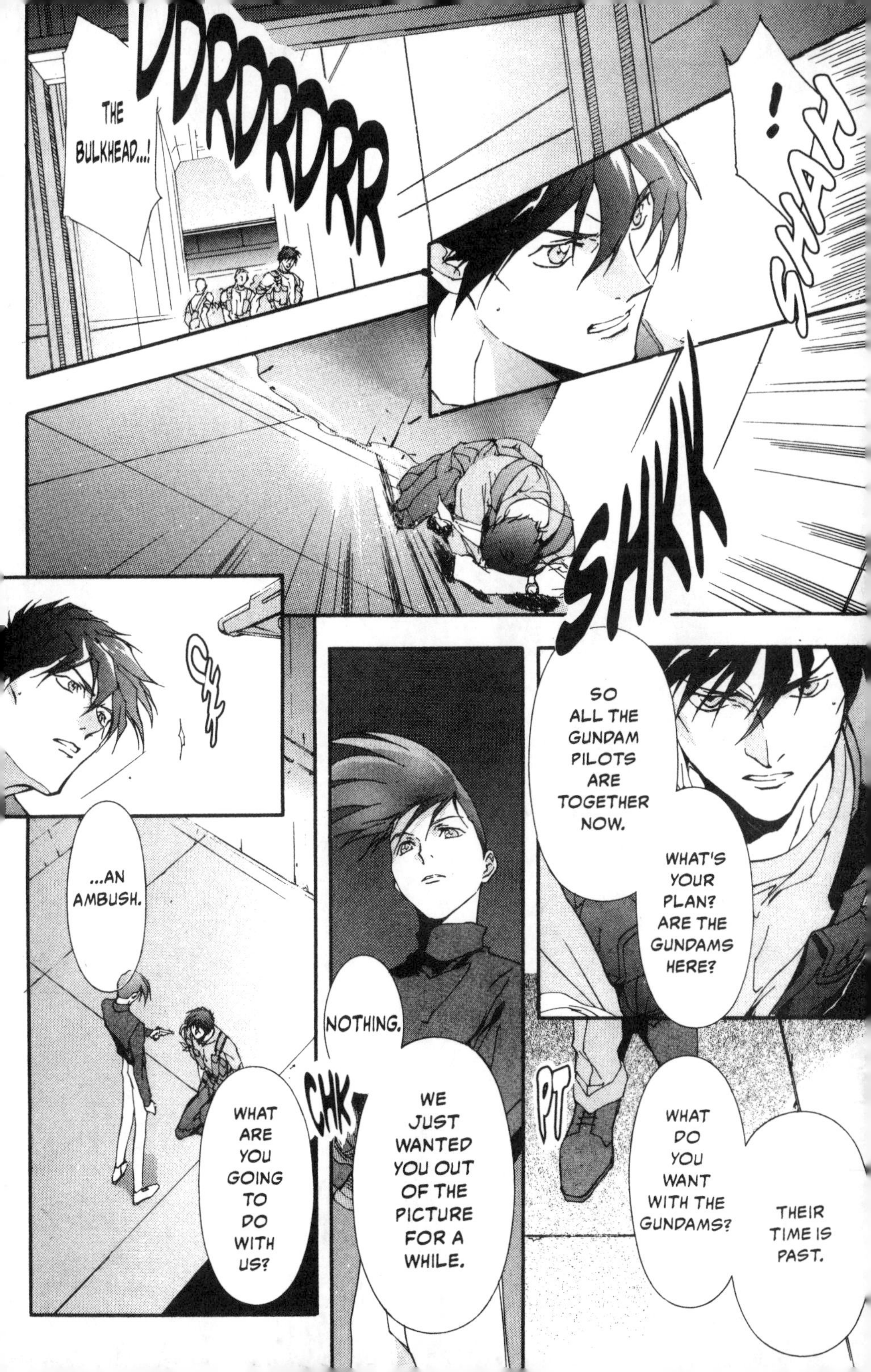
THE BULKHEAD...!
DRDRDRDRR
SHAH
!
SHKK
CH
...AN AMBUSH.
WHAT ARE YOU GOING TO DO WITH US?
NOTHING.
CHK
WE JUST WANTED YOU OUT OF THE PICTURE FOR A WHILE.
SO ALL THE GUNDAM PILOTS ARE TOGETHER NOW.
WHAT'S YOUR PLAN? ARE THE GUNDAMS HERE?
PT
WHAT DO YOU WANT WITH THE GUNDAMS?
THEIR TIME IS PAST.

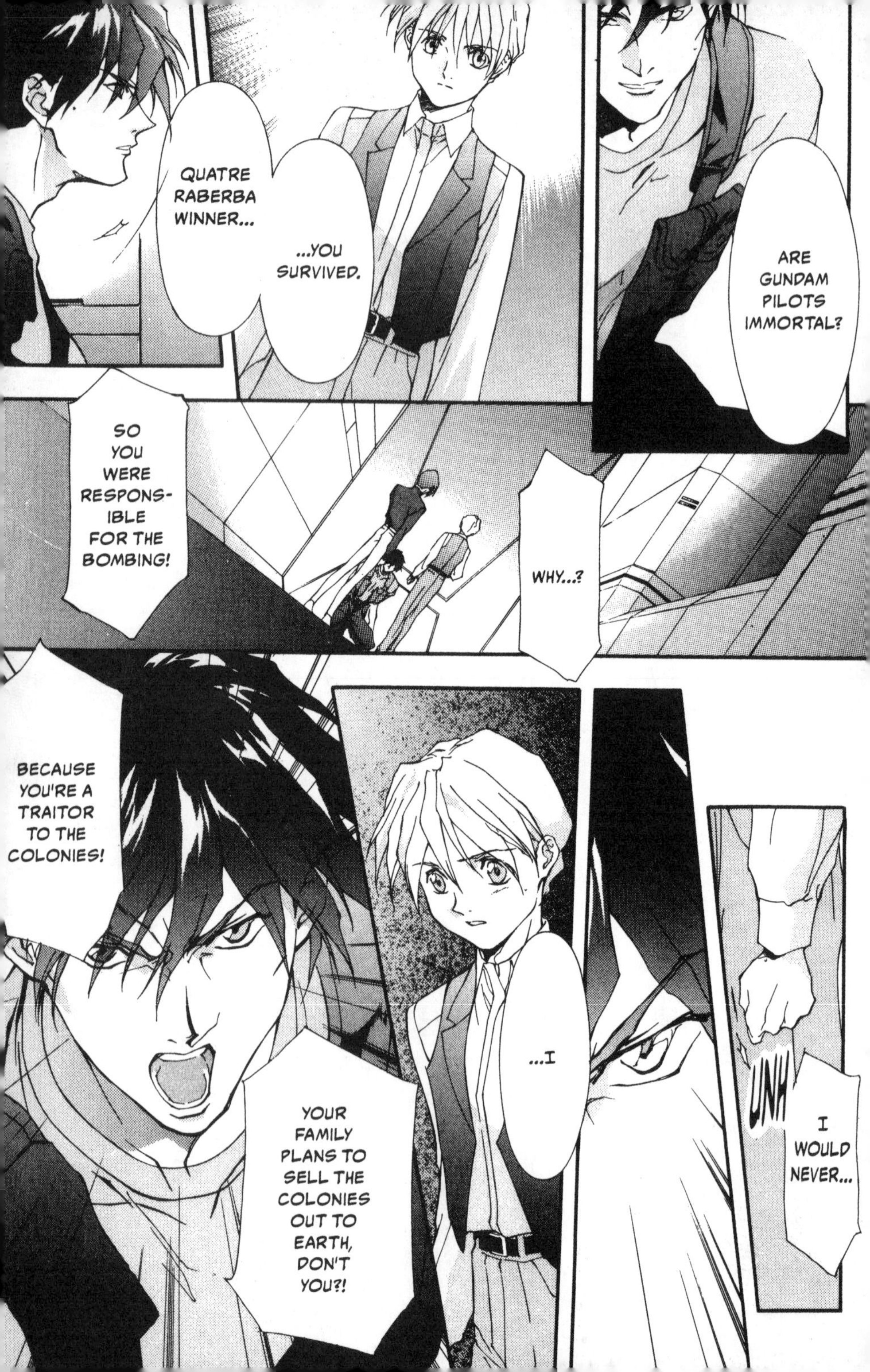
QUATRE RABERBA WINNER...
...YOU SURVIVED.
ARE GUNDAM PILOTS IMMORTAL?
SO YOU WERE RESPONS-IBLE FOR THE BOMBING!
WHY...?
BECAUSE YOU'RE A TRAITOR TO THE COLONIES!
YOUR FAMILY PLANS TO SELL THE COLONIES OUT TO EARTH, DON'T YOU?!
...I
UNH
I WOULD NEVER...

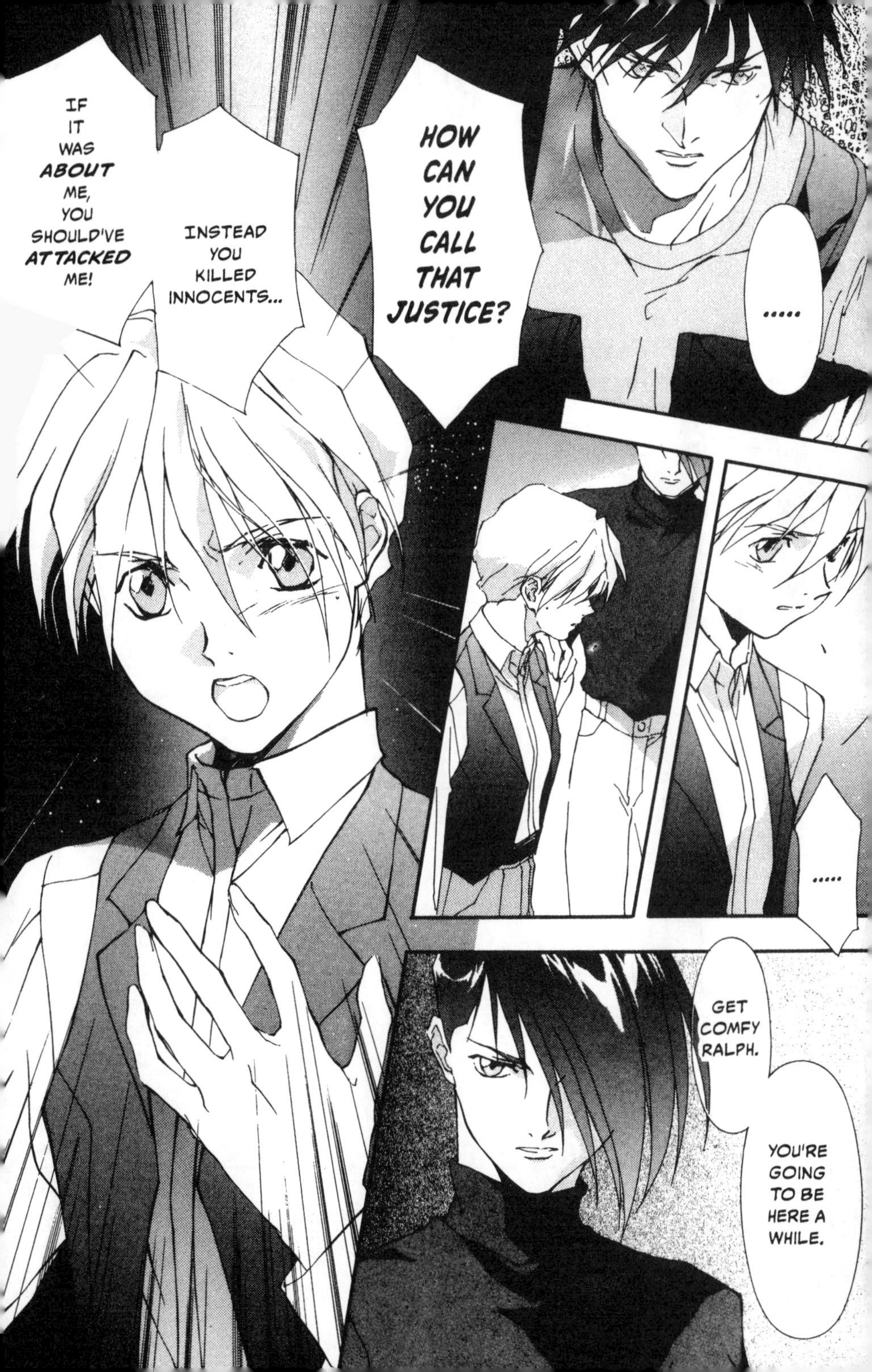
IF IT WAS ABOUT ME, YOU SHOULD'VE ATTACKED ME!
INSTEAD YOU KILLED INNOCENTS...
HOW CAN YOU CALL THAT JUSTICE?
.....
.....
GET COMFY RALPH.
YOU'RE GOING TO BE HERE A WHILE.

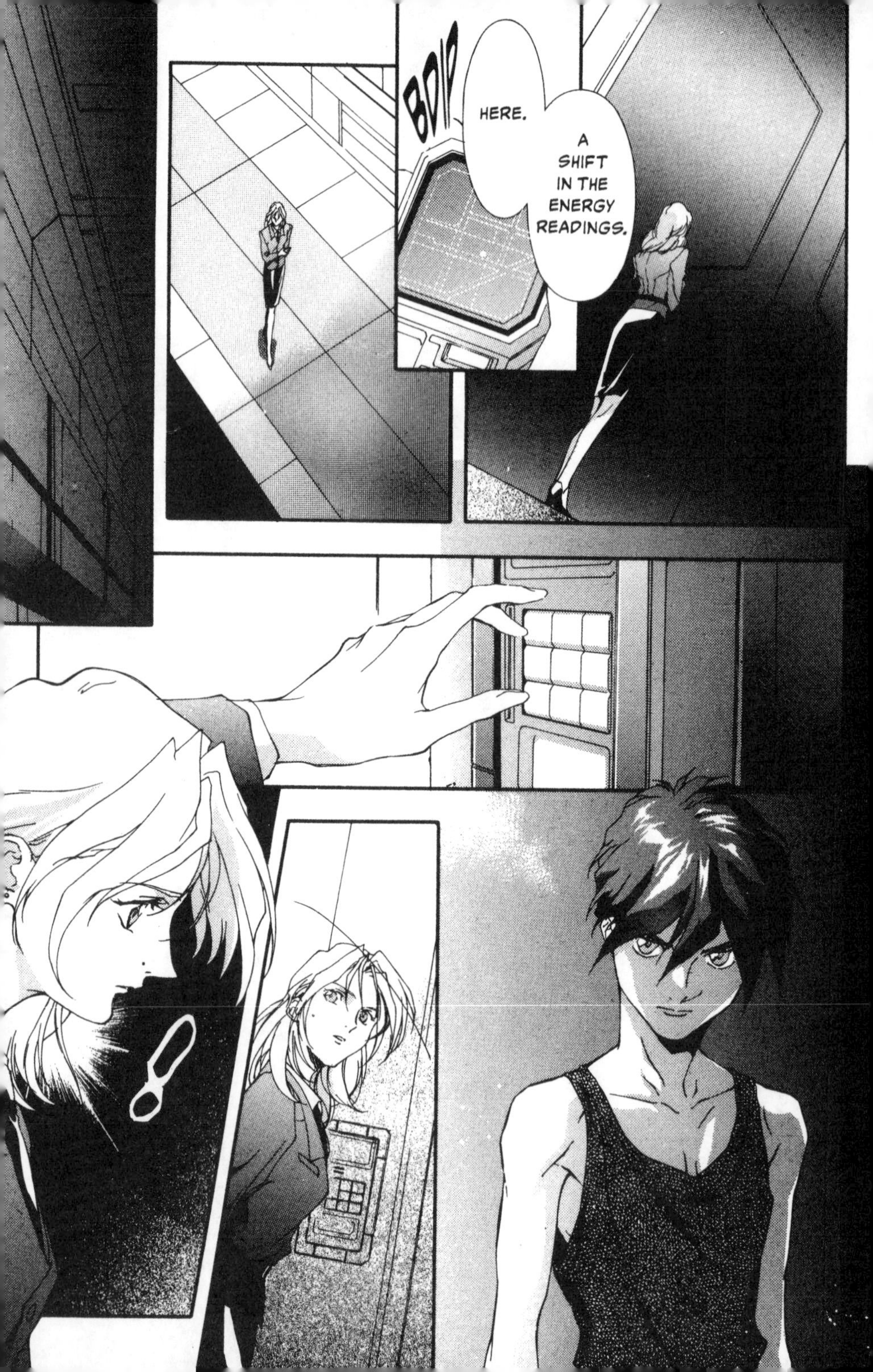

BDIP
HERE.
A SHIFT IN THE ENERGY READINGS.

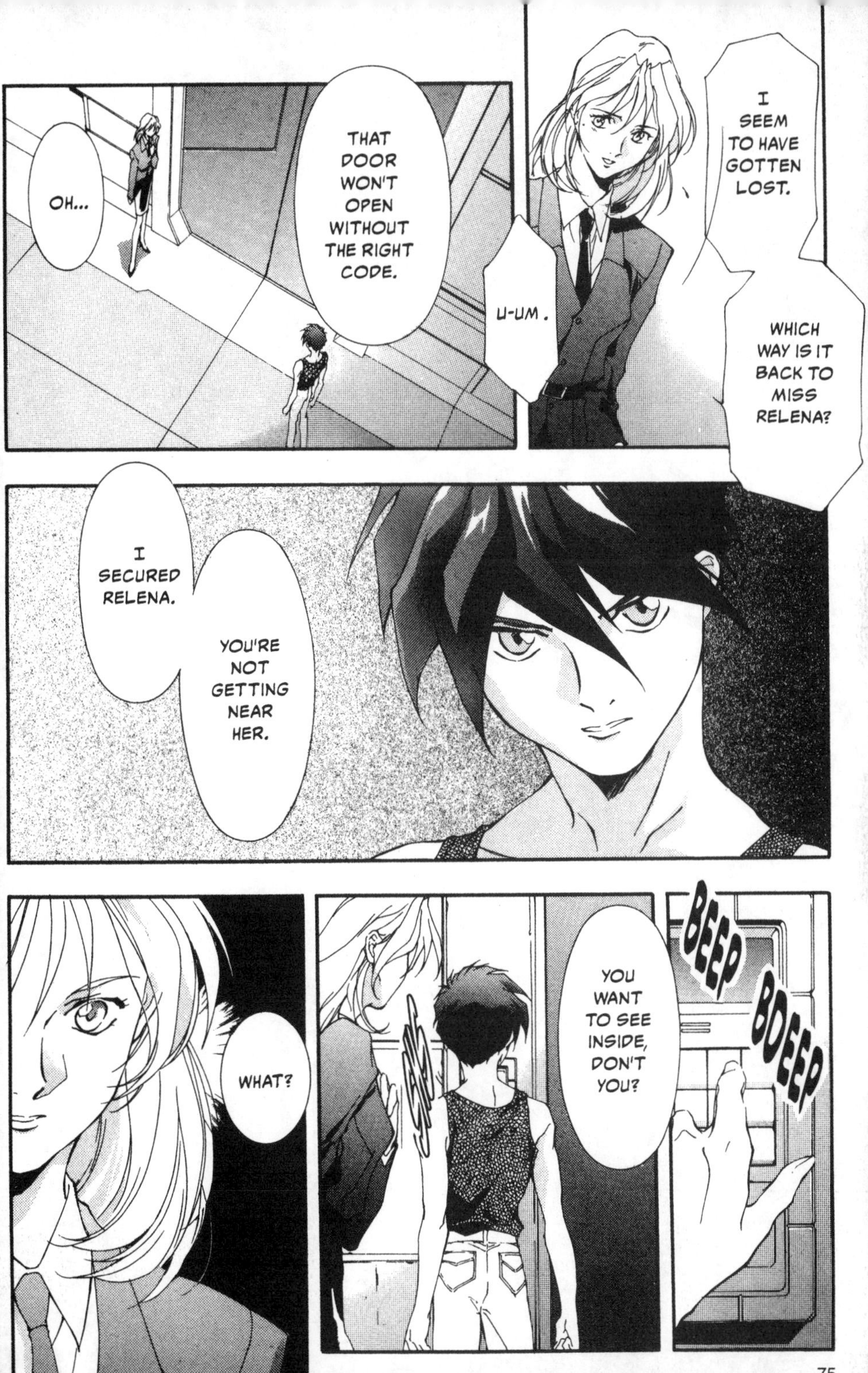
OH...
THAT DOOR WON'T OPEN WITHOUT THE RIGHT CODE.
U-UM.
I SEEM TO HAVE GOTTEN LOST.
WHICH WAY IS IT BACK TO MISS RELENA?
I SECURED RELENA.
YOU'RE NOT GETTING NEAR HER.
WHAT?
YOU WANT TO SEE INSIDE, DON'T YOU?
BEEP
BDEEP

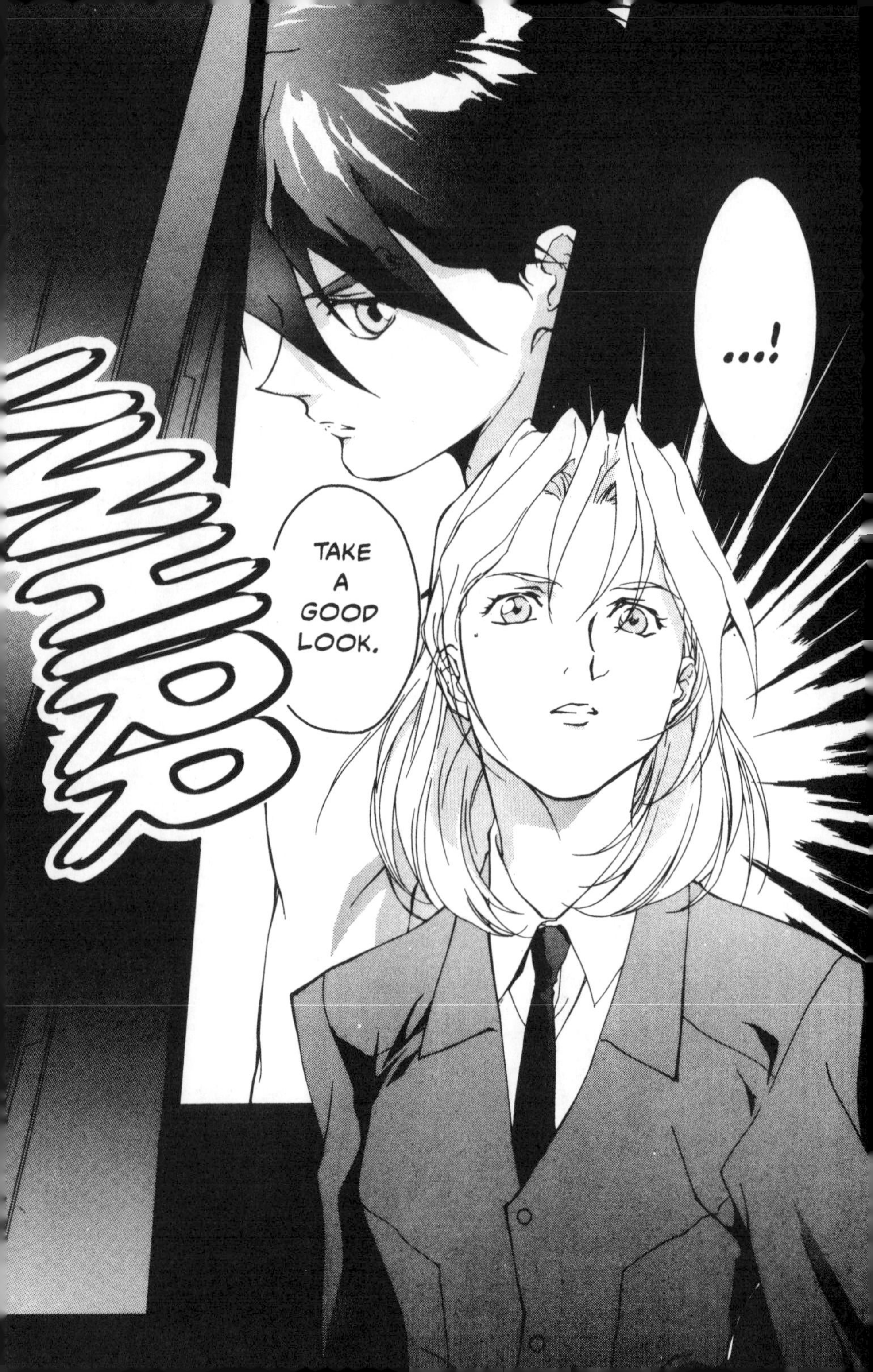
WHIRP
TAKE A GOOD LOOK.
...!

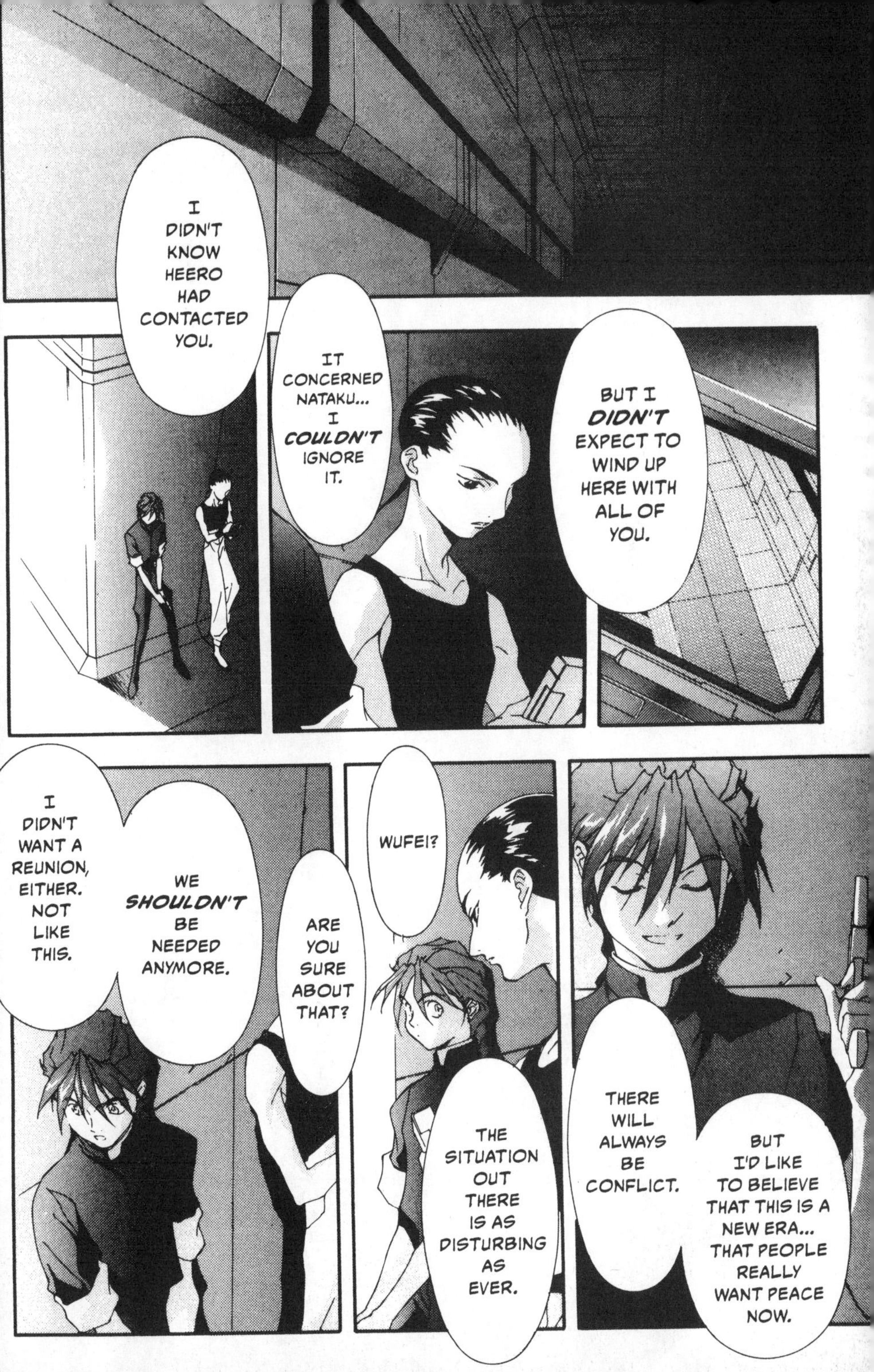
I DIDN'T KNOW HEERO HAD CONTACTED YOU.
IT CONCERNED NATAKU... I *COULDN'T* IGNORE IT.
BUT I *DIDN'T* EXPECT TO WIND UP HERE WITH ALL OF YOU.
I DIDN'T WANT A REUNION, EITHER. NOT LIKE THIS.
WE *SHOULDN'T* BE NEEDED ANYMORE.
WUFEI?
ARE YOU SURE ABOUT THAT?
THE SITUATION OUT THERE IS AS DISTURBING AS EVER.
THERE WILL ALWAYS BE CONFLICT.
BUT I'D LIKE TO BELIEVE THAT THIS IS A NEW ERA... THAT PEOPLE REALLY WANT PEACE NOW.

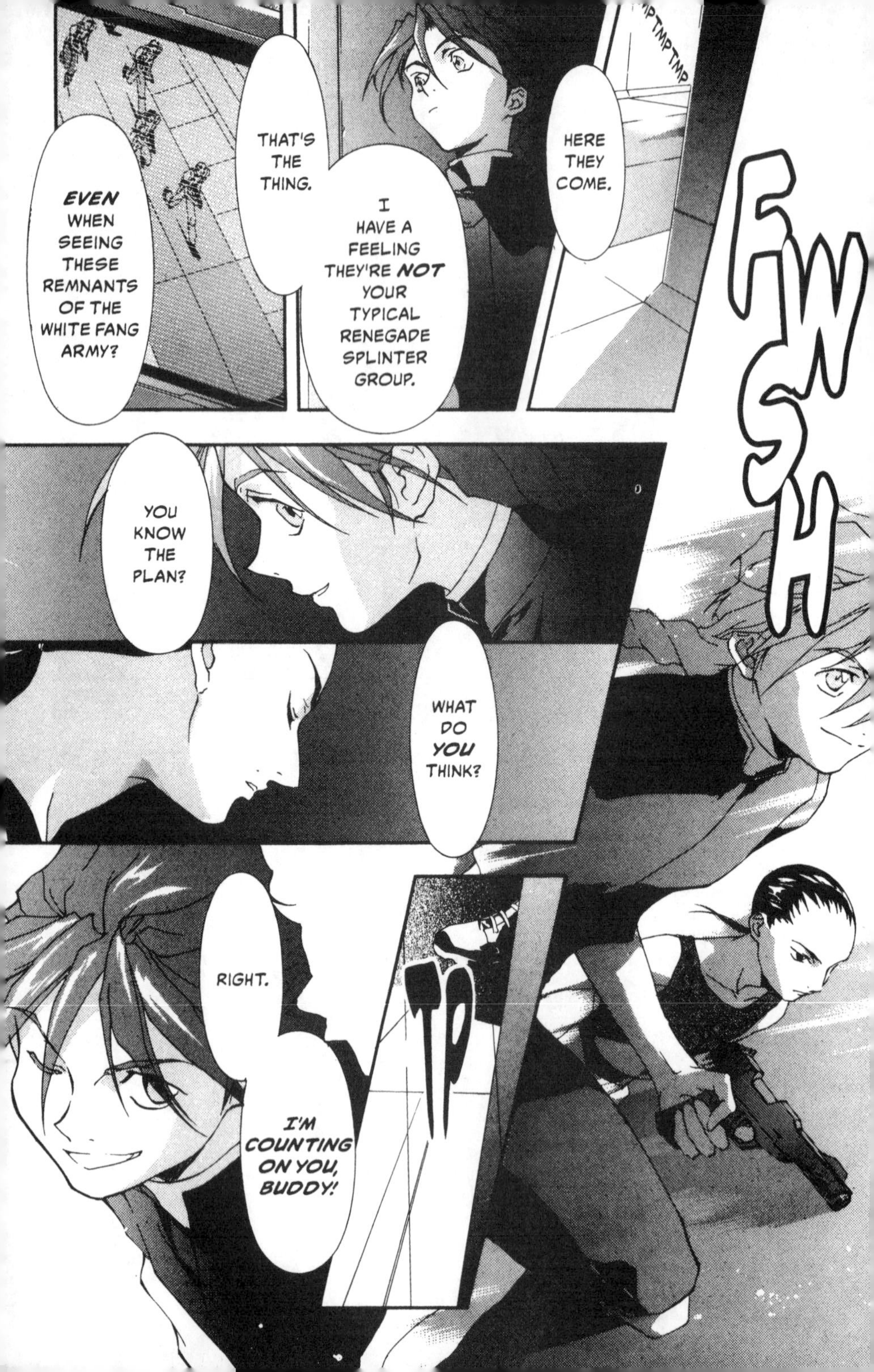

EVEN WHEN SEEING THESE REMNANTS OF THE WHITE FANG ARMY?
THAT'S THE THING.
I HAVE A FEELING THEY'RE *NOT* YOUR TYPICAL RENEGADE SPLINTER GROUP.
MPTMPTMP
HERE THEY COME.
YOU KNOW THE PLAN?
WHAT DO *YOU* THINK?
RIGHT.
I'M COUNTING ON YOU, BUDDY!
TP
FWSH

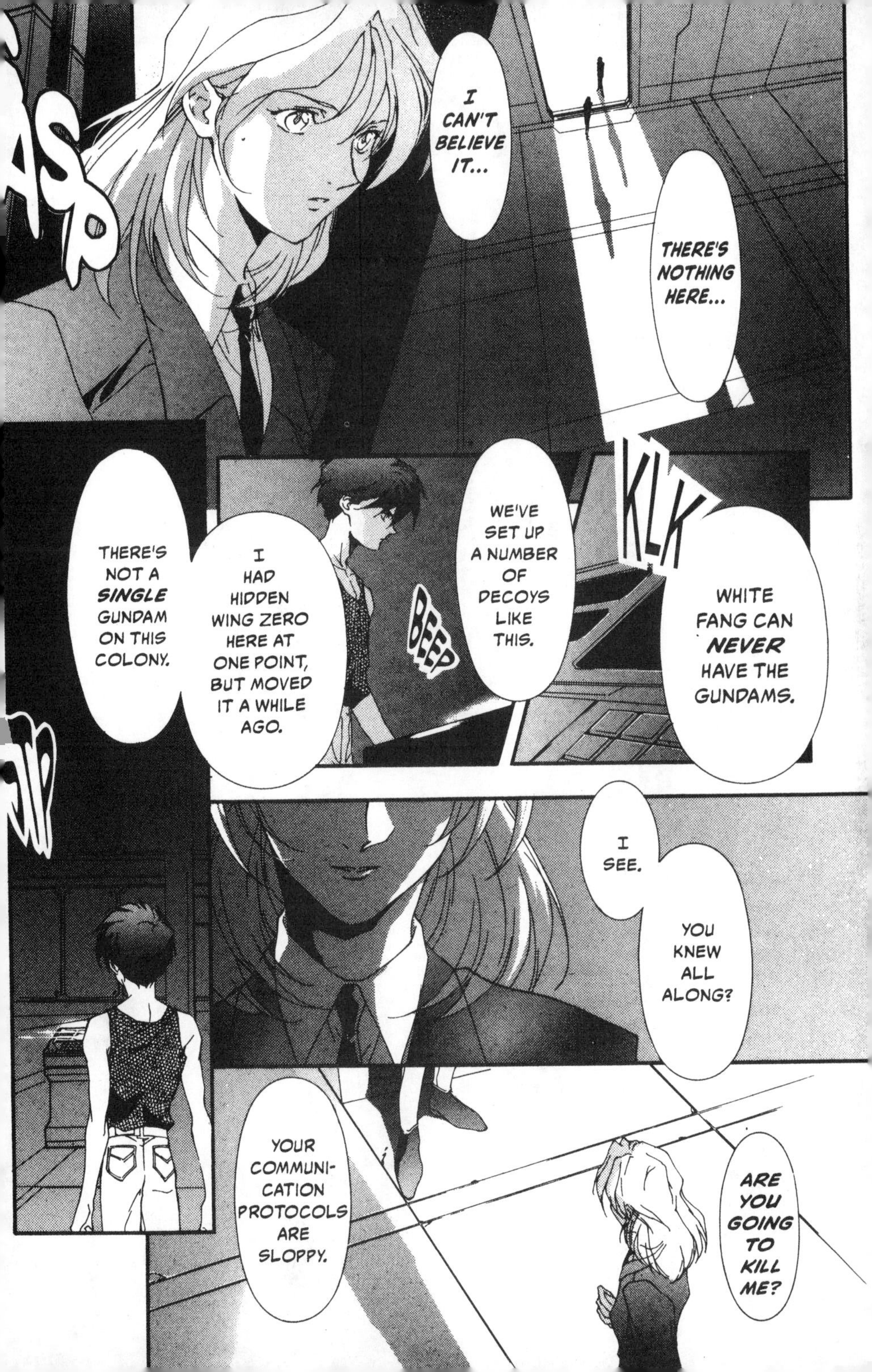
I CAN'T BELIEVE IT...
THERE'S NOTHING HERE...
THERE'S NOT A *SINGLE* GUNDAM ON THIS COLONY.
I HAD HIDDEN WING ZERO HERE AT ONE POINT, BUT MOVED IT A WHILE AGO.
BEEP
WE'VE SET UP A NUMBER OF DECOYS LIKE THIS.
KLK
WHITE FANG CAN *NEVER* HAVE THE GUNDAMS.
I SEE.
YOU KNEW ALL ALONG?
YOUR COMMUNI-CATION PROTOCOLS ARE SLOPPY.
ARE YOU GOING TO KILL ME?

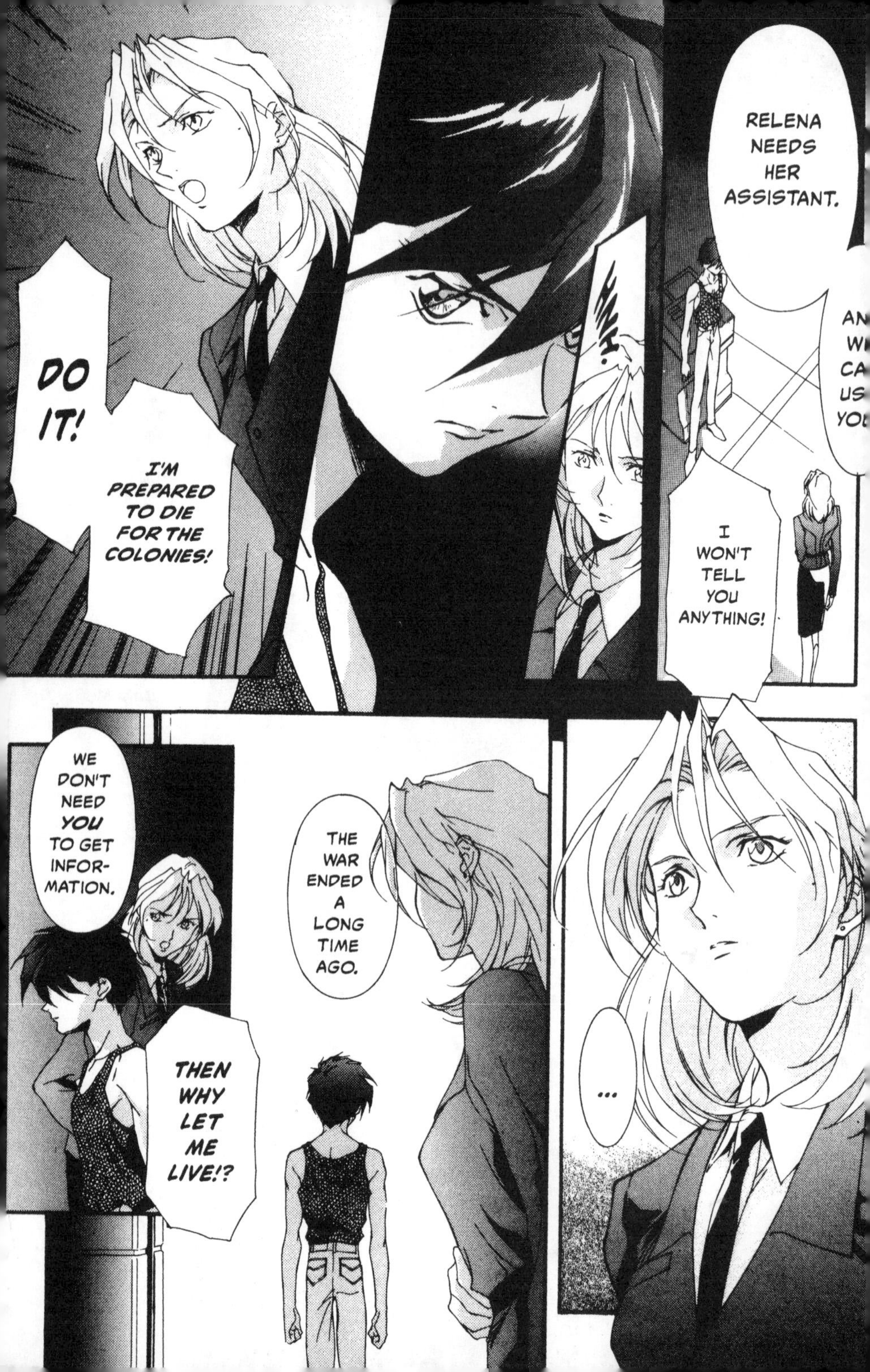
DO IT!
I'M PREPARED TO DIE FOR THE COLONIES!
HNH!
RELENA NEEDS HER ASSISTANT.
I WON'T TELL YOU ANYTHING!
WE DON'T NEED YOU TO GET INFOR-MATION.
THEN WHY LET ME LIVE!?
THE WAR ENDED A LONG TIME AGO.
...

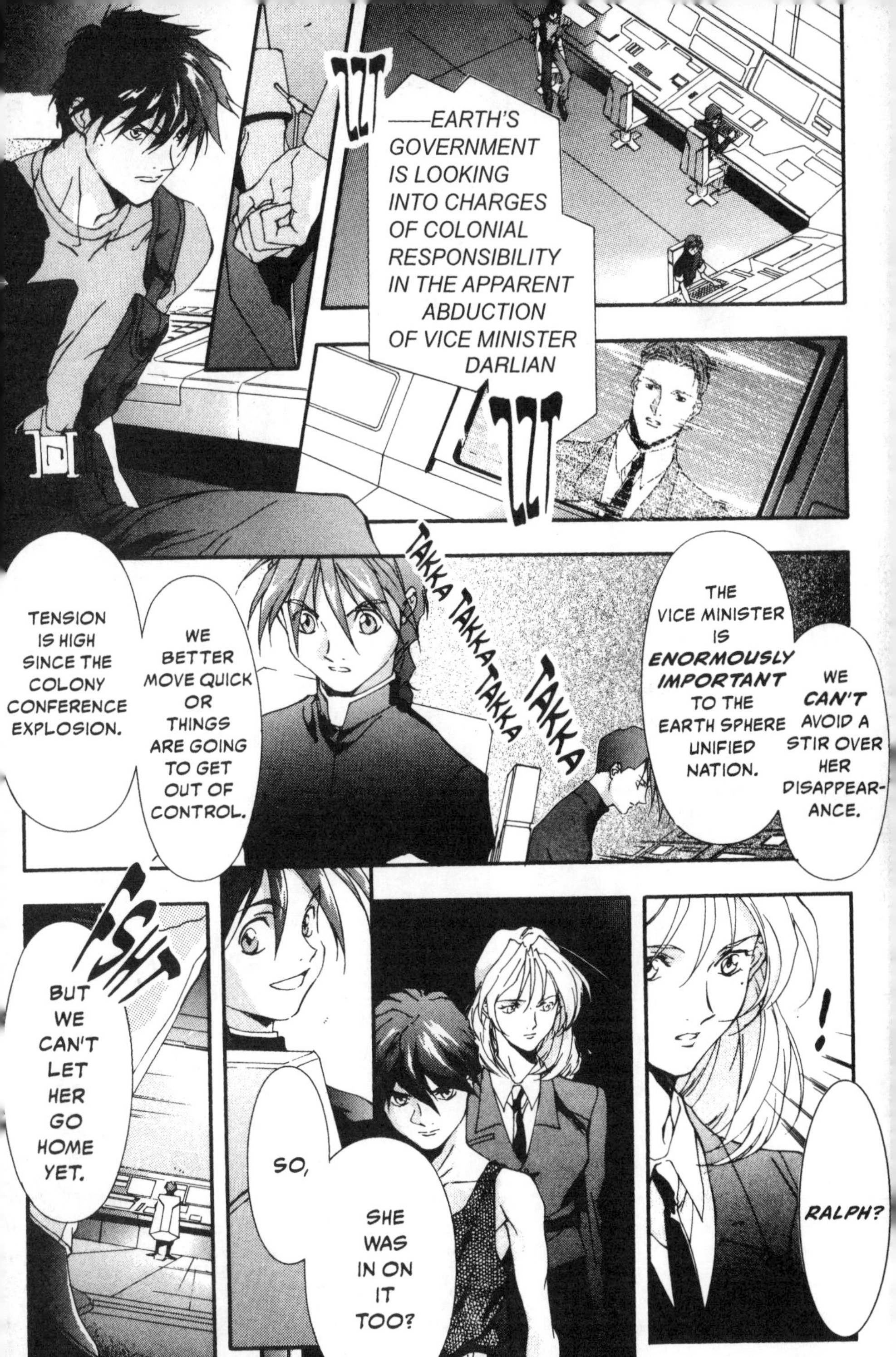
ZZT
——EARTH'S GOVERNMENT IS LOOKING INTO CHARGES OF COLONIAL RESPONSIBILITY IN THE APPARENT ABDUCTION OF VICE MINISTER DARLIAN
ZZT
TENSION IS HIGH SINCE THE COLONY CONFERENCE EXPLOSION.
WE BETTER MOVE QUICK OR THINGS ARE GOING TO GET OUT OF CONTROL.
TAKKA TAKKA TAKKA TAKKA
TAKKA
THE VICE MINISTER IS **ENORMOUSLY IMPORTANT** TO THE EARTH SPHERE UNIFIED NATION.
WE **CAN'T** AVOID A STIR OVER HER DISAPPEARANCE.
FSHT
BUT WE CAN'T LET HER GO HOME YET.
SO,
SHE WAS IN ON IT TOO?
!
RALPH?

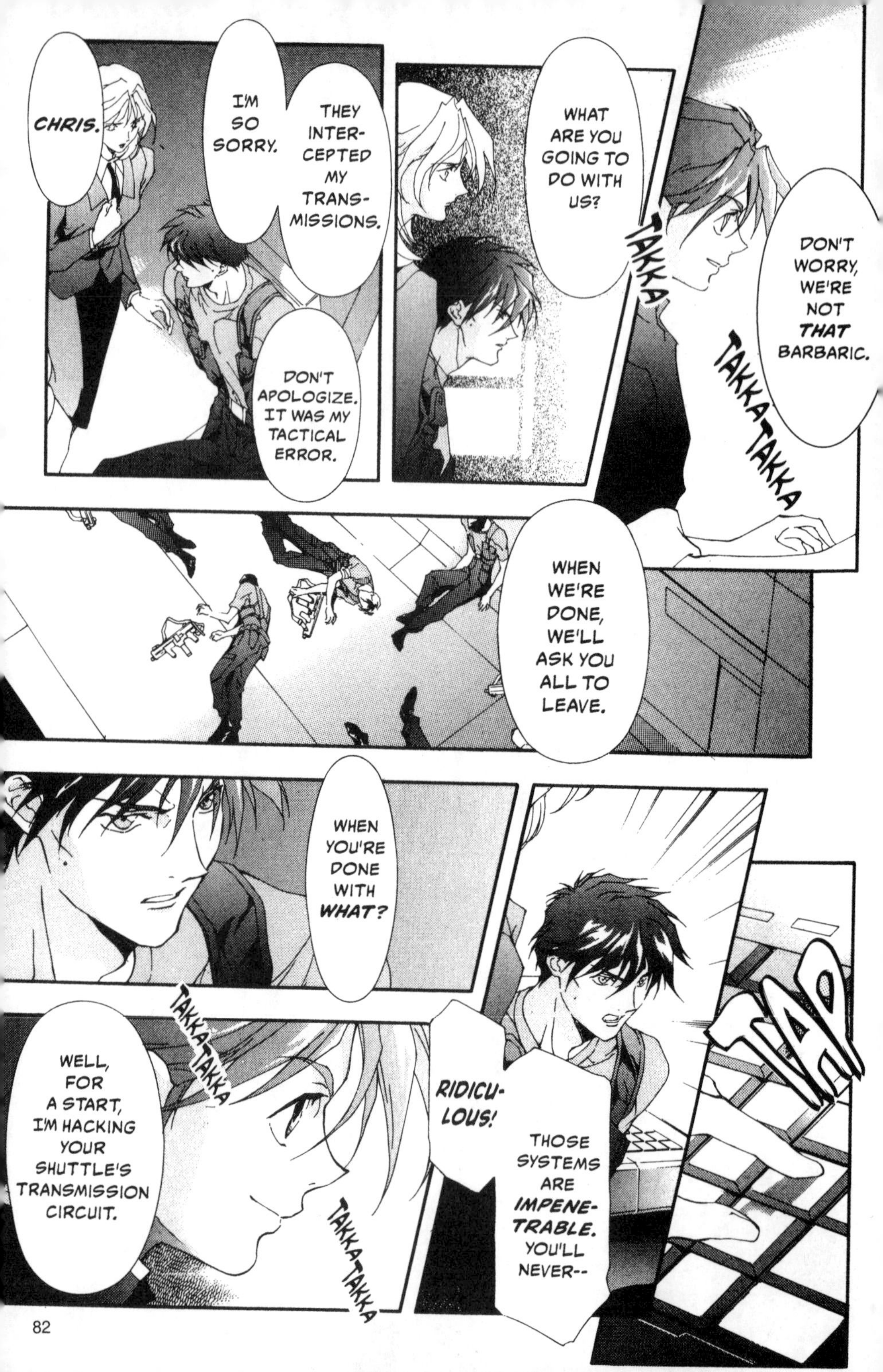
CHRIS.
I'M SO SORRY.
THEY INTER-CEPTED MY TRANS-MISSIONS.
DON'T APOLOGIZE. IT WAS MY TACTICAL ERROR.
WHAT ARE YOU GOING TO DO WITH US?
TAKKA
DON'T WORRY, WE'RE NOT *THAT* BARBARIC.
TAKKA-TAKKA
WHEN WE'RE DONE, WE'LL ASK YOU ALL TO LEAVE.
WHEN YOU'RE DONE WITH *WHAT?*
TAKKA-TAKKA
WELL, FOR A START, I'M HACKING YOUR SHUTTLE'S TRANSMISSION CIRCUIT.
TAKKA-TAKKA
RIDICU-LOUS!
THOSE SYSTEMS ARE *IMPENE-TRABLE.* YOU'LL NEVER--
TAP

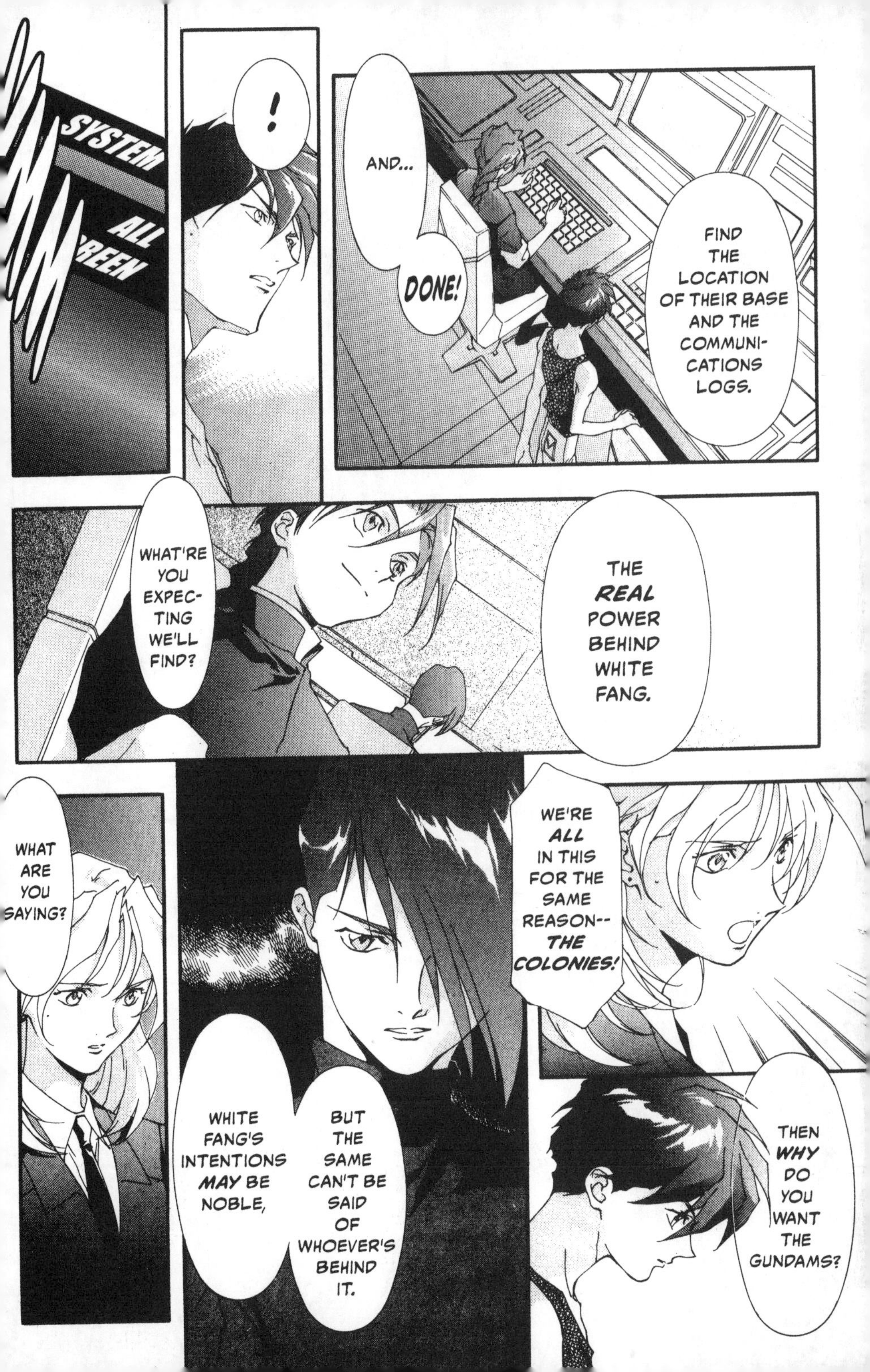
SYSTEM
ALL
REEN
!
AND...
DONE!
FIND THE LOCATION OF THEIR BASE AND THE COMMUNI-CATIONS LOGS.
WHAT'RE YOU EXPEC-TING WE'LL FIND?
THE *REAL* POWER BEHIND WHITE FANG.
WHAT ARE YOU SAYING?
WHITE FANG'S INTENTIONS *MAY* BE NOBLE,
BUT THE SAME CAN'T BE SAID OF WHOEVER'S BEHIND IT.
WE'RE *ALL* IN THIS FOR THE SAME REASON-- *THE COLONIES!*
THEN *WHY* DO YOU WANT THE GUNDAMS?

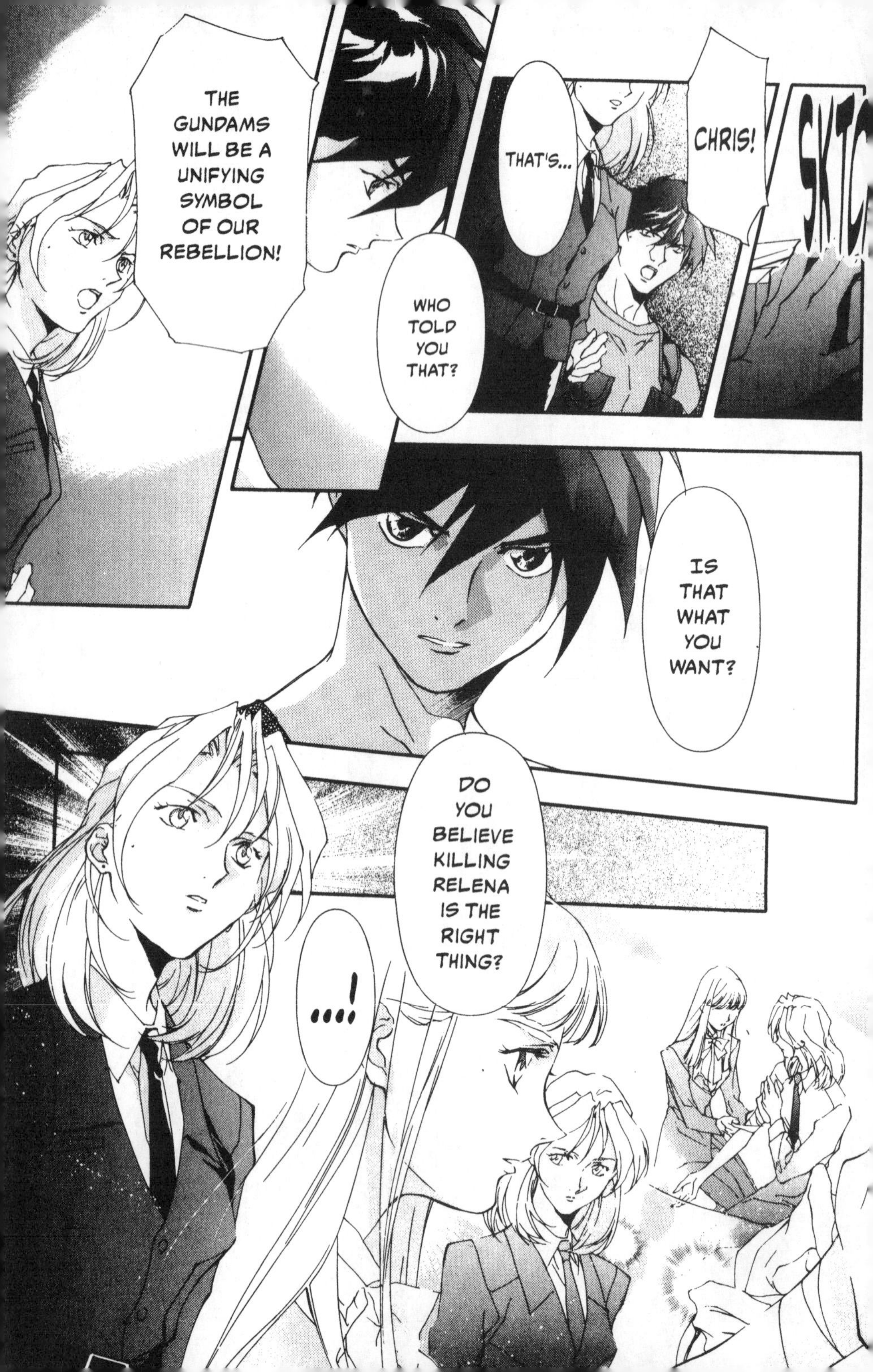
THE GUNDAMS WILL BE A UNIFYING SYMBOL OF OUR REBELLION!
WHO TOLD YOU THAT?
THAT'S...
CHRIS!
SKTC
IS THAT WHAT YOU WANT?
DO YOU BELIEVE KILLING RELENA IS THE RIGHT THING?
...!

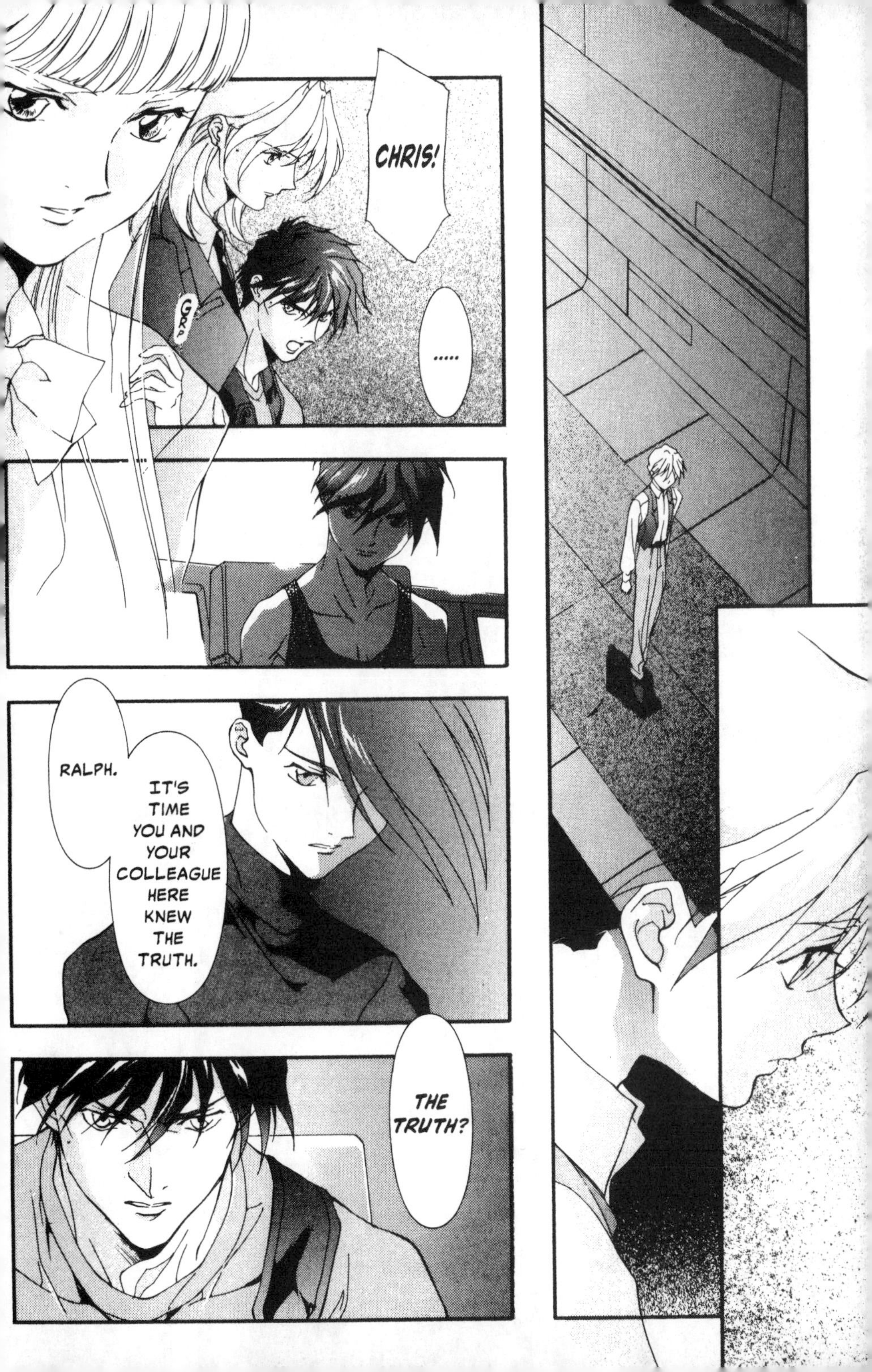
CHRIS!
GRP
......
RALPH.
IT'S TIME YOU AND YOUR COLLEAGUE HERE KNEW THE TRUTH.
THE TRUTH?

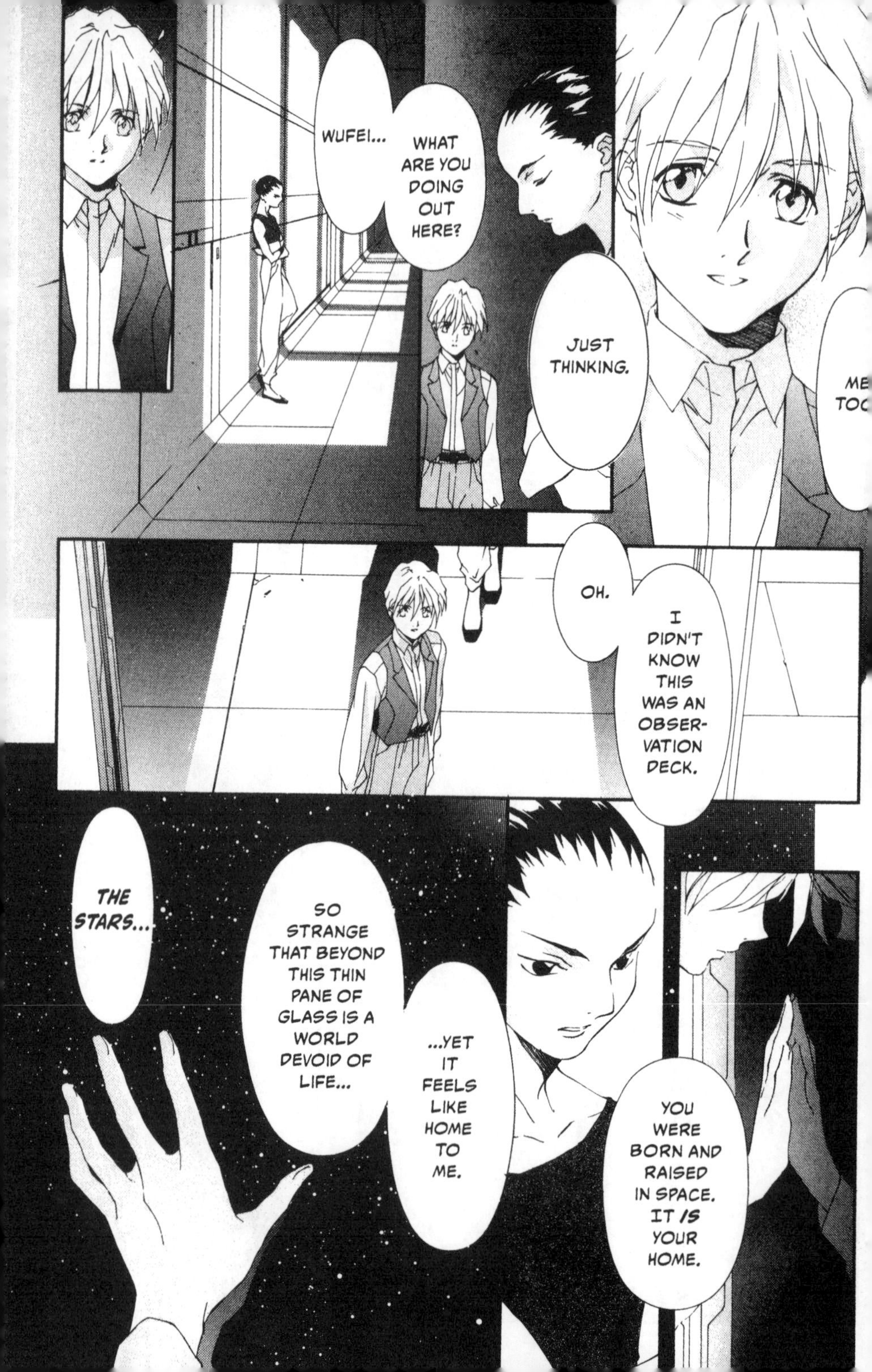
WUFEI...
WHAT ARE YOU DOING OUT HERE?
JUST THINKING.
ME
OH.
I DIDN'T KNOW THIS WAS AN OBSER-VATION DECK.
THE STARS...
SO STRANGE THAT BEYOND THIS THIN PANE OF GLASS IS A WORLD DEVOID OF LIFE...
...YET IT FEELS LIKE HOME TO ME.
YOU WERE BORN AND RAISED IN SPACE. IT *IS* YOUR HOME.

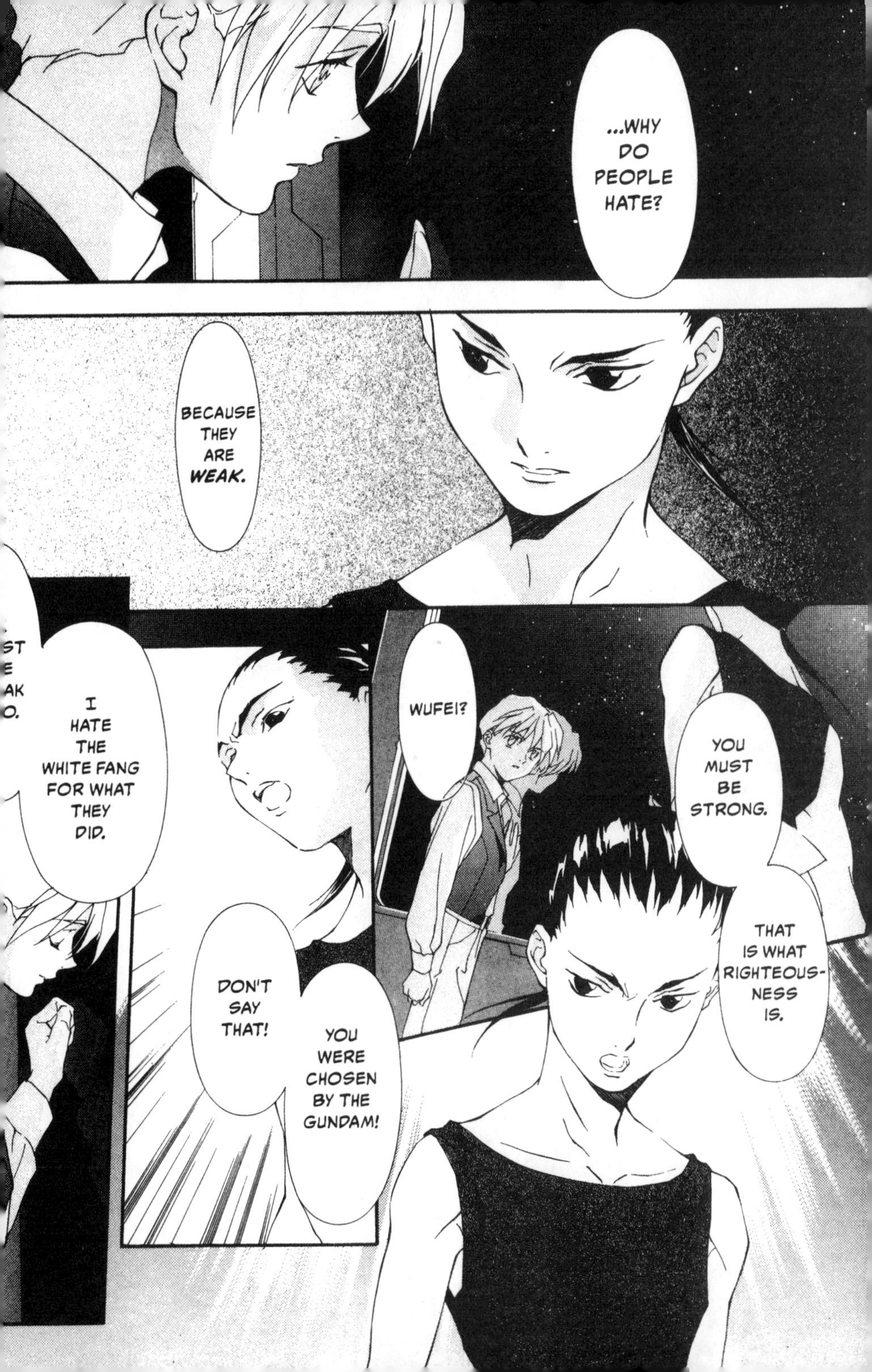
...WHY DO PEOPLE HATE?
BECAUSE THEY ARE *WEAK.*
I HATE THE WHITE FANG FOR WHAT THEY DID.
DON'T SAY THAT!
YOU WERE CHOSEN BY THE GUNDAM!
WUFEI?
YOU MUST BE STRONG.
THAT IS WHAT RIGHTEOUSNESS IS.

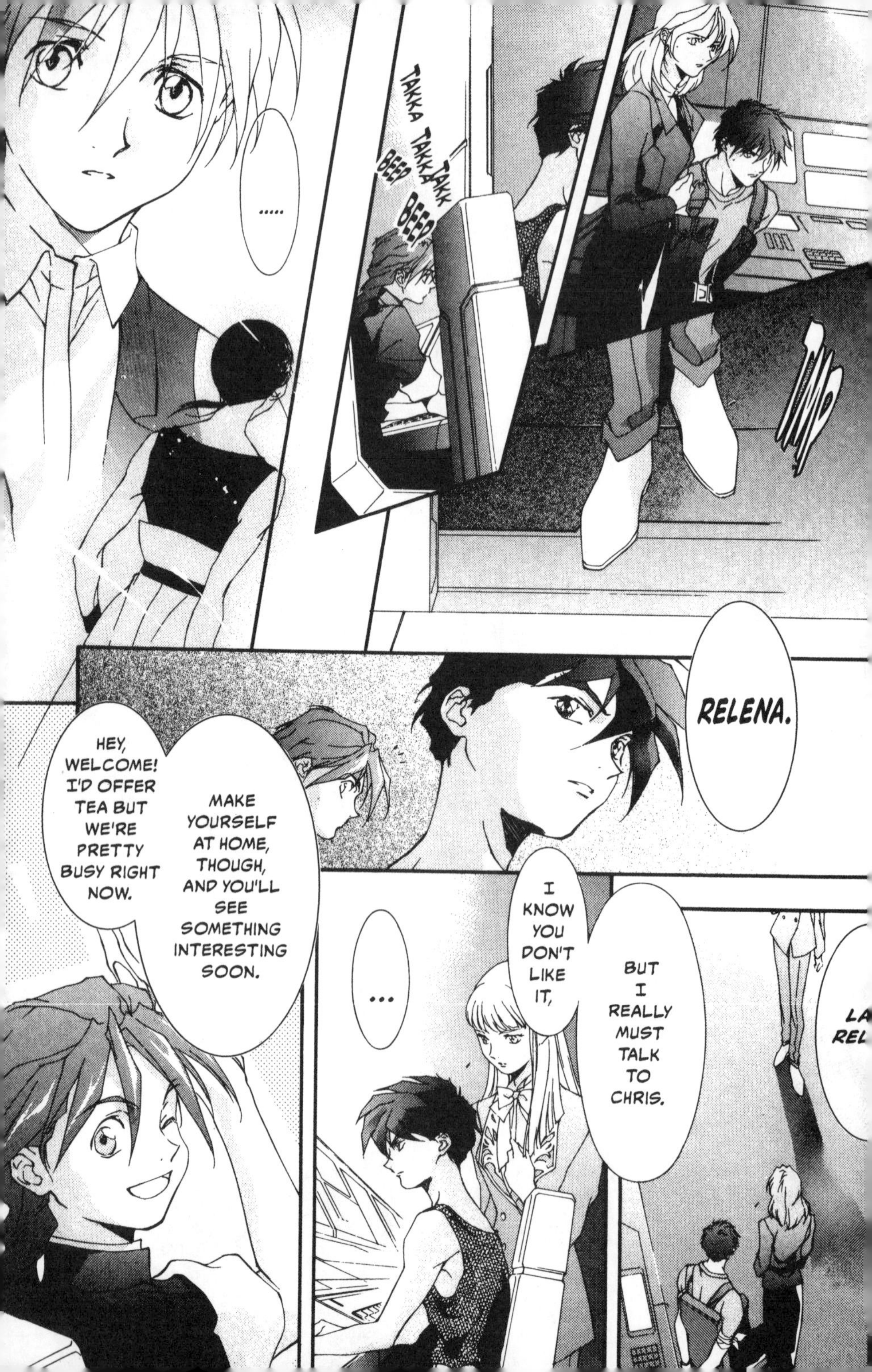
.....
TAKKA TAKKA TAKK
BEEP BEEP
RELENA.
HEY, WELCOME! I'D OFFER TEA BUT WE'RE PRETTY BUSY RIGHT NOW.
MAKE YOURSELF AT HOME, THOUGH, AND YOU'LL SEE SOMETHING INTERESTING SOON.
...
I KNOW YOU DON'T LIKE IT,
BUT I REALLY MUST TALK TO CHRIS.

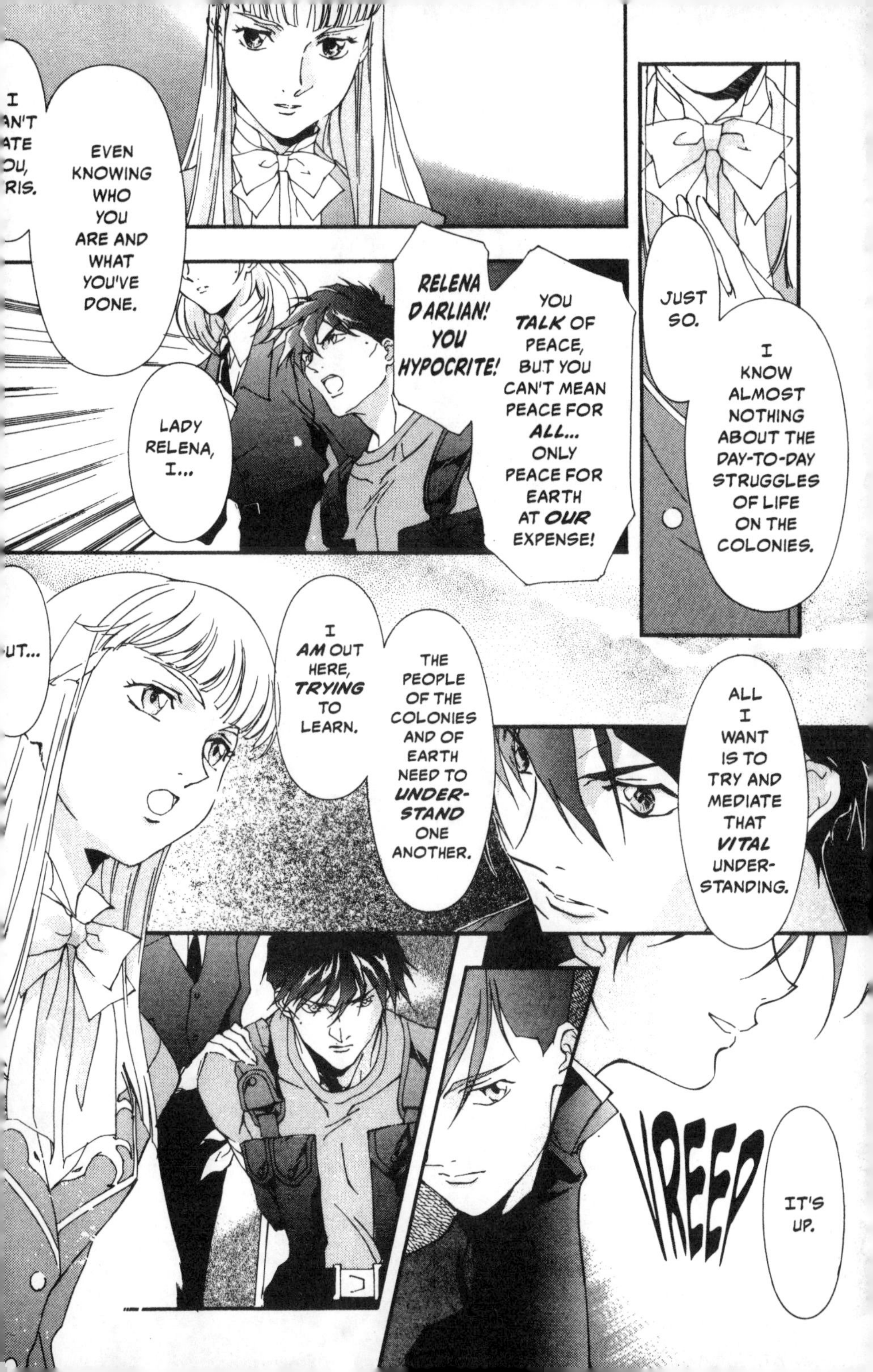
I
AN'T
ATE
OU,
RIS.
EVEN KNOWING WHO YOU ARE AND WHAT YOU'VE DONE.
LADY RELENA, I...
RELENA DARLIAN! YOU HYPOCRITE!
YOU TALK OF PEACE, BUT YOU CAN'T MEAN PEACE FOR ALL... ONLY PEACE FOR EARTH AT OUR EXPENSE!
JUST SO.
I KNOW ALMOST NOTHING ABOUT THE DAY-TO-DAY STRUGGLES OF LIFE ON THE COLONIES.
UT...
I AM OUT HERE, TRYING TO LEARN.
THE PEOPLE OF THE COLONIES AND OF EARTH NEED TO UNDERSTAND ONE ANOTHER.
ALL I WANT IS TO TRY AND MEDIATE THAT VITAL UNDERSTANDING.
VREEP
IT'S UP.

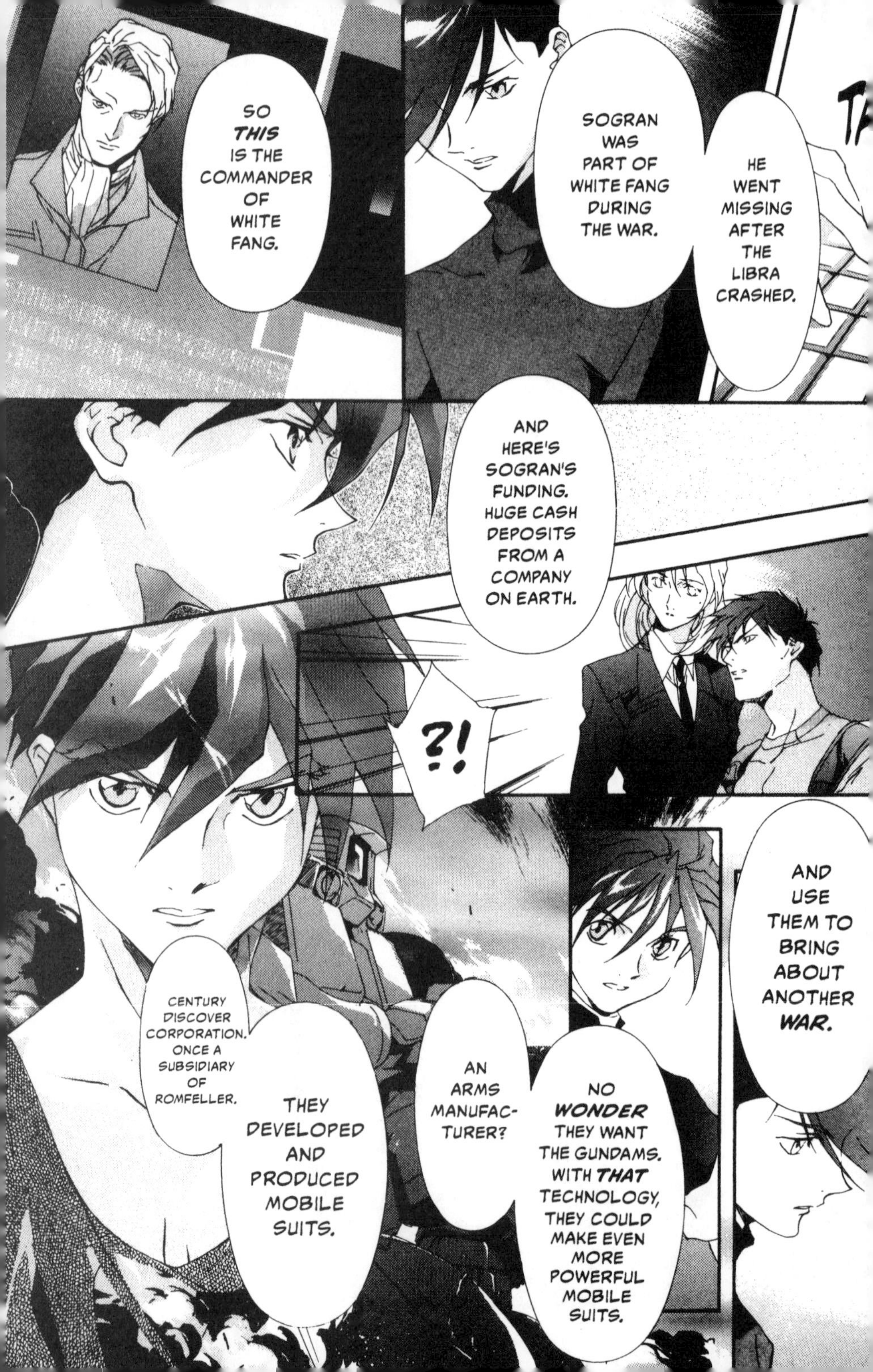
SO *THIS* IS THE COMMANDER OF WHITE FANG.
SOGRAN WAS PART OF WHITE FANG DURING THE WAR.
HE WENT MISSING AFTER THE LIBRA CRASHED.
AND HERE'S SOGRAN'S FUNDING. HUGE CASH DEPOSITS FROM A COMPANY ON EARTH.
?!
CENTURY DISCOVER CORPORATION. ONCE A SUBSIDIARY OF ROMFELLER.
THEY DEVELOPED AND PRODUCED MOBILE SUITS.
AN ARMS MANUFAC-TURER?
NO *WONDER* THEY WANT THE GUNDAMS. WITH *THAT* TECHNOLOGY, THEY COULD MAKE EVEN MORE POWERFUL MOBILE SUITS.
AND USE THEM TO BRING ABOUT ANOTHER *WAR.*

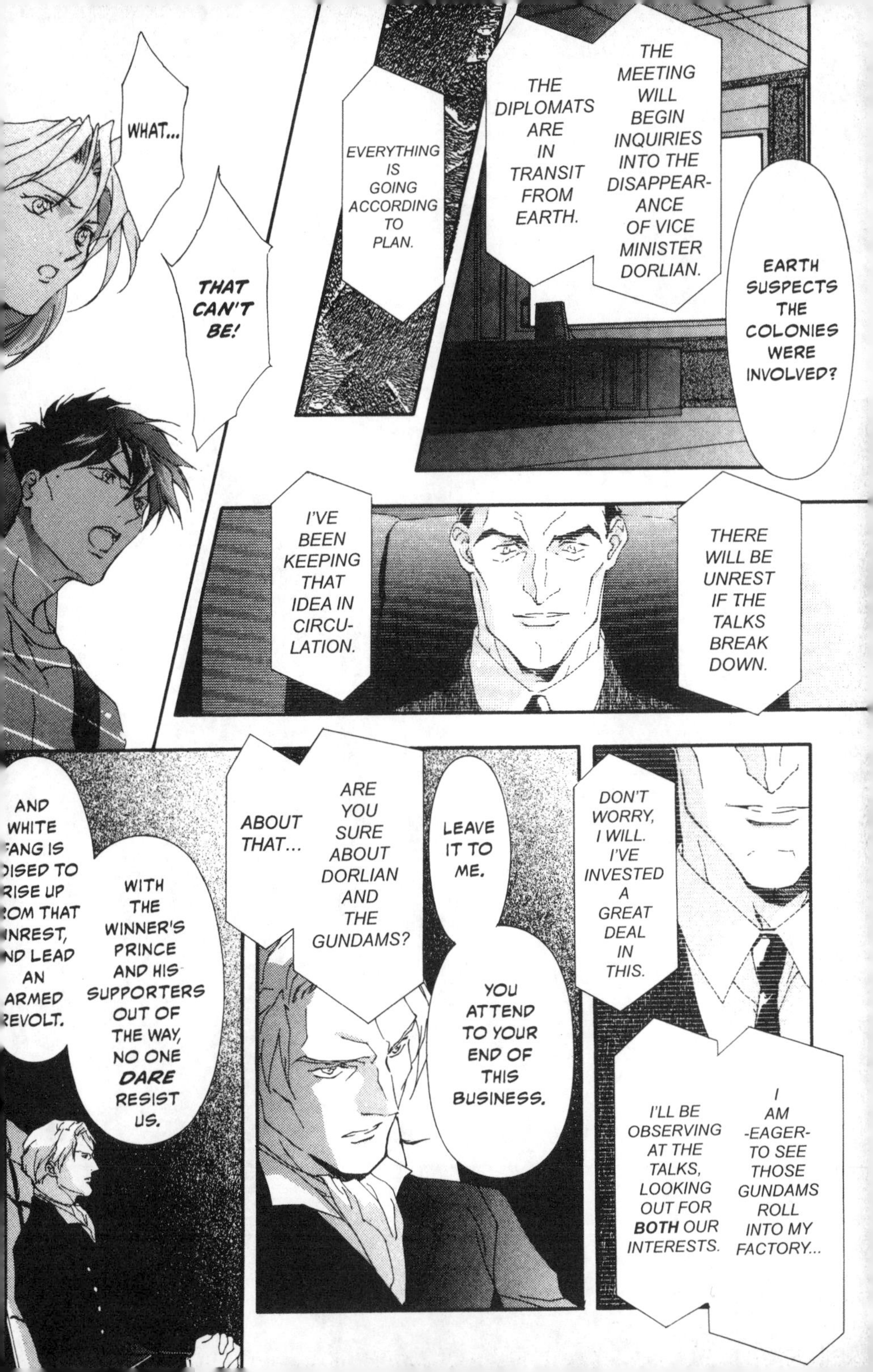

WHAT...
THAT CAN'T BE!
EVERYTHING IS GOING ACCORDING TO PLAN.
THE DIPLOMATS ARE IN TRANSIT FROM EARTH.
THE MEETING WILL BEGIN INQUIRIES INTO THE DISAPPEAR-ANCE OF VICE MINISTER DORLIAN.
EARTH SUSPECTS THE COLONIES WERE INVOLVED?
I'VE BEEN KEEPING THAT IDEA IN CIRCU-LATION.
THERE WILL BE UNREST IF THE TALKS BREAK DOWN.
AND WHITE ANG IS ISED TO RISE UP ROM THAT NREST, ND LEAD AN ARMED EVOLT.
WITH THE WINNER'S PRINCE AND HIS SUPPORTERS OUT OF THE WAY, NO ONE DARE RESIST US.
ABOUT THAT...
ARE YOU SURE ABOUT DORLIAN AND THE GUNDAMS?
LEAVE IT TO ME.
YOU ATTEND TO YOUR END OF THIS BUSINESS.
DON'T WORRY, I WILL. I'VE INVESTED A GREAT DEAL IN THIS.
I'LL BE OBSERVING AT THE TALKS, LOOKING OUT FOR BOTH OUR INTERESTS.
I AM -EAGER- TO SEE THOSE GUNDAMS ROLL INTO MY FACTORY...

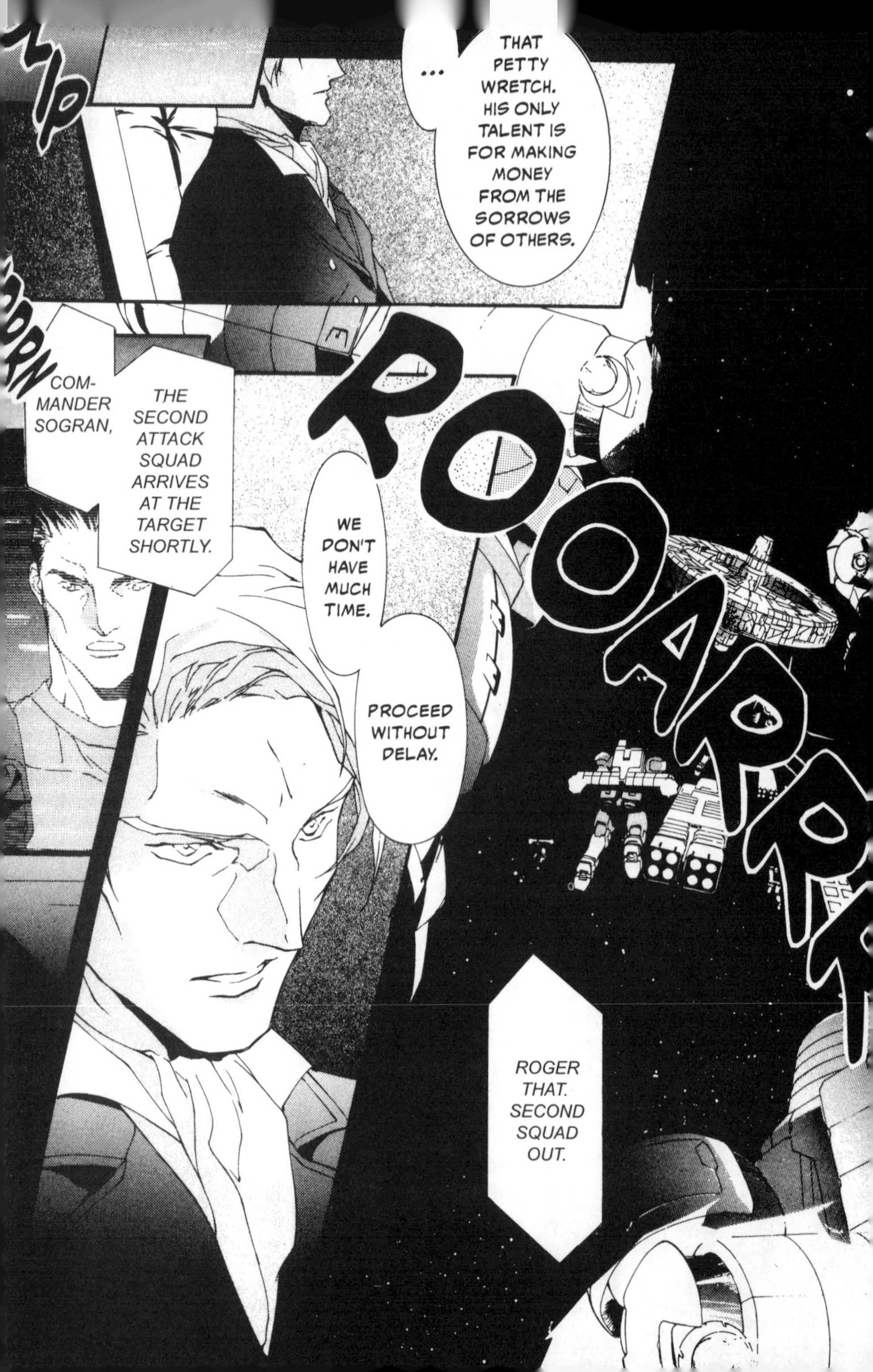
...
THAT PETTY WRETCH. HIS ONLY TALENT IS FOR MAKING MONEY FROM THE SORROWS OF OTHERS.
COMMANDER SOGRAN,
THE SECOND ATTACK SQUAD ARRIVES AT THE TARGET SHORTLY.
WE DON'T HAVE MUCH TIME.
PROCEED WITHOUT DELAY.
ROGER THAT. SECOND SQUAD OUT.

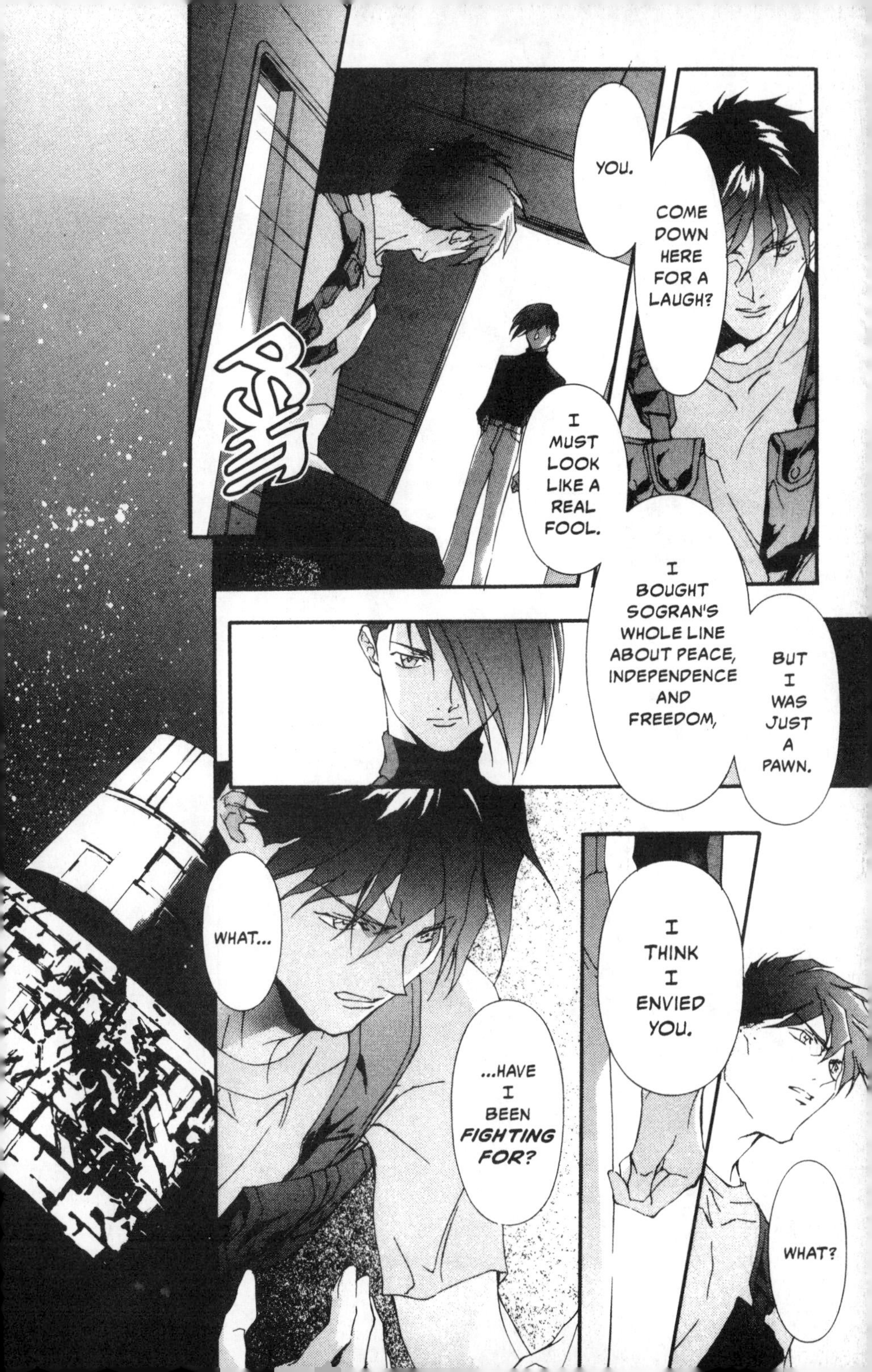
YOU.
COME DOWN HERE FOR A LAUGH?
I MUST LOOK LIKE A REAL FOOL.
I BOUGHT SOGRAN'S WHOLE LINE ABOUT PEACE, INDEPENDENCE AND FREEDOM,
BUT I WAS JUST A PAWN.
WHAT...
...HAVE I BEEN FIGHTING FOR?
I THINK I ENVIED YOU.
WHAT?

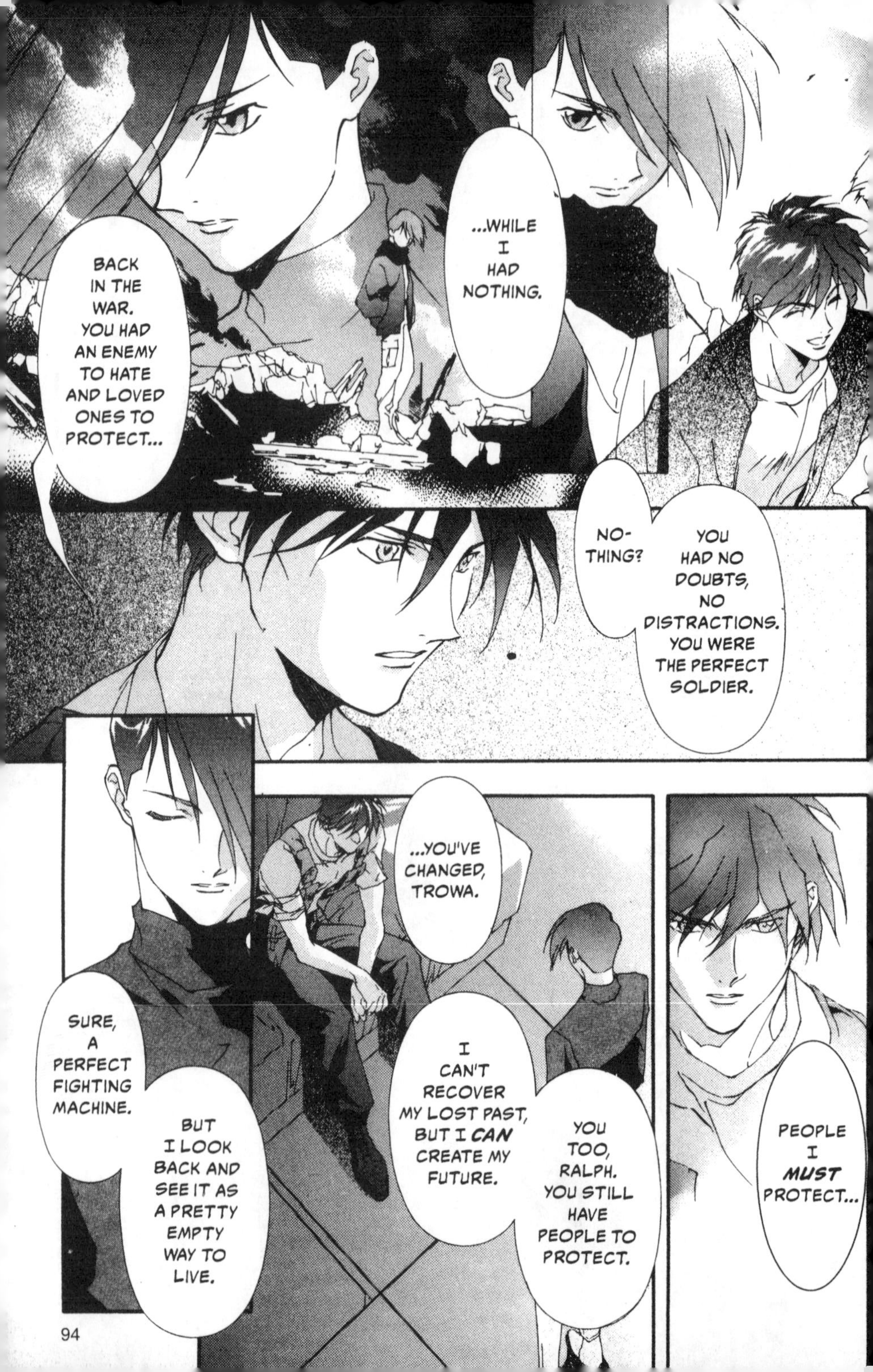
BACK IN THE WAR. YOU HAD AN ENEMY TO HATE AND LOVED ONES TO PROTECT...
...WHILE I HAD NOTHING.
NO-THING?
YOU HAD NO DOUBTS, NO DISTRACTIONS. YOU WERE THE PERFECT SOLDIER.
SURE, A PERFECT FIGHTING MACHINE.
BUT I LOOK BACK AND SEE IT AS A PRETTY EMPTY WAY TO LIVE.
...YOU'VE CHANGED, TROWA.
I CAN'T RECOVER MY LOST PAST, BUT I *CAN* CREATE MY FUTURE.
YOU TOO, RALPH. YOU STILL HAVE PEOPLE TO PROTECT.
PEOPLE I *MUST* PROTECT...

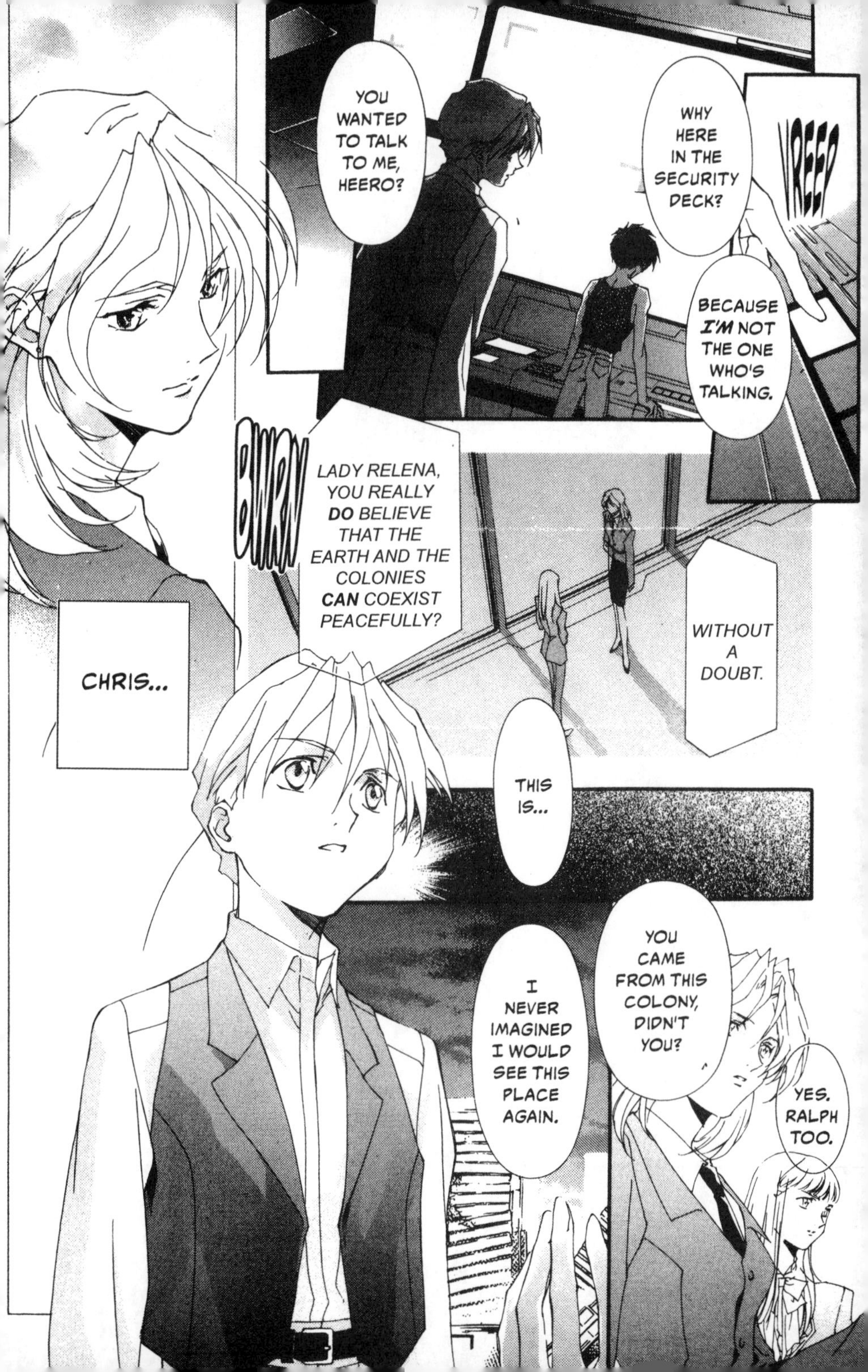
CHRIS...
YOU WANTED TO TALK TO ME, HEERO?
WHY HERE IN THE SECURITY DECK?
VREEP
BECAUSE I'M NOT THE ONE WHO'S TALKING.
GWRN
LADY RELENA, YOU REALLY DO BELIEVE THAT THE EARTH AND THE COLONIES CAN COEXIST PEACEFULLY?
WITHOUT A DOUBT.
THIS IS...
I NEVER IMAGINED I WOULD SEE THIS PLACE AGAIN.
YOU CAME FROM THIS COLONY, DIDN'T YOU?
YES. RALPH TOO.

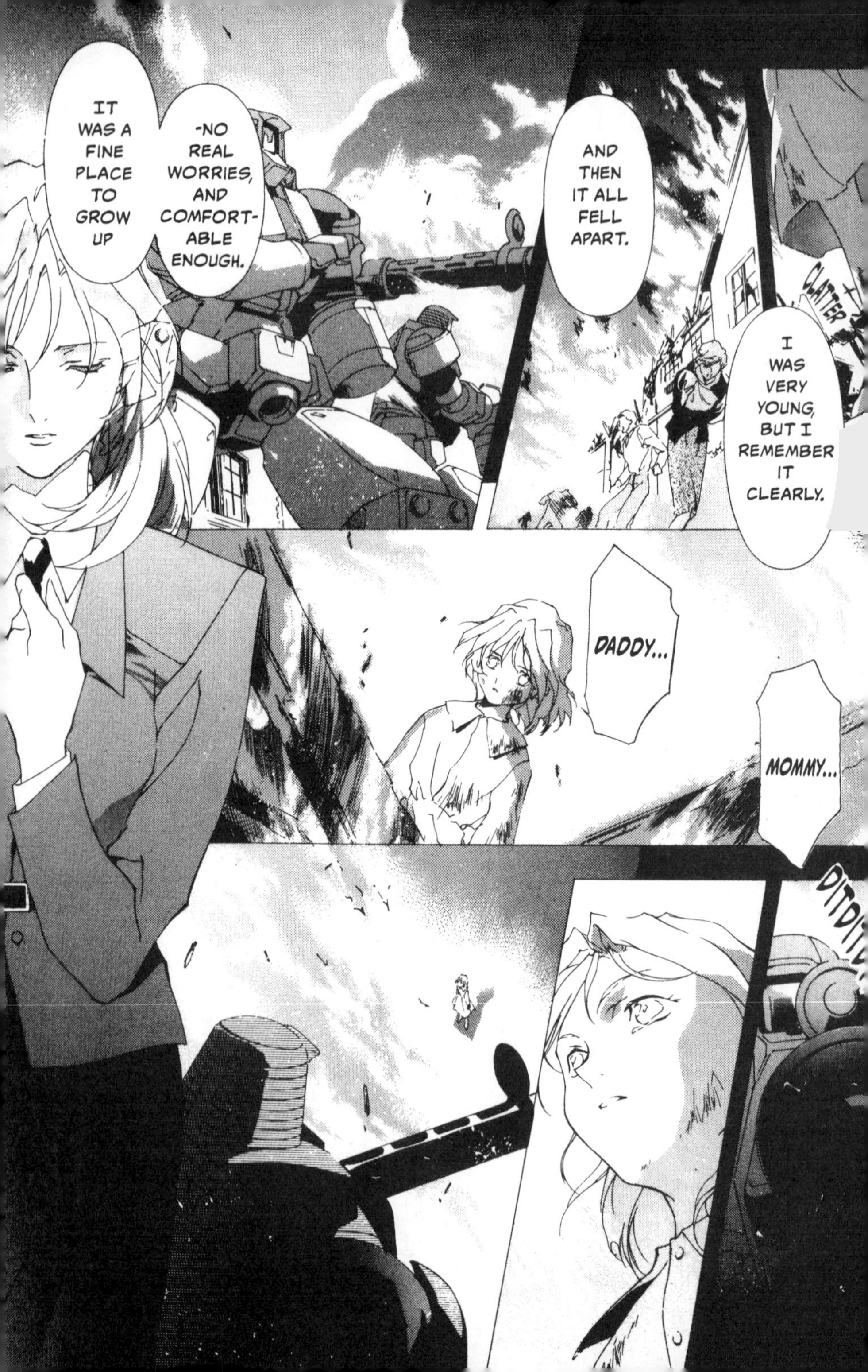
IT WAS A FINE PLACE TO GROW UP
-NO REAL WORRIES, AND COMFORT-ABLE ENOUGH.
AND THEN IT ALL FELL APART.
CLATTER
I WAS VERY YOUNG, BUT I REMEMBER IT CLEARLY.
DADDY...
MOMMY...
DITDIT

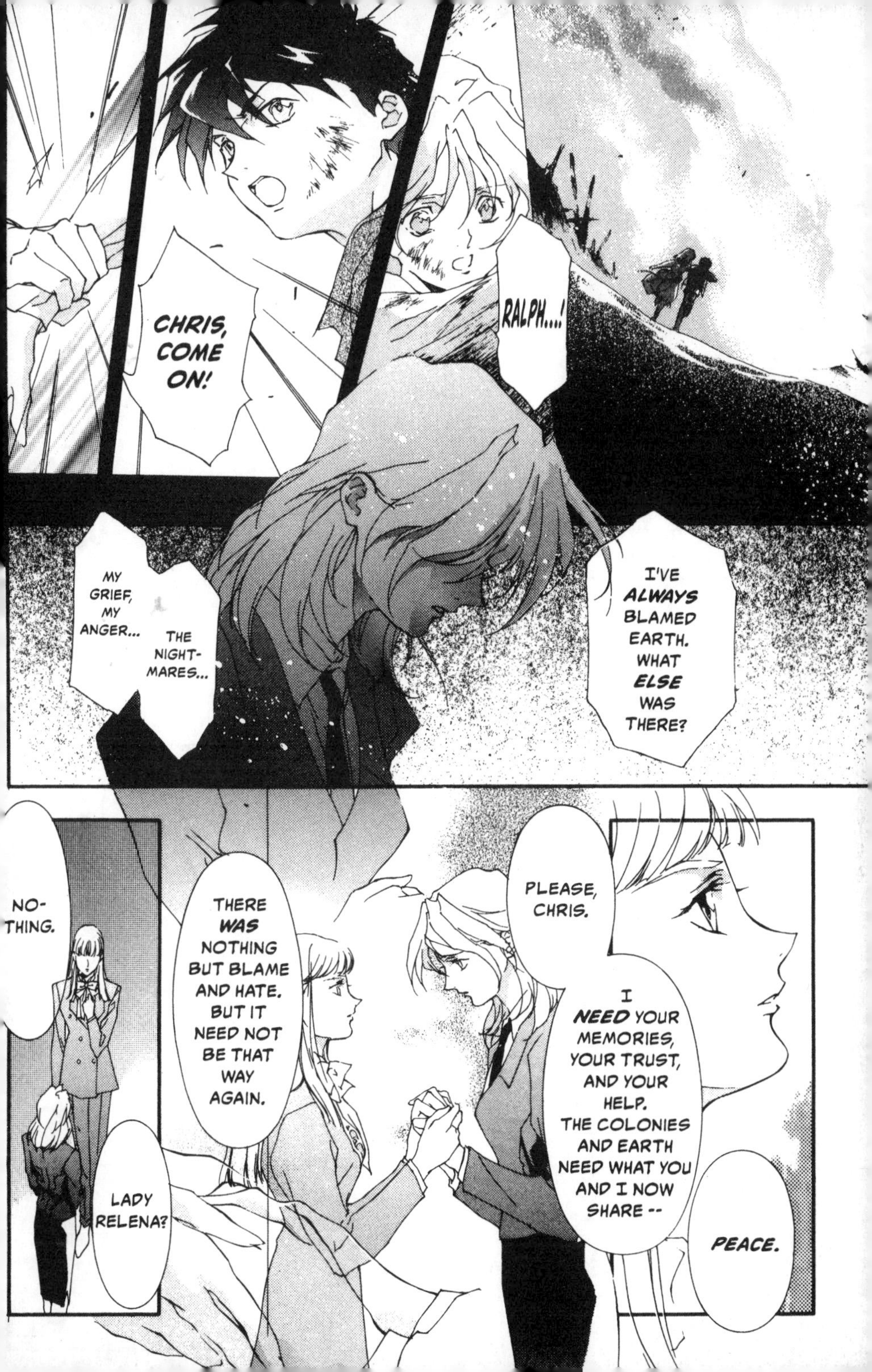
CHRIS, COME ON!
RALPH...!
MY GRIEF, MY ANGER...
THE NIGHT-MARES...
I'VE ALWAYS BLAMED EARTH. WHAT ELSE WAS THERE?
NO-THING.
LADY RELENA?
THERE WAS NOTHING BUT BLAME AND HATE. BUT IT NEED NOT BE THAT WAY AGAIN.
PLEASE, CHRIS.
I NEED YOUR MEMORIES, YOUR TRUST, AND YOUR HELP. THE COLONIES AND EARTH NEED WHAT YOU AND I NOW SHARE --
PEACE.

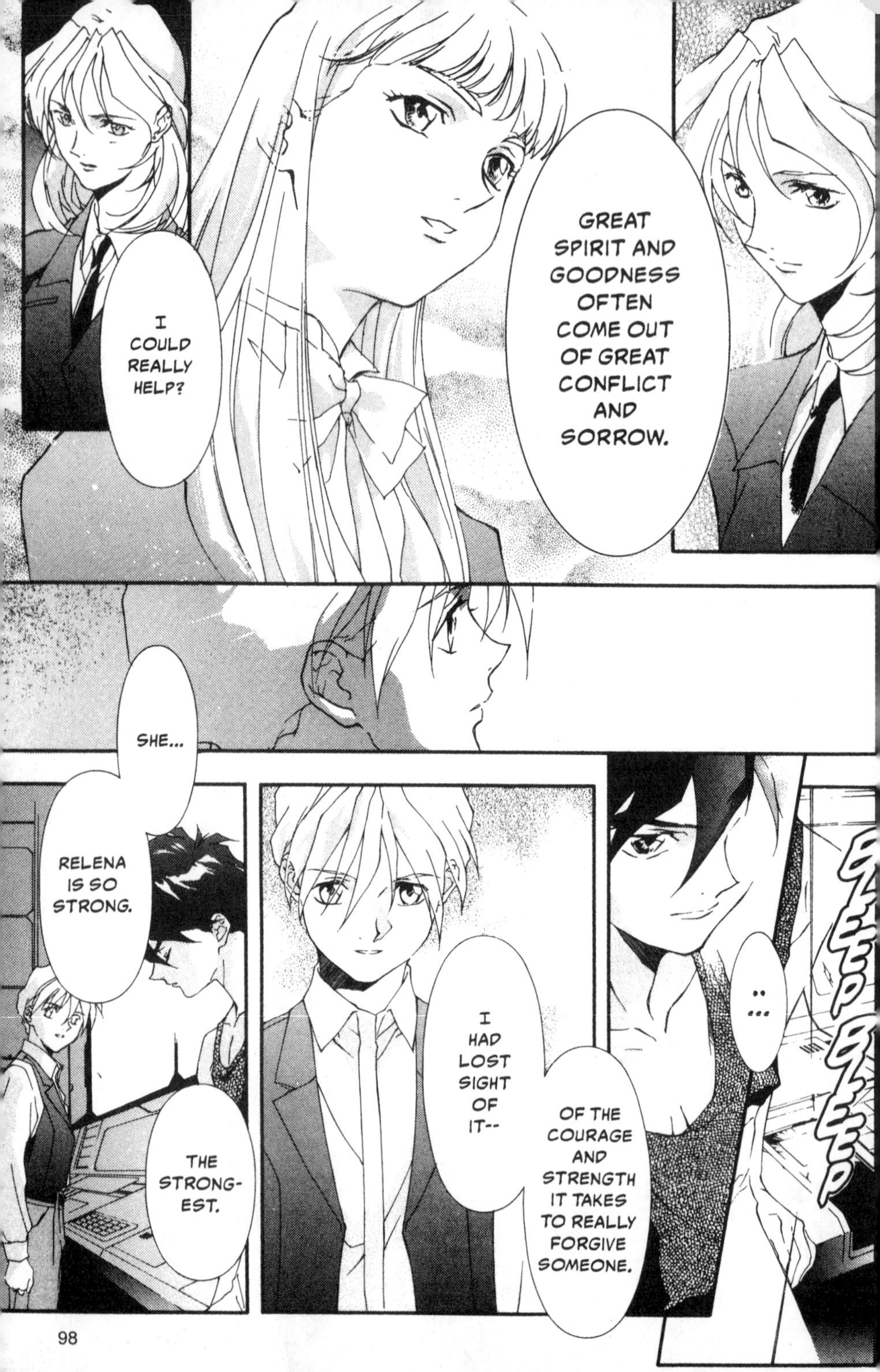
I COULD REALLY HELP?
GREAT SPIRIT AND GOODNESS OFTEN COME OUT OF GREAT CONFLICT AND SORROW.
SHE...
RELENA IS SO STRONG.
THE STRONG-EST.
I HAD LOST SIGHT OF IT--
OF THE COURAGE AND STRENGTH IT TAKES TO REALLY FORGIVE SOMEONE.
....
BEEP BEEP

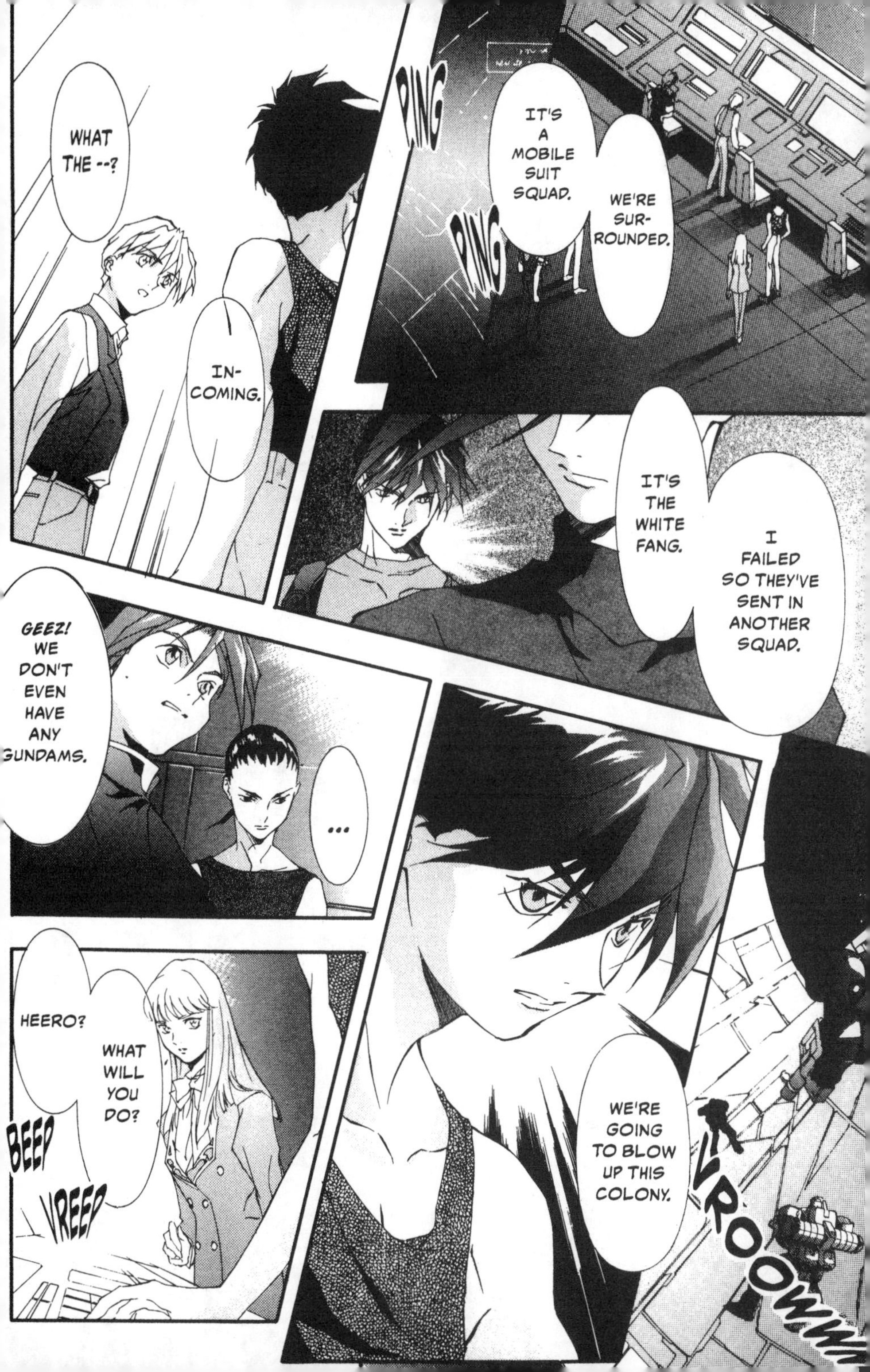
WHAT THE --?
IN-COMING.
PING
IT'S A MOBILE SUIT SQUAD.
PING
WE'RE SUR-ROUNDED.
IT'S THE WHITE FANG.
I FAILED SO THEY'VE SENT IN ANOTHER SQUAD.
GEEZ! WE DON'T EVEN HAVE ANY GUNDAMS.
...
HEERO?
WHAT WILL YOU DO?
BEEP
VREEP
WE'RE GOING TO BLOW UP THIS COLONY.
VROOOWWW

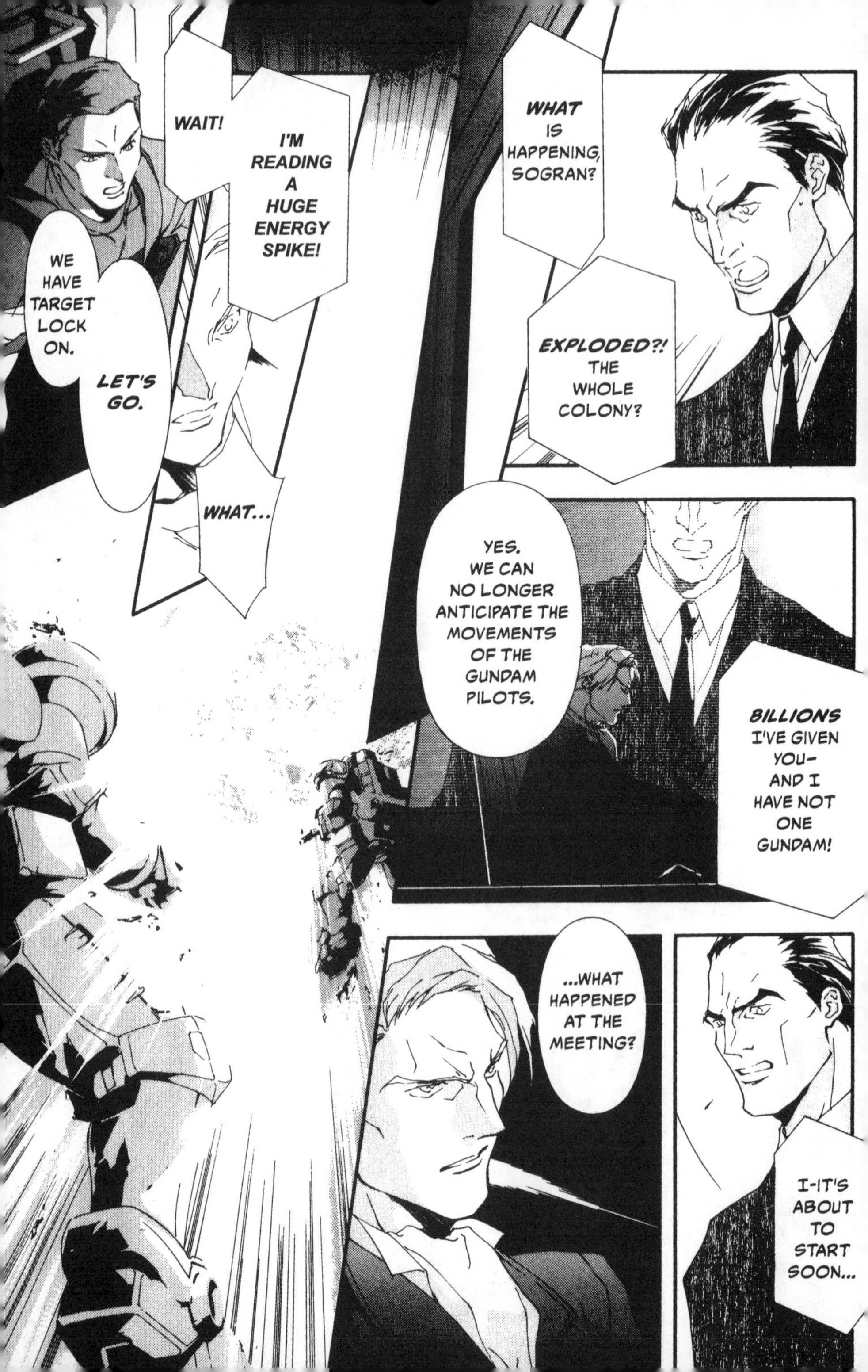
WAIT!
I'M READING A HUGE ENERGY SPIKE!
WE HAVE TARGET LOCK ON.
LET'S GO.
WHAT...
WHAT IS HAPPENING, SOGRAN?
EXPLODED?! THE WHOLE COLONY?
YES. WE CAN NO LONGER ANTICIPATE THE MOVEMENTS OF THE GUNDAM PILOTS.
BILLIONS I'VE GIVEN YOU— AND I HAVE NOT ONE GUNDAM!
...WHAT HAPPENED AT THE MEETING?
I-IT'S ABOUT TO START SOON...

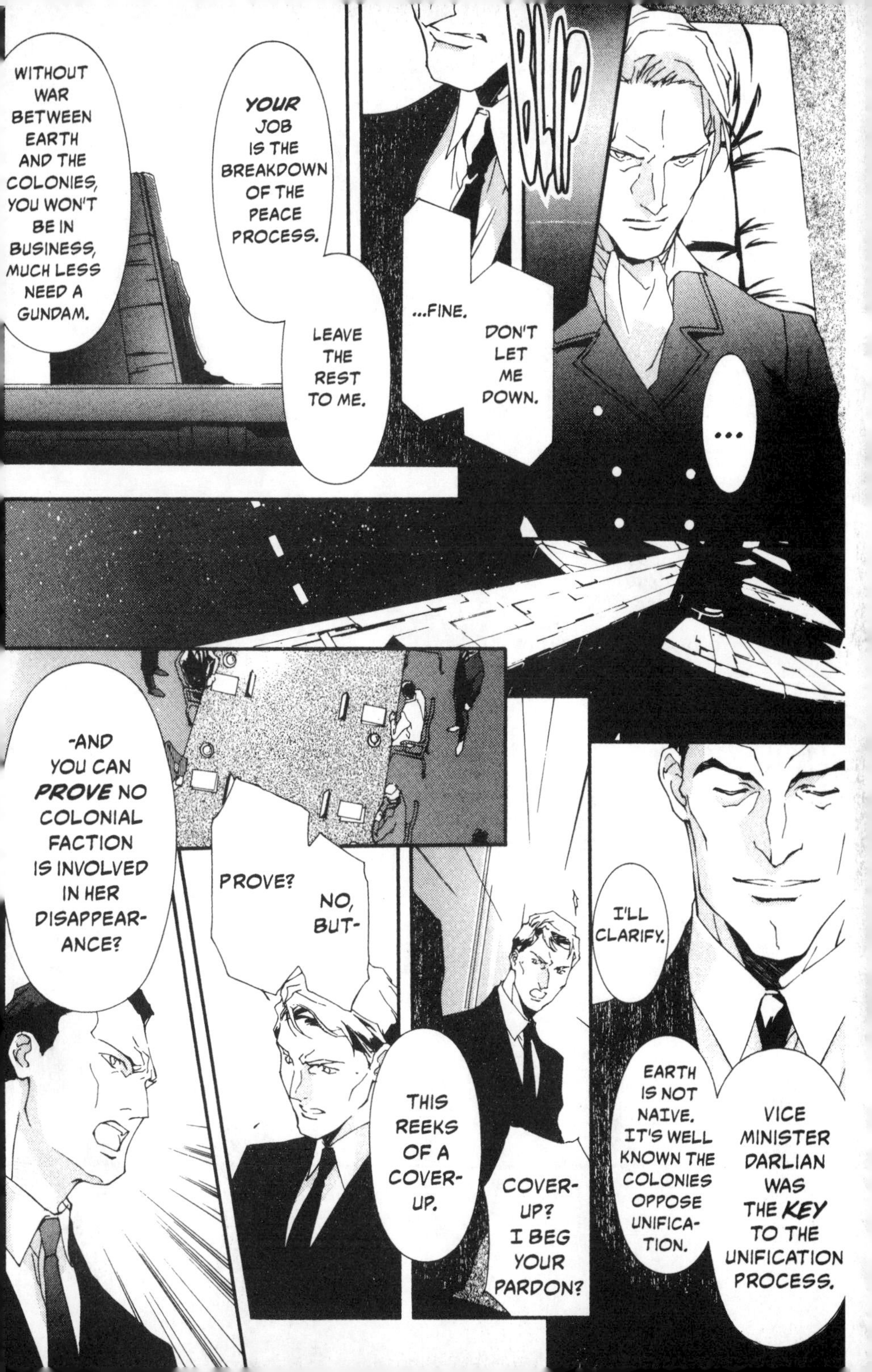
WITHOUT WAR BETWEEN EARTH AND THE COLONIES, YOU WON'T BE IN BUSINESS, MUCH LESS NEED A GUNDAM.
YOUR JOB IS THE BREAKDOWN OF THE PEACE PROCESS.
LEAVE THE REST TO ME.
BLIP
...FINE.
DON'T LET ME DOWN.
...
-AND YOU CAN PROVE NO COLONIAL FACTION IS INVOLVED IN HER DISAPPEARANCE?
PROVE?
NO, BUT-
THIS REEKS OF A COVER-UP.
COVER-UP? I BEG YOUR PARDON?
I'LL CLARIFY.
EARTH IS NOT NAIVE. IT'S WELL KNOWN THE COLONIES OPPOSE UNIFICATION.
VICE MINISTER DARLIAN WAS THE KEY TO THE UNIFICATION PROCESS.

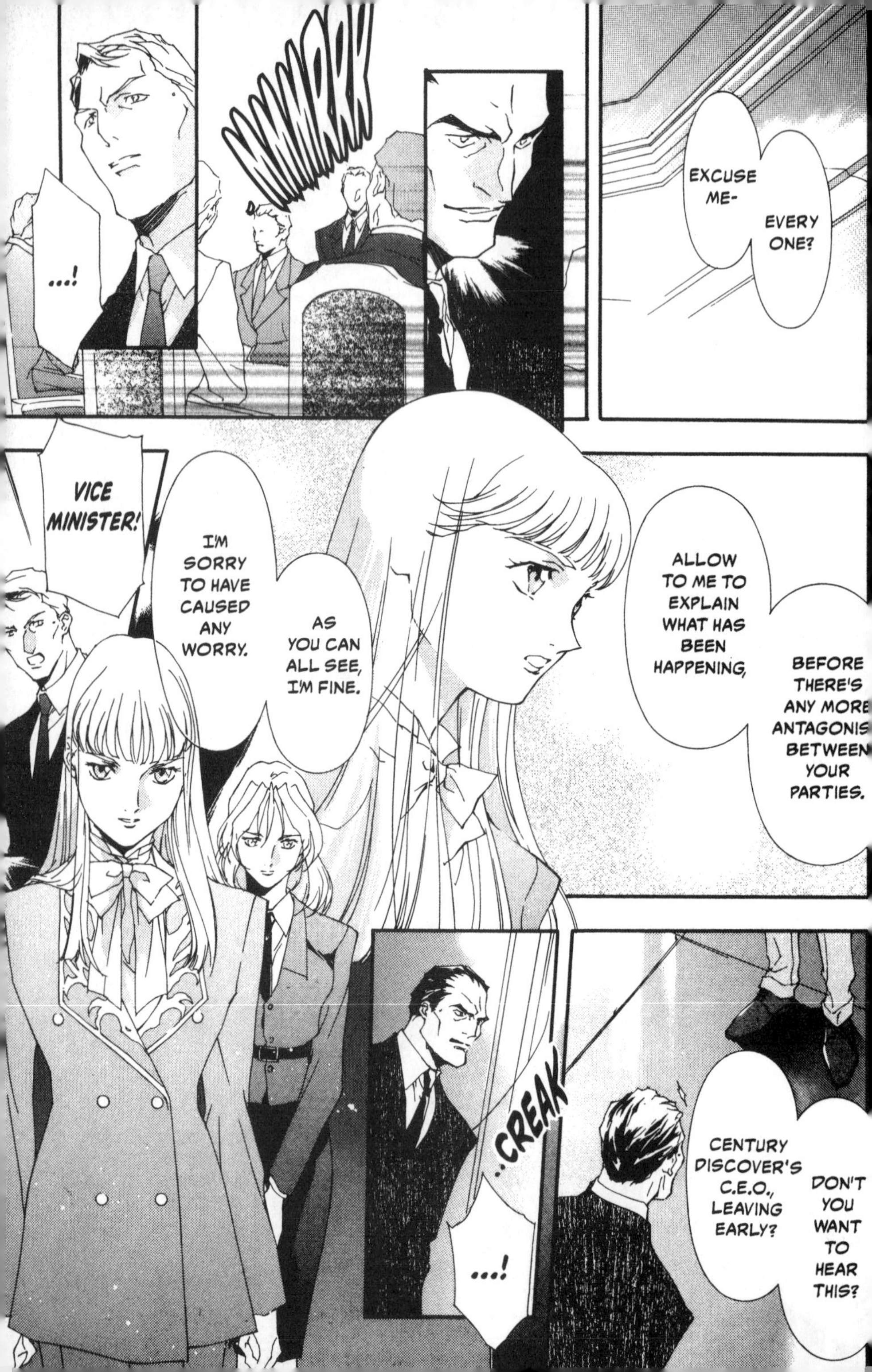
...!
EXCUSE ME- EVERY ONE?
VICE MINISTER!
I'M SORRY TO HAVE CAUSED ANY WORRY.
AS YOU CAN ALL SEE, I'M FINE.
ALLOW TO ME TO EXPLAIN WHAT HAS BEEN HAPPENING,
BEFORE THERE'S ANY MORE ANTAGONIS BETWEEN YOUR PARTIES.
CREAK
...!
CENTURY DISCOVER'S C.E.O., LEAVING EARLY?
DON'T YOU WANT TO HEAR THIS?

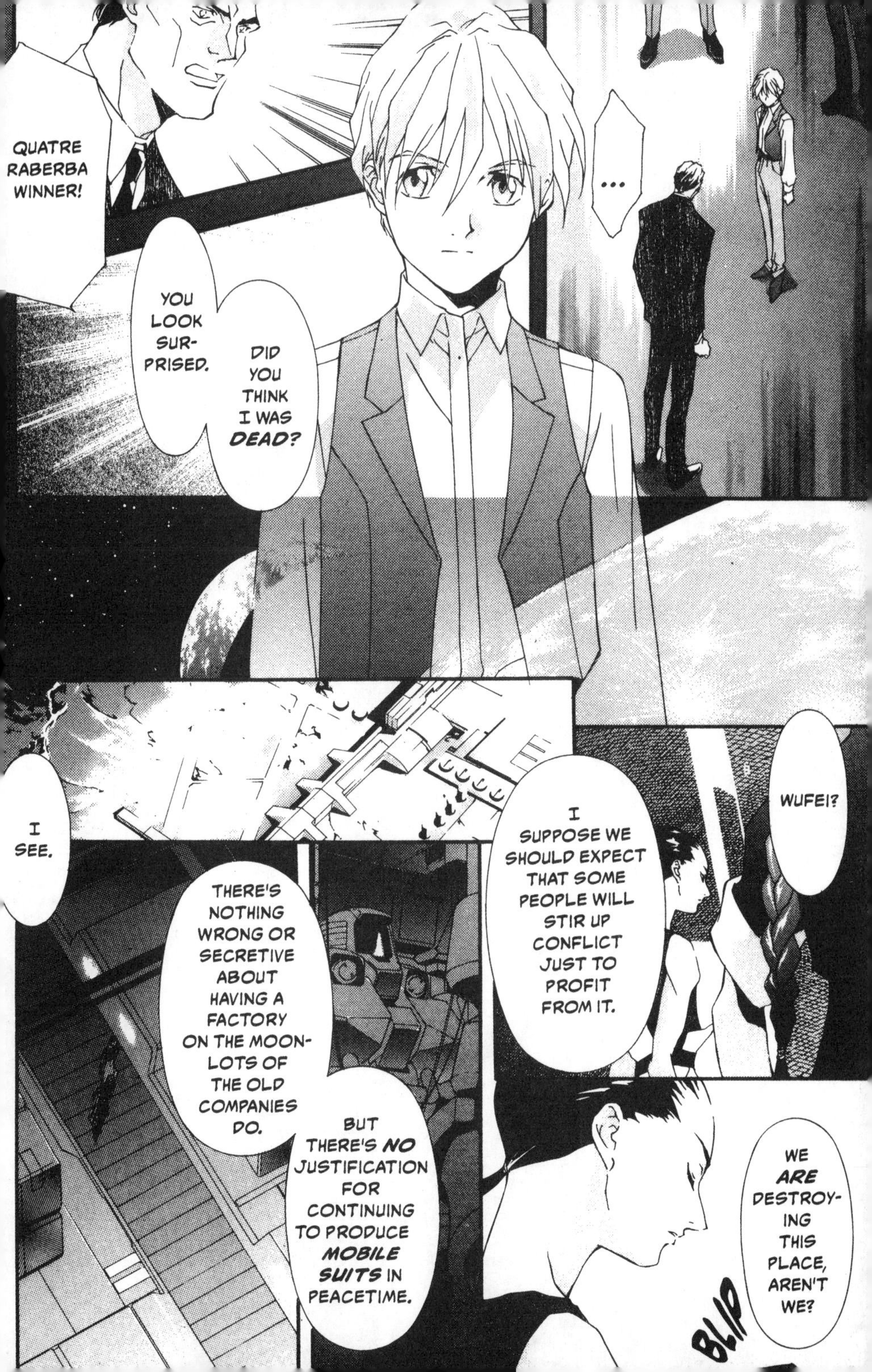
QUATRE RABERBA WINNER!
YOU LOOK SUR-PRISED.
DID YOU THINK I WAS ***DEAD?***
...
I SEE.
I SUPPOSE WE SHOULD EXPECT THAT SOME PEOPLE WILL STIR UP CONFLICT JUST TO PROFIT FROM IT.
WUFEI?
THERE'S NOTHING WRONG OR SECRETIVE ABOUT HAVING A FACTORY ON THE MOON-LOTS OF THE OLD COMPANIES DO.
BUT THERE'S ***NO*** JUSTIFICATION FOR CONTINUING TO PRODUCE ***MOBILE SUITS*** IN PEACETIME.
WE ***ARE*** DESTROY-ING THIS PLACE, AREN'T WE?
BLIP

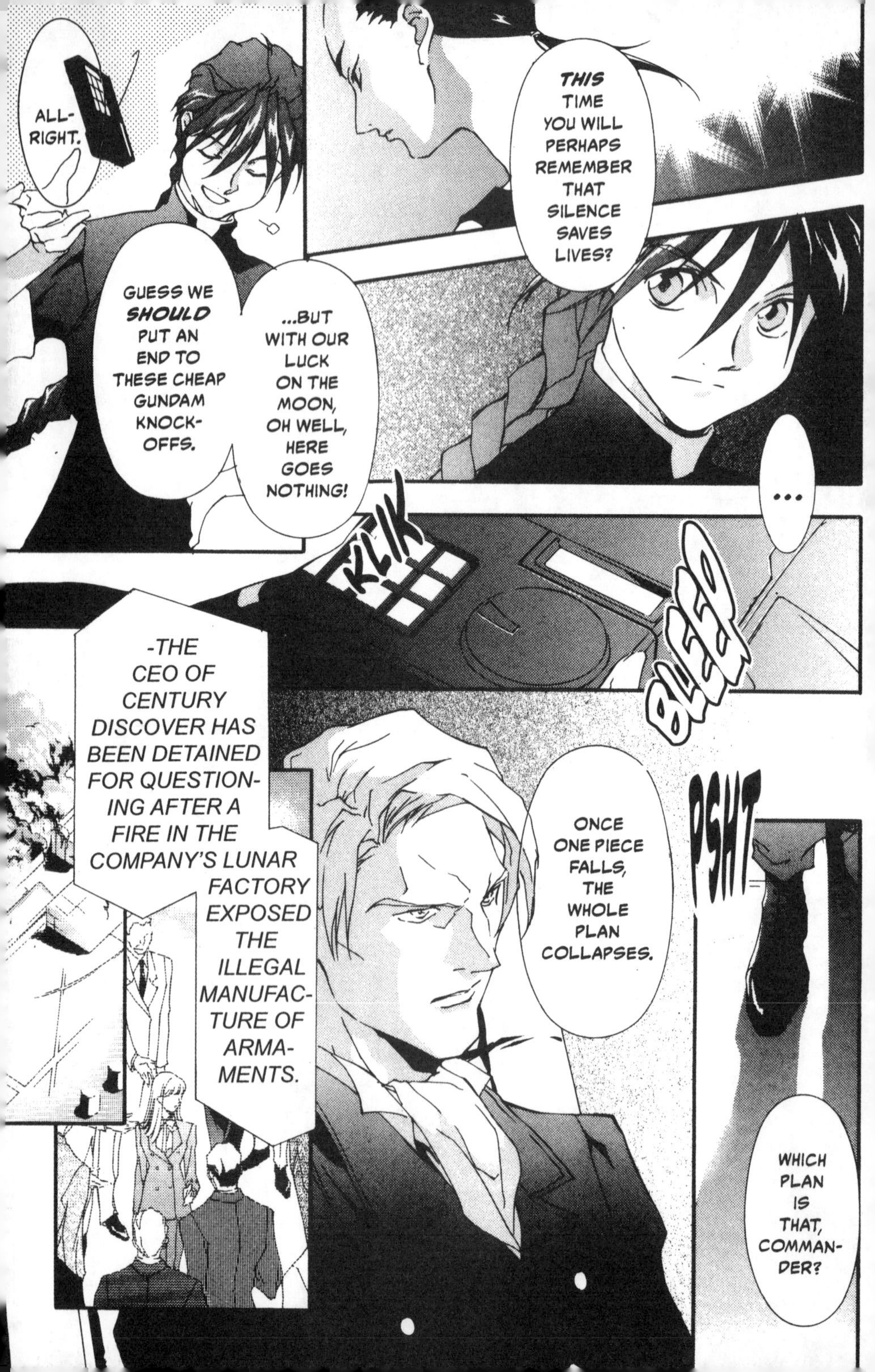
THIS TIME YOU WILL PERHAPS REMEMBER THAT SILENCE SAVES LIVES?
ALL-RIGHT.
GUESS WE SHOULD PUT AN END TO THESE CHEAP GUNDAM KNOCK-OFFS.
...BUT WITH OUR LUCK ON THE MOON, OH WELL, HERE GOES NOTHING!
...
KLIK
BLEEP
PSHT
ONCE ONE PIECE FALLS, THE WHOLE PLAN COLLAPSES.
WHICH PLAN IS THAT, COMMANDER?
-THE CEO OF CENTURY DISCOVER HAS BEEN DETAINED FOR QUESTIONING AFTER A FIRE IN THE COMPANY'S LUNAR FACTORY EXPOSED THE ILLEGAL MANUFACTURE OF ARMAMENTS.

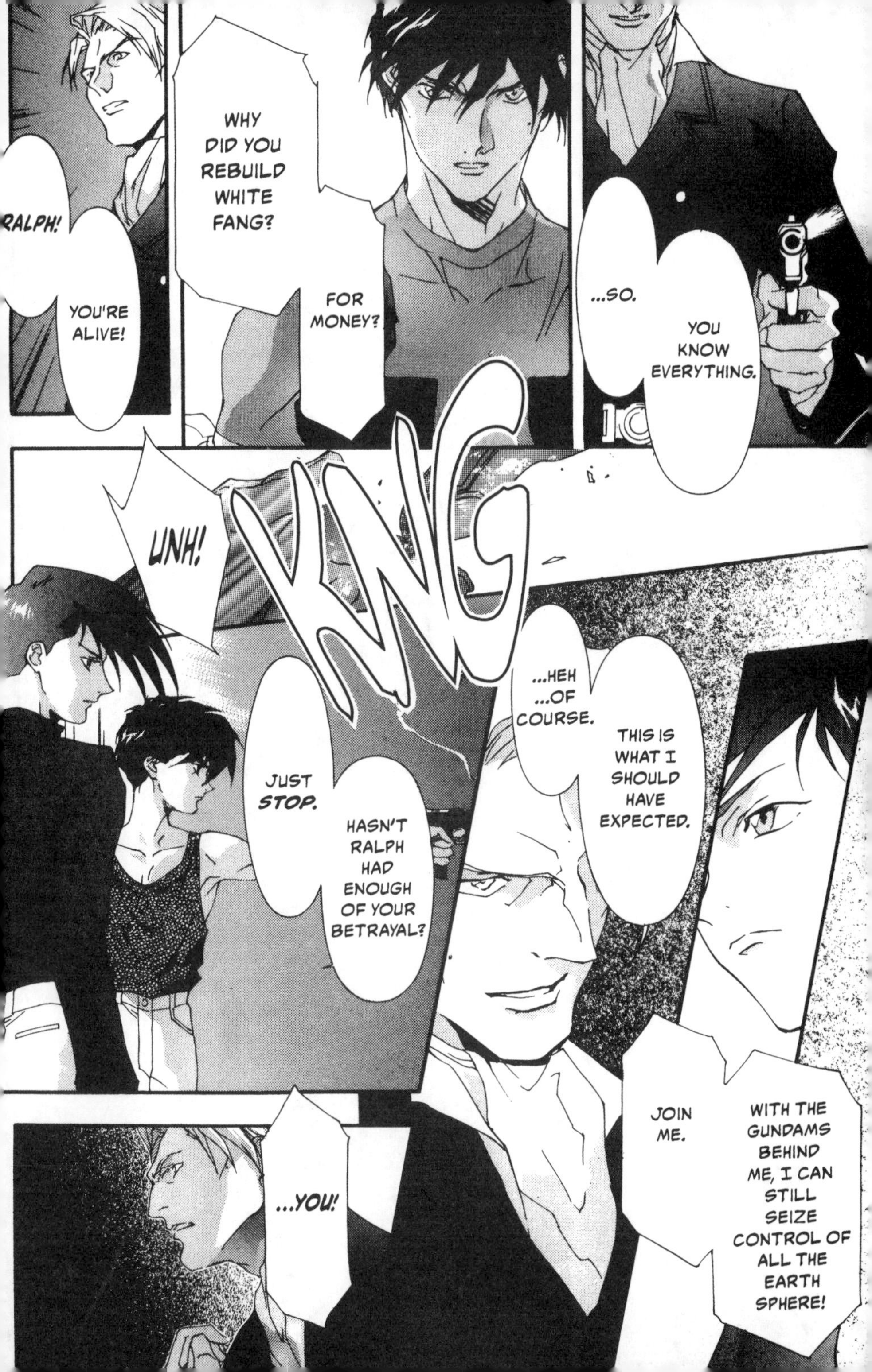
RALPH!
YOU'RE ALIVE!
WHY DID YOU REBUILD WHITE FANG?
FOR MONEY?
...SO.
YOU KNOW EVERYTHING.
UNH!
KNG
JUST STOP.
HASN'T RALPH HAD ENOUGH OF YOUR BETRAYAL?
...HEH ...OF COURSE.
THIS IS WHAT I SHOULD HAVE EXPECTED.
...YOU!
JOIN ME.
WITH THE GUNDAMS BEHIND ME, I CAN STILL SEIZE CONTROL OF ALL THE EARTH SPHERE!

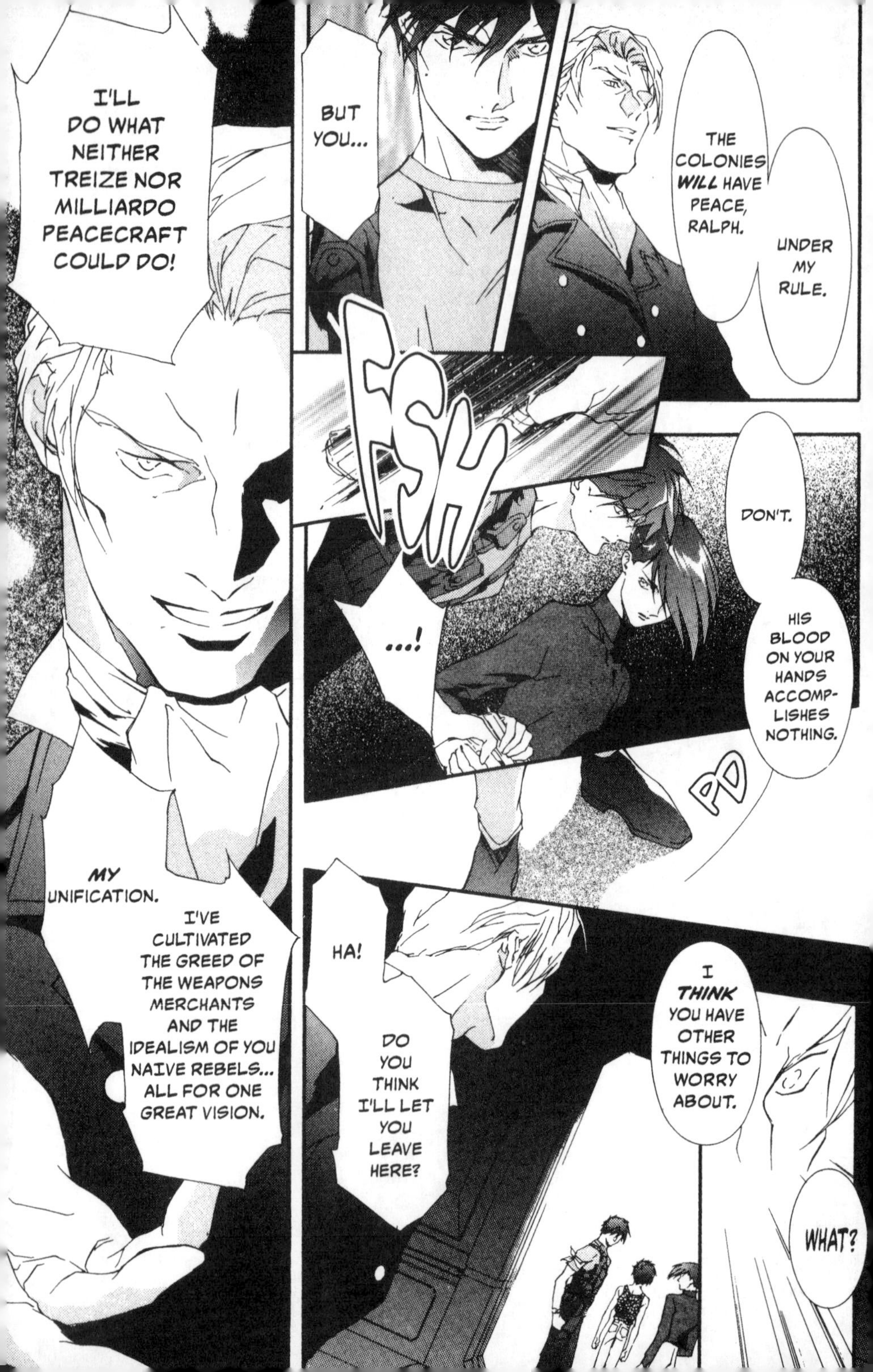

I'LL DO WHAT NEITHER TREIZE NOR MILLIARDO PEACECRAFT COULD DO!
MY UNIFICATION.
I'VE CULTIVATED THE GREED OF THE WEAPONS MERCHANTS AND THE IDEALISM OF YOU NAIVE REBELS... ALL FOR ONE GREAT VISION.
BUT YOU...
THE COLONIES *WILL* HAVE PEACE, RALPH.
UNDER MY RULE.
FSH
...!
DON'T.
HIS BLOOD ON YOUR HANDS ACCOMPLISHES NOTHING.
PD
HA!
DO YOU THINK I'LL LET YOU LEAVE HERE?
I *THINK* YOU HAVE OTHER THINGS TO WORRY ABOUT.
WHAT?

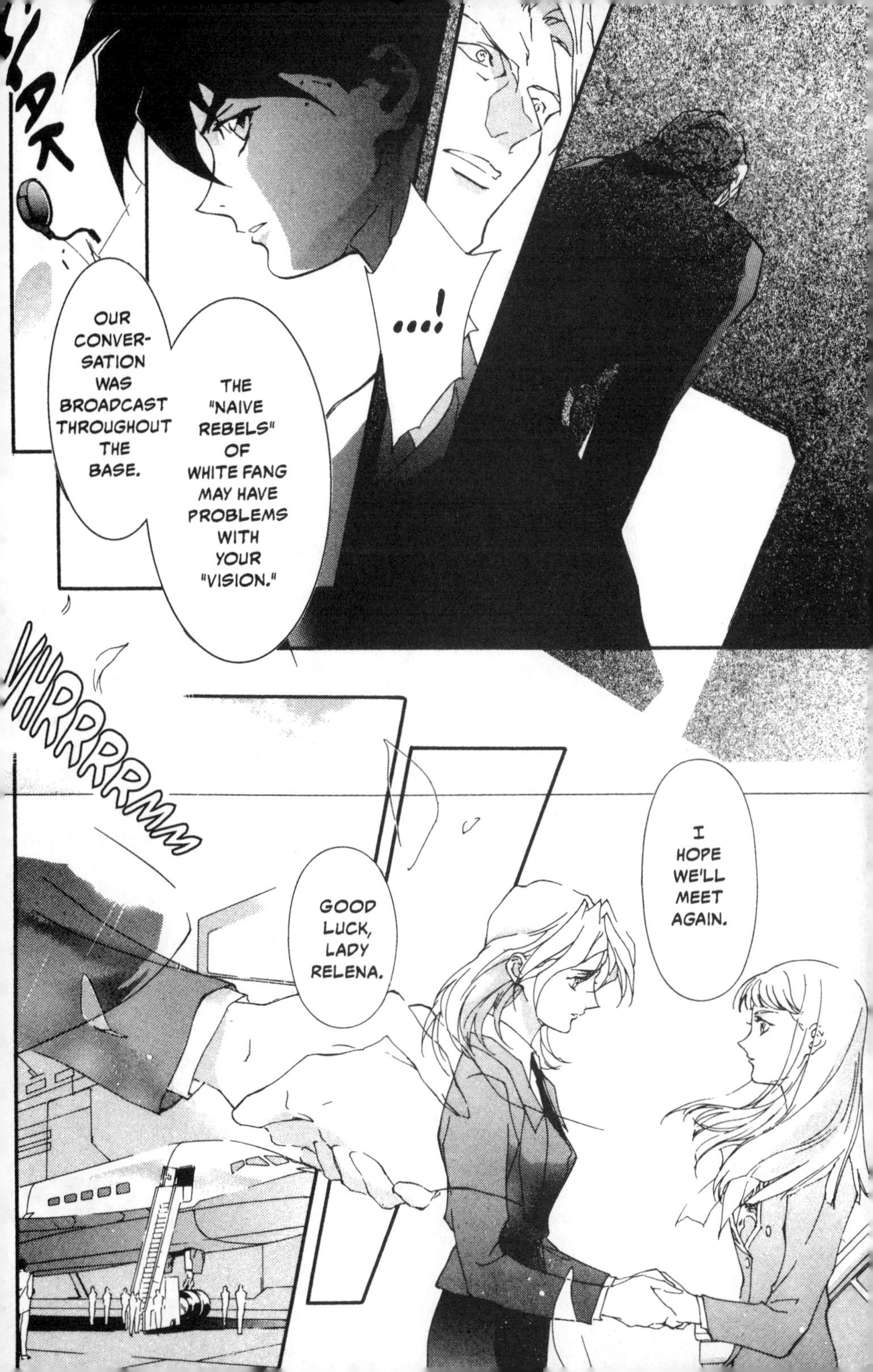
OUR CONVERSATION WAS BROADCAST THROUGHOUT THE BASE.
THE "NAIVE REBELS" OF WHITE FANG MAY HAVE PROBLEMS WITH YOUR "VISION."
...!
GOOD LUCK, LADY RELENA.
I HOPE WE'LL MEET AGAIN.

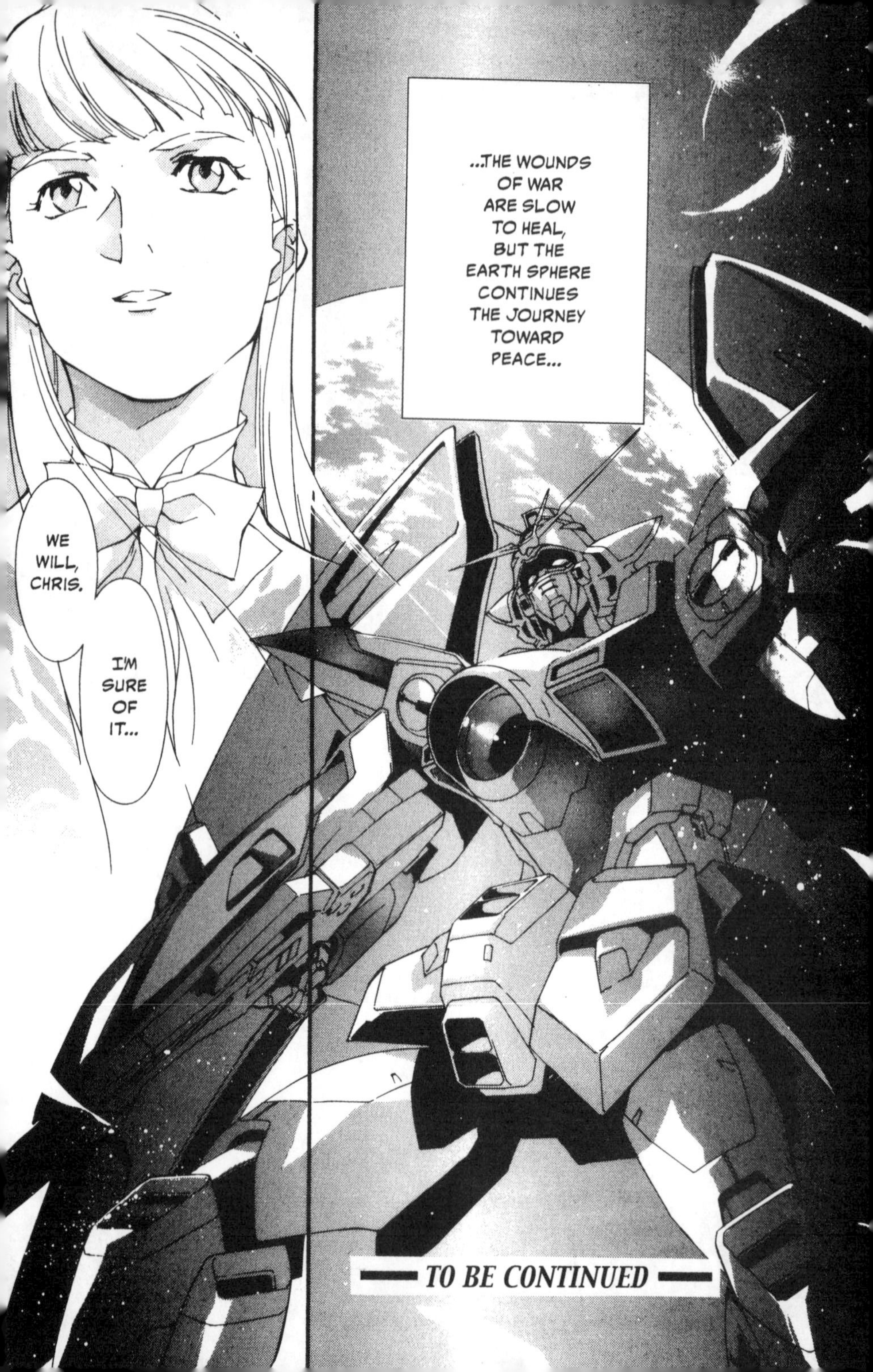
WE WILL, CHRIS.
I'M SURE OF IT...
...THE WOUNDS OF WAR ARE SLOW TO HEAL, BUT THE EARTH SPHERE CONTINUES THE JOURNEY TOWARD PEACE...
TO BE CONTINUED

MOBILE SUIT GUNDAM WING REMIX IV........

ANOTHER CROSS-MEDIUM LOOK AT OUR FAVORITE CHARACTERS!

1

CHANG WUFEI: THE TRUE PATH OF A WARRIOR

Wufei is particularly cryptic in "Blind Target," but why? In Gundam Wing, there's been a big debate about whether anyone who has not experienced the terrors of war first-hand can choose true pacifism. And here's Wufei trying to live quietly in a world where peace has been granted from outside, not born of a change of heart. Trained by Master O from childhood to be both a scholar and a fighter, Wufei had perfected the ways of a great warrior by the time he was 10. He probably struggles to understand his own existence in a world without war. Wufei may be thinking of himself only as a fighter now, but someday he may remember that half of being a warrior is about one's intellect.

That's why, one day, his path will lead him to work as an arbiter of disputes rather than a participant in them. He's a little near-sighted, too, so he can wear glasses if he ever wants to really emphasize his intellectual side.

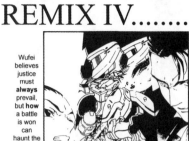

Wufei believes justice must **always** prevail, but **how** a battle is won can haunt the peace that comes after... ▶

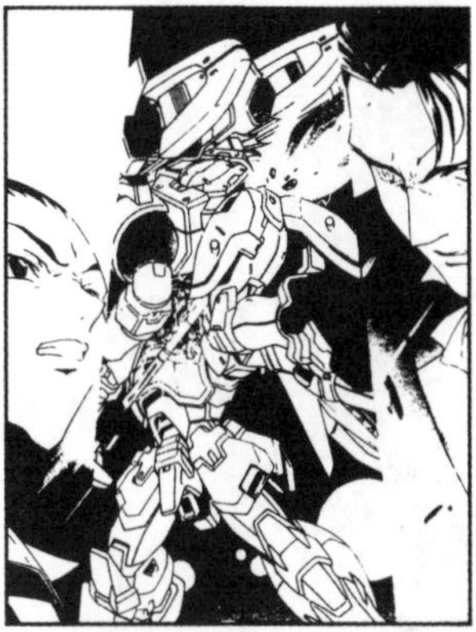

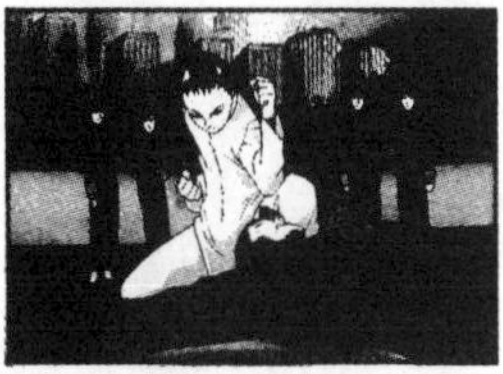

Wufei identifies with the ideal of justice so completely he believes he **too** must always prevail. You don't want to be there when he loses ▲

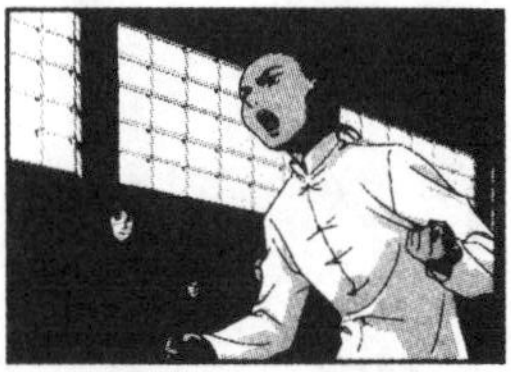

Living for the fight sometimes means Wufei doesn't see what else is going on. He **could** get caught off guard ▲

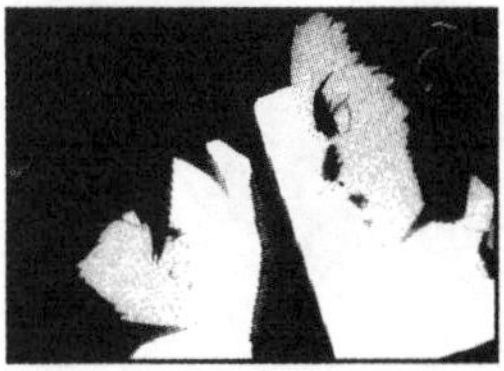

In Endless Waltz, Wufei was once so single-minded about his pursuit of justice that he was willing to fight even Heero. ▲

2

DEKIM BARTON: AVENGING A MURDERED HEERO?

The leader of Colony X-18999 might seem new on the scene, but he's been around for some time. Originally, Dekim was one of the two closest advisors to the first Heero Yuy, hero of the colonies. After Heero Yuy was asassinated, his other advisor, Quinze, swore revenge and made it his mission to fulfill the dreams of his fallen inspiration, leading the colonial revolutionary movement and the creation of White Fang. As the leader of the Barton family--and Marimaia's grandfather--Dekim's power is complicated by the Bartons' relatively low social status; they do not descend from nobility, nor have they got a very long history of public distinction. Well-born men much his junior, like Treize, sometimes treat Dekim with less respect than might seem appropriate; they do not view him as a superior.

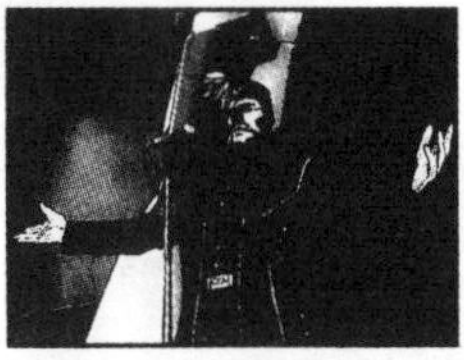

He does not stand alone before his followers always the memory of the fallen Heero is there with him. ▲

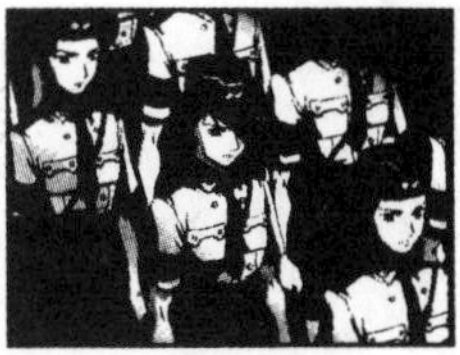

Marymaia's war orphan army. Trowa fit right in with these pretty boys! ▲

A shrine to a lost Heero in Dekim's quarters? ▶

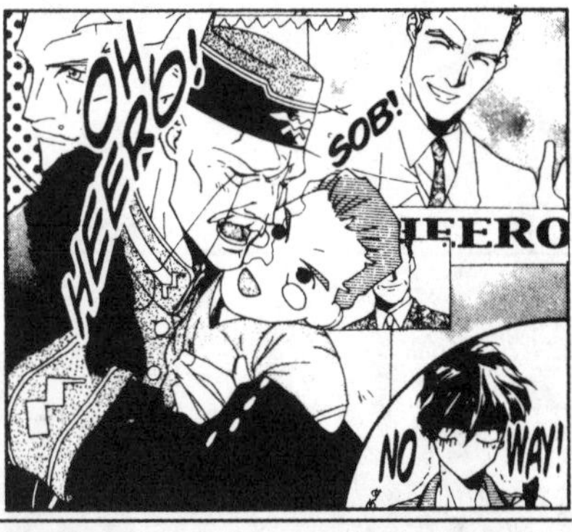
OH HEERO!
SOB!
HEERO
NO WAY!

The pictures were taken from the TV series and the video series "Endless Waltz."

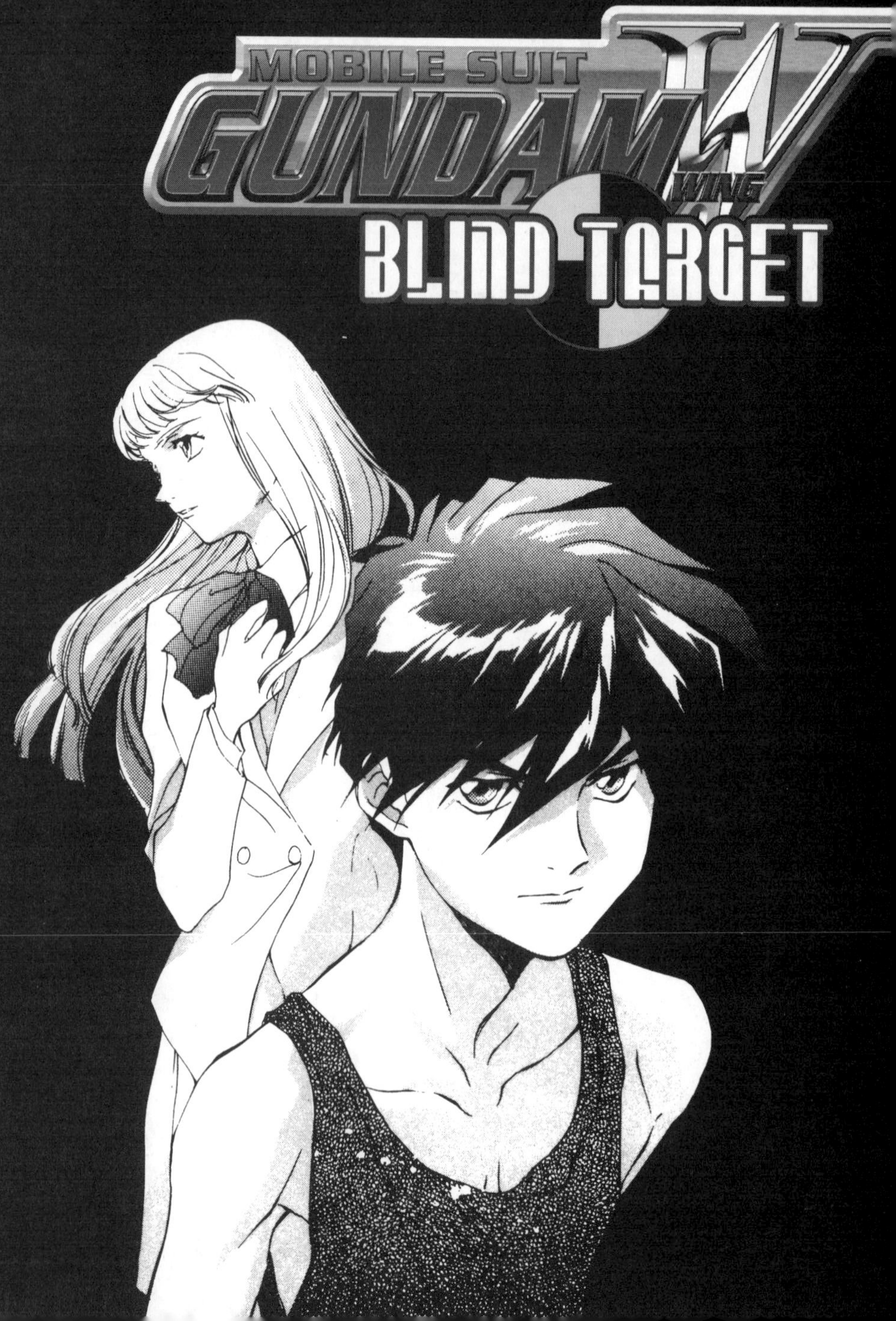
MOBILE SUIT GUNDAM WING
BLIND TARGET

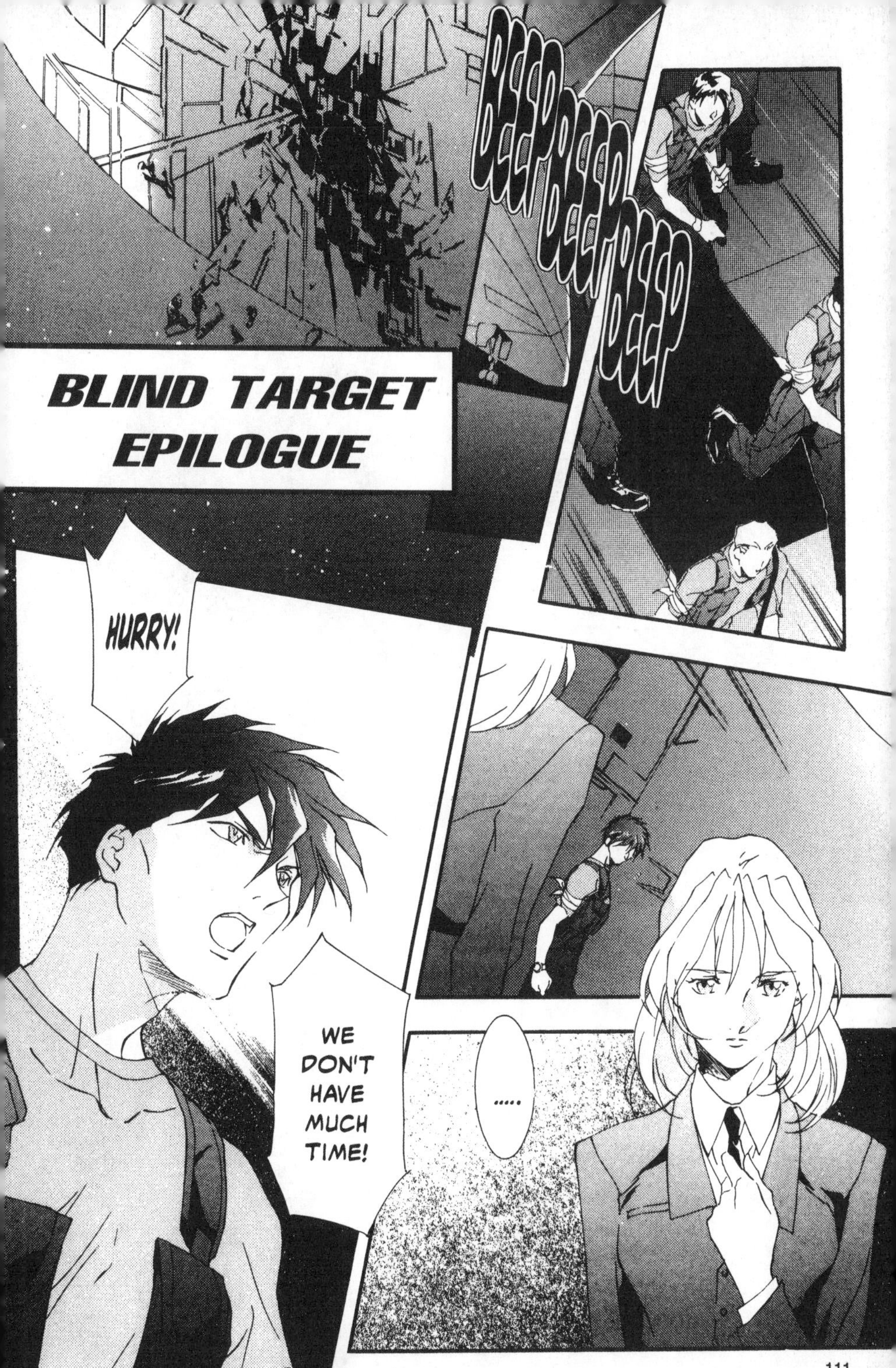

BEEP BEEP BEEP BEEP
BLIND TARGET EPILOGUE
HURRY!
WE DON'T HAVE MUCH TIME!
.....

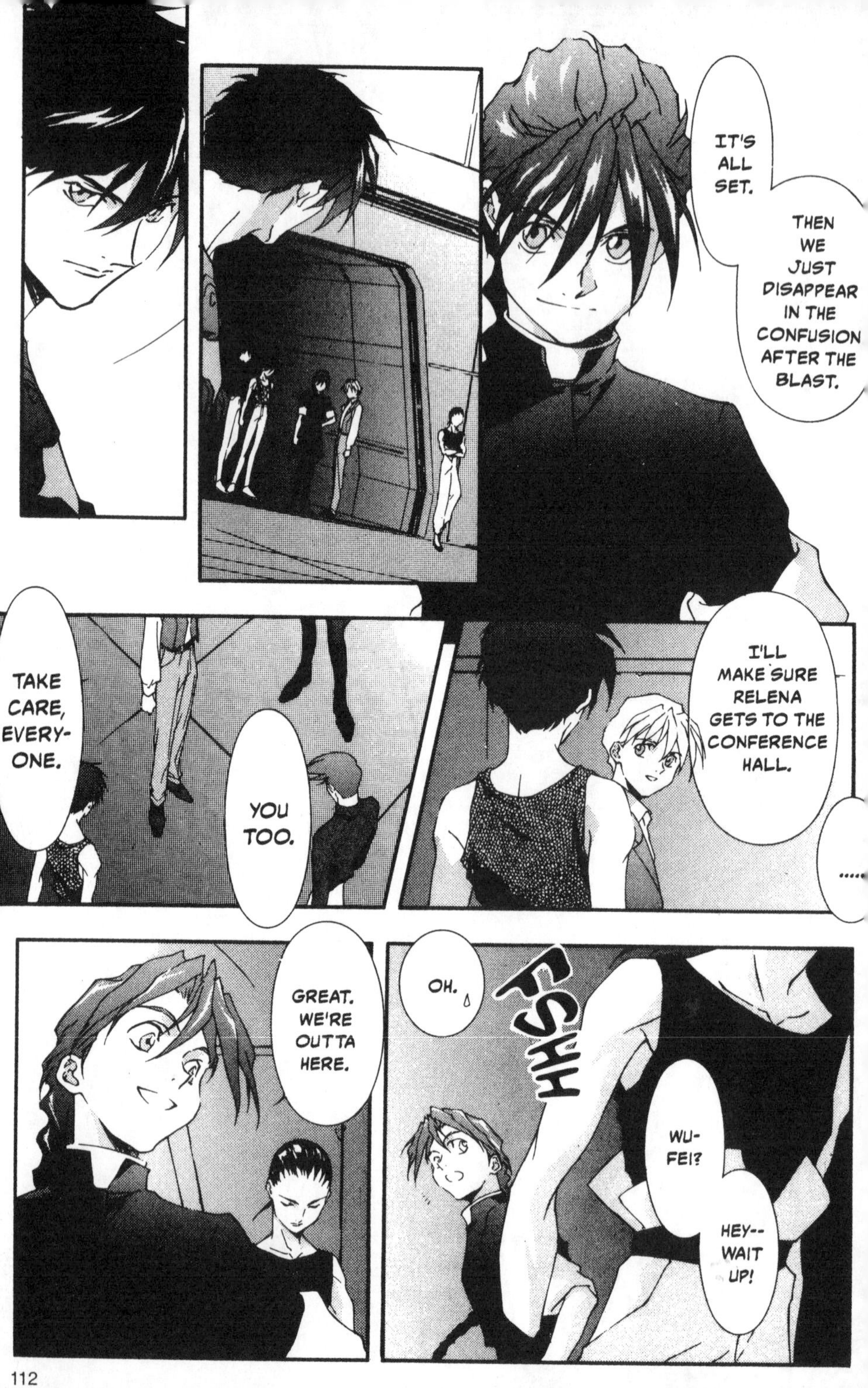
IT'S ALL SET.
THEN WE JUST DISAPPEAR IN THE CONFUSION AFTER THE BLAST.
TAKE CARE, EVERY-ONE.
YOU TOO.
I'LL MAKE SURE RELENA GETS TO THE CONFERENCE HALL.
.....
GREAT. WE'RE OUTTA HERE.
OH.
FSHH
WU-FEI?
HEY-- WAIT UP!

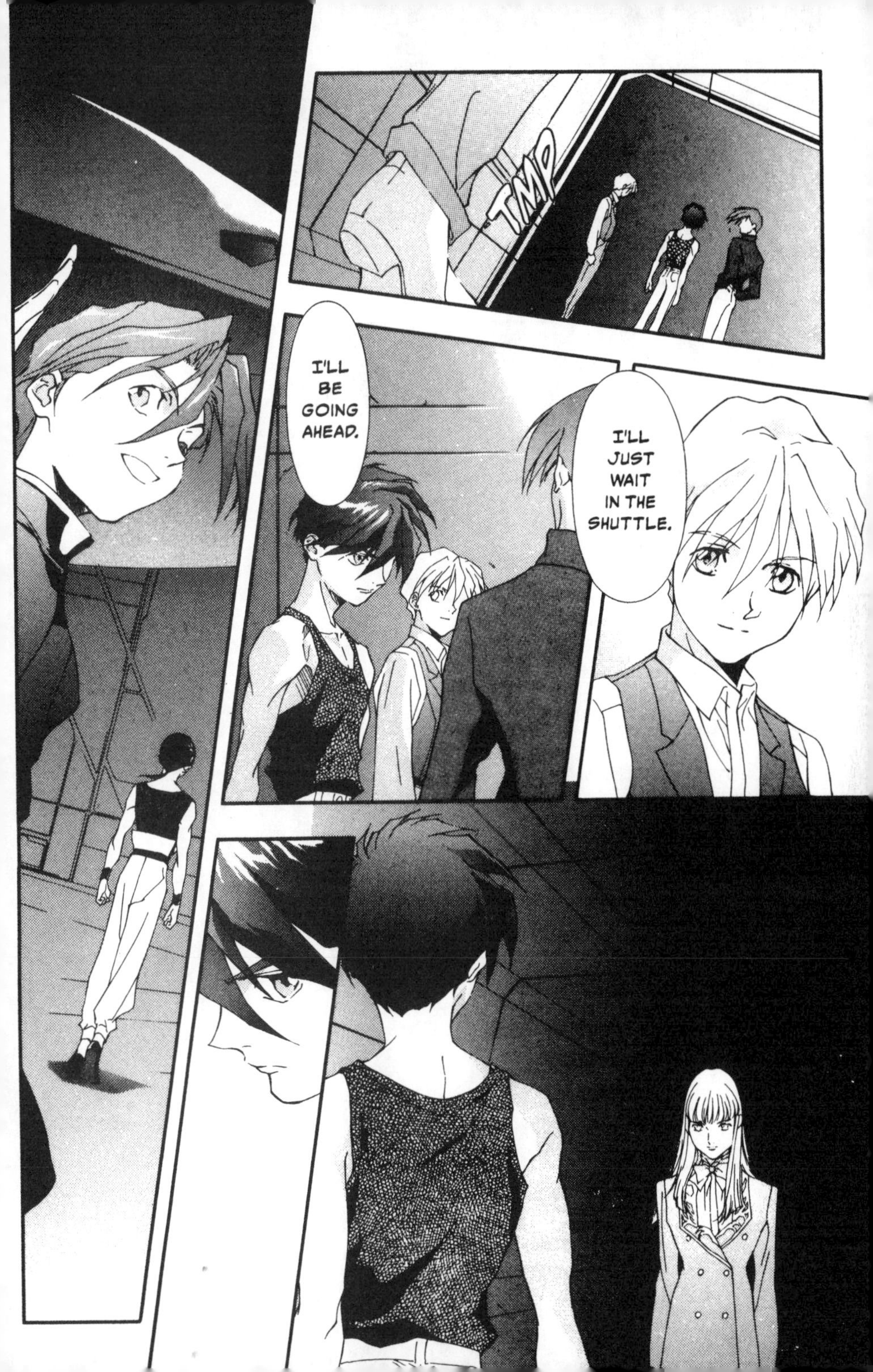
TMP
I'LL BE GOING AHEAD.
I'LL JUST WAIT IN THE SHUTTLE.

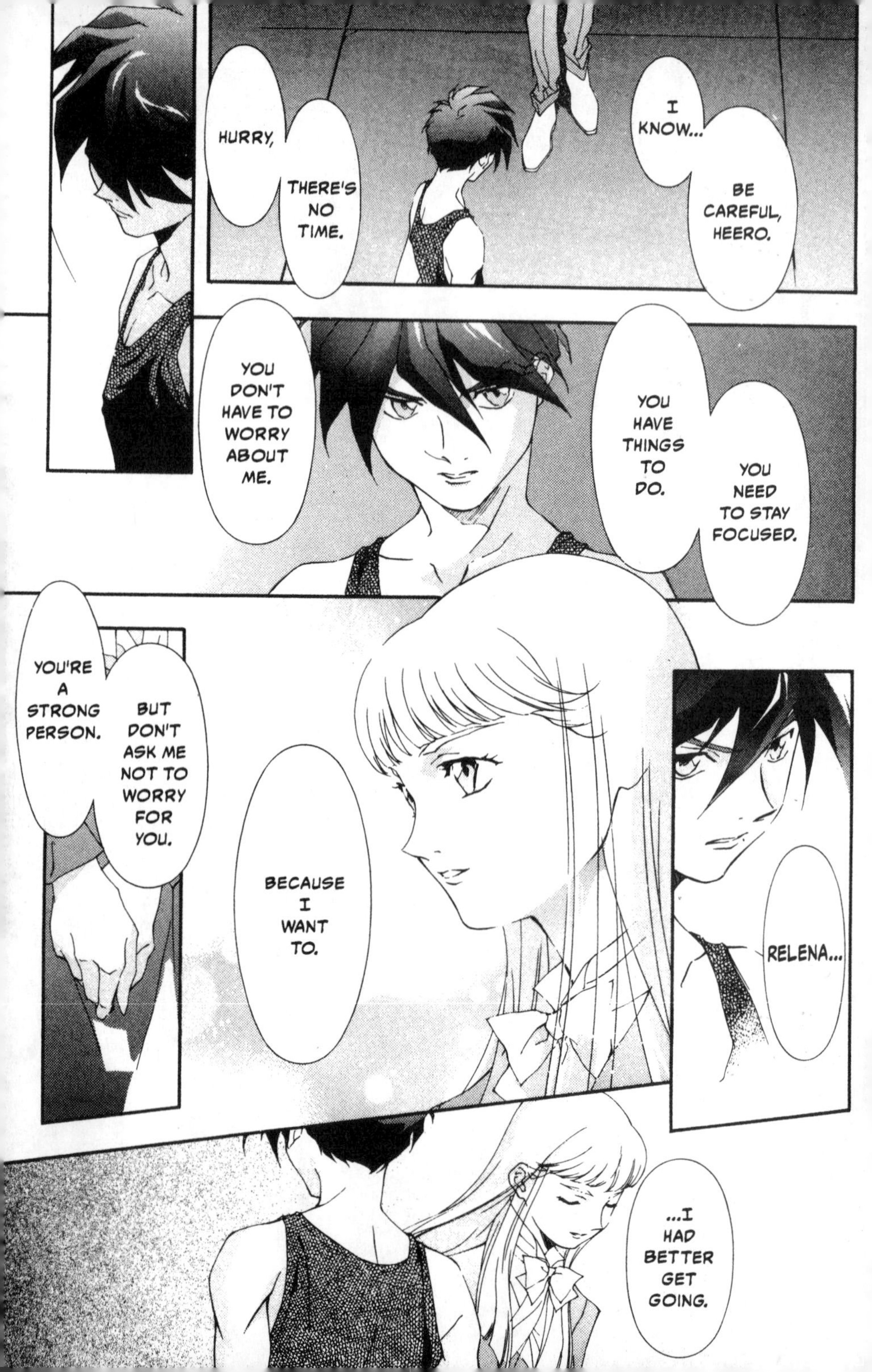
HURRY, THERE'S NO TIME.
I KNOW...
BE CAREFUL, HEERO.
YOU DON'T HAVE TO WORRY ABOUT ME.
YOU HAVE THINGS TO DO.
YOU NEED TO STAY FOCUSED.
YOU'RE A STRONG PERSON.
BUT DON'T ASK ME NOT TO WORRY FOR YOU.
BECAUSE I WANT TO.
RELENA...
...I HAD BETTER GET GOING.

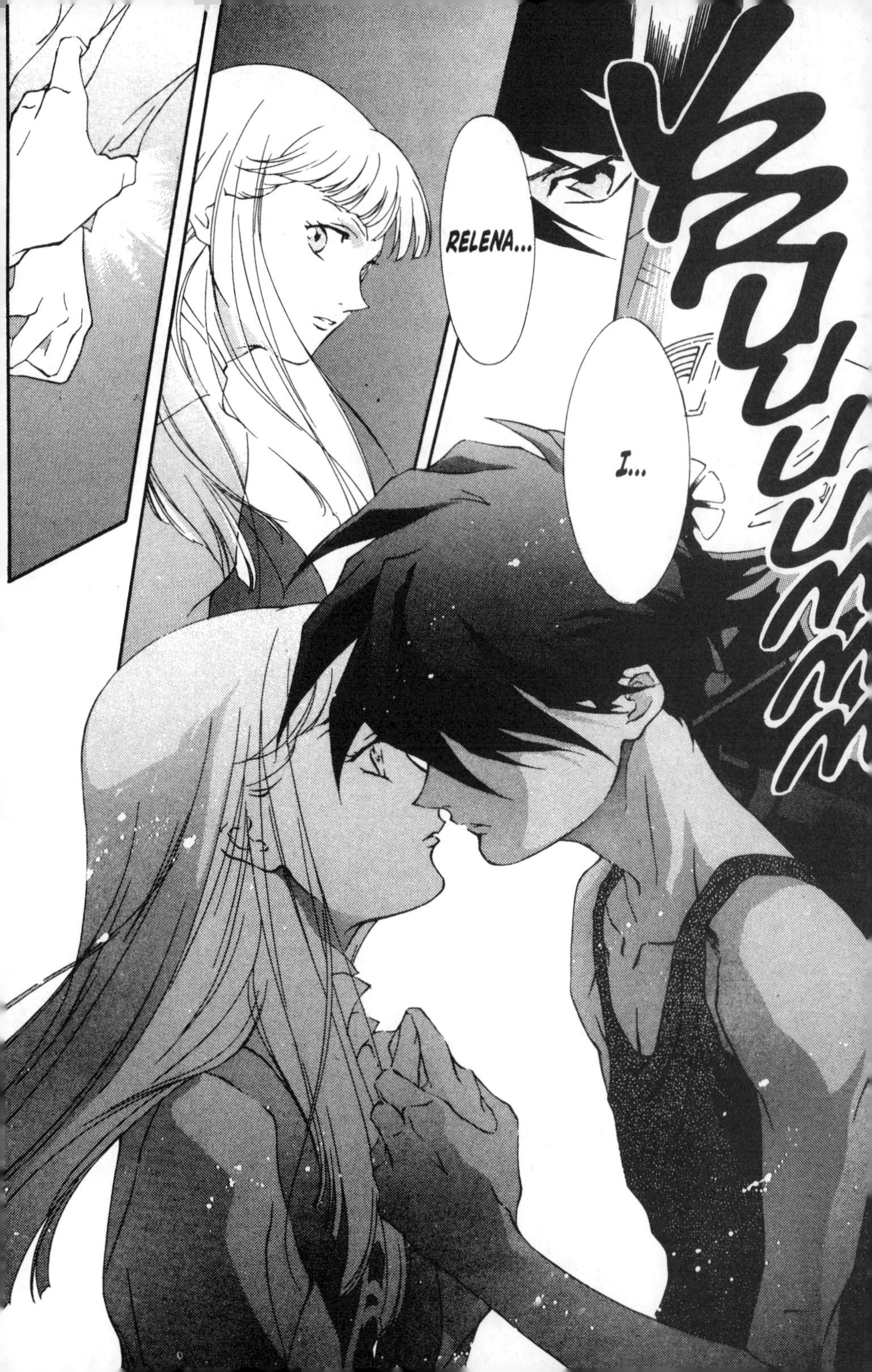
RELENA...
I...

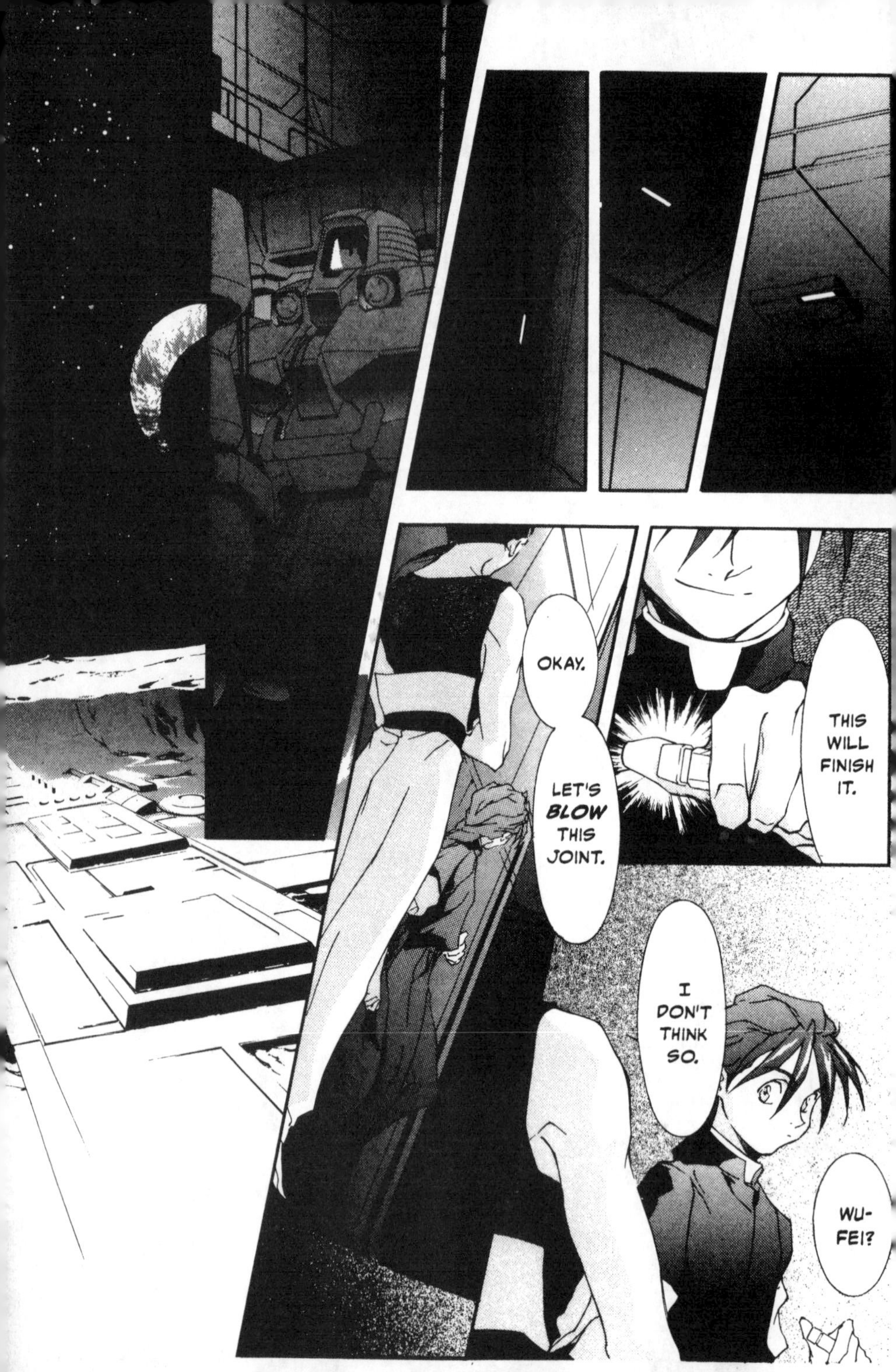
OKAY.
LET'S BLOW THIS JOINT.
THIS WILL FINISH IT.
I DON'T THINK SO.
WU-FEI?

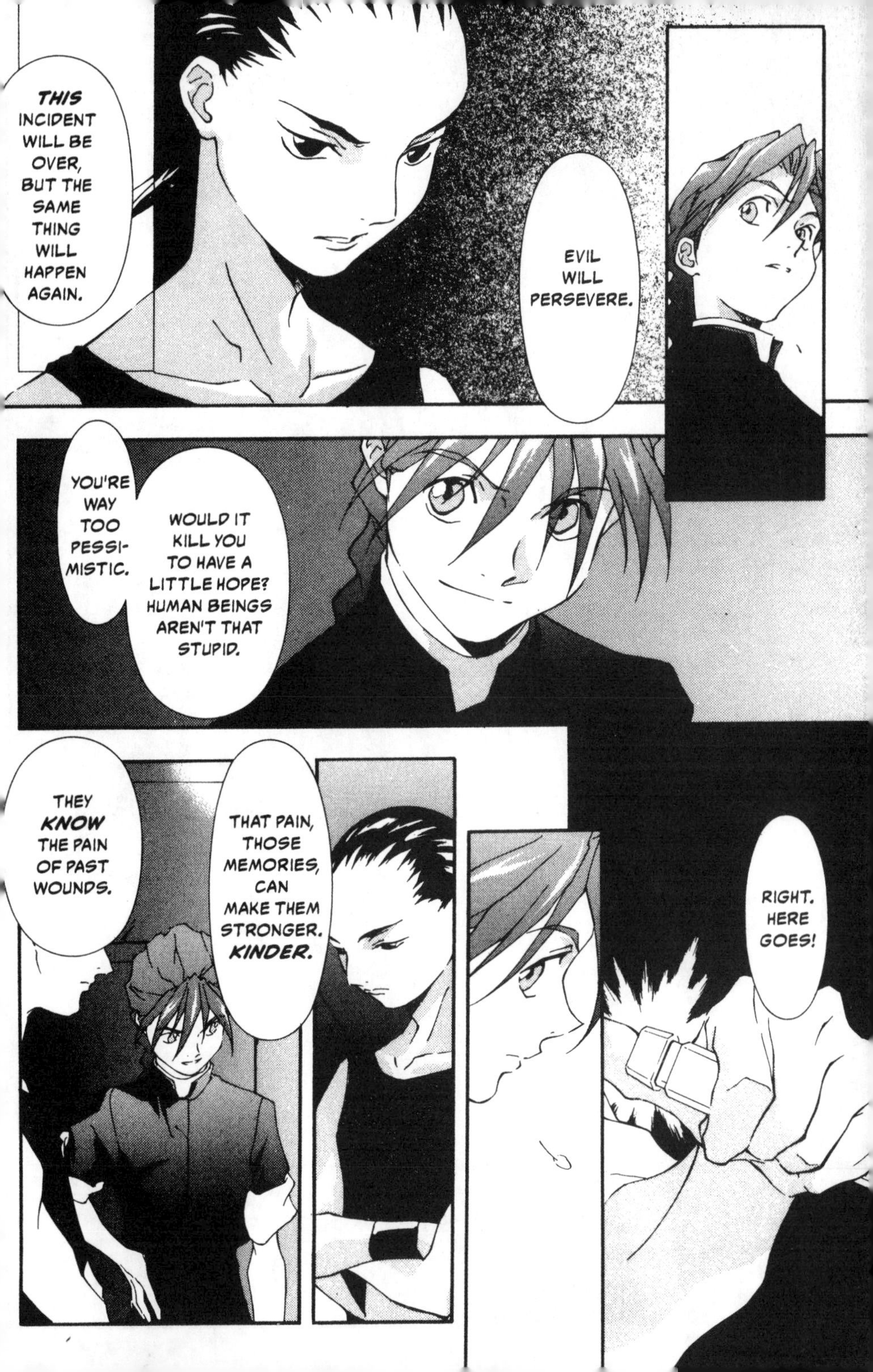
THIS INCIDENT WILL BE OVER, BUT THE SAME THING WILL HAPPEN AGAIN.
EVIL WILL PERSEVERE.
YOU'RE WAY TOO PESSI-MISTIC.
WOULD IT KILL YOU TO HAVE A LITTLE HOPE? HUMAN BEINGS AREN'T THAT STUPID.
THEY KNOW THE PAIN OF PAST WOUNDS.
THAT PAIN, THOSE MEMORIES, CAN MAKE THEM STRONGER. KINDER.
RIGHT. HERE GOES!

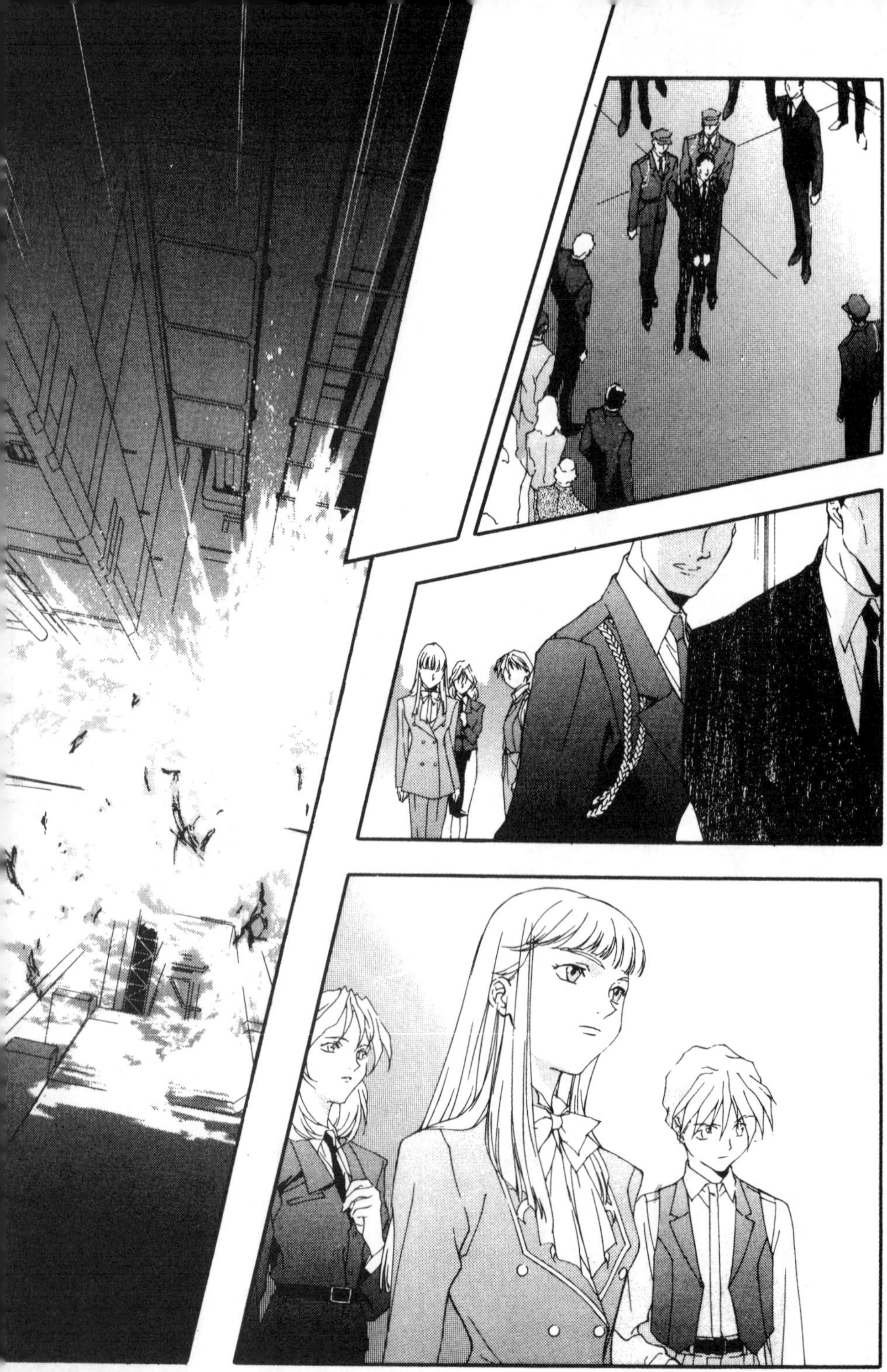

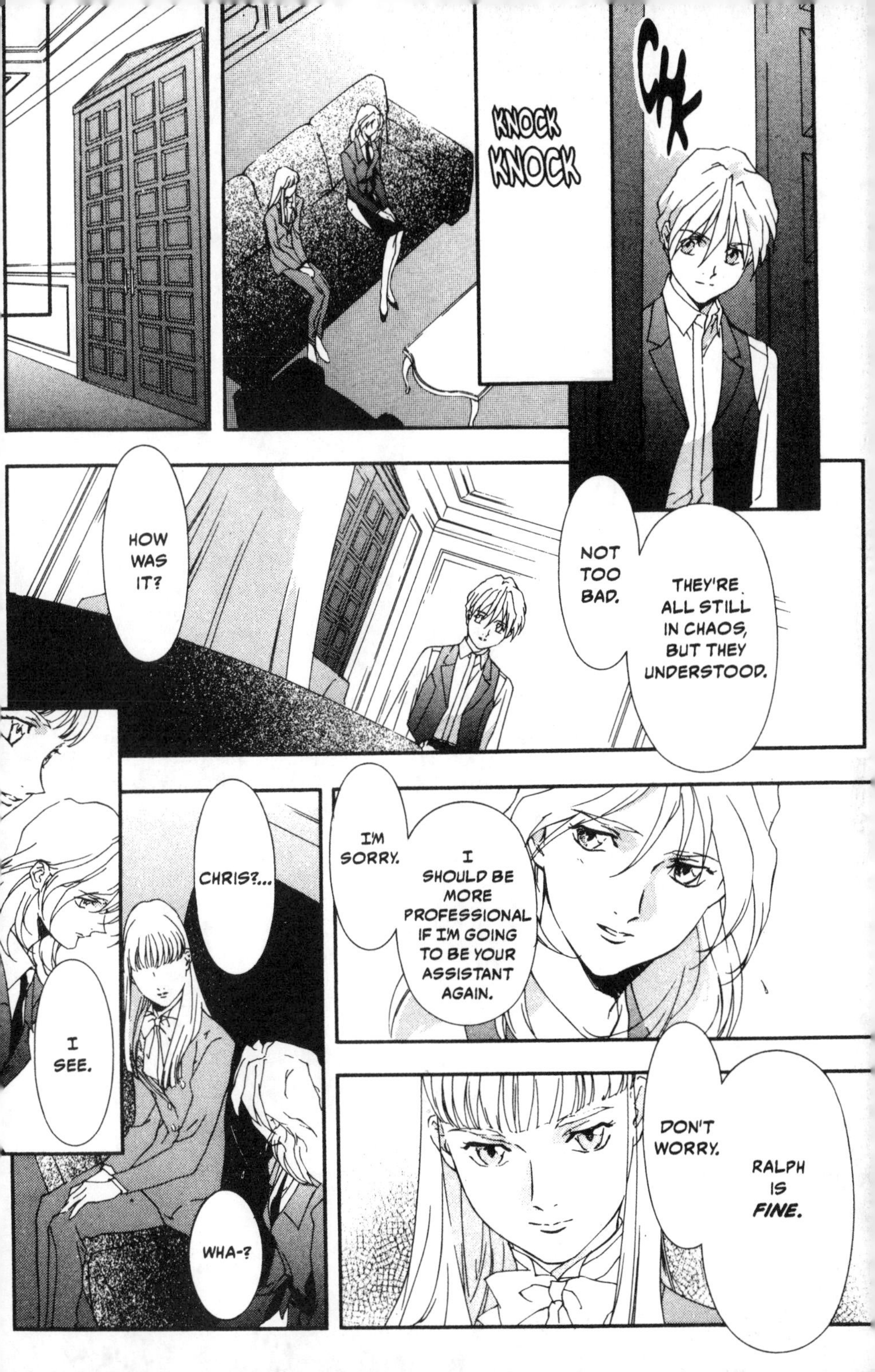
KNOCK KNOCK
CHK
HOW WAS IT?
NOT TOO BAD.
THEY'RE ALL STILL IN CHAOS, BUT THEY UNDERSTOOD.
I SEE.
CHRIS?...
WHA-?
I'M SORRY.
I SHOULD BE MORE PROFESSIONAL IF I'M GOING TO BE YOUR ASSISTANT AGAIN.
DON'T WORRY.
RALPH IS *FINE.*

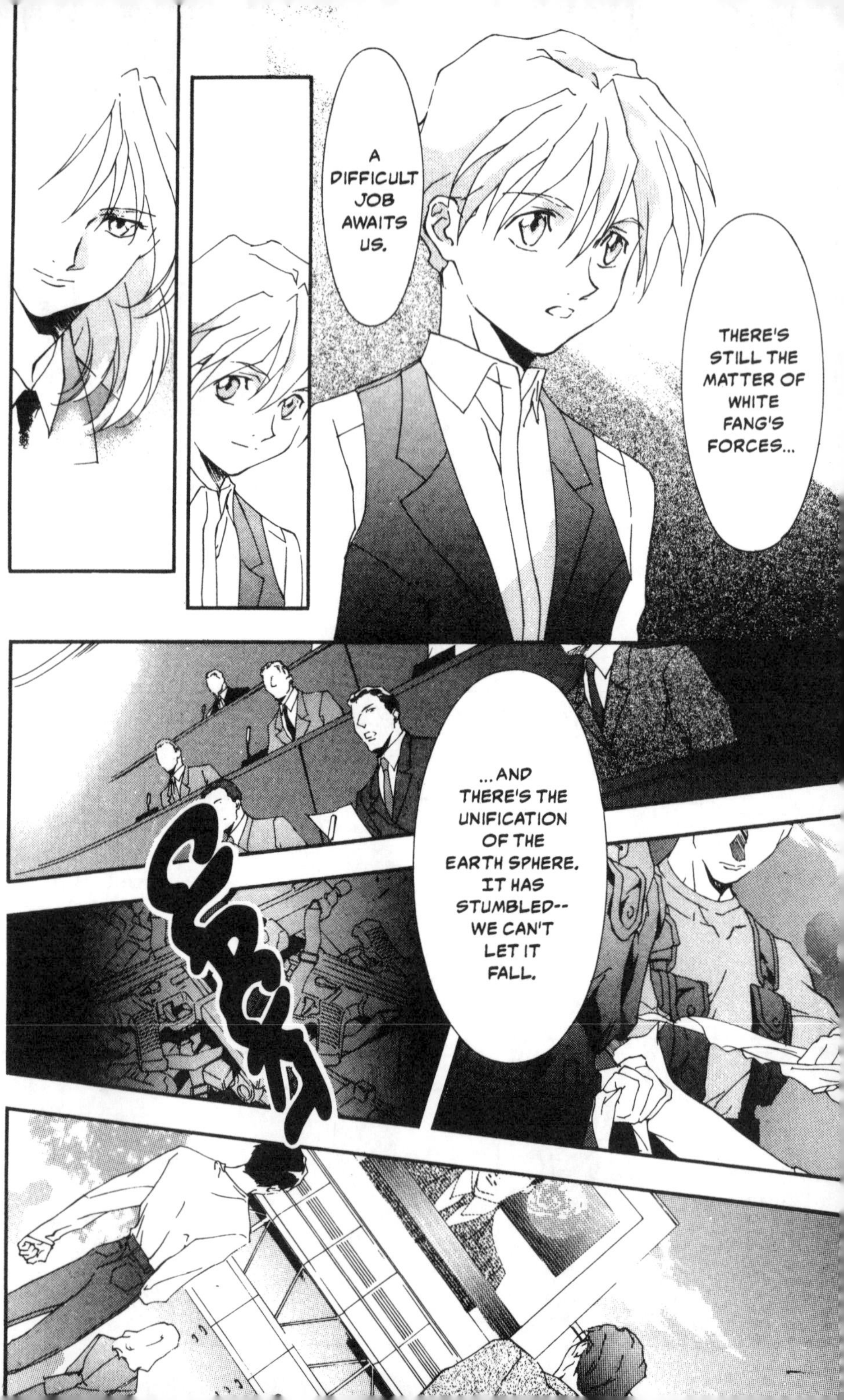
A DIFFICULT JOB AWAITS US.
THERE'S STILL THE MATTER OF WHITE FANG'S FORCES...
...AND THERE'S THE UNIFICATION OF THE EARTH SPHERE. IT HAS STUMBLED-- WE CAN'T LET IT FALL.

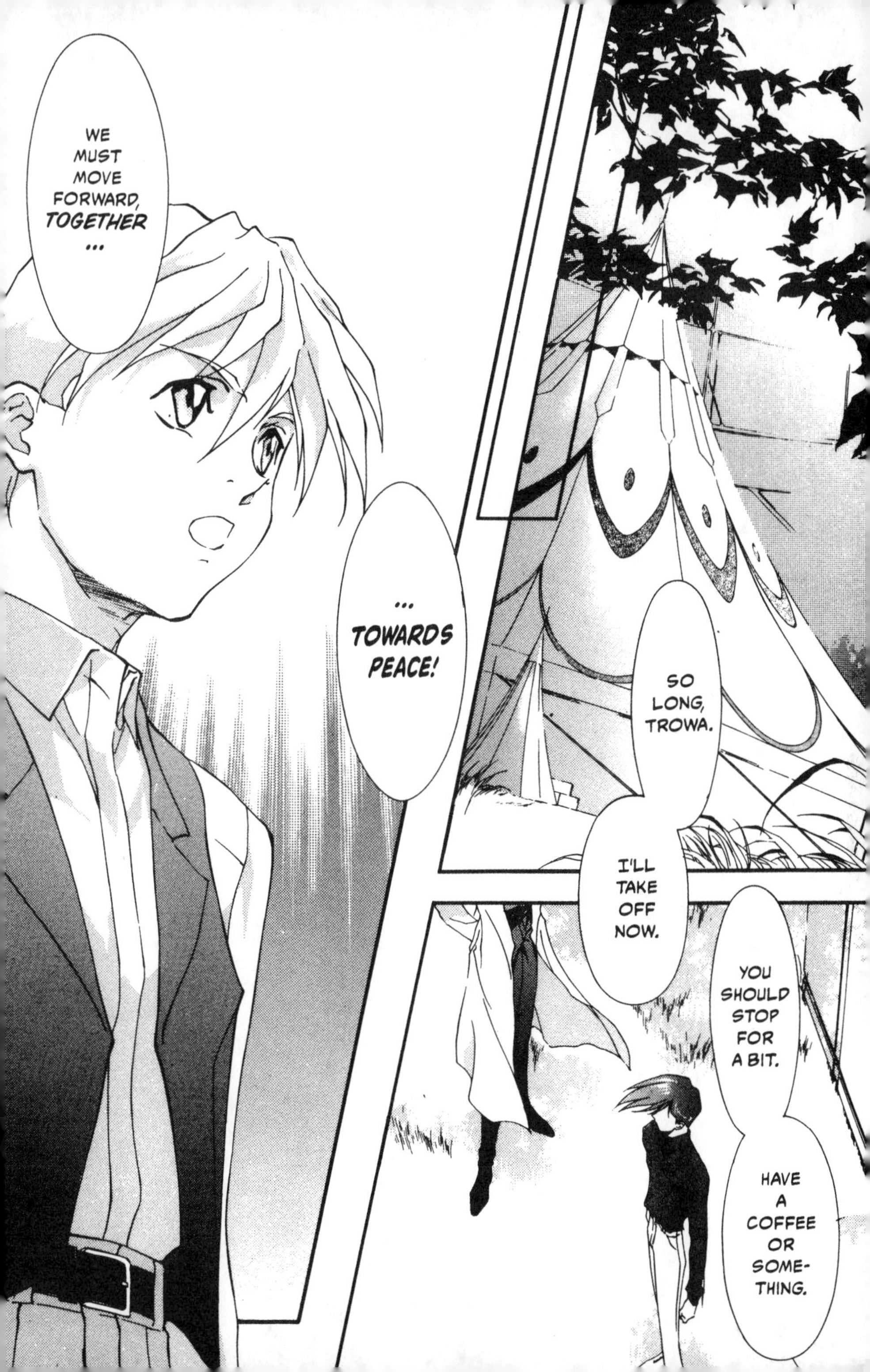
WE MUST MOVE FORWARD, TOGETHER...
... TOWARDS PEACE!
SO LONG, TROWA.
I'LL TAKE OFF NOW.
YOU SHOULD STOP FOR A BIT.
HAVE A COFFEE OR SOME-THING.

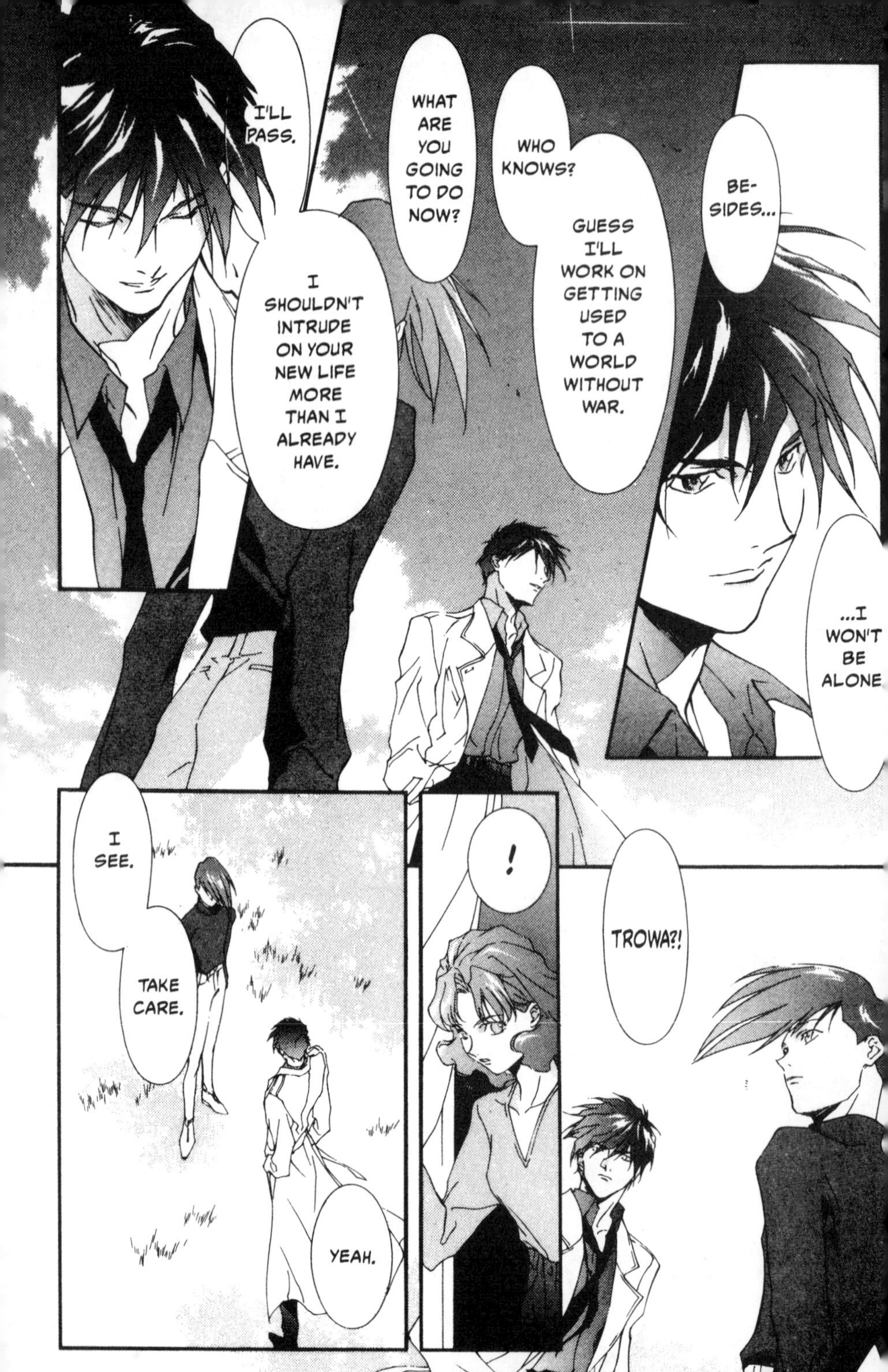
I'LL PASS.
I SHOULDN'T INTRUDE ON YOUR NEW LIFE MORE THAN I ALREADY HAVE.
WHAT ARE YOU GOING TO DO NOW?
WHO KNOWS?
GUESS I'LL WORK ON GETTING USED TO A WORLD WITHOUT WAR.
BE-SIDES...
...I WON'T BE ALONE
I SEE.
TAKE CARE.
YEAH.
!
TROWA?!

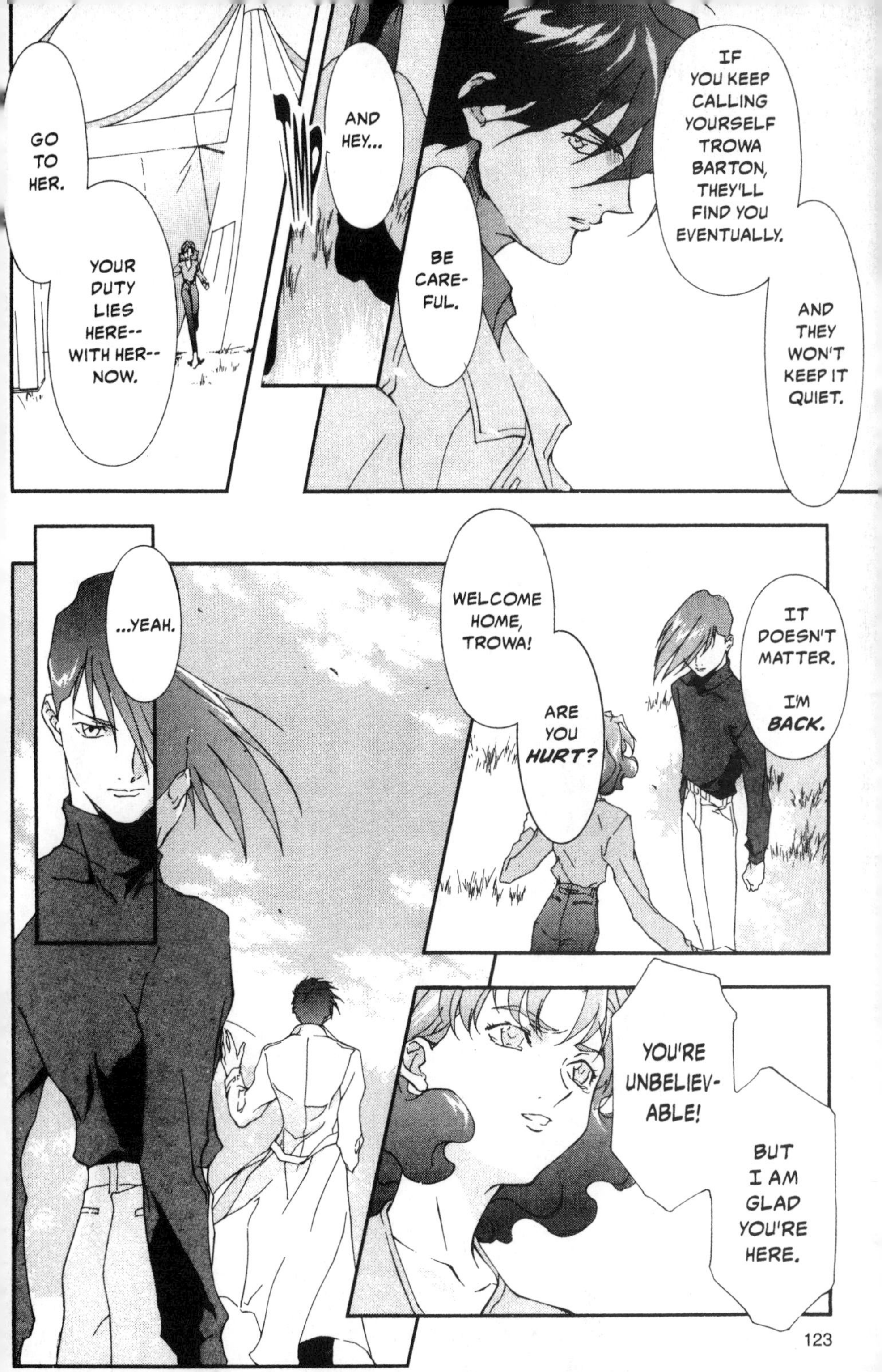
GO TO HER.
YOUR DUTY LIES HERE--WITH HER--NOW.
AND HEY...
BE CARE-FUL.
IF YOU KEEP CALLING YOURSELF TROWA BARTON, THEY'LL FIND YOU EVENTUALLY.
AND THEY WON'T KEEP IT QUIET.
...YEAH.
WELCOME HOME, TROWA!
ARE YOU *HURT?*
IT DOESN'T MATTER.
I'M *BACK.*
YOU'RE UNBELIEV-ABLE!
BUT I AM GLAD YOU'RE HERE.

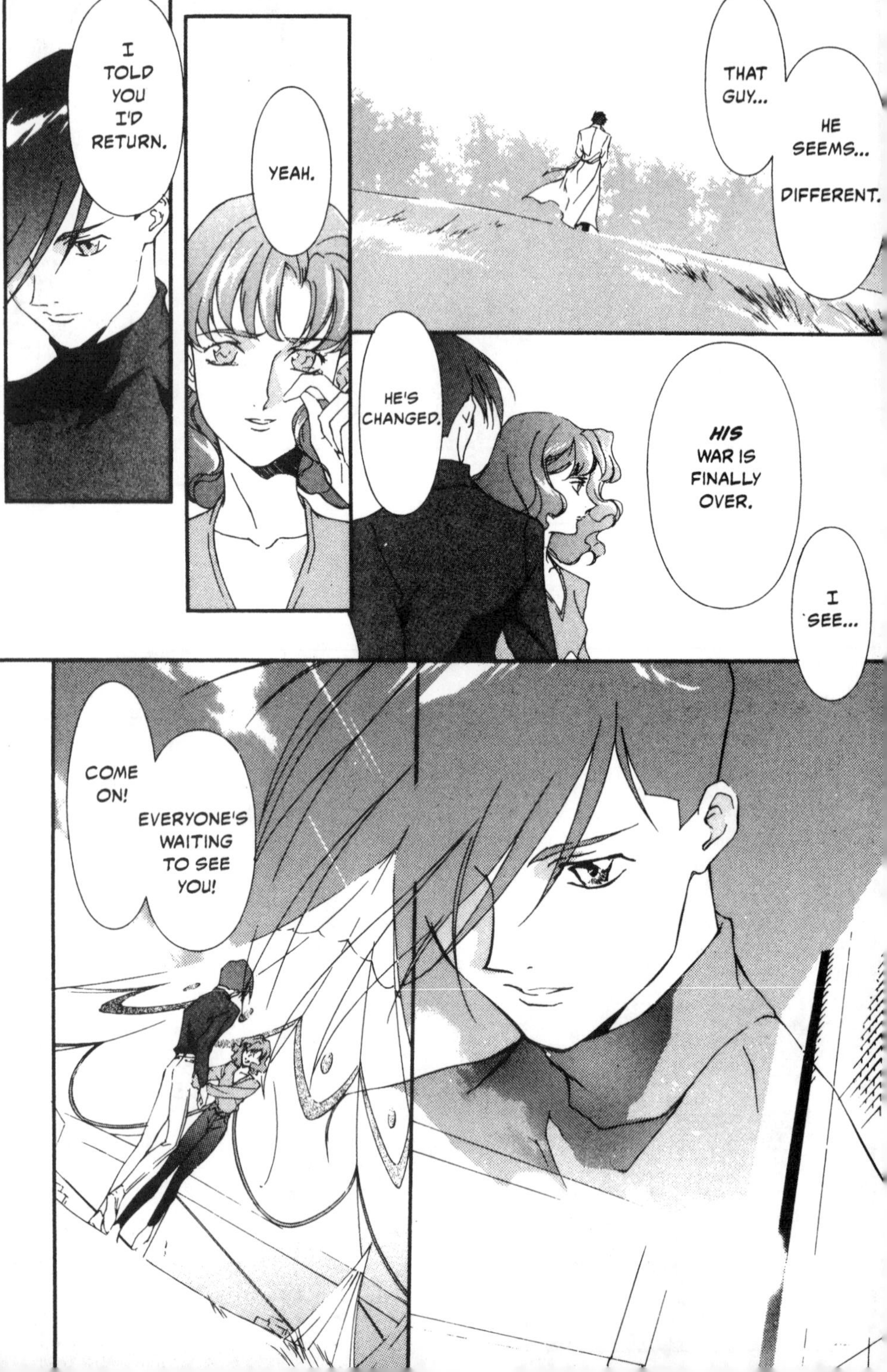
I TOLD YOU I'D RETURN.
YEAH.
THAT GUY...
HE SEEMS...
DIFFERENT.
HE'S CHANGED.
HIS WAR IS FINALLY OVER.
I SEE...
COME ON!
EVERYONE'S WAITING TO SEE YOU!

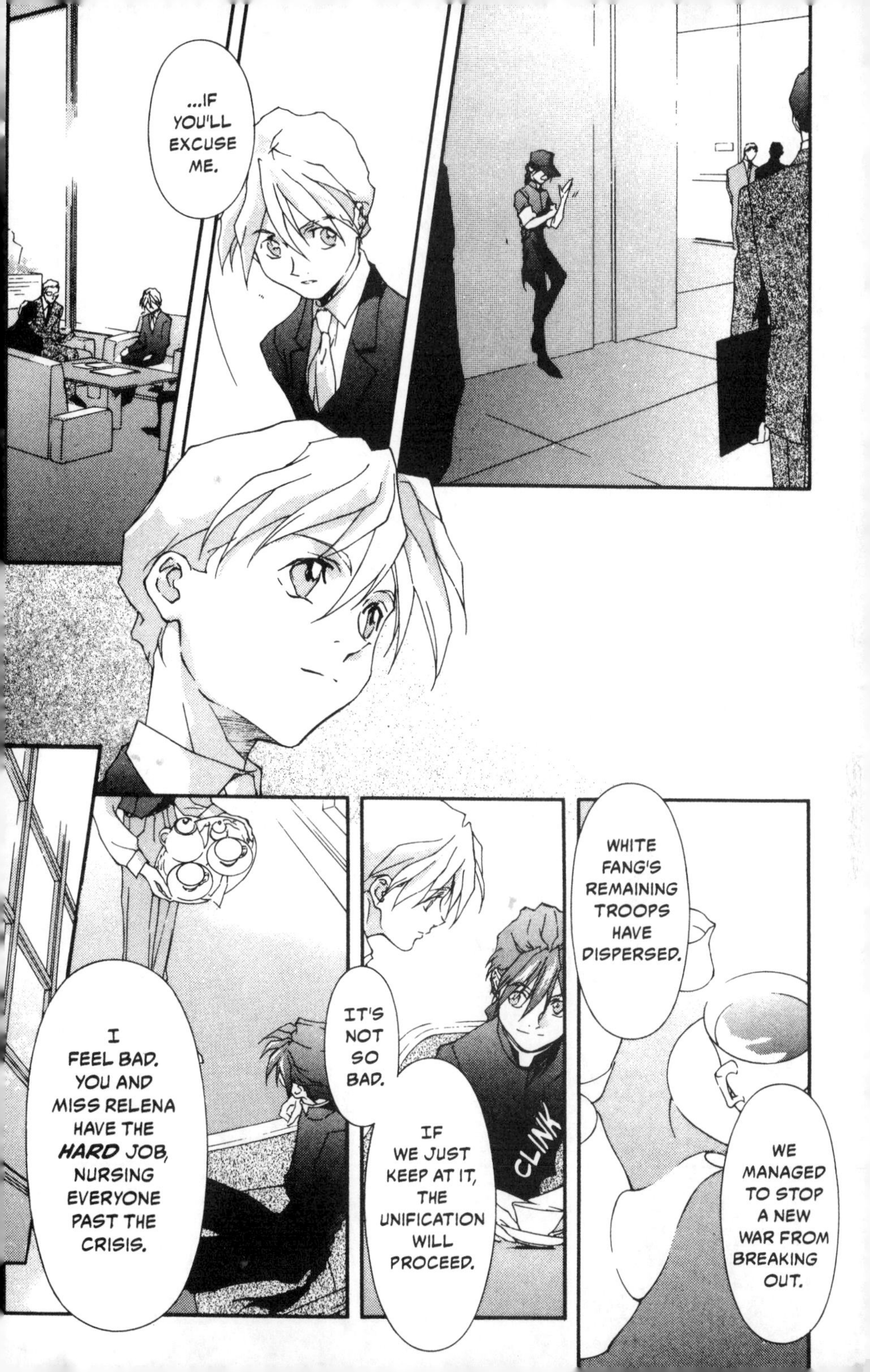
...IF YOU'LL EXCUSE ME.
I FEEL BAD. YOU AND MISS RELENA HAVE THE ***HARD*** JOB, NURSING EVERYONE PAST THE CRISIS.
IT'S NOT SO BAD.
IF WE JUST KEEP AT IT, THE UNIFICATION WILL PROCEED.
CLINK
WHITE FANG'S REMAINING TROOPS HAVE DISPERSED.
WE MANAGED TO STOP A NEW WAR FROM BREAKING OUT.

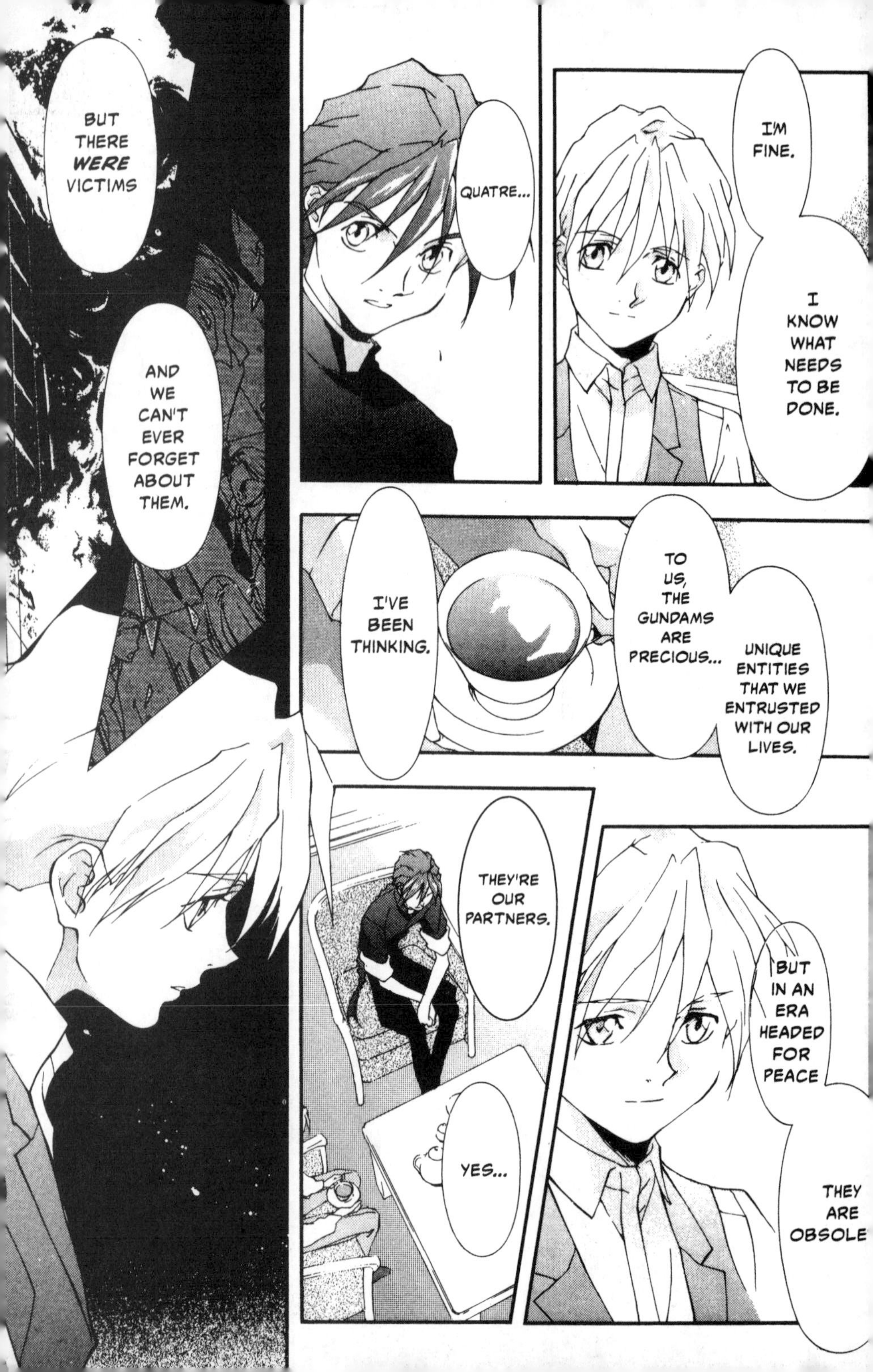
BUT THERE *WERE* VICTIMS
AND WE CAN'T EVER FORGET ABOUT THEM.
QUATRE...
I'M FINE.
I KNOW WHAT NEEDS TO BE DONE.
I'VE BEEN THINKING.
TO US, THE GUNDAMS ARE PRECIOUS...
UNIQUE ENTITIES THAT WE ENTRUSTED WITH OUR LIVES.
THEY'RE OUR PARTNERS.
YES...
BUT IN AN ERA HEADED FOR PEACE
THEY ARE OBSOLE

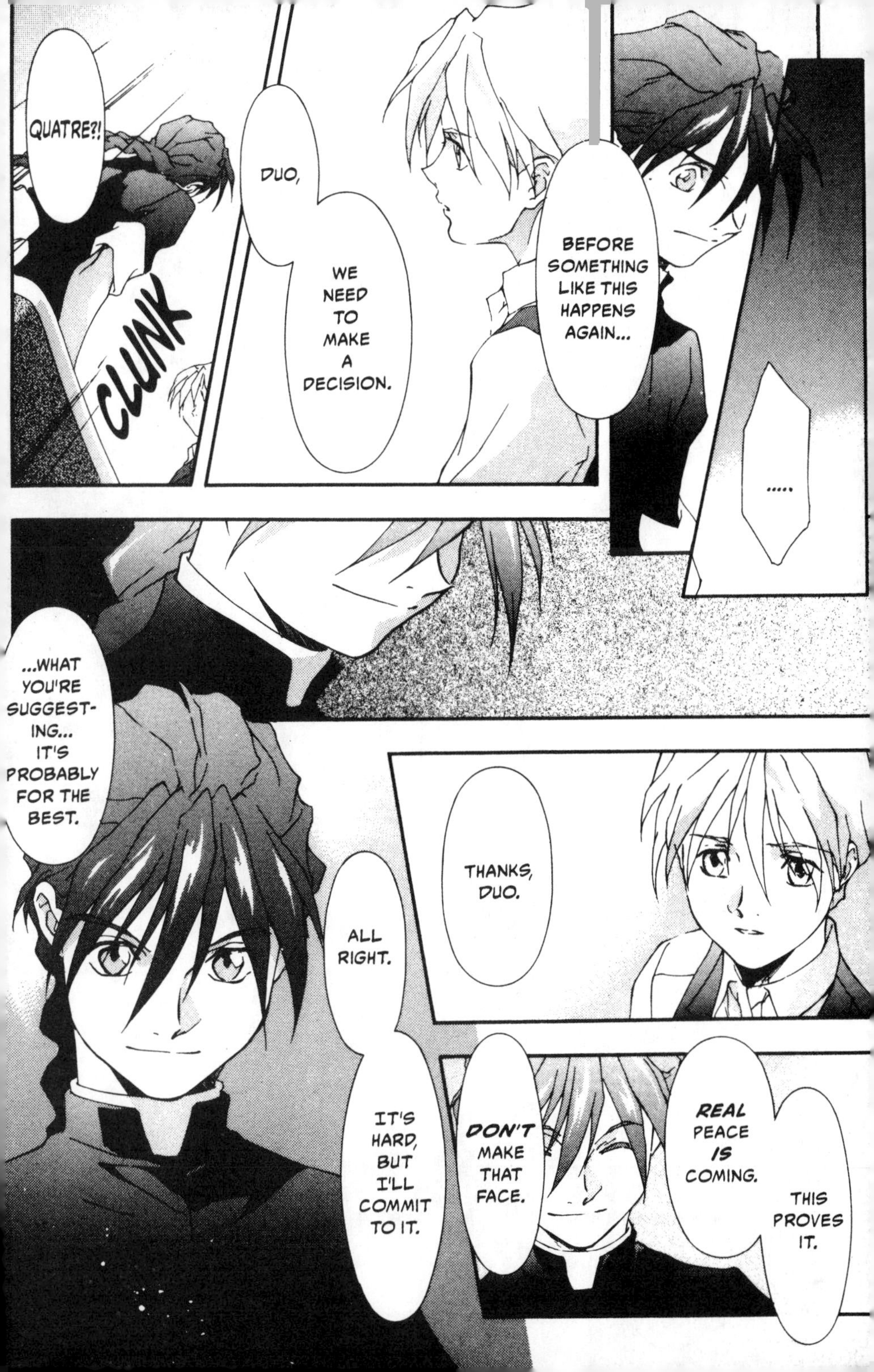
QUATRE?!
CLUNK
DUO,
WE NEED TO MAKE A DECISION.
BEFORE SOMETHING LIKE THIS HAPPENS AGAIN...
.....
...WHAT YOU'RE SUGGEST-ING... IT'S PROBABLY FOR THE BEST.
ALL RIGHT.
IT'S HARD, BUT I'LL COMMIT TO IT.
THANKS, DUO.
DON'T MAKE THAT FACE.
REAL PEACE IS COMING.
THIS PROVES IT.

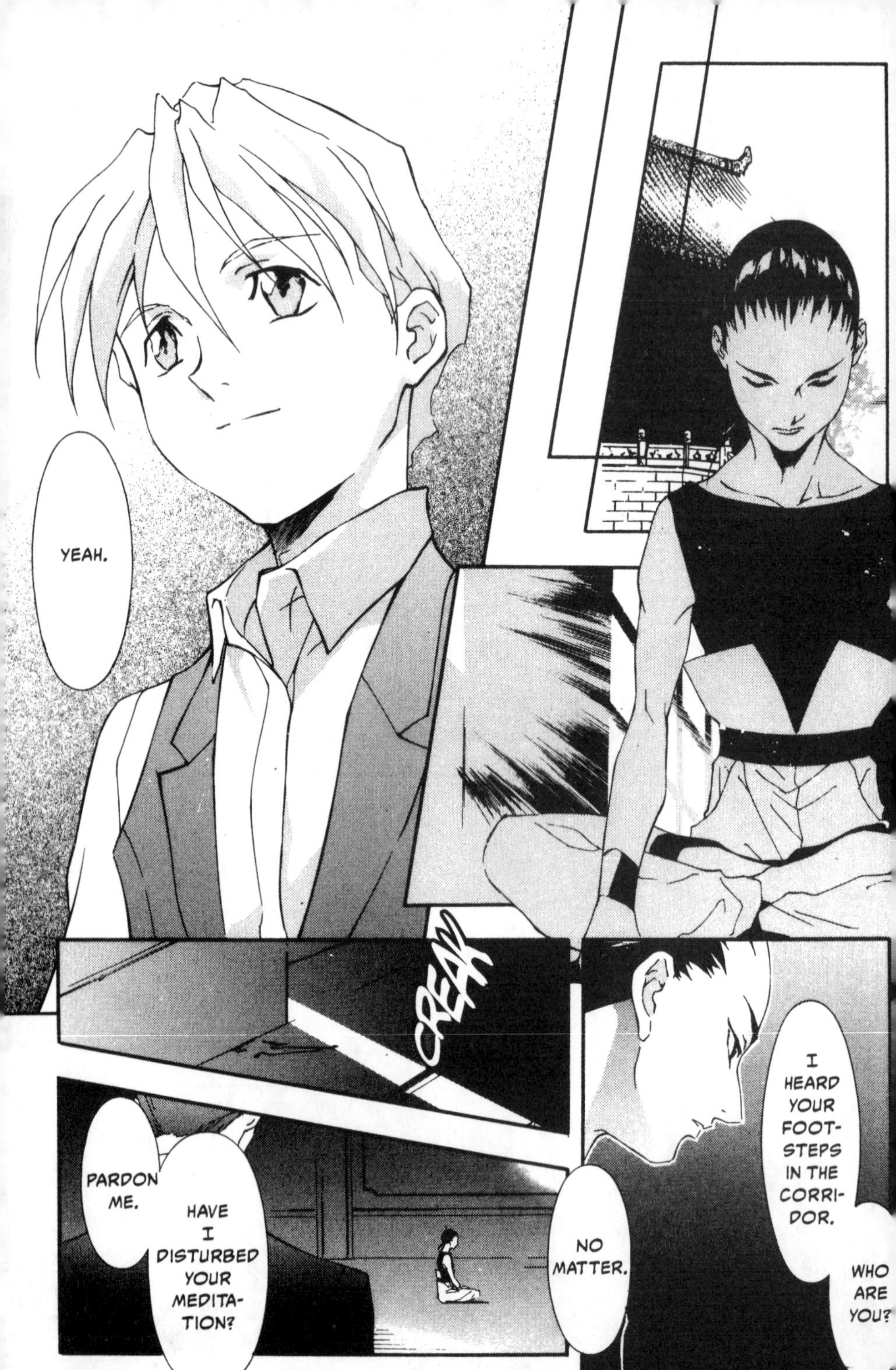
YEAH.
CREAK
PARDON ME.
HAVE I DISTURBED YOUR MEDITATION?
NO MATTER.
I HEARD YOUR FOOTSTEPS IN THE CORRIDOR.
WHO ARE YOU?

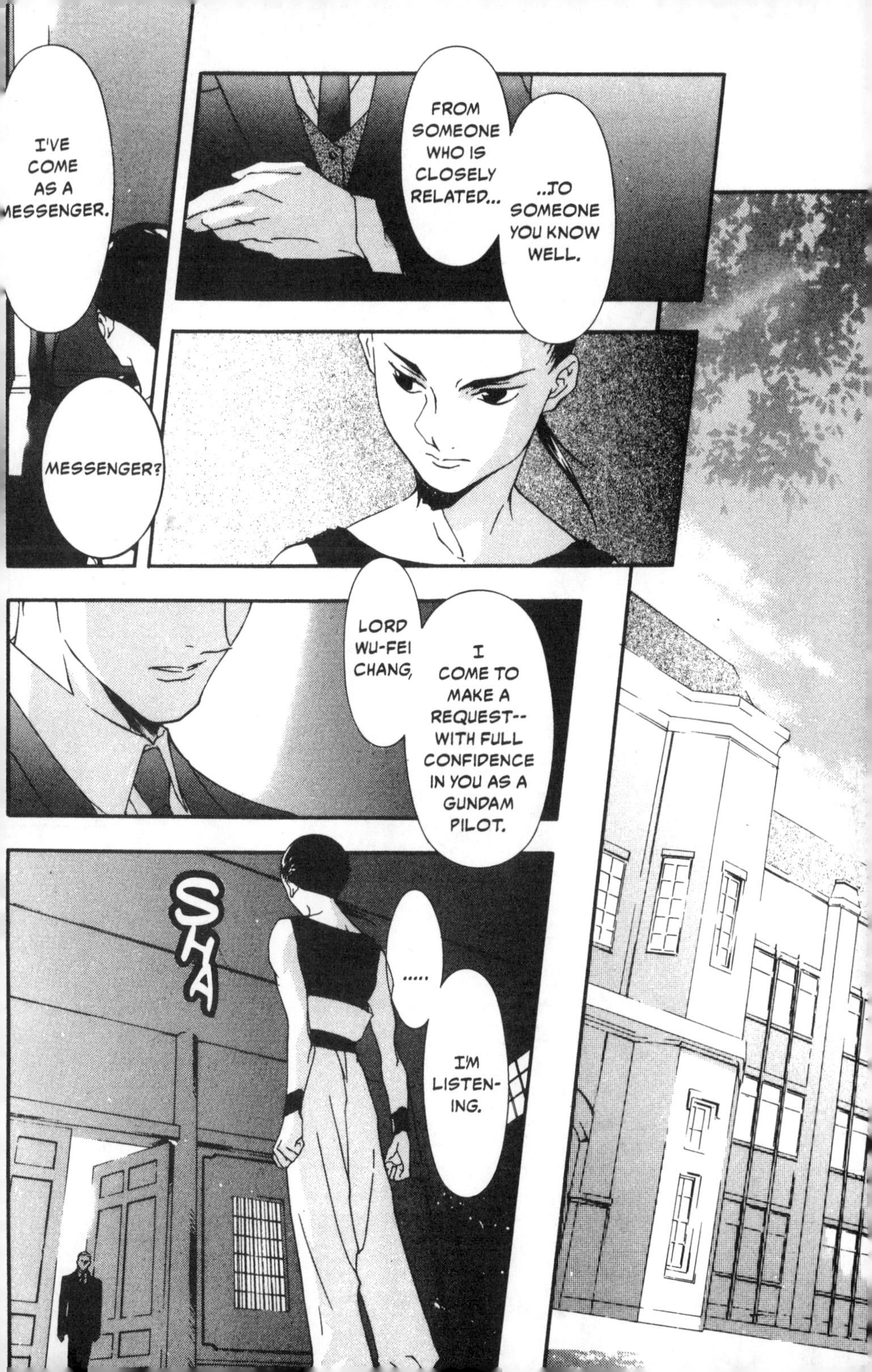
I'VE COME AS A MESSENGER.
FROM SOMEONE WHO IS CLOSELY RELATED...
...TO SOMEONE YOU KNOW WELL.
MESSENGER?
LORD WU-FEI CHANG,
I COME TO MAKE A REQUEST-- WITH FULL CONFIDENCE IN YOU AS A GUNDAM PILOT.
SHA
.....
I'M LISTEN-ING.

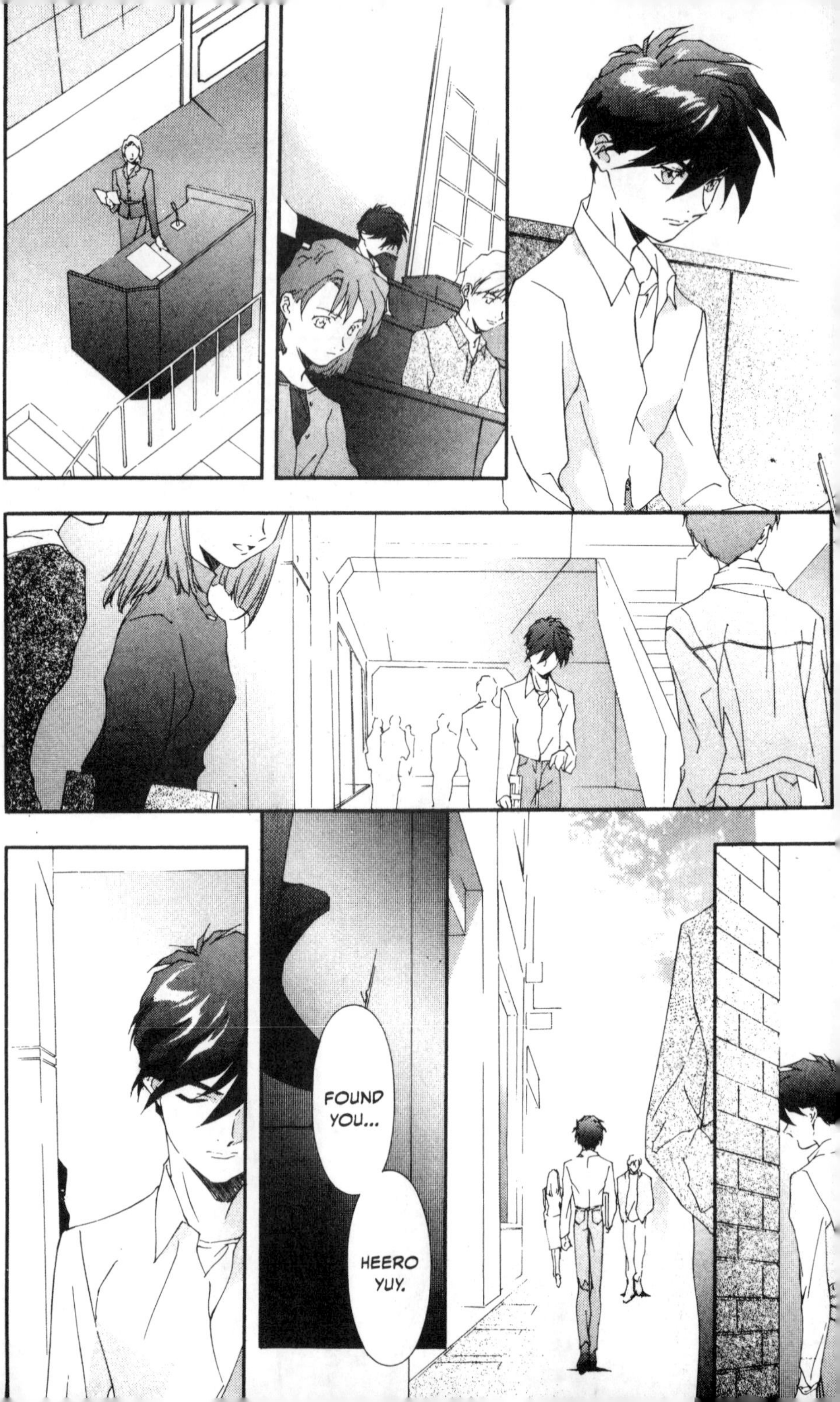
FOUND YOU...
HEERO YUY.

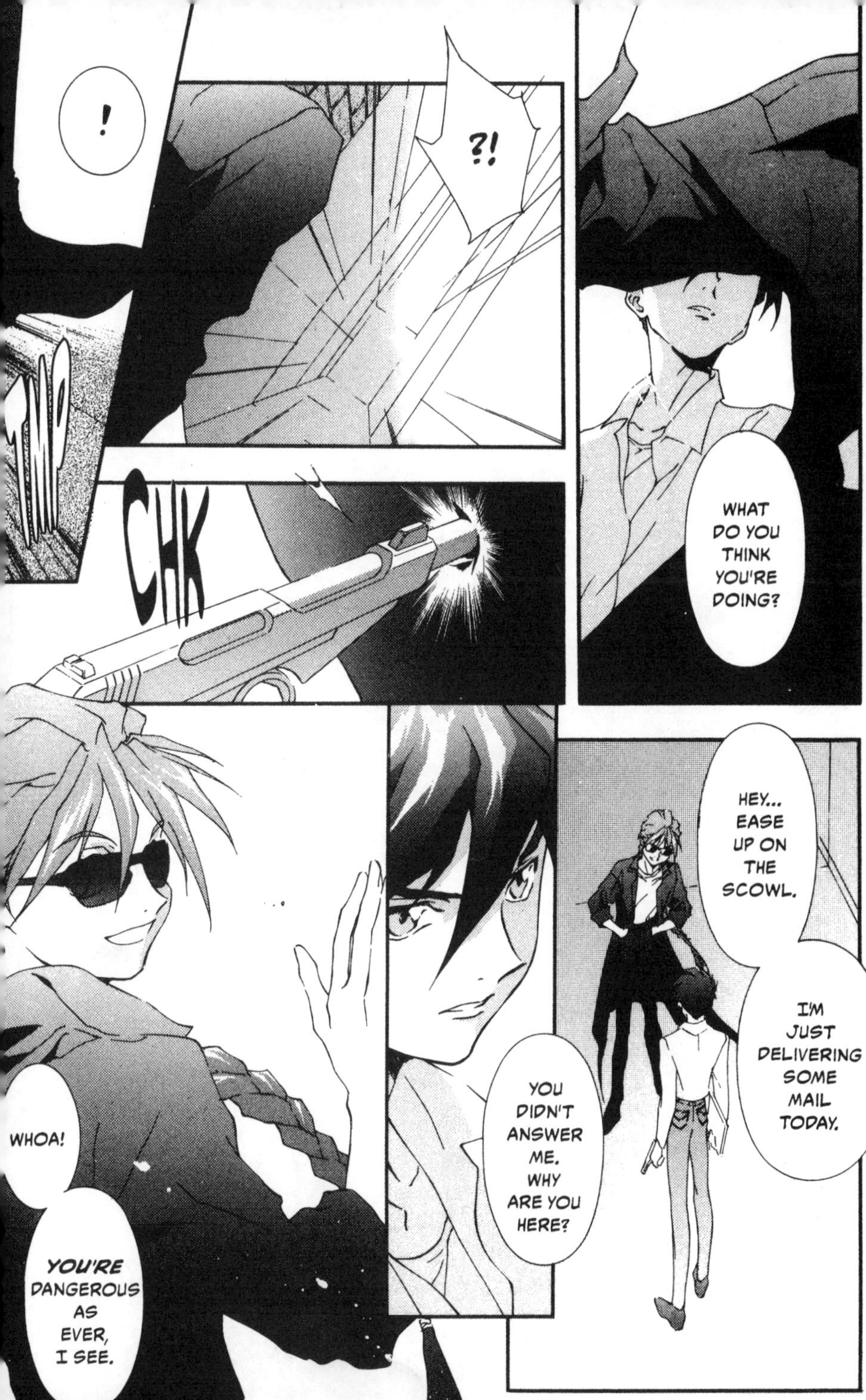
!
?!
TMP
CHK
WHAT DO YOU THINK YOU'RE DOING?
WHOA!
YOU'RE DANGEROUS AS EVER, I SEE.
YOU DIDN'T ANSWER ME. WHY ARE YOU HERE?
HEY... EASE UP ON THE SCOWL.
I'M JUST DELIVERING SOME MAIL TODAY.

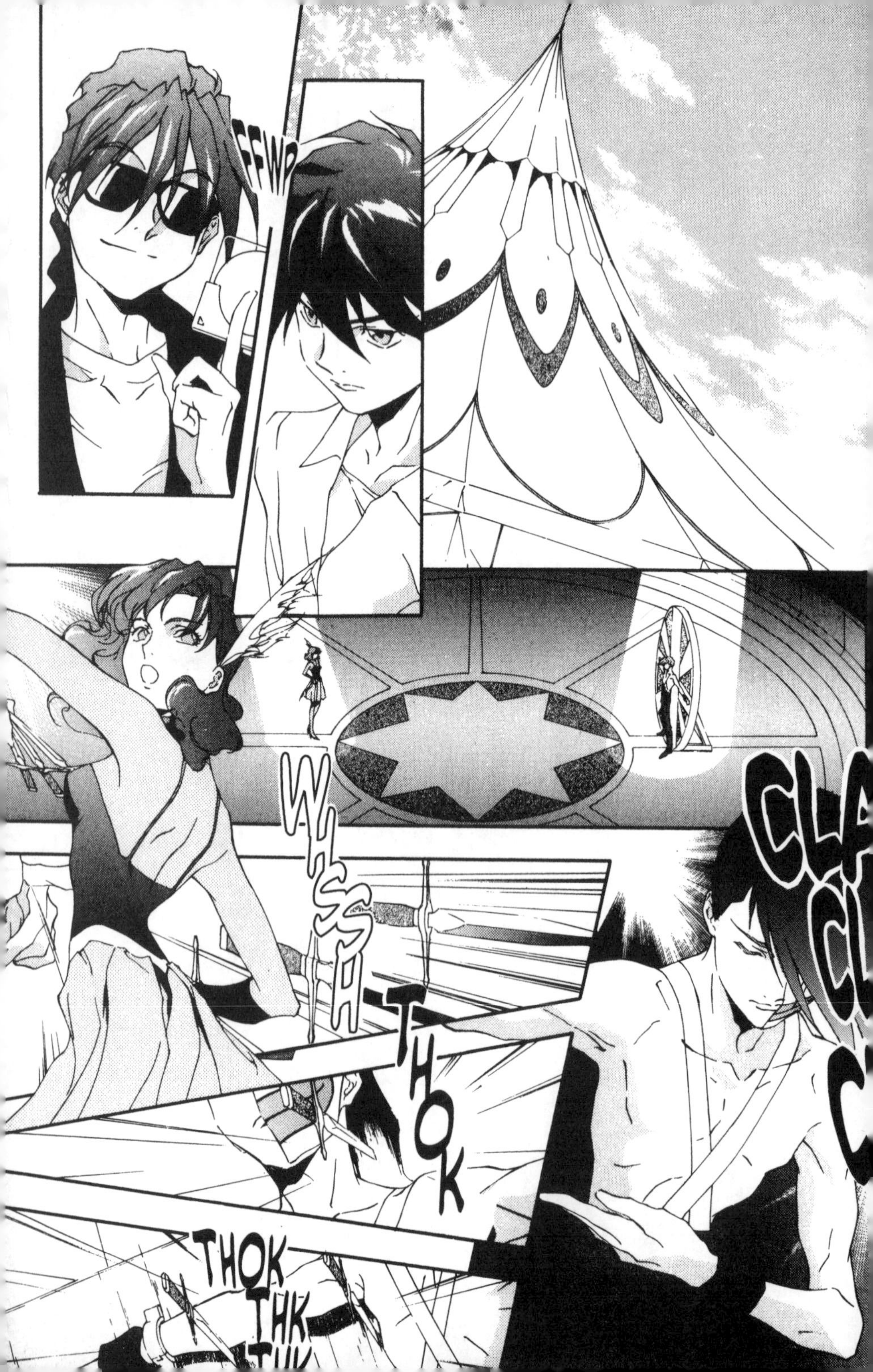
FFWP
WHSSH
THOK
CLA
CL
C
THOK
THK

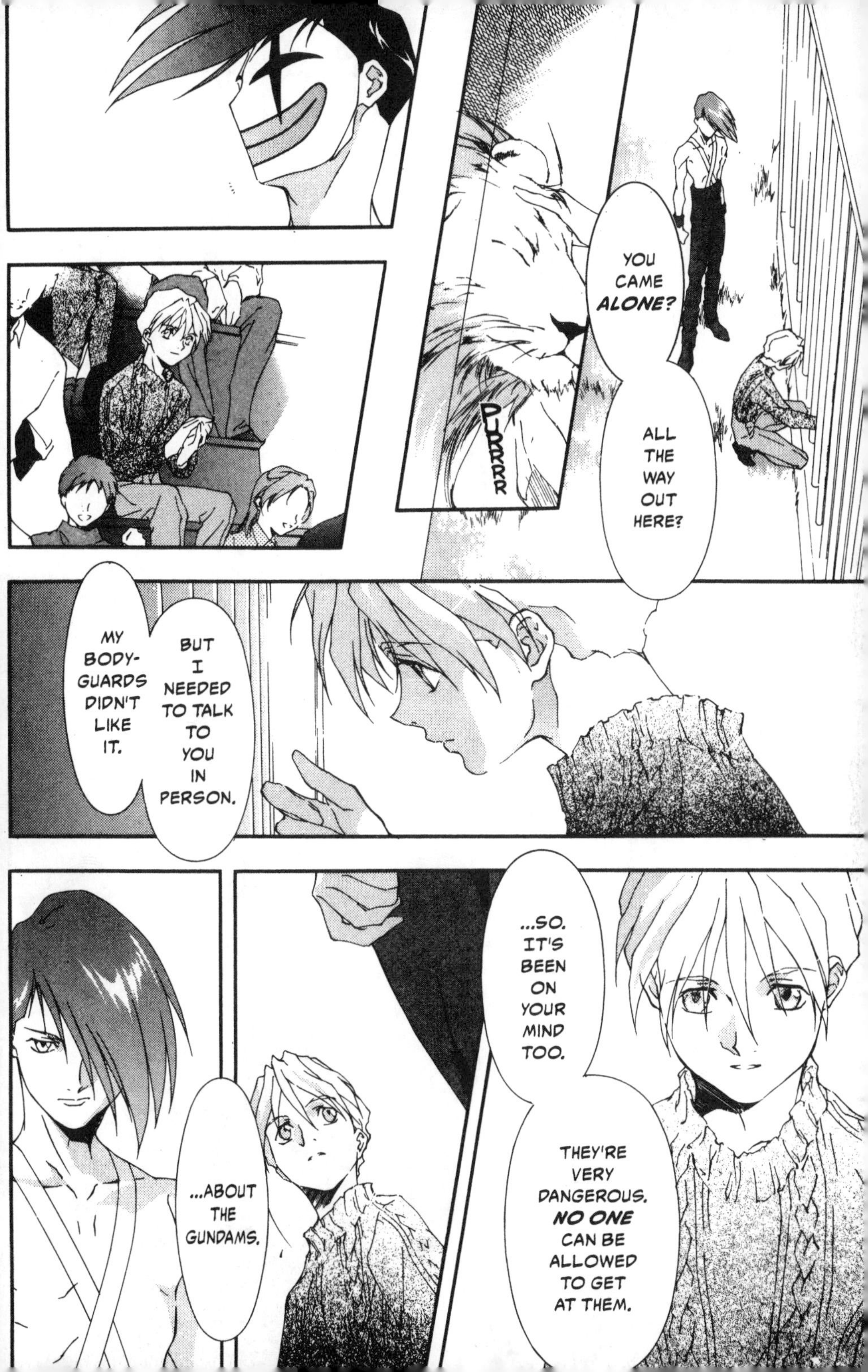
PURRRR
YOU CAME ALONE?
ALL THE WAY OUT HERE?
MY BODY-GUARDS DIDN'T LIKE IT.
BUT I NEEDED TO TALK TO YOU IN PERSON.
...ABOUT THE GUNDAMS.
...SO. IT'S BEEN ON YOUR MIND TOO.
THEY'RE VERY DANGEROUS. NO ONE CAN BE ALLOWED TO GET AT THEM.

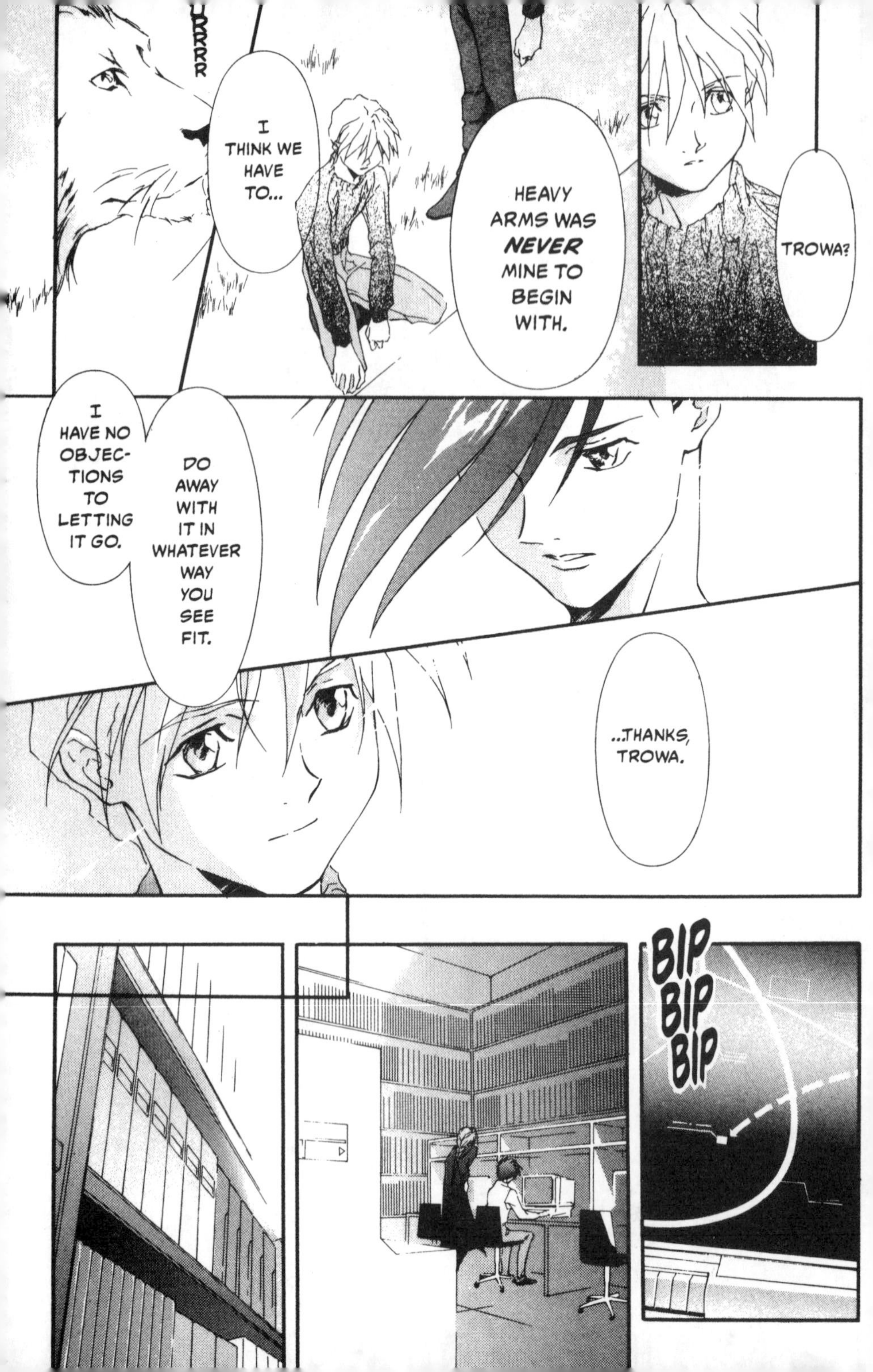
URRRR
I THINK WE HAVE TO...
HEAVY ARMS WAS **NEVER** MINE TO BEGIN WITH.
TROWA?
I HAVE NO OBJEC-TIONS TO LETTING IT GO.
DO AWAY WITH IT IN WHATEVER WAY YOU SEE FIT.
...THANKS, TROWA.
BIP BIP BIP

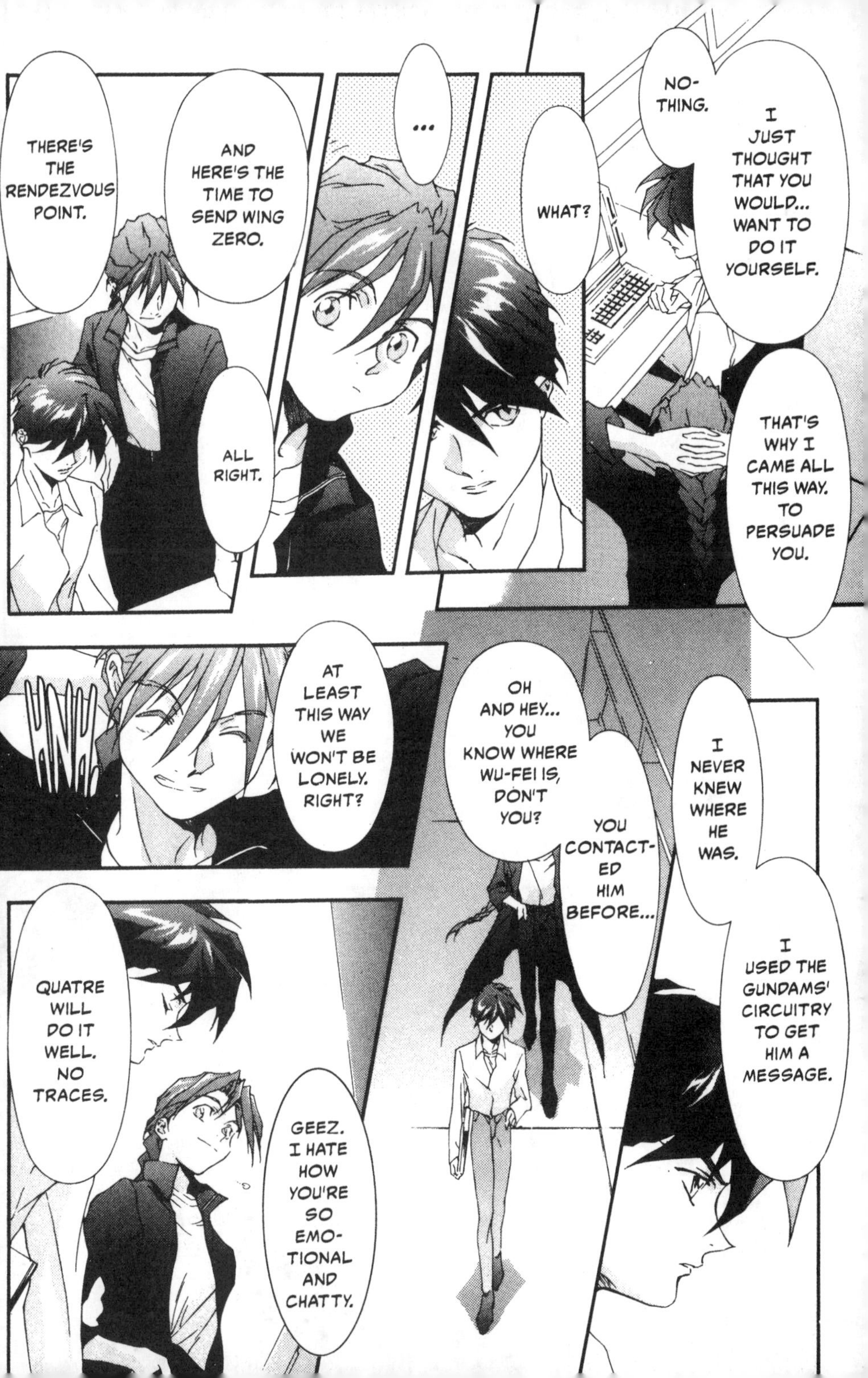
THERE'S THE RENDEZVOUS POINT.
AND HERE'S THE TIME TO SEND WING ZERO.
ALL RIGHT.
...
WHAT?
NO-THING.
I JUST THOUGHT THAT YOU WOULD... WANT TO DO IT YOURSELF.
THAT'S WHY I CAME ALL THIS WAY. TO PERSUADE YOU.
AT LEAST THIS WAY WE WON'T BE LONELY. RIGHT?
QUATRE WILL DO IT WELL. NO TRACES.
GEEZ. I HATE HOW YOU'RE SO EMOTIONAL AND CHATTY.
OH AND HEY... YOU KNOW WHERE WU-FEI IS, DON'T YOU?
YOU CONTACT-ED HIM BEFORE...
I NEVER KNEW WHERE HE WAS.
I USED THE GUNDAMS' CIRCUITRY TO GET HIM A MESSAGE.

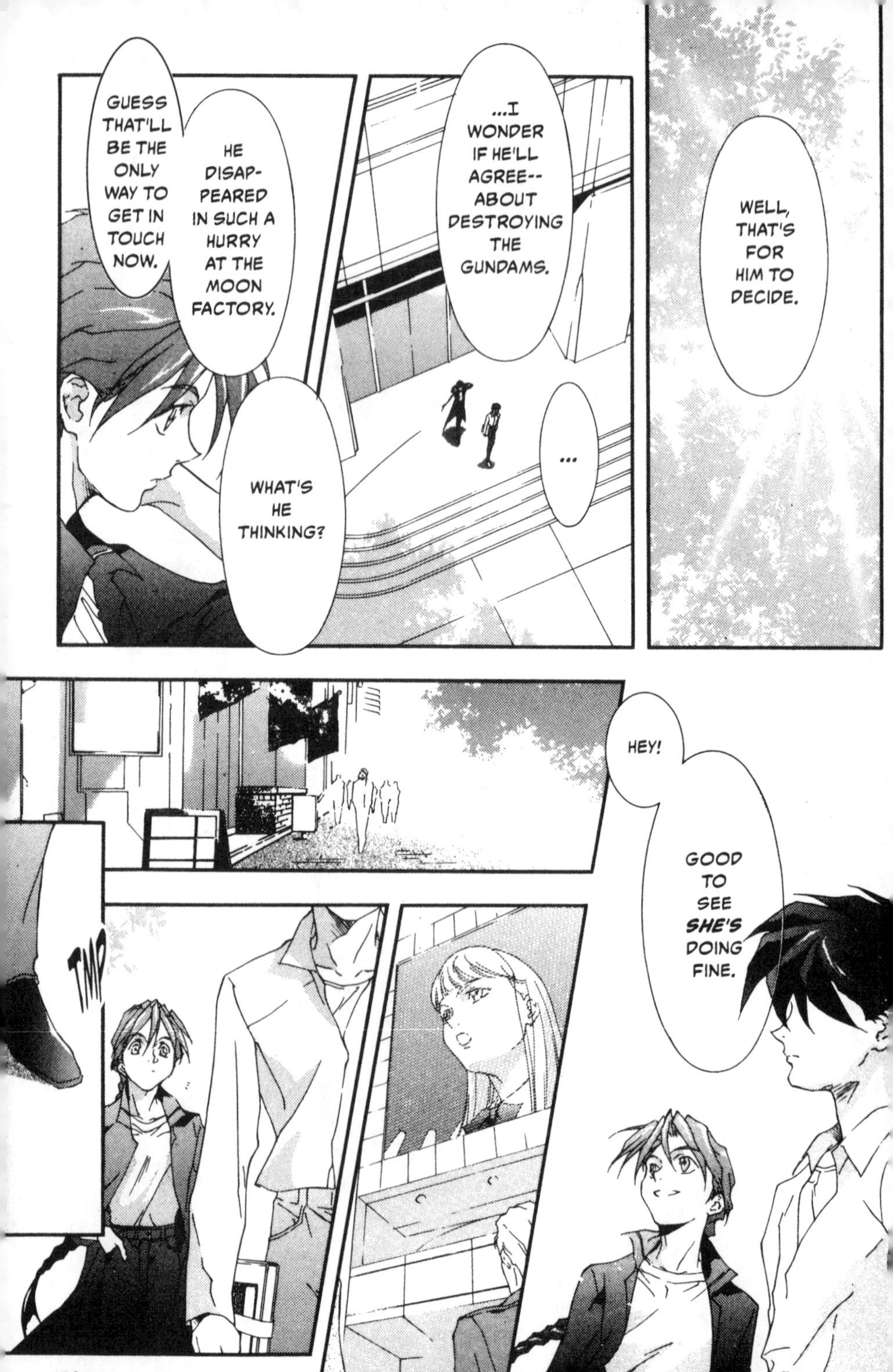
GUESS THAT'LL BE THE ONLY WAY TO GET IN TOUCH NOW.
HE DISAP-PEARED IN SUCH A HURRY AT THE MOON FACTORY.
WHAT'S HE THINKING?
...I WONDER IF HE'LL AGREE-- ABOUT DESTROYING THE GUNDAMS.
...
WELL, THAT'S FOR HIM TO DECIDE.
HEY!
TMP
GOOD TO SEE ***SHE'S*** DOING FINE.

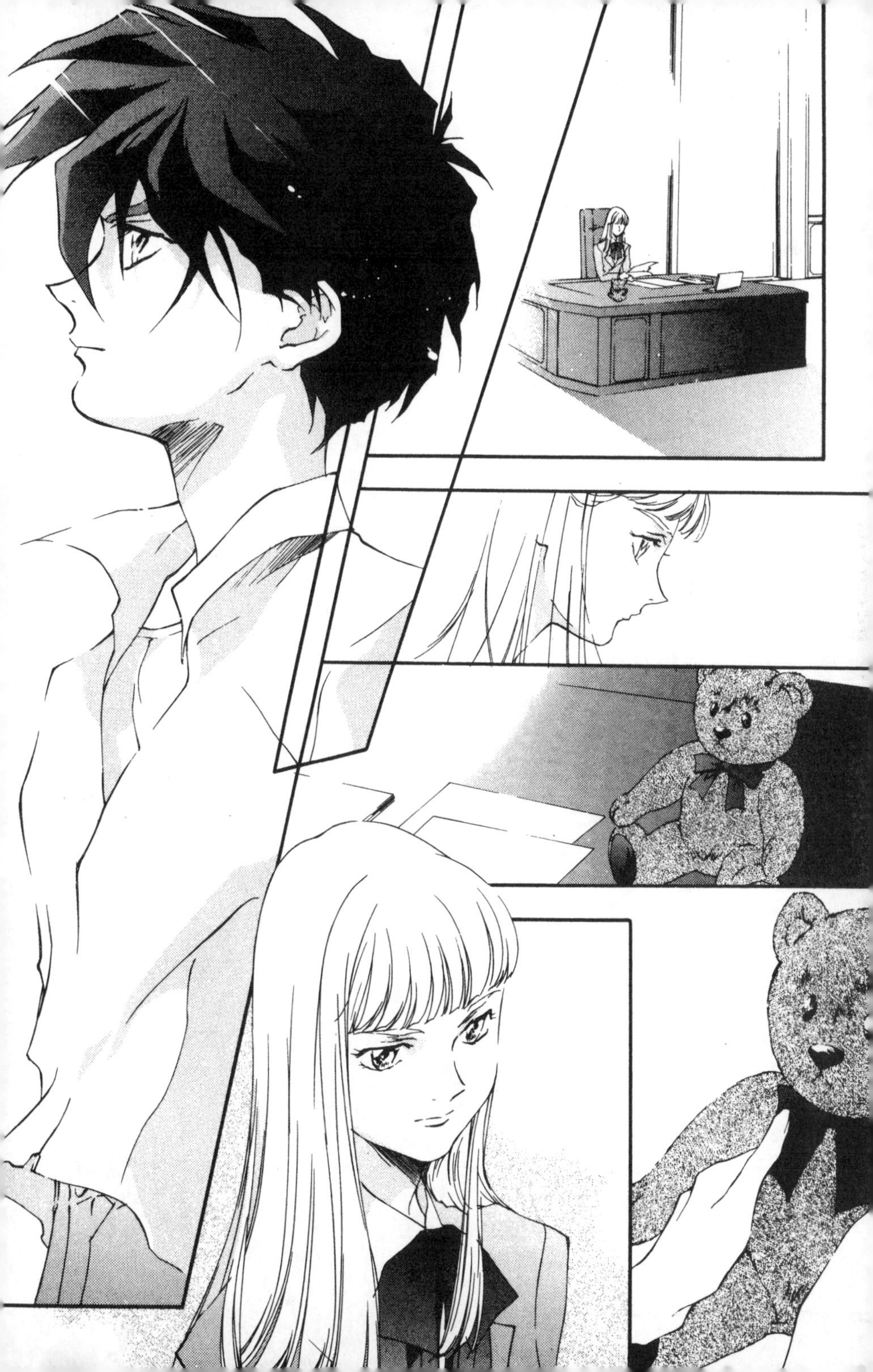

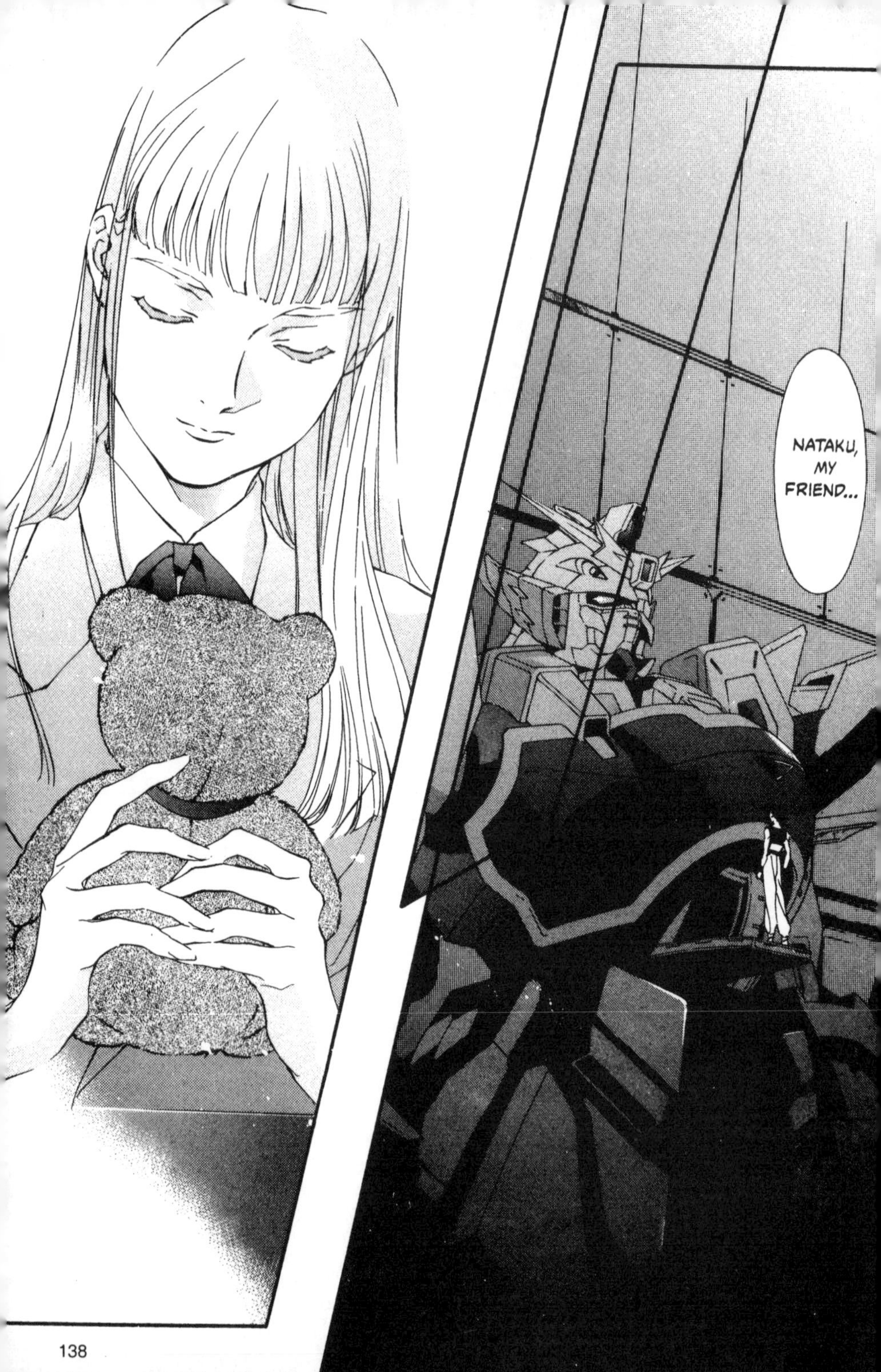
NATAKU, MY FRIEND...

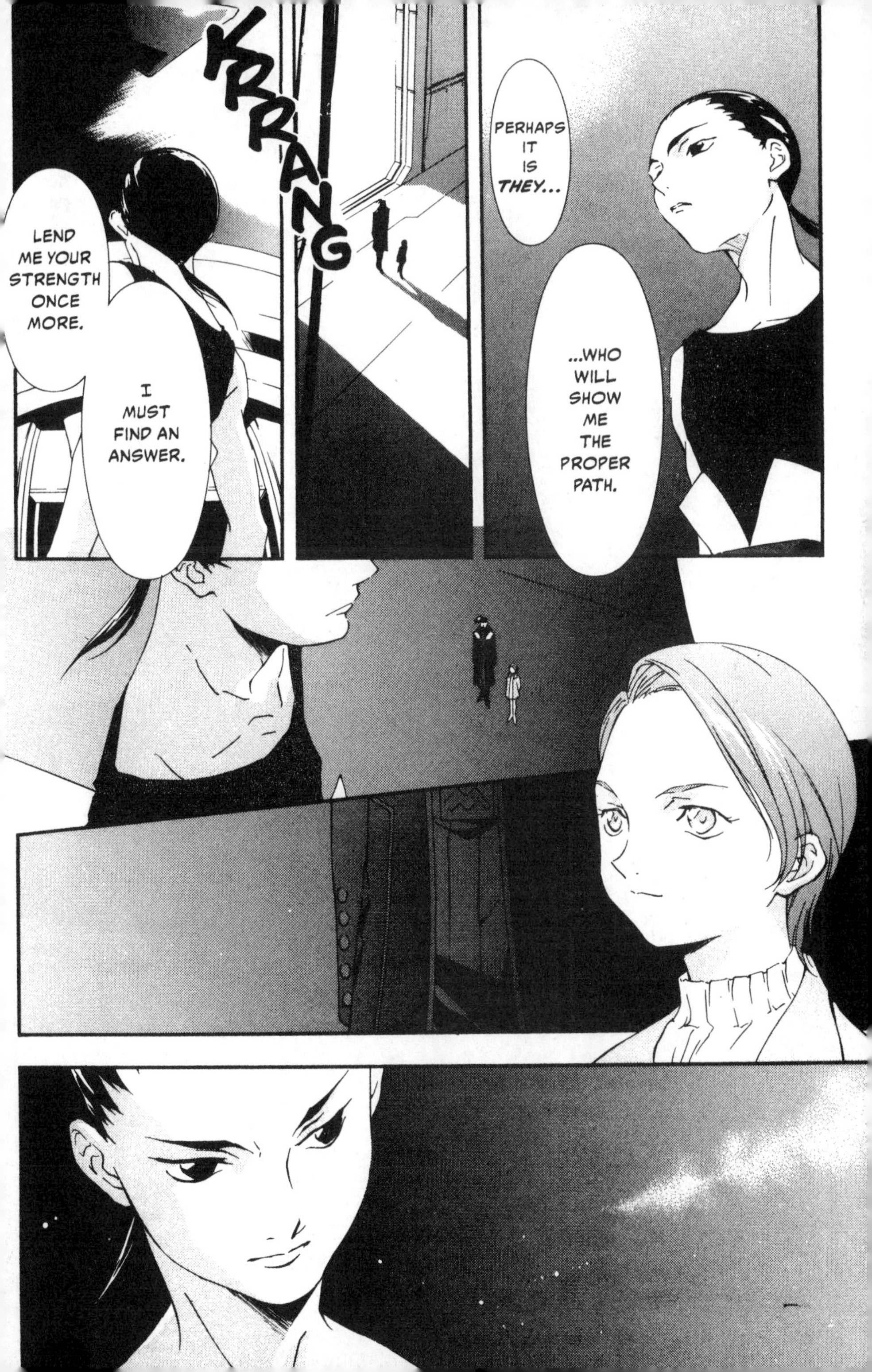
LEND ME YOUR STRENGTH ONCE MORE.
I MUST FIND AN ANSWER.
KRRANG
PERHAPS IT IS *THEY...*
...WHO WILL SHOW ME THE PROPER PATH.

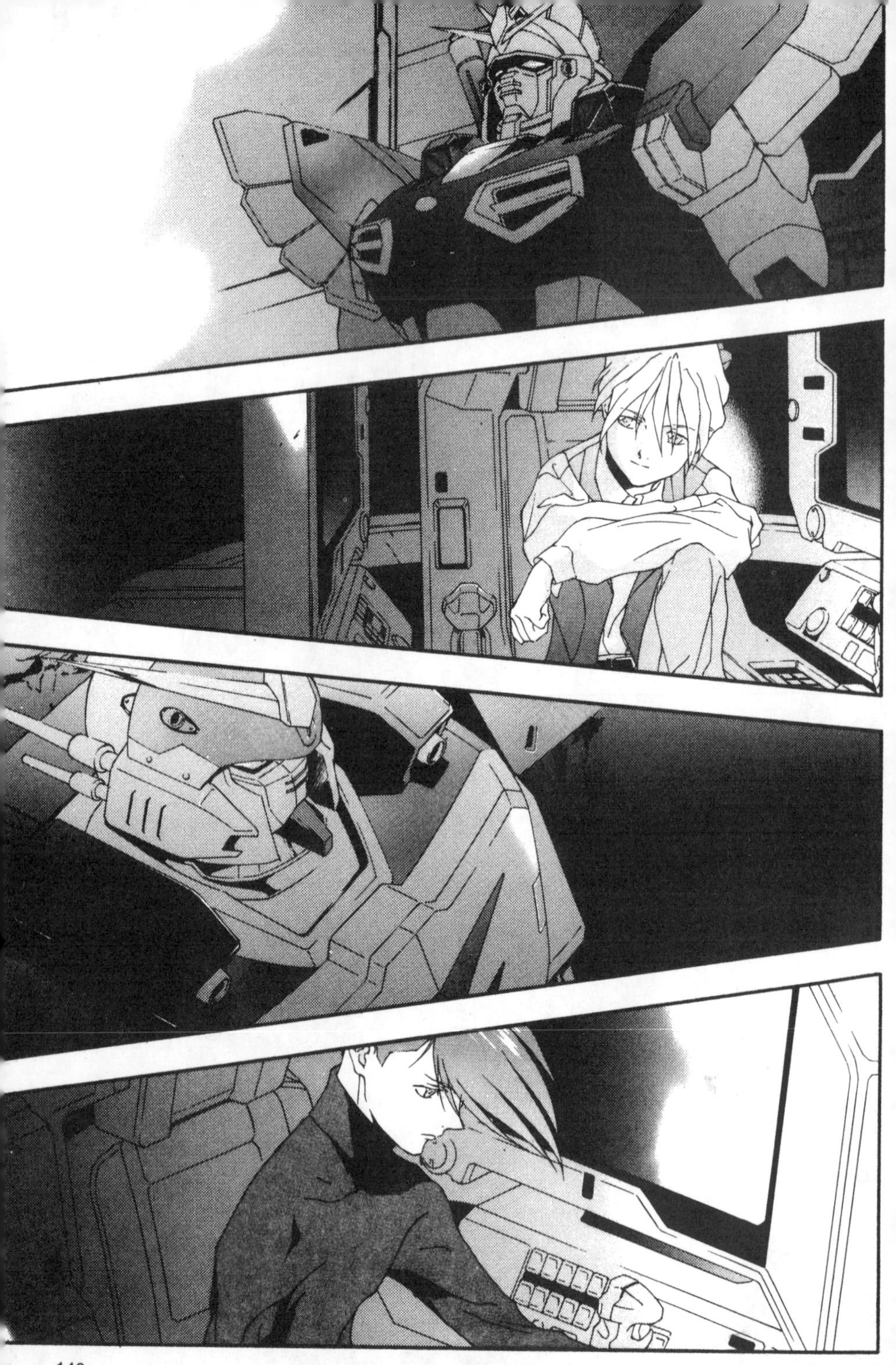

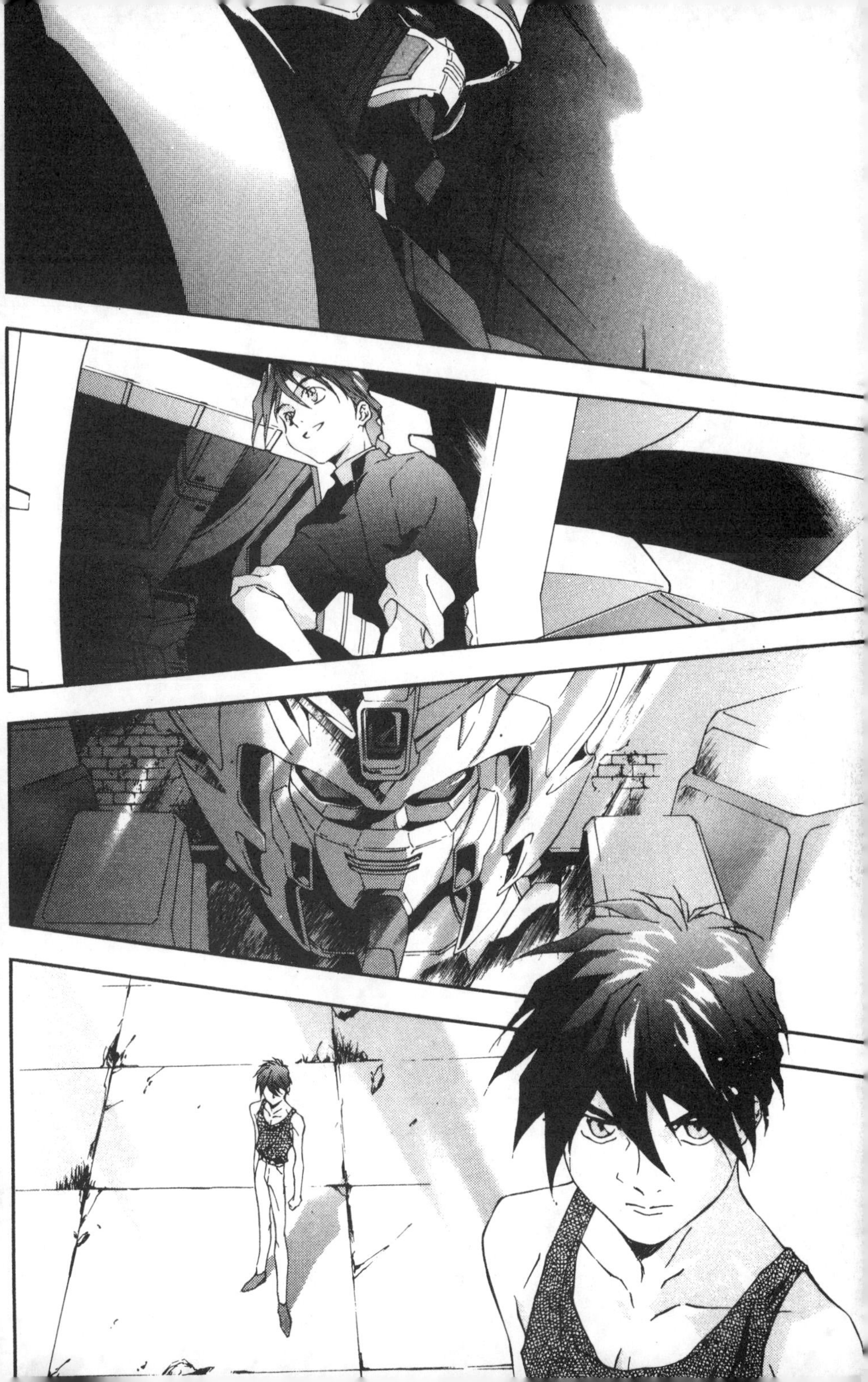

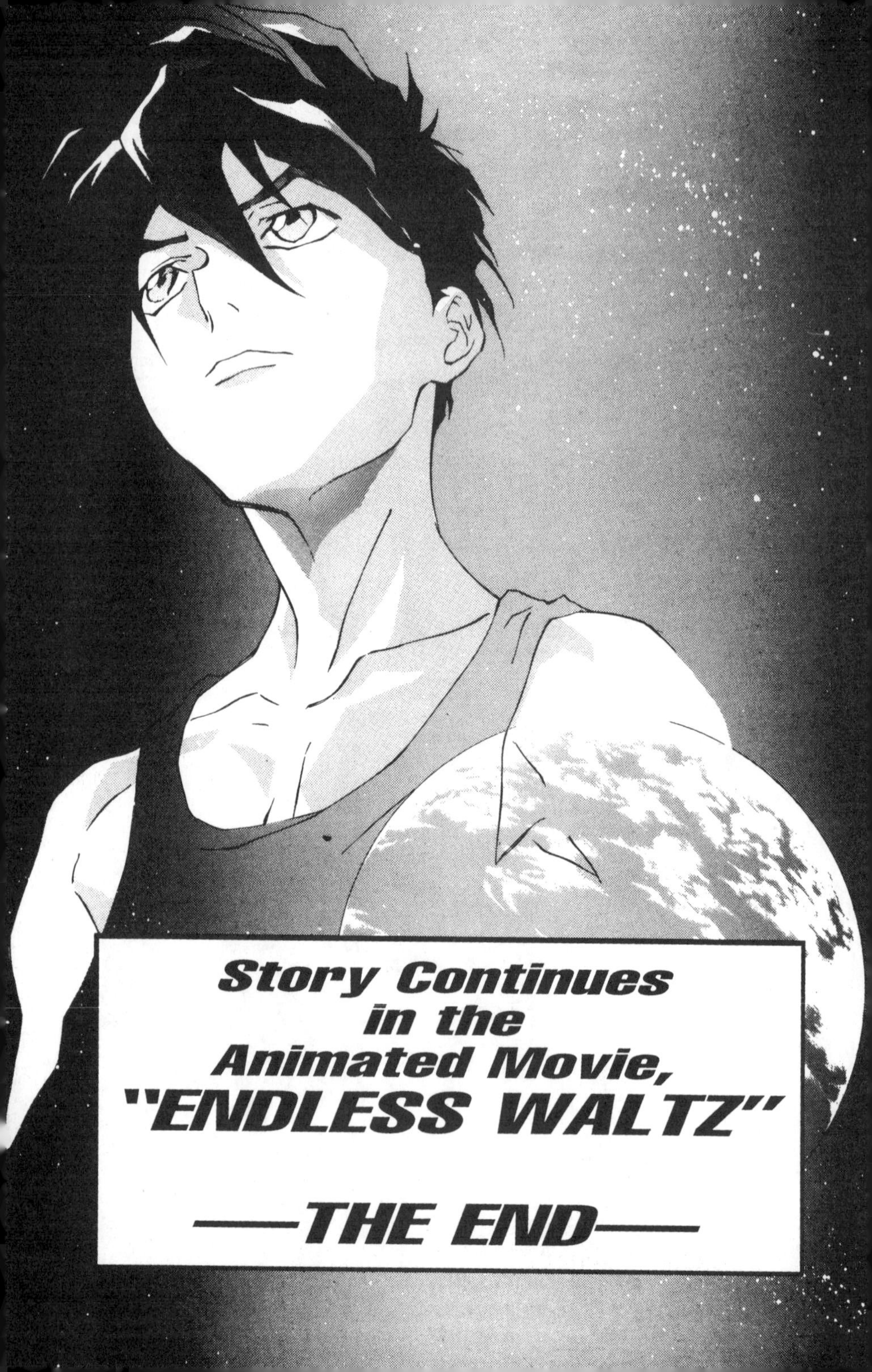
Story Continues
in the
Animated Movie,
"ENDLESS WALTZ"
——THE END——

MOBILE SUIT GUNDAM WING

BLIND TARGET

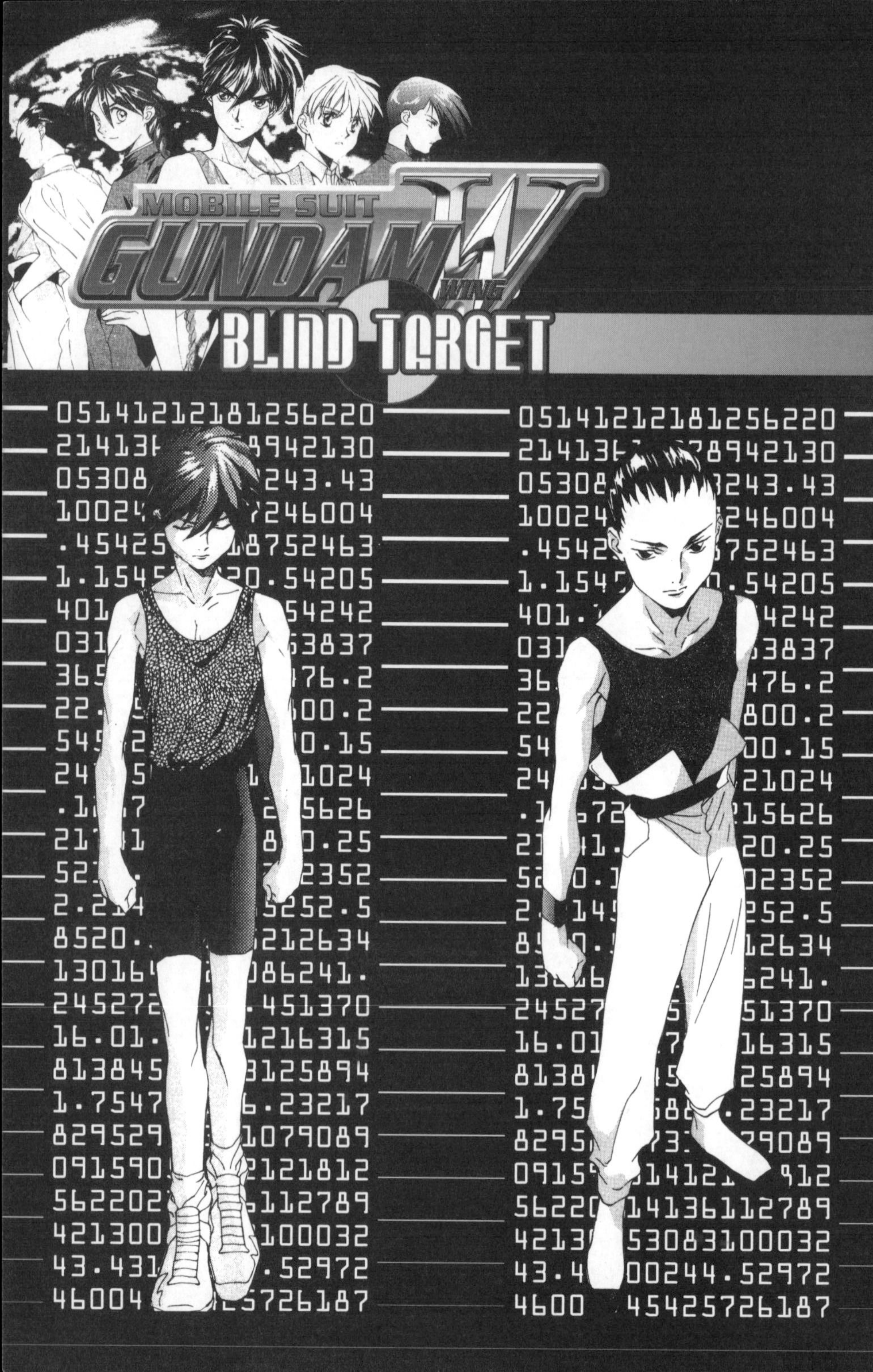
MOBILE SUIT
GUNDAM WING
BLIND TARGET

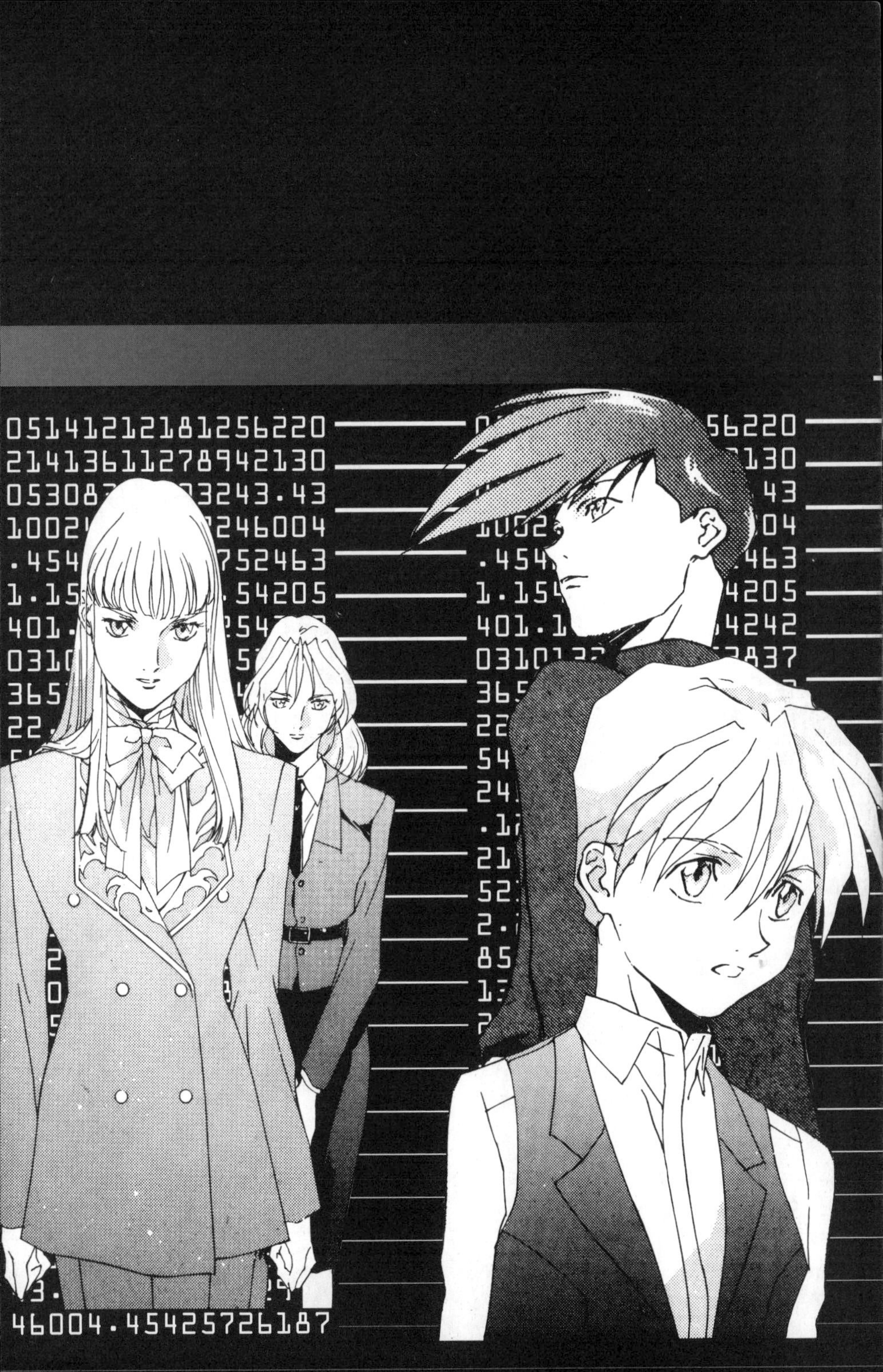
05141212181256220
21413611278942130
46004.45425726187

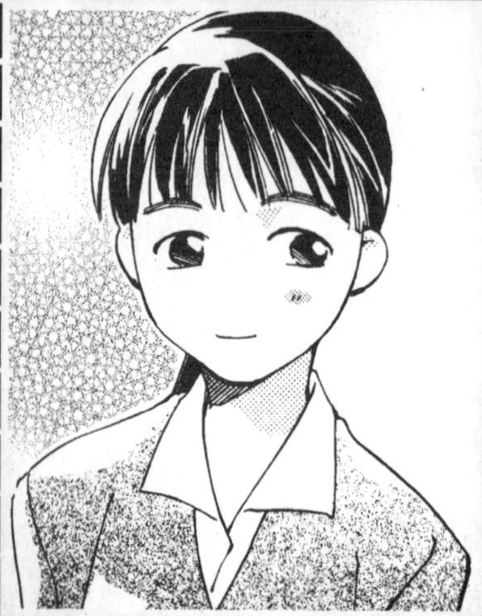

SCRIPT:
AKEMI OMODE

When it was decided that I was going to work on Gundam Wing, at first I felt a lot of pressure. But when I started writing the script, I got so caught up in the characters that I put my heart into the writing. I've ended up taking care of them for all this time. This work means a lot to me. I hope that love towards the characters will always remain in your hearts, as it does in mine.

DRAWING:
SAKURA ASAGI

My first encounter with Gundam Wing was, when the TV series was near its end, I got a job doing an illustration for a magazine. I think it's some kind of weird karma that I was able to be involved in the comics version too.

I took care to stick close to the original style in my drawings, since a lot of people put their hearts into the series. I'd be happy if you would accept it as just as real as the events in the TV series.

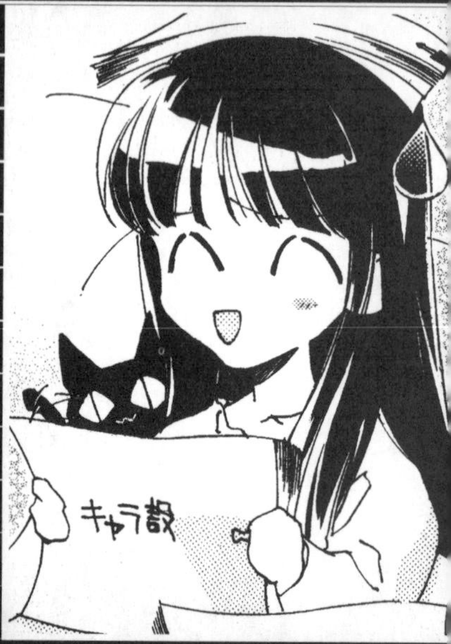
キャラ設

AVAILABLE FROM ▼ VIZ COMICS™
IN NOVEMBER!

Gundam Wing: Blind
Target takes place after
the TV series and before
Endless Waltz. Heero,
Wufei, Duo, Trowa,
Quatre and Relena are
determined to keep peace
in the midst of a terrifying
plot by a group who
wishes to obtain the
Gundams for their own
dubious ends.

By Akemi Omode
Art by Sakura Asagi
Graphic Novel
b&w, 152 pages
$12.95 USA/$20.95 CAN

Gundam Wing: Episode
Zero takes a look at the G
Boys' and Relena's origins
before Operation Meteor.
In Gundam Wing: Episode
#8, the latest installment,
gain some insight into
what events helped shape
and influence the
personalities and drive for
each member of the
Gundam team.

By Katsuyuki Sumisawa
Art by Akira Kanbe
monthly comic
b&w, 32 pages
$2.95 USA/$4.95 CAN

Why do you love NO NEED FOR TENCHI!?

It's the *greatest!* It's almost like a *shōjo* manga, with all those sparkly lights and zip-a-tone and big watery eyes!

Not to mention the *witty* writing and *sophisticated* romance... although I'm sure certain *space pirates* prefer the fight scenes...

I prefer the *comic relief* courtesy of certain *spoiled alien princesses!* I don't mind getting a few speed lines on me, if that's what you mean!

sigh... I like the letters and fan art...

I like the catering!

I don't even show up in the anime! But in the *manga* I get revenge on my arch-rival Washu!

Uhh...I was going to say I liked the science fiction elements...

AVAILABLE NOW IN MONTHLY COMICS OR GRAPHIC NOVELS!
GRAPHIC NOVELS • 176-184 pages • $15.95 each

As seen on the Cartoon Network!

CALL OR GO ONLINE FOR COMIC SUBSCRIPTIONS
(800) 394-3042 • www.j-pop.com

VIZ COMICS

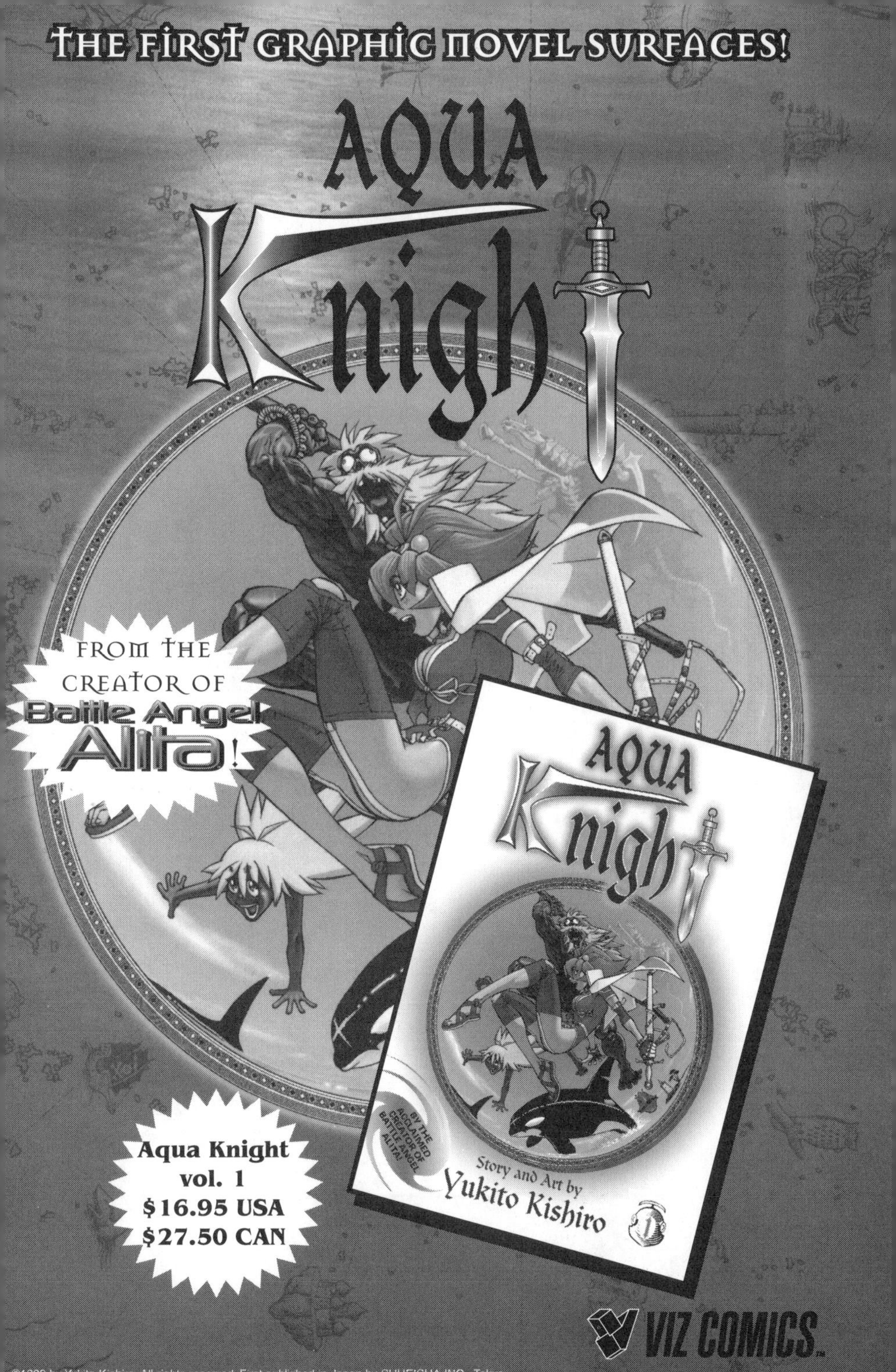
THE FIRST GRAPHIC NOVEL SURFACES!
AQUA Knight
FROM THE CREATOR OF Battle Angel Alita!
AQUA Knight
BY THE ACCLAIMED CREATOR OF BATTLE ANGEL ALITA!
Story and Art by Yukito Kishiro
Aqua Knight vol. 1 $16.95 USA $27.50 CAN
VIZ COMICS.